STORM TO VICTORY

STORM TO VICTORY

WAR OF THE ALLIANCE

5

TARA GRAYCE

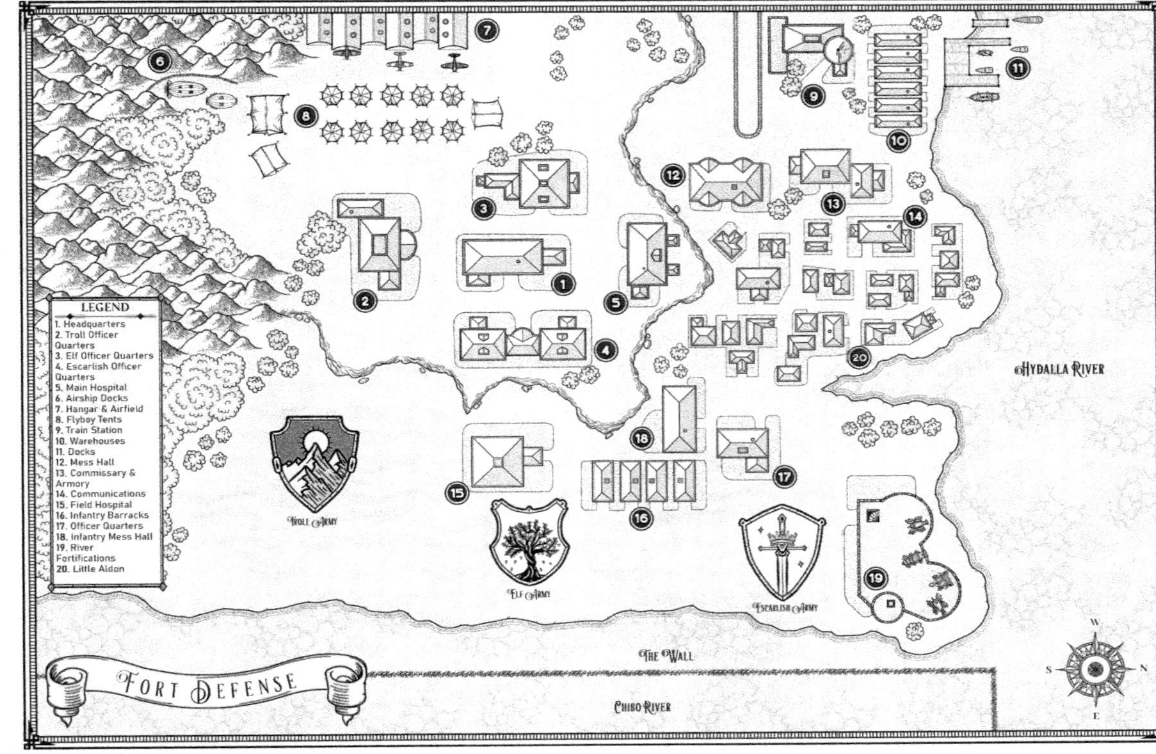

FORT DEFENSE
LEGEND
1. Headquarters
2. Troll Officer Quarters
3. Elf Officer Quarters
4. Escarlish Officer Quarters
5. Main Hospital
6. Airship Docks
7. Hangar & Airfield
8. Flyboy Tents
9. Train Station
10. Warehouses
11. Docks
12. Mess Hall
13. Commissary & Armory
14. Communications
15. Field Hospital
16. Infantry Barracks
17. Officer Quarters
18. Infantry Mess Hall
19. River Fortifications
20. Little Aldon
TROLL ARMY
ELF ARMY
ESCARLISH ARMY
HYDALLA RIVER
THE WALL
CHIBO RIVER

DWARVEN MOUNTAINS
OBAIKURA
DALORBOR
GULADEL
IDREKBOR
MT. DETMUK
AFRISTANI PLAINS
Milnissi River
WESTE
TERMI

KOSTARIA
OSMANA
TINENRESH
DAR GORANTH
DROGENVROH ISLAND
URIXIDOR ISLAND
BRENZUK ISLAND
PEACE BRIDGE
Gulmorth River
TARENHIEL
NINTHALOR
LETHOREL
ESTYRA
PERSATRA AERODROME
SYLMARE
DANORBIC OCEAN
RN RAIL NAL
BRIDGETOWN
FORT LINDER
Hydalla River
FORT DEFENSE
CHIBO RIVER
FYNE RIVER
AYRE
WINDERTON LAKE
ESCARLAND
TREEHAVEN
ALDON
FORT CHARIBERT
EMPIRE
LANDRI
BARRINGSTALL PASS
WHIREHURST MOUNTAINS
N
ENGLESTON GAP
W   E
LUDON
CARTMER GORGE
Frogg's Hollow
S
GROYRIA
MONGAVARIAN
THE WORLD OF THE
ALLIANCE KINGDOMS

ONE

Major Fieran Laesornysh peered over the side of his aeroplane, taking in the Whitehurst Mountains spreading as far as he could see. The Half-Breed Squadron roared in his wake with Merrik in position as his wingman and the others staggered into a formation stretching across the sky and several aeroplanes deep.

Far below, a river sparkled, carving its way through the mountains while thick green forests covered the mountains all the way to their peaks, the leaves tinged with the occasional hint of red or gold in the first blush of coming autumn.

On a dirt road winding through the Engleston Gap through the mountains, a line of dwarven tanks and Escarlish trucks rumbled over the dirt path, heading toward the front on the other side. Thanks to the troll and dwarven stone magic and to the dwarven skill in getting heavy armored vehicles through mountainous terrain, the Alliance had turned two of the main mountain passes into invasion routes into Mongavaria.

Puffs of smoke on the horizon marked where

Mongavarian soldiers attempted to hold off the invading Alliance armies. High in the sky above them, aeroplanes whirled and dodged as they fought, the handful of Mongavarian pilots putting up a good fight against the rather inexperienced Aerial Knights Squadron, the newest squadron in the Alliance Flying Corps. At least their captain had been picked from Capt. Fleetwood's squadron, so one of the pilots had some previous experience.

When Fieran glanced at the dashboard, the indicator lights for radio channels 1 and 2 were blinking, showing there was radio chatter in range. As his squadron was on channel 1, that must mean the Aerial Knights were on channel 2.

The newly installed, updated radio in his Defender had five channels compared to the two of the previous radio. The first three channels were reserved for the Flying Corps squadrons so that different squadrons could be on separate channels to reduce confusion during battle. The fourth channel was designated for communicating with ground troops and the fifth channel for airships.

The airships and ground troops had additional channels Fieran didn't have so that they could communicate without cluttering the channels used for coordinating between air and land. Lights on the dashboard showed when a channel was active.

Fieran flipped the switch to change from channel 1 to channel 2, and the chatter changed to a flurry of unfamiliar voices. "Aerial Knights, this is Maj. Laesornysh of the Half-Breed Squadron. We're coming up on your six and would appreciate it if you didn't shoot us. Over."

"Half-Breed, this is Capt. Crelford. Roger. Over." A high tenor voice with a highbrow Escarlish tone cut through the rest of the voices. He used the new alphabet code for R, meaning "received" or "message received."

"Need any assistance in the air before we proceed with our ground strike? Over." Fieran studied the battle both in the sky and on the ground as best he could from that distance.

"We have the skies handled, Half-Breed. Over."

Okay, so he'd probably mildly insulted the captain by asking if he needed help, but he'd had to ask. "Have any of those machines been spotted? Over."

"Not by my men. Over."

"Roger that. Out." Fieran flipped his radio back to channel 1. "Half-Breed, the Aerial Knights have the skies handled, but I'd like a rearguard to protect the rest of us when we make our run."

"Roger." Merrik, as the commander of Flight B, rattled off a few names to form the overwatch.

Fieran didn't wait for him to finish organizing, trusting Merrik to have it handled, before he flipped the radio channel again, this time to channel 4. "Half-Breed to Foe Hammer. Over."

Fieran waited for a moment before he repeated the call. A light on the truck-mounted radio used by infantry troops would be flashing, alerting the infantry's radioman that there was activity on the radio channel.

After another moment, a new voice answered, "Half-Breed, this is Foe Hammer. Over."

"We're a minute out and coming in hot." Fieran tried to judge the distances as he and the other aeroplanes neared the Mongavarian foothills, roaring toward the battle ahead. "Any update to the original strike coordinates? Over."

There was a pause. Probably the radioman reporting to his superior officers. After a few seconds, his voice came again. "We've pushed the enemy farther than expected. Do not—I repeat—do not strike the original coordinates." The man gave new coordinates about five hundred yards farther into Mongavaria.

"Roger." Fieran repeated the coordinates for confirmation, just to make sure. If he were to guess, the Alliance armies were now located at the old coordinates, and the last thing Fieran wanted to do was lead a strike on his own side.

Fieran probably should have been given the updated coordinates long before now, but the army was still getting used to the fact that they had radios for communication and that they could cooperate with those in the air. Everyone was still learning how to use everything from the radios to the military letter code to the system of coordinates.

The radioman's voice came over the radio again. "We're starting the shelling with the magic flares. Over."

"Roger that. Out." Fieran flipped back to channel 1, dropping into the middle of his squadron's lively chatter. They were a little infamous for cluttering up the radio with nonsense compared the far more proper radio communications of many other units. "Half-Breed, Foe Hammer should start shelling the Mongavarian line with the magic flares soon. We have new strike coordinates."

He repeated them to make sure everyone had them. His pilots would be following him and would do whatever he did, but he didn't want any mistakes, even if this was far from the first strike they'd executed in the past week.

With three warriors with the magic of the ancient kings—Dacha, Adry, and Rhohen—pushing the invasion from Fort Defense, the Alliance had sent Fieran to be the mobile warrior with that type of magic. He and the Half-Breed Squadron had flown back and forth between the two invasions through the Barringstall Pass and the Engleston Gap to provide a magical punch before the ground armies, greatly reinforced with dwarven heavy armor units, swept in with the hammer blow.

While only the dwarven kingdom of Dalorbor had signed a treaty with the Alliance, the other three dwarven kingdoms were still sending raw materials and work crews to the Alliance. Or at least to Dalorbor if they didn't want contact with the Alliance directly.

Still, even one kingdom of dwarves was enough to tip the military scales in the Alliance's favor.

Ahead, magical bursts flared all along the near horizon, brightening into red starbursts that lingered on the ground and in the air within one of the lines of men and artillery pieces that stretched across the churned-up ground of what had once been farm fields.

Over the past two weeks since Mongavaria had deployed those magic-grabbing machines, the Alliance had developed these magical test flares. Since a human magician's magic, once set into its final shape, wasn't tied to the magician directly, it was safe to use anything pre-prepared in the presence of the machines.

If the bomb exploded in a starburst, the magic going in all directions, then there weren't any of those machines in the area. But if the magic from the bomb was sucked in a particular direction, then not only would they know a machine was in the area, but they'd also know its location.

Even better, the magical flares also marked the enemy's location for air strikes.

Fieran studied the red flares of magic. None of it seemed to be wavering in any particular direction.

He released his magic from the tight hold within his chest, but he didn't unleash it yet. This test wasn't foolproof. The Mongavarians could have a machine but had it turned off, waiting for Fieran to release his magic before they switched it on.

But so far that hadn't been the case. With trolls, elves, and dwarves using their magic to push the invasion forward, the Mongavarians had plenty of other magic to combat and reasons besides Fieran to deploy any machines they had.

Overhead, the dogfight continued, although the Mongavarian resistance seemed to be failing. Between the Aerial Knights Squadron's dogged tenacity and the aeroplanes from the Half-Breed Squadron taking up a guarding overwatch, they were safe from that direction.

"Half-Breed, time to begin our run." Fieran let his magic burst from his fingers and curl around the protecting wires on his aeroplane. With another shove, he sent his magic outward until his squadron was protected by a network of his magic.

Then Lt. Rothilion and the elven pilots of Flight A rolled their aeroplanes into as steep of dives as they could manage without shredding their wings.

After a moment, Fieran and the pilots of Flight B put their aeroplane into dives as well. The wind whipped past Fieran's face, tugging at his silk scarf and snatching at his breath as it set up a whining noise through the various wing struts and supports.

Near the ground, Lt. Rothilion swerved toward the north to parallel the Mongavarian line. Fieran turned south to take that section. Below, a few Mongavarian artillerymen struggled to crank their guns' elevation high enough to point at the aeroplanes. It wouldn't do them any good if they managed it, however, thanks to Fieran's magic.

Fieran pressed the trigger for his machine guns, strafing the exposed soldiers even as he blasted his magic downward. His magic devoured metal, exploded ordnance, and ripped through men and artillery guns alike.

For good measure, he reached to one side and pulled on the levers beside him, releasing the two small bombs under his right wings. He quickly switched hands and released the bombs under his left wings as well, balancing the weight once again.

Behind him, Merrik's machine gun chattered before even more bombs exploded.

Cheers filled the radio.

"Yes!"

"Got 'em!"

"That will teach them to attack the Alliance!"

Across the farm fields, a line of tanks rumbled forward on their tracks. Dwarves hunched behind the armored vehicles, likely stomping and humming in rhythm since a protective shield stretched between the tanks, using the large chunks of metal as anchoring points. Behind them, ranks of elves, trolls, and humans crouched low as they hurried forward in a controlled charge.

Even as he turned his aeroplane toward the sky, wheeling it back toward the Alliance troops, Fieran shoved another wave of his magic outward. It danced over the dwarven magic, adding another layer of protection. It didn't merge quite as happily with the shield as it did with Pip's magic, but Pip's magic was rather special like that.

Fieran glanced over his shoulder, checking that the last of his Flight had finished their run and were lifting back into the sky once again.

Down below, the Alliance forces smashed into the Mongavarian line.

Fieran grinned as he toggled the radio back to channel 4. "Foe Hammer, come in. Over."

"Well done, Half-Breed!" The radioman sounded as if he might have been cheering a moment before. The vague sound of cheers and shouts could be barely heard in the background. The radioman must be with the rearguard command position rather than in the front lines currently engaged with the enemy.

"Do you need us to make another run? Over." With the armies so locked together, Fieran wasn't sure he and his squadron could make another strafing run. But they could join the overwatch and wait for an hour or two to see if another run was needed.

Fieran scanned the skies as his aeroplane climbed higher. The dogfight was over, and he couldn't spot a single Mongavarian aeroplane left.

There was a pause before a new voice came over the radio. "Half-Breed, this is Col. Fletcher. My commendations on a job well done. We've got it from here. Over."

"Yes, sir. Half-Breed out." Fieran switched back to channel 1. "Well done, Half-Breed. We can head back to Engleston Aerodrome."

Fieran perched on a log near one of the campfires, stretching out his bare feet toward the flames to warm them up after the flight. His socks lay on stones as close to the fire as he dared. Hopefully the dry heat would somewhat cut the smell while it dried them.

On the next log over, Merrik had his prosthetic leg off and in his lap as he cleaned out a few of the joints and fiddled with the adjustments. His socks, too, dried out near the fire, including the stocking he wore over his stump. As he stretched out his left leg, he wiggled his three remaining toes on that foot. A few scars wrapped around his foot and up his ankle from where he'd been pieced back together.

Lt. Rothilion, Lije, Stickyfingers, Tiny, and Murray lounged on the other logs around this campfire, although Stickyfingers was leaning so far backward that he was in danger of tipping over as he talked with Lt. Nellie Blair where she sat at a nearby campfire with most of the flygirls, both human and elven.

Lije sniffed at his shirt and grimaced. "I'm ready to get back to Fort Defense and get a proper shower."

The Engleston Aerodrome had a few outdoor showers behind makeshift curtains, but the water was ice cold. Laundry had to be scrubbed in a bucket and set out on a line to dry, something Fieran and his squadron had been too busy to do in the past few days.

"The return to proper accommodations will be much appreciated." Lt. Rothilion scrubbed at the mud splattered on the ends of his trousers and tilted his head toward where their two-person army tents were tucked beneath the trees at the very edge of this mountain meadow, the ground falling away to a gorge on the far side. To the other side of their fires, their aeroplanes were parked beside the airfield, scattered far enough apart that they wouldn't all be destroyed in case of a bombing raid.

Beyond the airfield, the haphazard buildings of the aerodrome perched amid piles of muddy earth while the skeleton of a half-finished hangar rose against the night sky.

"And away from the mud." Merrik peered into the small space at the ankle joint of his prosthetic.

"At least it isn't raining tonight." Fieran shot a glance at the clear night sky arching overhead, the stars winking. This high up in the Whitehurst Mountains, the night was somewhat chilly, even this far south in Escarland. At this time of early autumn, most of southern Escarland was still gripped in hot, humid weather, and as that air piled into the mountains, it resulted in frequent rainsqualls.

"Not yet," Lije grumbled as he shifted one of his damp boots closer to the fire.

"We'll be back at Fort Defense tomorrow." Tiny heaved a sigh, his eyes going somewhat distant. He was likely dreaming about donuts...and the troll girl who worked in the donut shop.

Lije rolled his eyes and elbowed Tiny.

Stickyfingers was so wrapped up with his conversation with the flygirls at the other campfire that he hadn't even noticed.

Fieran resisted the urge to heave a lovesick sigh of his own. He missed Pip. Missed joking with her. Missed tinkering on an aeroplane together. Missed evening walks with her hand in his.

For the little over a week that the Half-Breed Squadron had been supporting the southern two invasion forces, the squadron's mechanics had been left behind at Fort Defense, along with most of their gear. They'd camped in large fields, highland meadows, and makeshift aerodromes where they could borrow mechanics and purloin spare parts as needed, only occasionally having access to the luxuries of showers and hot food that they'd grown accustomed to at Fort Defense.

Now Fieran's squadron had finally been ordered to return to Fort Defense. The invasion was making good progress, and their aeroplanes were in need of maintenance and repairs.

Not to mention, all of them needed rest. They'd flown long hours, traveling up and down the border, and engaged in numerous battles both in the air and in support of ground troops.

It was beyond time for a day off. A plate of donuts. A walk with his girl.

And a hot shower. Definitely the hot shower.

TWO

Pip rocked from her heels to her toes as she shaded her eyes and peered upward at the black silhouettes of aeroplanes against the clear blue skies.

The Half-Breed Squadron was finally coming home.

"Is that them?"

Pip jumped at the voice and turned to the tall young woman with long red-gold hair flowing around her shoulders and over the hilts of the twin swords sheathed across her back. "Yes. Finally."

Fieran's sister Adry grinned, her stance relaxing as she, too, peered upward. She wore the evergreen uniform of the Tarenhieli Army, while lieutenant's stripes marked her shoulders. "They're going to be all noble and land last, aren't they?"

"Yes." Pip resisted the urge to sigh as two of the aeroplanes circled down before lining up on the airfield. Unless there were extenuating circumstances, Fieran always waited to land until all his pilots were safely on the ground.

She and Adry waited at the edge of the airfield, standing to one side of the large hangar doors to avoid blocking them as the ground crew wheeled the returned aeroplanes inside. As the flyboys and flygirls climbed from their aeroplanes and entered the hangar, Pip waved greetings to them, sharing a few longer, shouted greetings with Lije, Stickyfingers, Tiny, and Aylia, although none of them lingered. They were too intent on heading straight to the showers. Not that she blamed them. She wasn't about to get too close to any of them.

At last, the final two aeroplanes circled down from above, gliding to gentle landings, the aeroplanes going from graceful warbirds to bumping, unwieldy contraptions as they rolled to a halt before the hangar.

"Merrik!" Adry dashed forward, leaping onto the toe step in the side of the aeroplane before it had fully stopped.

Pip followed much more slowly, waiting for Fieran's aeroplane to stop before she approached. She might be half-elf, but she hadn't inherited the extreme athleticism from her elven side that Adry had from hers.

Fieran yanked off his flight cap and goggles before he scrambled out of the aeroplane. As he turned, his gaze landed on her, that broad grin spreading on his face and sparkling in his bright blue eyes.

"Fieran!" Pip flung herself into his arms, her feet lifting from the ground as he wrapped his arms around her.

Then he kissed her, and Pip clung to him as she kissed him back. For the first few heartbeats, she was too happy to have him back to pay attention to anything else. But then she grew more aware of just how in need of a shower he was, his hair greasy against her fingers.

She broke off the kiss, propping herself up on her elbows on his chest, her feet still dangling as he gripped her around the waist. "You're gross."

"Too gross for kissing?" Fieran's grin turned lopsided.

"Yeah." She grimaced and tried to take shallow breaths. "Sorry. No more kissing until you've had a shower."

"Fine, fine." He lowered her back to the ground and took a step away. He waved at where Merrik was climbing down, Adry stepping back into his arms as soon as he had both feet —left foot and right prosthetic foot—firmly on the ground. "The lack of showers doesn't seem to be bothering them."

"I saw Adry when she returned from her week at the front. I think her standards for cleanliness have been broken." Pip shuddered just thinking about it. Life as a mechanic behind the lines was far preferable to the life of frontline troops. She got clean sheets and regular showers. Not a week of living in mud. Even with the troll and elven warriors firming up the ground with both stone and roots, the repeated thunderstorms and the two armies churning up the ground had created more mud than could be contained.

"These look good on you." Fieran plucked at one of her shoulders, where bars decorated her jumpsuit coveralls.

"Thanks. I'm still getting used to them." She tugged on the green coveralls, which were her official day uniform. She had a dress uniform and everything in her locker in the barracks.

Shortly after the Wall had come down, the Army made the decision to turn her unit from the civilian contractor Mechanics Auxiliaries to an official army unit, the Ordnance Corps.

Since she'd volunteered and had a degree from Hanford University, she'd been listed as an officer. More than that, she'd been bumped straight to captain, given that she'd served from the beginning of the war and that she was already considered the commander of her unit.

Her brother Mak had been made a sergeant while the

latest mechanics recruits that now served under her and her original team of mechanics had been drafted as privates.

Even after two weeks, she wasn't quite used to thinking of herself as a captain in the Tarenhieli Army, thanks to her Tarenhieli citizenship, on official detachment to the Alliance Army.

Thankfully, she had been made an officer, and she wasn't under Fieran's direct command. As of yet, there wasn't anything in Alliance military regulations to bar them from courting.

Given how invested Fieran's family was in their relationship, she suspected that if any such regulation got handed down, it would include a clause to grandfather in any relationships formed prior to the regulation.

Although, she probably was supposed to greet Fieran with a salute instead of a kiss. Somehow, she didn't think he would report her for insubordination.

Adry and Merrik had finally stopped kissing, and the two of them ambled past Fieran and Pip, hand-in-hand. Merrik's gait was only slightly hitched.

Adry gave Fieran a wave as they passed. Fieran waved back.

Fieran set off for the hangar, his flight cap and goggles dangling from one hand. "Is my dacha back as well?"

He held out his free hand, and Pip took it, although she still left plenty of space between the two of them.

"Yes." Not that Pip had sought Prince Farrendel out. She could talk with Adry easily enough, even if Adry was far more intimidating than Louise. But Prince Farrendel was another matter. "I'm surprised he isn't waiting here to greet you."

With three warriors of the magic of the ancient kings at Fort Defense, they had been rotating in pairs through one-week stints at the front lines to avoid taxing any warrior too much. Adry and Prince Farrendel had just completed a week of fighting, pushing the Mongavarian troops back each day. Now King Rharreth and Prince Rhohen had taken over at the front, giving Adry and Prince Farrendel a week to rest at Fort Defense before they returned. While King Rharreth didn't have the magic of the ancient kings, he was Rhohen's dacha, and he had incredibly strong troll magic, wielding both ice and stone.

"He's probably waiting to greet me until after I've had a shower." Fieran grinned again as they stepped into the hangar.

"Wise of him." Pip dared get close enough to Fieran to bump his arm with hers. The hangar had its own lingering odor of grease and gunpowder, sunbaked metal and equally sunbaked men. Fieran was hardly the only man here who reeked of sweat.

"He is an experienced warrior." Fieran shrugged. "He knows how it is."

She debated for a moment before she tugged on Fieran's hand, pulling him toward Bay 5. "I have something to show you."

"It can't wait until after I've showered?" Fieran shook his head with a chuckle as he followed her, unresisting.

"Nope. I've been waiting days to show you." She kept hauling him along, dodging around an aeroplane as the ground crew rolled one of Flight B's Defenders into Bay 4.

"But you said no kissing until I've showered, and this thing you want to show me sounds like it might deserve a celebratory kiss or two." Fieran's expression was probably his attempt at a smolder, but he was grinning too broadly to pull it off.

"Now I understand why you're so motivated to shower

first." Pip rolled her eyes as they neared the large door separating the two hangar bays. "Well, tough. Besides, all the showers will be taken at this point. You might as well be productive while you wait."

"I suppose you'll just have to put up with my stink." Fieran sniffed at his shirt and gave an exaggerated grimace.

She hurried through the door into Bay 5 and gestured at the rows upon rows of the gleaming new Althidon aeroplanes, which had arrived for the elven half of the squadron while they'd been gone. "They came!"

Lt. Rothilion and a handful of the elven pilots of Flight A —those unlucky enough not to claim a shower—meandered through the hangar bay, inspecting their new aeroplanes. They weren't quite as effusive as the human flyboys had been when receiving their new Defenders, but Pip caught a few of the elves gazing at their new aeroplanes with the adoration they might give to a particularly beautiful tree.

Fieran released her hand and strode to the nearest aeroplane, halting next to where Lt. Rothilion stood.

At Fieran's approach, Lt. Rothilion grimaced, his nose flaring, and eased back a step. "You are rather malodorous."

"Yes, yes, I know." Fieran flapped a hand at him and rolled his eyes. "As if you elves still smell like a sparkling fresh forest even after a lack of showers and fresh laundry."

"Of course we do. Elves are superior." Lt. Rothilion spoke completely flat and straight-faced, that tilt to his nose giving away that he was being just as sarcastic as Fieran, in his own elven way.

Pip positioned herself upwind of the two of them. Neither of them smelled like a bouquet of roses.

Fieran sobered and studied the new aeroplane before them. "These new aeroplanes look like they will keep up with the Defenders better than your old Yshendars."

"Yes." Lt. Rothilion gave a sharp nod.

Fieran's expression turned even more somber as he waved at the nose of the aeroplane. "I suppose without Pretty Face…"

Pretty Face. Pip swallowed at the now familiar ache. There still had been no word of him. If he was going to walk out of Mongavaria, he would've done it by now. They could only hope he'd been captured rather than killed.

Rothilion gave a slight sniff. "We elves are capable of painting our own aeroplanes. We will not forgo the badge of the Half-Breed Squadron."

How far Lt. Rothilion and the other elves of Flight A had come since the Half-Breed Squadron had been formed, almost haphazardly, at Dar Goranth.

"Ah, yes. Then I will leave the artwork in your capable hands." Fieran shared a nod with Lt. Rothilion before he turned back to Pip. "This was worth putting off a shower."

"The new aeroplanes are nice, but not all I wanted to show you." Pip grabbed his hand again and dragged him away from Lt. Rothilion. She didn't figure the elf lieutenant would mind the abrupt departure.

She led Fieran to the corner of the hangar where she'd had the ground crew pull one of the new aeroplanes closer to a workbench.

Fieran chuckled and gestured as they approached. "How long were these new aeroplanes parked here before you started fiddling with one?"

"A day." Pip squirmed under Fieran's look. "Well, a few hours. I had nothing else to do with the squadron away."

She'd helped the mechanics for the other two squadrons after a few bombing raids, but even that hadn't been enough to keep her busy.

But helping out those mechanics and seeing how shot up

the aeroplanes of the other squadrons got had sparked this idea.

"Do you remember how I tried to create a magical shield for the aeroplanes back at Dar Goranth?" Pip halted beside the aeroplane.

"Yes. The magic of the ancient kings kept burning the aeroplane. And it drained the magical power cell too quickly." Fieran stopped as well, studying the wires she'd rigged on the side of the aeroplane.

Those problems were the reasons they had stuck with him providing an active shield for the aeroplanes. That way he could control the magic directly.

"Yes, exactly. But I finally figured out how to overcome those problems." Pip hopped onto the toe step of the aeroplane and patted the side, where a strip of aluminum lay beneath the protective wire, even though Fieran had probably already noted it. "Louise sent me a roll of thin aluminum. It isn't enough on its own, but once I infused it with my magic, it prevents the magic from leaping from the wires and burning the canvas."

"Smart." Fieran nodded, his gaze taking in the strips of aluminum.

"And as for the other problem, that was even simpler." Pip pointed toward the aeroplane's nose. "I added a second magical power cell. The older aeroplanes didn't have the space for it, but these do. I've rigged it so that the shield runs exclusively from this second power cell. The shield still drains the power cell quickly, but that power cell can be safely used up without risking engine power. I added a switch so the shield can be turned on and off as needed to conserve power or if one of those magic-grabbing machines is in the area."

The solutions were so obvious that she'd almost kicked

herself for not thinking of them sooner. But the older aeroplanes back at Dar Goranth hadn't been sturdy enough to add anything else to them, nor had there been space for an additional magical power cell. It hadn't been until aeroplane technology had progressed enough that she had been able to make these modifications.

"You're making me obsolete. Again." Fieran gave her an exaggerated scowl.

"Hardly." She struggled to keep her expression solemn. "Each aeroplane will use twice as many power cells. More, probably. You're going to be needed to fill magical power cells more than ever."

Fieran huffed a breath, muttering, "Oh joy."

She felt a little bad teasing him about that, knowing that not all of his frustration was feigned. He filled magical power cells because it was his duty, but he didn't particularly enjoy it. "Besides, your direct shield is still superior. A pilot can't leave the shield on during a full battle. It will drain out in minutes that way. It's like the machine guns. It needs to be used in short bursts only."

Fieran's grin returned, and he patted the side of the aeroplane. "Still, this will be a lifesaver for the other squadrons."

"Yes, well, it will be. Eventually." Pip dropped back to the concrete floor. "It can't be certified as safe for installing on more aeroplanes until a pilot with a magical engineering degree—preferably one who can shield himself if something should explode—runs it through a few tests."

"Ah." Fieran gave her that lopsided grin again. "Now I know why you were so excited to see me. It wasn't because you missed me. It was because you needed your test pilot."

"You caught me." Pip clasped her hands in front of her, trying to put on an innocent expression.

"I knew your friendship with Louise was going to be

trouble." Fieran shook his head, chuckling with resigned mirth. "But I suppose I'm used to being a test subject. First for Louise and Bennett, and now you. It's my lot in life."

"You're just so good at it." Pip braved his grossness again to elbow him. Getting that close, she caught a whiff of him again. She grimaced and hurried backward once again. "Now, you really need to test out the showers."

"Yes, Captain." Fieran didn't salute her, not even in jest—he was a major, after all—but he nodded to her before he spun and marched toward the nearest outer door.

THREE

Fieran parked the large army truck on the side street next to the donut shop run by Tiny's girlfriend and her father. After he shut off the engine and made sure the truck wouldn't roll away, he grinned at Pip sitting on the bench seat squished next to him, her legs hugged to her chest to keep them out of the way of the gear shift on the floor. "Ready to stretch your legs?"

"Yes. I'm small, but even I have my limits for squishing into tight spots." Pip glanced at Adry and Merrik, who were squashed onto the bench seat on the other side of her before she began scooting along the bench to follow Fieran out the driver's door.

He pushed the door open and hopped down, holding the door for her as she jumped to the dirt road after him.

Across the truck, Merrik had opened the passenger door, and he lowered himself to the ground more slowly than Fieran had. For a moment, he gripped the truck's door, as if he was making sure his legs would hold him before he let go.

The canvas flap at the back of the truck's covered bed

was shoved aside, and the flyboys and flygirls, both human and elven, tumbled out. They'd piled nearly the whole squadron in there as few of them had opted to stay behind in Fort Defense when their squadron had been given a pass to Defense City. Mak hopped out last, likely having been crammed in a corner to take up as little space as possible.

"All right, everyone, if you want to ride back in the truck to Fort Defense, make sure you're back here by 17:00," Fieran called to them as they began scattering into the town. "If you aren't back here, I'm assuming you want to walk back."

He, Pip, Merrik, and Adry had a planned dinner with Dacha and Uncle Iyrinder, and he didn't want to be late. Not when this would be Pip's first dinner with Dacha.

While Defense City was only three miles inland from Fort Defense—walkable or jog-able in a pinch—he wasn't going to ask Merrik to make the walk. Merrik's left ankle was healing well, but it still ached if he did too much. And after all the long hours of flying and living in unwashed and dirty clothing, Merrik had chafed the skin of his stump. After spending the day in Defense City, Merrik would need the truck back to the fort more than any flyboys or flygirls who wanted to stay in the city longer.

"Well, I'm off." Tiny hurried toward the back steps of the donut shop. His girlfriend was already opening the door and grinning at him. She waved to the rest of them, but her smile was focused solely on Tiny.

"I heard there is a new two-reeler at the theater." Stickyfingers turned toward Nellie Blair. "Would you like to go?"

"Sure." She stepped slightly closer to Stickyfingers.

That was something Fieran was going to have to keep an eye on. While his courtship with Pip wasn't against regulations, courting within a unit was. If Stickyfingers and Nellie went past mild flirting, he'd either have to put a stop to it or offer to transfer one of them.

Which he'd hate to do. Stickyfingers was part of the core of the Half-Breed Squadron, and their squadron was Nellie's only option for a combat unit.

Lije strolled over to join Stickyfingers and Nellie. "A moving picture show sounds great." Lije didn't seem to notice the way Sticky's expression fell slightly.

"Yes!"

"Let's go!"

Within a few minutes, a large group of the flyboys and flygirls had set off down the street toward the theater, whisking Stickyfingers and Nellie along with them. Aylia, too, had gone with them, as well as a few of the other elves.

Most of the elves mentioned they were going to head toward the river where there was a small stretch of relatively untouched riverfront that still had some trees.

As a few of the other groups drifted away, Fieran mentally ticked off his list, checking that no one was being left out. It seemed everyone had found a group to hang out with for the day except for Lt. Rothilion, who was shifting his feet and glancing around as if he wasn't quite sure where he belonged.

Fieran suppressed a sigh and glanced at Pip. He'd imagined spending this day with Pip. A day-long date with no work and no intrusions.

Pip looked up at him, and their gazes met. Was that a hint of regret in her own eyes? Then she turned and gestured to Lt. Rothilion. "Saranthyr, you can tag along with us."

"With all of us." Adry was tugging Merrik closer. Apparently this was going to be a double date, even if Rothilion didn't come along.

Rothilion sighed and shook his head, a hint of a resigned-but-pretending-to-not-be curl to his mouth. "I have no wish to find myself the extraneous person."

"You won't be extraneous." As much as he'd hate to do it, Fieran would send Pip off with Merrik and Adry and see to it that Lt. Rothilion wasn't without a friend, if it came to that.

"You won't be the only one not paired up." Mak drifted over to them as well, clearly staking his spot as part of their group.

Fieran bit back another sigh. And now he was going to have Pip's big brother breathing down his neck. Granted, Merrik too would have Adry's big brother breathing down *his* neck, so it was only fair.

"Fine." Rothilion joined them with a faint roll of his shoulders. "I suppose it will not be entirely unpleasant. Where do you intend to go?"

"My cousin Draenelynn said that some of the dwarven crafters tagged along and are setting up shop here in Defense City." Pip took one of Fieran's hands, although her gaze remained on Rothilion. "We were hoping to find some of their booths."

Rothilion gave a nod, and the six of them set off. Mak led the way with Merrik and Adry falling in behind him.

Fieran waited until last to make sure Rothilion came along. But he hadn't needed to worry. Adry was already walking backward, somehow managing to do that and hold Merrik's hand. Merrik steered her around a loose cobblestone, as if this wasn't anything unusual.

"I haven't had the chance to get to know Merrik's squadron yet." Adry shot Rothilion a grin, walking and talking in a way that forced Rothilion to fully join their group rather than trail awkwardly behind. "I'm Adry. Fieran's sister. You're Saranthyr..."

Rothilion hesitated, shooting a glance over his shoulder at Fieran. "Rothilion."

Adry's eyebrows shot up. "Related to—"

"Yes." Lt. Rothilion cut her off before she could finish. "But considering my damasha is on the verge of disowning me, that connection is hardly worth mentioning."

Next to Fieran, Pip stumbled. "Your father is threatening to disown you? Why?"

Rothilion glanced at her before shooting Fieran a look. "You did not tell them?"

"No. I can keep my mouth shut when something is told to me in confidence." Fieran shrugged, trying to ignore the twinge at Rothilion's surprise. Yes, Fieran talked a lot. But that didn't mean he blabbed other people's secrets.

"Linshi." Rothilion dipped his head in a nod before he turned back to Pip. "My father and uncle are a part of the most traditional among the elves. He was angry that I stayed in the squadron under a Laesornysh, and he was even more angry when he heard I had flown with Prince Farrendel."

"And there's your uncle's strange resentment toward my whole family." Adry rolled her eyes. "I'm not sure why he's the one with his knickers in a knot since *he* was the one who broke off his engagement to Aunt Melantha, not the other way around."

Rothilion made a small choking noise at Adry's reference to undergarments. Merrik just shook his head in a resigned kind of way, even as he steered her around another pedestrian since she was still walking backward.

After another polite cough, Rothilion dipped his head. "My damasha has likely only held off because openly taking such a stand against Laesornysh would be politically disastrous."

"That's messed up." Adry flexed her fingers, as if she

wanted to give Rothilion's father a piece of her mind…and perhaps acquaint him with her magic.

Not that Fieran wasn't fully prepared to join her in that, if the occasion should arise.

"I'm sorry." Pip's fingers tightened on Fieran's hand.

"I knew the consequences when I made my choices." Rothilion faced forward, rolling his shoulders in the elven shrug.

His tone said that the conversation was over. All of them paused for a moment before Adry smiled and made the elven forehead to mouth greeting gesture. "Well, it's good to meet you."

She finally faced forward and began a conversation with Mak.

Fieran slowed his steps so that he and Pip dropped somewhat back from the others. "This isn't quite the day-long date I was planning."

"It's all right. Spending time with everyone is also nice." Pip swung their clasped hands before she leaned slightly closer. "And seeing the way you squirm around Merrik and Adry is hilarious."

Fieran heaved a sigh, his gaze drifting to where Merrik and Adry walked ahead, their hands clasped, Adry leaning into Merrik as she pointed at something. "Glad someone finds it funny. It isn't even that I'm against it or anything. It's Merrik. I couldn't ask for someone better for my sister. It's just…"

Pip peered up at him, her eyes searching his face. "What?"

"You're going to laugh. It's ridiculous." Fieran didn't really want to admit the truth out loud. He already knew how silly it would sound.

Pip opened her mouth, as if to promise that she

wouldn't, before she closed her mouth and shrugged. "Okay, yes, I probably will laugh. But you still need to tell someone and get it out of your system."

Fieran swung their hands again, letting some of the bustle of Defense City come between them and the others. "When Merrik and I were little, I resented when Adry got old enough to join us. It felt like she was stealing my friend, and I just wanted to hang out with Merrik without my little sister tagging along."

"And now it kind of feels the same way. Like your sister is stealing your best friend from you." Strangely, Pip didn't laugh. Instead she wrapped her free hand around his arm, tugging him closer.

"It's silly, I know." Fieran exhaled, trying to relax the tightness inside him. "Their romantic relationship is completely different than our friendship. And I'm not losing a friend. I could gain the best brother a man could ask for. It's just..."

"Complicated, given how long the lot of you have been friends. And family." Pip paused for a moment before she burst into laughter.

"See. I told you that you'd laugh." Fieran found himself smiling. Talking it over with Pip was helping. He didn't want to resent Merrik and Adry's relationship at all. Especially since he was rather in favor of it. This was his own problem he had to work through.

"I'm not laughing at that." Pip waved a hand at where Merrik and Adry had paused at an open-fronted booth selling elven shampoos and conditioners. "Let me guess. Merrik was the one who played the peacemaker and tried to stop your childhood fights with Adry?"

"Yes..." Fieran dragged out the word, his smile growing.

"Poor man. He's willingly signing up to keep doing that

the rest of his life." Pip shook her head, an exaggerated sorrowful expression on her face.

"He'd likely do that anyway. This just makes it more convenient." Fieran found himself grinning and hurrying his and Pip's pace so that they could catch up with the others.

Just as they caught up with Merrik and Adry, Lt. Rothilion and Mak meandering a few paces ahead of them, a voice called out over the crowd a moment before Stickyfingers, Lije, and Aylia hurried up to them.

"No moving picture?" Fieran raised his eyebrows.

"The tickets for the first few showings were already sold out." Lije dug into a pocket before he pulled out a ticket. "But we got tickets for the 14:00 showing. It should end just in time for us to catch the truck back."

"Most of the others who didn't get tickets decided to go to one of the taverns." Stickyfingers shrugged, his hands stuck in his pockets, a rather disappointed slump to his shoulders.

"We decided to track all of you down instead." Aylia grinned, her long hair drifting around her. "So where are you headed?"

"Some of the dwarves set up booths, and we were going to try to find them." Pip gestured at the street ahead of them.

"See? I knew you'd be doing something fun." Aylia fell into step with them, Lije and Stickyfingers falling in behind them.

Well, this date was getting rather crowded. Fieran shared a look with Pip, shrugged, and they set off once again.

After wandering the narrow dirt streets for a while and finally asking for directions, they located the street where the dwarves had set up open-fronted, rather ramshackle booths.

This alley was quieter, tucked far into the labyrinth of the growing entertainment town. The booths left the street too narrow for vehicles, leaving the pedestrians free to wander as they wished. With such a large group, they spread out among the various booths.

Stickyfingers, Lije, and Aylia wandered a section of booths with various dwarven foods and drinks. Mak waved and halted by a booth, striking up a conversation in dwarvish with the male dwarf behind the booth. Perhaps he was another Detmuk dwarf since he and Mak seemed to know each other.

Lt. Rothilion drifted with his hands clasped behind his back, staying several feet away from the booths as he perused without taking a specific interest in any of them.

Fieran gripped Pip's hand and let her tug him where she wanted. First across the street to try dwarven salt taffy. Then kitty-corner across the way to look at an array of metal objects. Across the street again to look at a booth with small figurines carved out of rock. The random, scattered, excited way of viewing the booths suited him just fine.

Pip tugged him to the next booth over, their clasped hands still somewhat sticky from the taffy. "Ooh! Look at these!"

This booth held an array of leather armor items. Merrik and Adry were already there, examining one of the leather bracers.

"Those look great." Fieran reached to pick up one of the bracers, but Adry bumped him hard enough to halt him.

She shot him a look that was part annoyed, part teasing. "I was looking at them first."

"Doesn't mean I can't look too."

"It does if I intend to buy a set." Adry's eyes flared with more heat. "You don't need to have the same things as me."

On the other side of Adry, Merrik huffed. "The two of you can share, you know."

Adry raised an eyebrow at him. "You're supposed to be on my side now."

"I am on the side of sense. As I have always been." Merrik spoke in a flat tone, but the slight upward curve to his mouth gave him away. "Which, in most cases, is neither side."

"Ouch. I'd be offended but…" Adry smirked at Fieran. "He has us there."

Fieran nodded and grinned back. "Admit it. We wouldn't know what to do without Merrik's sense."

Pip nudged Fieran's arm and whispered, "Like I said. Poor Merrik."

Fieran laughed, the mirth bubbling inside him washing away the last of his snappiness with his sister. He really shouldn't be childish about this.

He picked up a bracer with dwarven, geometric designs tooled into the leather. The bracer weighed more than he'd expected, and he nearly dropped it.

The dwarf behind the booth, still shooting glances between Fieran and Adry, gestured. "The bracers are layered with reticulated, thin metal reinforced with dwarven magic. Guaranteed to stop an ax from chopping off your hand."

"Handy if you are invested in not losing any more limbs." Merrik reached out and traced a finger over a bracer with an elven tree design.

"How about this?" Pip placed a hand on Fieran's arm, glancing from him to Adry. "As long as the two of you don't have the same design…"

Merrik shot Pip a grateful look, as if he was thankful that he would have at least one sensible ally in his peacekeeping.

"Works for me." Adry picked up another set of the bracers with the elven trees on them. She dug into her pocket. "I'll take two sets in this design."

"Adry…" Merrik's low voice held a fond warning.

"Don't blame me for wanting to spoil my boyfriend." Adry pressed a kiss to Merrik's cheek before she plunked the money down on the table before the dwarf, claimed her two sets of bracers, and tugged on Merrik's hand. "You can always spoil me right back if you feel you must."

Merrik was still grinning as Adry dragged him away to the next booth.

"Decided to join Merrik in playing peacemaker?" Fieran rubbed a thumb over the geometric design on the bracer.

"If this is going to be the way of things, I figured Merrik might as well not stand alone in that." Pip grinned before she pointed at the bracer in Fieran's hand as she turned toward the dwarf. "And I'll take that set."

"Pip, I…" Fieran wasn't sure how to protest. Or if he wanted to. "You don't have to."

"I can't let Adry be the only one spoiling her boyfriend." Pip touched the wrench pendant on the necklace he'd given her. "Besides, you've already spoiled me. It's time I returned the favor."

"Then, linshi." Fieran collected the bracers from the dwarf. With the geometric dwarven designs, it would be as if he wore Pip's colors.

As they stepped away from the booth, a fit of hacking and coughing broke out across the street.

Stickyfingers, gagging and choking, stuck his head halfway into a nearby trash barrel and retched. Lije was coughing, eyes watering, as he braced himself against the post of the booth.

"What's going on? Are you guys all right?" Fieran called to them, taking a step in that direction.

"They're fine. Probably." Pip winced as Lije made a gagging sound, though he didn't run to join Stickyfingers at the barrel. "I think they made the mistake of trying a sip of dwarven mushroom brew. Let's just say, it's strong."

"Remind me to stay away from the stuff." Fieran shuddered as he fell into step with Pip. "Where to now?"

AFTER EATING lunch at a café and joining Aylia, Stickyfingers, and Lije for the moving picture—a rather horrible production that couldn't decide if it wanted to be a slapstick comedy, a romance, or a heartfelt look at industrialization—Fieran drove the truck back to Fort Defense and returned to his tent.

After a quick cleanup from walking the dusty streets for most of the day, Fieran paused before leaving his tent. Hesitating another moment, he picked up his swords, shrugged them on, and buckled the straps. He buckled the bracers on as well.

He didn't necessarily need his swords for a family dinner —although carrying them at least fulfilled the army regulations to be armed—but he was trying to wear them more. To get more used to the feel of them on his back and in his hands.

As he strolled out of his tent, Merrik was stepping out of his, a small wince twisting his face.

"Are you all right?" Fieran hurried closer, though he didn't offer an arm. If Merrik wanted help, he'd ask for it.

"Fine." Merrik's gait had more of a hitch to it, a limp that he'd nearly erased most days. "That was just a lot of walking. I'll be fine tomorrow."

Fieran opened his mouth, not quite sure what to say. Before he had the chance, Merrik's gaze swung past him. With a smile, Merrik nudged Fieran.

Turning, Fieran found Pip strolling toward the two of them, dressed in her uniform shirt and skirt. She halted and smoothed her skirt in what seemed to be a nervous gesture. "Do I look all right?"

"You look great. Not that Dacha will even notice." Fieran held out his hand to her, resisting the urge to pull her closer or kiss her.

"You do not have to be nervous." Merrik fell in on the other side of Fieran. "The table will be so crowded that Uncle Farrendel's attention will not be on you."

Pip gave a slight nod, but she was still walking close to Fieran, her grip tight on his hand.

Continued distraction was in order. Fieran nudged Merrik with an elbow. "Is it weird, still calling my dacha Uncle Farrendel while you're courting Adry?"

"A little, yes." Merrik shrugged, breathing out a light chuckle. "That is something we are still sorting out. It is too soon to claim him as Dacha yet, especially while he and my dacha are in the same room. That would get confusing for everyone involved. But he is too much family to take a step back to call him *Amir* or *General*."

And perhaps this was why Merrik courting Adry was both complicated and strangely simple. Merrik was family already.

When he, Merrik, and Pip crested the rise, Adry was waiting for them, pacing in the grassy space between the rise and the elven officer quarters, where she had a room. As soon as Adry's and Merrik's gazes met, a smile burst across Adry's face. A glance at Merrik beside him showed a similar smile.

Pip leaned closer to Fieran and whispered, "They're so cute together."

"Yes." Fieran hadn't realized how often Merrik and Adry

had gravitated toward each other until he'd searched his memory. The signs had been there. He'd simply missed them.

Adry hurried toward them, taking Merrik's hand and whispering something to him. He smiled back, their pace slowing.

Fieran shared a glance with Pip and hurried ahead.

Two elven guards, neither of them Uncle Iyrinder, guarded the door. They nodded to Fieran, stepping aside to give him and Pip more room, as Fieran knocked on the door.

"Come in," Dacha's voice called from inside.

Fieran opened the door. He would have gone inside, but Pip remained rooted to the spot, her eyes wide. He leaned closer. "Breathe, Pip."

She shuddered in a breath and muttered something that sounded almost like *I can do this.*

"Could you hold the door?"

Fieran glanced over his shoulder, then hurried out of the way, holding the door open. He tugged Pip out of the way as well, since she was still shaking off her hero-worship paralysis.

Uncle Iyrinder approached, carrying a chair. He nodded to them before he walked inside.

Fieran rested a hand between Pip's shoulder blades, his other arm crooked at an awkward angle since Pip had a death grip on it, and steered her inside.

In the main room of Dacha's suite, Uncle Iyrinder set the chair down next to the small table. Dacha adjusted one of the other chairs, as if attempting to create more space. But with four chairs around a table designed for two and one side of the table pulled up to the cushioned bench set into the wall for the final two seats, they would be rather crowded.

Dacha's silver-blond hair lay long down his back and

around the hilts of his swords. When he turned to face Fieran, there were shadows beneath his eyes, his mouth set in a grim line.

And the look in his eyes...it had Fieran halting, wondering if perhaps this wasn't a great night for a large family dinner. The set of Dacha's shoulders was somewhere between hard and fragile.

But then Merrik and Adry piled into the room after them, and there was no chance to duck out and call the dinner off.

After a few minutes of awkward shuffling, everyone squished into seats around the table. Adry and Merrik took the cushioned bench with Pip in the chair next to Adry. Fieran sat on the other side of Pip with his dacha on the other side of him. Uncle Iyrinder took the last chair between Dacha and Merrik. With the table so small, all of them were basically elbow to elbow, everyone's feet and knees knocking into each other.

"Well, this is cozy." Adry nearly elbowed Pip as she grabbed one of the covered dishes.

Merrik reached beneath the table, a moment later straightening with his prosthetic foot in hand. He tucked it onto the bench next to him. "One less foot to worry about."

His joking tone didn't fully hide the edges of pain lingering around his eyes.

Fieran shifted on his chair until he was only half on the seat. To most of those around the table, it probably looked like he just wanted to get closer to Pip. But he met Merrik's gaze across the table and tilted his head toward the open spot he'd created.

Merrik nodded, and a moment later he propped his left foot on the chair beside Fieran where he could elevate the ankle after their long day of walking.

Beside Fieran, Pip had shrunk small onto her chair, as if

hiding. On Fieran's other side, Dacha was stiff and silent. This was going to be one long, awkward meal if Fieran and Adry couldn't spark some kind of conversation.

"Look at these bracers Adry, Merrik, and I got in the market. Well, Adry and Pip got them. Merrik and I were given them." Fieran held out his arm to show off his new bracer to Dacha.

Dacha made a small noise of approval in the back of his throat as he examined the bracer on Fieran's arm. "The dwarves do excellent work."

"Perhaps we will need to venture into Defense City ourselves if we get the chance." Uncle Iyrinder glanced at the bracers Merrik was wearing.

Dacha made another noise in the back of his throat, part agreement, part discomfort. As if he wasn't sure he wanted to agree and lock himself into a commitment.

But the conversation had broken the ice somewhat, and laughter and talking took over between the clink of forks and knives on the plates.

Fieran took in the table, squished as it was, and he could imagine this scene after the war. His family gathered around the much larger table at Treehaven, yet with Pip and Merrik added to their numbers.

It was strange, getting used to his family expanding and growing like this. But he wouldn't have it any other way.

FOUR

Fieran wandered into the hangar, dodging around the bustle of the ground crew returning the aeroplanes to their places.

He finally found Pip in Bay 7, one of the bays claimed by the Fighting Second, beside one of the newly-rigged aeroplanes. "How is installing the new shields going?"

"Going almost too well." Pip checked off something on her clipboard. "The mechanics for the Fighting Second have nearly all of their aeroplanes rigged, and I'm just doing the final checks for them. But they have things well in hand. Honestly, they don't need me to check their work."

The military command had waited for only the most cursory of tests by Fieran to give approval to move forward with protecting all the fighter aeroplanes. Pip trained both the mechanics under her and those in the other squadrons on how to install the protective shield system, and the other mechanics had done most of the work. She hadn't even had to create the wire and aluminum shielding since several dwarves with metal magic had infused their magic into the metal similarly enough to Pip's version to function the same way.

"Glad it's going smoothly." Since Pip was working, Fieran kept his hands firmly clasped behind his back instead of pulling her close. This wasn't the time for distractions.

"The Wardogs will have their aeroplanes rigged within a day or two." Tucking the clipboard under her arm, Pip climbed onto a ladder and peered into the engine compartment. "The bomber squadrons are coming up with a spare aeroplane that I can experiment with to figure out how to rig a shield over it."

"Want help?" Fieran grinned, rocking back on his heels to keep himself from leaning closer to the ladder.

"Always." Pip shut the hatch for the engine compartment and jotted a few notes on her clipboard. After climbing down the ladder, she pointed at it. "You can carry that for me."

Fieran's grin widened before he followed her, toting the ladder, as she made her way to the next aeroplane needing the final check.

"Maj. Laesornysh." A clipped, tenor voice called from behind him.

Fieran turned and found Lt. Busher, Col. Dentley's adjutant, standing at attention there with his customary clipboard and crisply ironed uniform. "Yes?"

"Col. Dentley requests that you, Lt. Rothilion, and Lt. Loiatir report to his office, sir." Lt. Busher's starched posture and blank expression gave away nothing.

"We'll be there shortly." Fieran waited for Lt. Busher to spin on a heel and march away before he sighed and glanced up at Pip. "I guess I'd better round up Rothilion and Merrik."

Pip halted in her inspection, worrying her lower lip as

she peered down at him. "Do you think everything is all right?"

"Hopefully. I can't think of anything I've done wrong lately." Fieran shrugged and pushed away from the ladder.

After winding his way back through the massive nested hangar, he located Rothilion in Bay 5, overseeing the elves as they put the finishing touches on painting the nose art on their new aeroplanes.

Only a few minutes later, the two of them fetched Merrik. He'd been keeping an eye on the flyboys and flygirls where they'd been indulging in their latest obsession: learning wood carving from Mak and Lije. So far, only three of the flyboys had had to report to the hangar's elven medic with sliced hands.

Adry, enjoying her last day before she and Dacha returned to the front, had joined the wood carving lesson with gusto. Merrik whispered to her before he pushed to his feet from where he'd been sitting on a crate.

At least this was an improvement over the sourdough takeover. And better than the group lockpicking session Stickyfingers had taught a few days ago. They'd be fine.

Leaving Mak in charge of making sure no one bled out, Fieran, Merrik, and Rothilion strode back through the hangar, walking all the way to Bay 12, where Col. Dentley had set up an office.

The table in the center of the space was covered in charts and maps while a radio sat in one corner, manned at all times. Several lieutenants hurried in and out as Col. Dentley coordinated with both of the bomber squadrons and with headquarters. Long gone were the days when this room was mostly empty.

Fieran stood at attention before Col. Dentley's desk. "Sir."

Col. Dentley motioned for the three of them to stand at ease, even as he dismissed the rest of the bustle from the office. Once the door was shut, Col. Dentley slid a piece of paper across the desk toward Fieran. "The front lines have pushed far enough into Mongavaria that they can no longer be effectively supported in the air from Fort Defense. Headquarters, too, has deemed Fort Defense too far behind the lines now. A new operations base is being set up in one of the captured Mongavarian towns, and command has requested that I assign one squadron to move forward. Since you and your squadron have proved how capable you are at working independently, I'm assigning the Half-Breed Squadron to this mission. The Wardogs and Fighting Second will remain here to continue providing escort to the bomber squadrons."

"Thank you, sir." Fieran picked up the official orders.

It was the station he would have picked, if given the chance. Escorting the bombers was becoming rather boring lately, as Mongavaria struggled to field enough aeroplanes or airships to put up any real resistance. Now that the fighters and soon the bombers would be rigged with Pip's wiring, Fieran truly wasn't needed for those runs any longer.

Pip…Fieran's stomach sank. He swallowed, not sure how to ask this delicately. "Will one of the Ordnance units be sent forward with us?"

For the first time, a hint of a sardonic smile broke through Col. Dentley's professional mien. "Yes. Capt. Detmuk-Inawenys and her mechanics will be sent forward as well."

Fieran resisted the urge to do anything as visible as heave a sigh of relief. Instead he merely repeated, "Thank you, sir."

Col. Dentley pushed two more pieces of paper forward, the smile disappearing once more. "To more effectively support the ground troops, you may need to split your squadron up more often. To make that easier, I'm promoting both Rothilion and Loiatir to captain."

Rothilion and Merrik stepped forward to pick up the papers. Rothilion's expression never wavered, but Merrik's eyes had widened, as if he hadn't expected he'd ever become a captain.

With that, Col. Dentley dismissed the three of them, turning back to his paperwork.

After they had stepped out of the room, Fieran elbowed Merrik. "Capt. Loiatir has a good ring to it. As does Capt. Rothilion." He shot a grin at Saranthyr. "It's about time, isn't it?"

"Yes." Rothilion's expression had fallen into that too-dour look that meant he was playing along with the banter.

Merrik was still staring at the paper in his hands. "I did not think they would promote me. Not after…" He gestured down at his right leg.

"You're still one of the best pilots in the entire Flying Corps." Fieran draped an arm first over Merrik's shoulders, then Rothilion's. "Now come on. Let's go tell the squadron the good news."

"Good news?" One of Rothilion's eyebrows went up. "The news that we will likely be going back to lack of bathing facilities and sleeping in tents in the mud?"

Right. There was that.

FIERAN SWEPT his aeroplane in a long curve over Fort Defense, taking in all the changes.

Below, the damage from the bombing had been repaired as if it had never happened. The warehouses had been rebuilt, the rubble cleared away. The Escarlish officer quarters had been repaired as well.

Instead of dug-in front lines beside the Chibo River, the Escarlish border was now a massive staging area with a constant stream of trucks rumbling across bridges over the muddy trench of what had once been the river. A single set of train tracks even stretched across to the Mongavarian border, carrying more soldiers and supplies to the battling Alliance Army.

Cargo ships, guarded by small river warships, plied the Hydalla River with more war material.

Now that the invasion of Mongavaria had begun, the Alliance was ensuring that their supply lines remained robust, even with the relentless drive pushed forward by the magic of the ancient kings.

The Chibo River remained dammed with the landslide, the floodplain caused by diverting the river now providing a protected flank for the Alliance Army as it marched into Mongavaria.

Even the air section of Fort Defense had changed. The new hangar for the bomber squadron was now completed and bustled with activity. More bombers clustered to one side of the expanded airfield. A second squadron of bombers had been sent to Fort Defense, and Capt. Fleetwood's Fighting Second was currently escorting a bombing run on targets deep within Mongavaria, their aeroplanes protected with Pip's new shielding mechanism.

A lump formed in Fieran's throat as he took in the sprawling fort that he'd called home for months. He'd fought so hard in these skies and on that ground. He'd nearly died here. Merrik, too, had nearly died and had lost a leg. If Fort Linder had been his squadron's first taste of the fight and Dar Goranth had forged them into a unit, then here at Fort Defense they had come into their own as a fighting force.

But now it was time to move forward. They would sleep in Mongavaria tonight.

As the last aeroplane of the squadron rose into the air, Fieran wheeled his aeroplane out of the circling pattern and pointed the nose east toward Mongavarian skies.

The muddy trench where Fieran had held off the Mongavarian advance flashed by below, followed by the marshy floodplains where the Mongavarian army had been camped for so long and where Fieran had nearly died after falling from the sky.

Then he was out over the scarred and abandoned farm fields. Craters from bombs and mortar shells dug pits within the shattered stalks of corn and wheat while trampled sections marked where armies had charged and retreated. Still more patches of dug up earth showed the places where hundreds were buried in mass graves. The blackened remains of aeroplanes, airships, trucks, artillery guns, and other armaments of war lay scattered across the land.

So much death and destruction. And still more would come before the end.

"I wonder where we'll be bunking." Lije's voice broke through the unusual silence on the radio, as if they'd all been caught in a moment of reverie saying goodbye to Fort Defense. "Hopefully somewhere better than a tent in the mud."

"And somewhere with showers." Aylia conveyed a shudder in her voice.

"The human half of the squadron grew rather pungent the last time we were at a temporary aerodrome," one of the male elven pilots piped up with a disdainful sniff that he somehow managed to get across even over the crackle of the radio. Despite the appearance of derision, the fact that he was joining in the banter showed how far the squadron had come during their time at Fort Defense.

"Hey! We weren't the ones whining about how crusty our hair was getting," Stickyfingers snorted.

"If I had wanted to forgo showers, I would have remained in the infantry." The elf's comment set off a round of laughter and agreement.

Fieran grinned and simply listened to his squadron's banter as he and Merrik led the way through the sky.

After slightly over an hour of flying, they neared the location Fieran had been given of the new aerodrome.

Below, a line of trucks clogged the one road into what had once been a Mongavarian village. The set of train tracks ended at the town while a smaller gauge rail line had been built as a spur leaving the town, likely to carry men and material onward to the front lines themselves.

With Fieran's squadron and much of headquarters moving to this new location, the people in charge of logistics must be tearing their hair out trying to find transportation for everyone.

In the distance, puffs of smoke and the blaze of blue magic marked the front, still miles ahead of even this forward position.

Just outside of town, a large brick manor house dominated the area around it with a large stable set back from it. A line of trucks parked in the circle drive in front of it, tiny figures carrying items from the trucks into the manor house.

The front lawn stretched in a huge expanse of cut grass, marked by flags and elven lights to designate it as an airfield.

"Are we going to be staying in the manor house?" Lije sounded as if he was gawking.

"Naw. We couldn't be that lucky." Sticky's voice held a scoffing laugh. "We're probably going to be camping in the stables or the horse pasture behind it."

While Fieran would normally wait until last to land, he gave the order for Merrik and Rothilion to stay in the air while he led the way toward the ground. He would need to be on hand to officially report in and oversee setting up their new accommodations, wherever they happened to be.

After gauging the wind, he turned into it and lined up on the airfield, easing lower to the ground until his wheels touched down on the unfamiliar patch of grass. Moments later, his tail bumped onto the ground, the tailskid biting into the earth to slow his aeroplane.

Coasting, he turned his warbird toward the edge of the airfield to get it out of the way of the rest of the incoming squadron. Once he'd fully rolled to a stop before the stable, he pulled his goggles off his forehead, then tugged off his flight cap. Leaving both in the cockpit, he scrambled from his aeroplane and hopped to the ground, taking in the bustle. Voices came from the stable, including what he thought might be Pip's, but he couldn't be sure.

A lieutenant hurried toward him and saluted. "Maj. Laesornysh?"

"Yes, that's me." Fieran returned the salute.

"I've been assigned to show you around." The lieutenant, far more jumpy and less starched than Lt. Busher, gestured around them. "The manor house and the grounds have been requisitioned for you and your squadron. It has more than enough rooms to house all your pilots, mechanics, and ground crew. Healing stones have been provided for the elven members of your unit. You'll take your meals there, and a cook and assistants have been assigned to your unit. The stable isn't large enough to house your aeroplanes, so those will be kept under tarpaulins outside, but Capt. Detmuk-Inawenys seemed to think it would be possible to get one aeroplane inside as needed for maintenance."

"Capt. Detmuk-Inawenys and the other mechanics have already arrived?" Fieran glanced at the stable, this time sure he'd heard Pip's voice giving orders. She, the mechanics, the ground crew, and the trucks holding the squadron's gear had left before first light since they'd take far longer to travel the hundred miles into Mongavaria than Fieran's squadron had.

"Yes, sir. They arrived only half an hour before you, sir." The lieutenant pointed toward the south where the town lay only about a mile away. "All of the Mongavarian civilians had fled long before we arrived, so the entire town is ours. Headquarters is setting up in the town, designated as code-name Dungeon on the signs. One small personnel truck has been assigned for your use if you need to travel between here and headquarters."

"Thank you." Fieran surveyed the area with new eyes, trying to calculate how best to park the aeroplanes without keeping them too close together or hampering their ability to reach the airfield quickly.

"Do you need anything else, sir? I can show you around the manor house or fetch anything else you need?" The lieutenant rocked back on his heels.

"No, I can take it from here. Please see to it that the cook, assistants, and other new personnel being assigned here have what they need. Then you may return to your unit." Fieran dismissed the lieutenant before he strode to join the cluster of flyboys that was forming at the edge of the grass lawn as more and more of them landed. He glanced around before he pointed at the manor. "The manor is ours."

With a whoop, the whole pack of flyboys rushed off, shouting about picking rooms and exploring.

Fieran shook his head. Some things never changed whether one was a child or an adult. Leaving the flyboys to sort out the chaos, or cause it as the case might be, he strode toward the barn, halting in the doorway to take in the scene without getting in the way.

Pip stood in the center of the space next to a large stack of crates. Her mechanics, Mak, and what looked like a work crew of enlisted men sent from a nearby unit bustled about under her orders, unboxing each of the crates and placing the items in their new spots.

Fieran smiled and leaned against the large beam framing the doorway into the stable. Pip had come such a long way since those early days at Dar Goranth where she struggled to give orders to five mechanics. Now she gave orders without a blink.

Yet she wasn't barking commands in a harsh manner either. When one of the mechanics made a suggestion different than her original order, she nodded and gave her approval. The enlisted men paused to ask her questions about where items went, and she answered with a smile and a wave of her hand in the direction of where she wanted the item.

She glanced up, and when her gaze landed on him, a warm smile blossomed across her face.

Fieran pushed away from the beam and strode farther into the bustle.

That bustle instantly died as everyone realized a major had just stepped into the barn. They came to attention, facing him.

Fieran dismissed them to go back to what they were

doing and joined Pip. "Looks like you have things well in hand."

Pip grinned and gestured around the space. "It isn't as spacious as the hangar bays at Fort Defense, but it will do nicely."

Fieran took a closer look at what she'd organized. In the front open space where the carriages would have been parked, Pip had cleared everything away, besides the crates still waiting to be sorted and put away. The wall to the left of the door had several wooden worktables lined up before it, their surfaces now covered with tools. Across the way, the empty crates had been turned on their sides and stacked, forming makeshift shelving where spare parts had been stashed.

The back of the barn was the actual stable portion with three stalls on either side of a short walk and a back door that opened into a pasture. Three of the stalls held a pile of what appeared to be junk, as if everything that wasn't needed had been shoved there. The other three stalls held horses, who had their heads over the half wall of their stalls, ears pricked, as they watched all the bustle. Perhaps they'd been issued by the army in addition to the truck. Or perhaps the owner of this mansion had left them behind when he fled. Either way, they would give the squadron another option for transportation.

The loft above the horse stalls held bales of hay, stacked all the way to the front. At least there would be plenty of food for the horses. If there wasn't already someone assigned to the squadron to care for the horses, Fieran would have to set up a work rotation among the squadron, ground crew, mechanics, and everyone else here.

Pip gestured at the doorway. "I measured. If the barn

doors are opened as far as they will go, the doorway is thirty and a half feet wide, just wide enough for the fighter aeroplane's thirty foot wingspan if we're careful about wheeling them inside for maintenance. The scout aeroplanes that are coming tomorrow won't fit—they have a thirty-five foot wingspan—but that's all right. We'll just have to get used to performing basic maintenance outside. We can at least park any aeroplanes needing more than basic maintenance on the gravel drive in front while we're working on them. And there's this…" Pip grinned as she pointed upward at a track set into the center of the ceiling, a chain with a hook dangling from it. "That's for hauling the hay into the loft. But it will be handy for any heavier maintenance we need to do."

"Glad the barn will work." Fieran resisted the urge to pull her close, the happy excitement in her voice and on her face enticing.

But she was working, and there were men who weren't a part of the Half-Breed Squadron present. She needed to remain a commanding officer in their eyes.

The point was further hammered home as one of the men approached, carrying a stack of replacement propellers. "Where would you like these, Captain?"

Pip shared one last look with Fieran before she turned away and pointed toward the wall with the crates. "Stack them over there."

Leaving her to her work, Fieran ducked out of the stable and strolled up the gravel drive toward the mansion.

Aeroplanes lined up at the edge of the front lawn beneath the shelter of the trees beside the lane toward the mansion, and the ground crew was wheeling one last aeroplane into place. No more aeroplanes circled overhead.

As he neared the front of the mansion, he met Rothilion

and Merrik strolling up the drive from where their aeroplanes had been parked.

Rothilion regarded the brick mansion rising before them. "It appears the army has greatly improved our accommodations."

"Yes, though I haven't been inside yet to see what the owner left us." Fieran shrugged and gestured at the building ahead of them as Rothilion and Merrik fell into step on either side of him. "I've been told healing stones were left for any of Flight A who need them."

While man-made brick wasn't as bad to elves as natural stone, it could cause headaches over a long period of time, such as living in the building.

Rothilion nodded. "That is surprisingly organized of them."

"I know, right? Remember how chaotic it was when we were sent to Dar Goranth? We had to build our own aeroplanes." Fieran shook his head with a sigh.

On his other side, Merrik gave a snort.

"That was *your* army. My army adequately provided aeroplanes and healing stones then as well." Rothilion tilted his nose slightly skyward, his tone overly supercilious. "However, your army is running this invasion. Hence my surprise."

Fieran laughed and slapped him on the back. "It seems you elves have been a good influence."

"Of course." Rothilion sniffed, but he couldn't fully hide his smile.

One of the second story windows opened. Stickyfingers stuck his head out and hollered, "Fieran! You'd better hurry if you don't want all the good rooms to be claimed! Aylia already claimed the family wing for the flygirls."

Rothilion gave another sniff. "It appears you are still in need of our good influence."

Farther along the second story, Aylia opened a window and hung halfway out, shouting just as raucously toward Stickyfingers, "Of course I claimed the family wing! It makes the most sense for we ladies to have our own private hall!"

Merrik raised his eyebrows at Rothilion. "Such a good influence."

Rothilion heaved a sigh.

Fieran struggled to contain his laughter long enough to actually think about the room situation.

As the senior three officers, he, Merrik, and Rothilion were entitled to pick whatever room they wanted. It was probably expected that they take the nicest rooms in the place.

But...Fieran resisted the urge to glance at Merrik. Unless this mansion had a lift installed, there would only be stairs to the second floor. While Merrik could walk well now, there were times in the evenings when he used a peg leg, crutches, or even his wheelchair to fully rest his legs. Stairs would be a hindrance, and he'd probably pick a room on the main floor.

It would make the most sense for all three of the commanding officers to room in the same general area, so they could be located easily.

Besides, it wasn't like Fieran, Merrik, or Rothilion needed the novelty of sleeping in a luxurious room. They'd grown up wealthy. Might as well leave the ostentatious rooms for those who would appreciate the experience more.

"Take whatever rooms you want on the second or third floors." Fieran gestured between himself, Merrik, and Rothilion. "We'll be rooming on the main floor."

Stickyfingers grinned, nodded, and shut the window, as did Aylia.

"Main floor." Merrik's voice was too carefully neutral.

"Yes. There should be the rooms for the upper staff there." Fieran set out for the mansion once again, and the other two caught up a moment later. "We'll be easy to find if headquarters sends someone with a message or orders, and I can take over the butler's office for all the paperwork the higher-ups keep demanding. It might even have a telephone for communicating with headquarters."

"Quite logical." Rothilion quickened his pace. "I will ensure the healing stones are distributed to those who need them. Once I can locate the stones."

"If I were to guess, there's probably a massive pile of crates and rucksacks dumped in the foyer." Fieran matched his pace to Merrik's.

Rothilion nodded as he headed for the main door.

"You did not have to pick our rooms on the main floor on my account." Merrik crossed his arms and halted, turning to face Fieran with both boots firmly planted on the gravel.

"I didn't..." Fieran cut off his instinctual protest as he met Merrik's gaze. "It was one factor. But everything else I said to Rothilion is also true. It makes the most logical sense. Besides, Lije, Stickyfingers, and the others will enjoy having fancy sheets and luxury furnishings far more."

"Still having fun slumming it like a regular person?" Merrik's flat look disappeared into a hint of his smile.

"Exactly." Fieran crossed his arms too as he faced Merrik, his smile dropping. "As the commanding officer, it's my job to make sure the members of my unit have what they need to operate at their best. That means I make sure the elves have healing stones, the flygirls have privacy in their own wing, and, yes, that you have a room that is optimal for you. I'm not coddling you; I'm making sure you can operate at your best."

Merrik sighed and shook his head. After a moment, his smile returned. "And what are you doing to make sure you operate at your best?"

"Ensuring that I have you, Rothilion, and Pip around to be the voices of sense." Fieran grinned and set out for the mansion once again. "Speaking of sense, I have a feeling it's going to take all three of us to bring order to whatever chaos the flyboys have turned the mansion into."

"Very true." Merrik matched his grin.

FIVE

As more of the Half-Breed Squadron rose into the sky to join their circling pattern, Fieran could almost feel Merrik's impatience wafting from his aeroplane in the wingman position behind Fieran's.

In the days since they'd arrived at their new station, Fieran had set up a rotation with Flight A flying overwatch one day and Flight B the next day. That way, everyone had one day on, one day off. Besides overwatch, they'd flown numerous scouting missions.

But today, the Alliance armies were making a big push, and the whole squadron was taking to the sky to provide air support.

When the last of Flight B took to the sky to join the formation, Fieran pressed the button for the radio. "Flight B is in the air and headed for the front. Flight A, head for the front after you've formed up."

Rothilion acknowledged, even as Fieran swung his aeroplane toward the east, the formation of aeroplanes forming around and behind him.

Trampled and torn ground lay below as their aeroplanes

flashed overhead. Lines of trucks rumbled over rutted, makeshift roads. A tiny Mongavarian town was ringed with vehicles, under martial law now that the Alliance had captured it.

The explosions of dirt and fire grew closer until they flashed over the meandering, dug in trenches and foxholes that formed the current front lines. The front stretched for as far as Fieran could see in either direction with one flank anchored against the flooded farm fields from the re-routed Chibo River and the other end stretching toward the Hydalla River.

With each day that passed, the Alliance armies forged deeper into Mongavaria, swinging the front down and forward from the northwest. To the north, another army of elves and trolls had crossed the Hydalla River, led by Fieran's cousin Ryfon, to form another invasion spearpoint.

A few Alliance airships hovered high over the battlefield, providing more protective air cover. Although at the moment, Mongavaria had mustered neither airships nor aeroplanes to harass the advancing Alliance army.

At the vanguard, a blaze of blue magic surged outward, covering miles in either direction even as a storm of magic whirled in the center. Somewhere in that maelstrom, Dacha and Adry were fighting as the warriors of the ancient kings had always fought: with blades and blood, magic and steel.

If Fieran had made other choices, he would have been down there with them. He well-remembered what it had been like, holding his dacha's swords, the weight of history in his hands, as he faced down the Mongavarian Army.

He didn't regret the choices that led to him taking to the sky instead of fighting at his dacha's side. But there was just a hint of a bittersweet could-have-been stirring in his chest regardless.

Giving himself a good shake, he flipped the radio to channel 4. "Half-Breed reporting in. Any changes to the strike points? Over."

"Half-Breed, standby. Over." A voice came over the radio.

Fieran flew along the front lines, taking in the way the Alliance Army was pressing forward. At one point along the line, the trolls had created a blizzard of snow and ice, driving the Mongavarian Army back. At another spot, the elves turned a small forest against the Mongavarians, and the enemy were in full retreat as they ran, likely screaming, from the vengeful trees. And, of course, the dwarven armored unit formed a wedge behind their armored vehicles as they slammed into the enemy line.

After several minutes of waiting, the voice came again. "No changes to the strike coordinates. Over."

Fieran acknowledged. He'd spent far too long in the past few days in the nearby town, standing in on the various planning meetings for this offensive. If he'd known how many meetings he'd have to attend, he might not have been as eager for this assignment.

After he flipped back to channel 1, he sent off the squadron in groups of six to hit the various strong points and villages that lay in the Alliance Army's path. Once Rothilion arrived with Flight A, he divided them up as well until finally just he, Merrik, Lije, Stickyfingers, Rothilion, and Aylia remained.

"I saved the best spot for us." Fieran grinned as he unleashed his magic, shoving it outward into a protective network over their six aeroplanes.

With the lack of Mongavarian aerial attacks, he hadn't shoved his magic over the squadron. They would be too scattered along the miles of front for him to hold the network once they started their strikes. Instead, this would be an additional test for Pip's protective shields.

"It is hardly the best spot if only those protected directly by your magic would be able to make this run." Rothilion's voice was just as flat and calm as he always was when going into battle. Seemingly not at all worried that his aeroplane might be incinerated in the next few minutes, if Fieran couldn't hold his magic against the coming onslaught. The Mongavarian guns would be the least of his worries.

"We have faith in you, Fieran." Lije's voice was a cheerful note.

"It's going to be spectacular!" Aylia punctuated her words with a whoop.

"Are we going to keep talking or are we going to make our run?" Merrik's voice sliced with an almost stern, lecturing tone instead of joining the banter.

"Someone is eager to impress his girlfriend," Stickyfingers hooted into the radio.

Fieran didn't have to see Merrik to know he was gripping the stick in white knuckles, his jaw working. "All right, everyone. Let's put Merrik out of his misery. Starting my dive...now."

Then he rolled his aeroplane and dove, the force pressing him into his seat, the wings straining.

This was exactly where he was meant to be. In the sky. The control column of an aeroplane gripped in his hands. The wind rushing past his face and tugging at the strands of hair that had fallen free of his flight cap.

As he neared the ground, he plunged into the edge of the crackling blue magic. The bolts lashed at him, clashing against his magic. He gritted his teeth and poured more magic into the shields around the six aeroplanes, preventing Dacha's and Adry's magic from incinerating them.

Large armored vehicles, more clunky and rudimentary than the dwarven-built ones, rolled forward with the Mongavarian Army huddled around them. The armored vehicles must have had some of that deflecting magic on them for Dacha's and Adry's magic skipped off of them, bouncing back into the sky.

Fieran leveled out and headed toward the leading armored vehicle, skimming only a few yards over the ground. Dropping the bombs from underneath his wings was horribly imprecise, so the closer he was to the ground, the more likely he was to actually hit one of those vehicles.

He mentally counted the seconds before he gripped the control column with his knees so that he could grasp the bomb levers. When his countdown hit zero, he pulled first the lever on the right, then the one on the left.

His aeroplane shot upward as the weight dropped from the wings. He quickly grasped the control stick in his hands again and pulled back, pointing his nose toward the sky.

He'd barely gained altitude before an explosion shoved against his aeroplane, shrapnel bursting against his magical shield.

He didn't dare glance over his shoulder until he'd roared higher into the sky. Once he had enough height, he rolled his aeroplane onto its side.

The first of the armored vehicles lay on its side, two others tangled together as if they'd collided while trying to avoid the explosion. Even as Fieran watched, Merrik dropped his bombs on those armored vehicles and, within moments, they disappeared into a fireball.

Even as Fieran and Merrik rose upward, Lije, Stickyfingers, Aylia, and Rothilion dropped their bombs on the other armored vehicles, the bombs striking close enough to destroy or disable all but one of them.

The magical storm parted, and Dacha stepped into view, followed by Adry. Adry lifted one sword in salute before she and Dacha descended on the advancing Mongavarian Army.

Merrik circled one last time, waggling his aeroplane's wings, before he returned to his spot as Fieran's wingman.

Fieran grinned and shook his head. Showing off for his girlfriend was right.

Voices burst over the radio, reporting that the various coordinates had been hit. As they sounded off, Fieran balanced a small pad of paper on a knee and checked off the strikes. "Remain in station above the various points along the line and await further orders. The ground forces might request additional strikes."

Even if they didn't, the army would need the aerial protection, and the generals at headquarters would want a final scouting mission over the length of the front at the end of the day to confirm the new location of the front lines.

Fieran settled as comfortably as he could on the thin leather padding. This was going to be a long day now that most of the fun was over, at least for those in the sky.

As the sun hung low on the western horizon, Fieran climbed out of his aeroplane, his legs wobbling slightly at actually having to hold his weight after hours flying. For a moment he just stood there, holding on to his aeroplane while his legs remembered how to work.

A few yards away, Merrik climbed out of his aeroplane and sagged against it, shifting from leg to leg as if he couldn't decide which leg was better suited to hold him up at the moment.

Fieran managed to push away from his aeroplane and tottered to Merrik. "How are you holding up?"

"Still standing." Merrik leaned his back against the fuselage of his aeroplane. "That is about all you can expect at the moment."

"True." Fieran gave a weary laugh and clapped Merrik on the shoulder, although he made sure not to put any actual weight behind the gesture. Should he offer to let Merrik lean on him for the walk back? He was still figuring out exactly how and when Merrik wanted Fieran to help and when he should back off.

Merrik pushed away from his aeroplane, his gait unsteady as he moved toward the mansion. Then again, Fieran's stride was unsteady, and his only excuse was stiffness.

As they neared, Pip stepped from the stable. "How did today go?"

"We hit all the points we were supposed to, no Mongavarian aeroplanes even dared show their noses, and the front is now several miles deeper into Mongavaria than it was this morning." Fieran resisted the urge to rub the numb stiffness out of his rear end. A hot shower was sounding rather good at the moment.

"Sounds like a successful day." Pip grinned, the expression turning somewhat lopsided as she took in the way they were all tottering and stiff.

Merrik waved as he passed, but he kept going, disappearing through the front door into the mansion.

Since Merrik seemed fine, Fieran headed toward Pip. "How was your day?"

"Boring." Pip shook her head, rolling her shoulders in a shrug. "There isn't much to do while I'm waiting for all of you to return. But now that I have an entire squadron of aeroplanes to inspect, my boredom is at an end."

"There likely won't be much to do after your inspections either." Fieran kneaded his thigh, trying to work out the cramping. "Probably some burnt-out engine wires after all our flying, and all the magical power cells for the shielding wires are likely empty. Did you manage to get a station rigged up so I can fill our magical power cells myself without waiting on shipments?"

"I started on it, but I don't have all the parts I need." Pip jabbed a hand in the direction of the stable.

"Fill out a requisition form and put it on my desk so I can add my signature to yours." Fieran shifted to his other foot. His other leg was cramping now.

"Done and done." Pip raised her eyebrows at him.

"Of course. Should have known." Fieran cradled her face and gave her a quick kiss, pulling away as the ground crew wheeled one of the aeroplanes down the gravel drive to park it before the stable. "I see you need to get to work."

"Yes." Pip sighed and turned toward the stable.

"A walk under the stars in a few hours?" Fieran called after her.

Pip turned back toward him, walking backward for a moment. "Sounds like a plan. I'll find you once I'm free." With a wave, she disappeared into the stable, her voice giving orders drifting back to him.

After strolling to the mansion, Fieran stepped inside the marble-floored, mahogany-paneled foyer, the grand staircase rising before him. In the nearest parlor, Tiny sprawled on one of the couches, snoring uproariously as he slept. A few others lounged on the other couches or even the soft carpet on the floor, also sleeping soundly after the long day of flying.

Very few of the elven pilots were around, but the rush of water through the pipes sounded throughout the house. The elves must have beaten the humans in the race for the showers.

After turning down the corridor that held the rooms for the upper staff, Fieran found Merrik pacing back and forth in the modest hallway. Merrik had replaced his prosthetic limb with the straight-shafted peg leg that strapped to his knee, letting him rest his stump and his magic.

"You're restless." Fieran slouched against the wall. All he wanted to do was get to his room, take a shower, and crash for an hour before supper. "I was expecting you to be headed for the showers or relaxing like the others."

Merrik sighed and leaned against the wall a few feet away. "I know. I should. But..." He sighed again, his gaze dropping to the floor. For a long moment, he didn't speak, as if gathering himself. "I was worried during her first week on the front lines. But we were so busy flying up and down the border that I could set my worries aside. Today, I saw the battle she faced. And I just...I need to know she is all right. I know it is foolish. If she were injured, you would have been informed. I need to trust that she can take care of herself. I just wish I could see for myself."

Fieran squeezed his eyes shut and let his head fall back. If Pip were the one fighting, it would eat him alive not to see her at the end of the day to reassure himself she was all right. He remembered all too well the fear gripping him when Pip had gone into battle to retrieve those machines a few weeks ago.

Pip wasn't a trained warrior like Adry was, although Pip's magic still meant she could take care of herself amid everything from battles to bombings.

Adry was a warrior. Trained by Dacha and wielding the

magic of the ancient kings. It would take a lot before she was hurt. Yes, Fieran was worried about his little sister facing battle, but it was easier for him, given that he knew the strength of magic she wielded. Not to mention, Dacha was with her. Fieran knew exactly how far Dacha would go to protect his children.

Fieran suppressed a sigh. The last thing he wanted to do was fly more today after all the hours they'd spent in the cockpit.

But this was Merrik. And Adry. And Fieran would do anything for the two of them.

He pushed away from the wall. "Then let's commandeer an aeroplane, go AWOL, and steal Adry away from her commanding officer."

That familiar thrill at doing something impulsive glowed in his chest. Incandescently warm and heady and crackling like his magic.

Merrik gaped at Fieran, his mouth working slightly.

With a shake of his head, Fieran stuck his hand out to Merrik. "And before you break your brain trying to figure out if your love for Adry outweighs your love of common sense, remember, I'm the highest ranked officer here at our temporary aerodrome. I'm pretty sure I can authorize a scouting mission whenever I want. If we want to land near the front lines to consult with one of the generals, who's going to stop us? Dacha certainly isn't going to stop Adry from leaving her post for a few minutes to talk to you."

It would probably be more than talking, but Fieran wasn't about to say "kiss you" out loud.

His grin spreading slowly across his face and into his eyes, Merrik gripped Fieran's hand and let him pull him upright. "I suppose I will let you drag me into something reckless. Again."

"Admit it. You don't mind this kind of recklessness as much as you pretend." Fieran's grin was so wide it hurt, buoyed as he was by that thrill.

"I am not going to confirm or deny anything." But Merrik, too, was grinning that way he always did when Fieran was about to drag them into something fun.

This time, they likely weren't going to get into trouble, and that dimmed the excitement somewhat. Besides, Fieran had turned over a new leaf. Nothing reckless that would endanger others. Since this wouldn't do that, it was perfectly fine.

"I'm flying. Grab your leg and a camera. You can snap a few photographs on our way over to cover our butts if anyone questions us." Fieran patted Merrik's shoulder before he headed outdoors once again.

THE TWO-SEATER BIPLANE soared over the darkening fields and roads that stretched between their small haven and the battlelines. The front lines had been pushed miles deeper into Mongavaria over the course of the day, but now both armies were busy digging in, fortifying their positions with trenches and earthworks.

Fieran flew high over the new lines, tipping the aeroplane so that he could locate where Dacha and Adry were holed up and give Merrik a chance to take a few photographs. The low light wasn't ideal, but the long shadows would reveal features that would be hidden in pictures taken in better light.

He sensed the crackle of magic before he spotted the faint blue glow embedded into the ground far below. Dacha or

Adry must have placed an alert around where the two of them were camped.

Luckily, there was a nice open farm field only a few hundred yards behind the Alliance lines at that point. Perfect spot to land an aeroplane and still be able to take off again afterward.

Fieran circled once before he lined up on the farm field, easing the scout aeroplane lower. The wheels touched down, then bumped over the rough rows. Something squished and spattered up onto the aeroplane. Was that a pumpkin? Great. This aeroplane was going to be splattered with pumpkin guts by the end of this trip.

The aeroplane rolled to a halt at the far end of the field, its nose pointed toward the front lines.

Fieran unbuckled his lap belt and peeled off his cap and goggles. Yet Merrik was already scrambling out of the aeroplane, his boots hitting the ground before Fieran had so much as levered himself out of his seat.

A leather- and armor-clad figure was already dashing toward them, her red-gold hair flying behind her. "Merrik!"

Merrik dodged several large pumpkins and swept her up into his arms, holding her close as she pressed her face against his shoulder.

Fieran hopped to the ground, his boots sinking into the soft soil of the field. Great. He was going to have to wash his flight boots after this.

He did his best to avoid looking at Merrik and Adry. Last he'd seen, they were talking quietly. While standing rather close in an embrace. But he wasn't going to look to see if they'd moved from talking to kissing.

Instead, he circled around them and strode toward the edge of the field, reaching it as Dacha did, Uncle Iyrinder trailing behind him.

Dacha halted, his shoulders slumped, his gaze holding a haunted weariness, weighted with the toll this war was taking on him.

Until Dacha had been knocked unconscious a few weeks ago, it had never occurred to Fieran that he could lose Dacha in this war.

But now, seeing Dacha like this, his chest hurt with the knowledge that there was more than one way to lose his dacha to war.

"Sason." Dacha shot him a look. "I did not expect to you see you here tonight."

"Merrik was missing Adry." Fieran gestured vaguely in that direction, though he didn't look. "And it had been far too long since I dragged Merrik into something impulsive. Sadly, I don't think we'll even get into trouble for this."

Dacha shook his head with a sigh, but a hint of a smile creased his otherwise hard face.

Good. The war might be taking a toll, but as long as Fieran could talk his way into making his dacha smile, perhaps they'd all come through this just fine.

By the time he and Merrik climbed back into the scout aeroplane and took to the sky once again, the sun had sunk fully behind the distant Whitehurst Mountains in the west. But thanks to all the new gauges installed in the aeroplane—an altimeter, a gyroscopic ball that showed his position relative to the horizon, his compass, the light so he could see what the gauges said—Fieran could actually fly back in the gray of the coming night with relative safety.

After flying in silence for a few minutes, Merrik's voice came over the radio that connected the front and rear seats. "Linshi."

"Anytime. Really." Fieran flexed his fingers on the

control column, trying to pretend his throat wasn't going tight.

Merrik paused. "Especially because...because I know you have been uncomfortable with me and Adry courting."

"It isn't *that*." Fieran shook his head vigorously enough that Merrik would be able to see the motion easily from the rear seat. "My discomfort has nothing to do with you. I had a few childhood resentments between me and Adry to resolve in my own mind. That was it. Besides, this is the new, more mature me. If I can be mature about Rhohen, then surely I can be mature about you and Adry courting."

Instead of saying *I will believe it when I see it*, as Fieran expected, Merrik chuckled. "Believe it or not, that is actually reassuring. You have been surprisingly civil to Rhohen. Especially since he is growing closer to Pip's cousin."

"Don't remind me." Fieran scowled. He'd been doing his best to avoid Rhohen. Easy enough during the week that Rhohen had been at the front. But now that Rhohen was enjoying a week of rest in the small headquarters town and likely to spend time with Pip's cousin Draenelynn, Fieran was going to have to work even harder at it.

Ahead, the mansion was a darker speck in the gloom, all the windows blacked out so that it wouldn't be as visible from the air.

Fieran toggled the radio to call ahead to let the ground crew know to turn on the elven lights for the airfield.

Time to land, finally take that shower, enjoy a walk with Pip, and get some sleep.

CHAPTER

SIX

P ip clasped Fieran's hand, her steps light, as the two of them strolled through the streets of the head-quarters village after Fieran had parked the small truck, Merrik and Rothilion trailing behind them. Merrik's shoulders were slumped, his hands in his pockets. He wasn't about to admit it, but he was mopey since Adry was still at the front.

With her free hand, Pip smoothed her uniform skirt, which she'd opted to wear instead of the uniform pants for this evening. It was as fancy as she could dress, here in this forward operating base. Not that this was a date. Just a showing of an entertainment troupe visiting the army to provide a morale boost.

They paused at the intersection to check the signs to figure out which way they needed to go. A line of army trucks rumbled past, filled with infantry likely also headed in the direction of the small park where the entertainment would be held.

After they turned the corner, they caught up with the pack of other elven pilots, flyboys, flygirls, mechanics, and members of the ground crew, who had walked the mile from the aerodrome. Stickyfingers, Lije, Tiny, Aylia, and Mak drifted back so that they followed the larger group.

On the other side of Merrik, Rothilion strolled with a step that was almost…peppy. His mouth curved into the broadest smile she'd ever seen on him.

Pip tugged on Fieran's arm. When he glanced down at her, she pointed at Rothilion.

Fieran followed her pointing finger and grinned. "Rothilion. What has you grinning like a cat that just noshed on a mouse?"

Rothilion's grin snuffed out as he lifted his nose slightly into the air. "I am merely anticipating the fact that all of you will finally get a taste of what sophisticated and refined culture is like."

"Is elven entertainment really that much better than an Escarlish moving picture?" Lije sounded more curious than offended.

"It is superior, of course." Rothilion's tone might have sounded haughty, if one didn't know him that well.

"It's something, all right," Fieran muttered under his breath, too low for anyone but Pip to hear.

She nudged him gently in the ribs, shaking her head. The others would just have to see for themselves.

They rounded a corner and found themselves at the edge of a broad green in the center of town, a few large trees breaking up the expanse. At the far end of the park, a beautifully painted silk backdrop was suspended between two of the largest trees with more rolls of backdrops rigged to be released when needed. Rows upon rows of assorted chairs, benches, and stools had been set up facing the stage. Most of the homes and businesses in the town must have been emptied of furniture to provide enough seating.

Along the edges of the park, tables with refreshments had been set up, and they appeared to hold a variety of traditional elven foods and drinks.

"Good thing your dacha is at the front. He would not have appreciated all of this going on right outside of his door." Pip leaned closer to Fieran as they shuffled between the various groups of people.

The townhouses surrounding this park had been turned into the quarters for the various generals and other commanding officers traveling forward to this base. Dacha, Uncle Iyrinder, and Adry had stayed in one of these townhouses before they returned to the front, with Uncle Julien and Aunt Vriska in the one next door. Uncle Rharreth and Rhohen probably had one of the townhouses, now that they were taking their week of rest from the fighting.

"No, he wouldn't have." Fieran headed down one of the rows that was mostly empty, gesturing for her to take a seat in a spot nearly in the middle of the row where they would have a good view.

After she sat on the bench, Fieran took the seat next to her with Merrik on his other side. Lije and Stickyfingers claimed chairs on the other side of Merrik while Mak worked his way past all their feet and knees to claim the seat on Pip's other side. Tiny, Aylia, and Rothilion found seats on the other side of Lije and Stickyfingers.

Fieran wrapped his arm around her shoulders, and Pip snuggled into him, resting her head on his shoulder. She didn't care what the elven entertainment was going to be. She was here for the snuggles and whispering with Fieran until they got yelled at.

More people found seats as the evening darkness closed deeper around them while elven lights in the trees set the stage area aglow in a soft light.

A few rows ahead, a slim figure with gray skin and long black hair shuffled between the benches, holding the hand of a young dwarf woman.

Fieran's cousin Rhohen and her cousin Draenelynn. Pip tightened her grip on Fieran's hand, not sure if she expected Fieran to start something or not.

Fieran stiffened, his breath hitching as his gaze locked in that direction.

Merrik elbowed Fieran, causing him to *oof* and squirm. "Remember. Mature."

"Yes, yes, I know." Fieran slouched even more on the bench. "But did he have to sit right there?"

"Just keep your eyes on the stage." Pip poked him in the ribs, making him squirm again.

"He'd better not kiss her." Fieran's mumble was almost sullen.

"Hush. Now you're starting to sound as petulant as Prince Rhohen." Pip poked him again. "Be the mature one."

Merrik shot her a grin, and she grinned back, already feeling a hint of what the future might look like. She was going to enjoy teaming up with Merrik to keep the Laesornysh siblings on the path of good sense.

"I knew you'd gang up on me." Fieran sighed and shook his head, but he, too, was smiling.

An elf glided to the center of the stage and made some elaborate pronouncement about their production. The only really important bit being that the elves were, magnanimously, performing for the Escarlish for the sake of their esteemed allies. They had just completed a tour with the elven armies along the Hydalla River border.

The announcer elf glided back into the wings as lights swung to illuminate a male elf standing in the branches of the tree on the left. Another light flared to focus on a female elf perched in the branches of the tree on the right.

The male elf began the recitation of a traditional elven ballad. This particular ballad was a woven story, written to be recited by a male and female as if speaking in a dialogue.

On the stage between the two trees, more elves poured into view, the females wearing flowing dresses with just as flowing sleeves while the males had the traditional tunics and trousers with abbreviated pieces of armor. Their motions were somewhere between a dance and acrobatics as they performed.

One of the male elves lifted a female elf, her skirts floating around her like the petals of a flower in a breeze. It was strangely mesmerizing, even if Pip had seen similar performances before.

The voices of the recitation flowed around them, telling the story of young elves who desperately loved each other but could not be together because their families were political enemies.

As they got to the part where the two lovers tragically died, ribbons of red silk pooling on the stage, Pip found herself sniffing as she squeezed Ficran's hand tighter. The loss in the story hit a lot harder now that she had Fieran, the memories of his crash still far too fresh.

Fieran held out a white handkerchief. She took it and dabbed at her eyes. "How did you know to bring a handkerchief?"

"It's an elven troupe. It was guaranteed that at least one of their performances would be something morbidly sad." Fieran tugged her closer, as if he knew she needed a bit more snuggling.

On the stage, the performers ended with a dramatic

flourish, the two lovers both lying dead in each other's arms, her skirt spread around her and his sword still in his hand.

As the elf announcer came back on the stage to proclaim an intermission and the soothing notes of elven flutes provided background music, most of the audience remained frozen in their seats.

Lije gaped at the stage, his eyes wide, his mouth hanging open. "What *was* that?"

"That was a traditional elven ballad." Merrik had his arms crossed as he slouched in his seat more than he usually did. Perhaps he, too, didn't exactly appreciate something about lovers dying in each other's arms.

"That was…was…" Lije flapped his hand, seemingly at a loss for words.

"That was art." Rothilion gave something that was very nearly a happy sigh.

"But…*why*?" Stickyfingers had tear tracks streaked down his face, even though he kept scrubbing at his cheeks with his sleeve. "I thought this was supposed to be a morale boost for the troops. Not…not…"

"Morbid and tragic?" Fieran's sigh brushed Pip's hair. "Most traditional elven ballads and stories tend to be. Don't ask me why elves thrive on tragedy."

"Perhaps our long lives give us the perspective to appreciate such things." Rothilion gave a slight sniff, although he couldn't fully hide the curve to his mouth behind his haughty expression.

"Or the long lives make you melancholic." Fieran shook his head.

"Not a trait you will ever have to fear." Rothilion somehow made a snort sound sophisticated. "I suspect the centuries will make you more nonsensical."

"Absolutely." Fieran began to ease his arm from around

Pip. "I suppose we should hit up the refreshment tables before they're too picked over."

Merrik sighed and pushed to his feet. "Stay and save our seats. I will fetch refreshments."

Pip probably should have protested and sent Fieran off with Merrik but she didn't mind just staying there, snuggling, kept warm against the increasing chill of the evening.

Most of the other flyboys filed out as well after Merrik, including her brother Mak. Leaving her and Fieran semi-alone for the first time in far too long.

As Fieran settled his arm more securely around her again, she happily snuggled against him. "Poor Merrik. He's moping."

"Why do you think I made such a big deal about Rhohen and Draenelynn?" Fieran murmured before brushing a light kiss against her hair. "Thoroughly distracted him."

"It worked." Pip glanced at the spot a few rows down. Draenelynn was sitting alone now. Rhohen must have gone for refreshments. Probably just as well Merrik had gone alone, then. She could only imagine how Fieran's maturity level would have been tested if he and Rhohen ran into each other at the refreshment tables. "Though don't deceive yourself. You aren't as mature about Rhohen as you pretend you are."

"Fine, fine. You know me too well." Fieran rubbed his thumb on her upper arm before he stilled. "Do you think that's why Merrik volunteered to fetch food?"

"He knows you too well too." Pip clasped Fieran's free hand, her grip tightening as Rhohen appeared again, two plates and two glasses balanced in his hands. He was smiling as he handed one plate and glass to Draenelynn.

Thankfully, Fieran was further distracted when the whole group of flyboys returned, Rothilion leading the way as he pointed at something on his plate with the hand holding a teacup of all things. "This is an elven *ishikal*, a heavy pastry filled with honey."

"And what's this one?" Lije pointed to a square formed of flaky pastry on the bottom and topped with a layer of red berries.

"*Alalah*," Lt. Rothilion informed him with a dignified tilt of his head.

"It's a lemon-raspberry bar." Fieran straightened so that he wasn't so slouched in his seat.

Pip released Fieran's hand and also straightened so that she wasn't as slumped against him.

Mak shuffled past them and sank onto the seat next to Pip. He held out one of the two glasses he carried. "I got you a cherry cranberry juice."

"Perfect." Something more tart than too sweet. Pip claimed the glass and took a sip.

Merrik held two plates and two glasses. He twisted his wrist to turn one of the glasses toward Fieran. "And raspberry strawberry for you. The sweetest juice the elves make."

"Linshi." Fieran took the glass with his free hand. Then with a glance from Merrik to Pip, he withdrew the arm he'd had around her shoulders to take the second plate from Merrik, the plate piled with enough tasty treats for two.

"I did not think you would mind sharing a plate." Merrik raised an eyebrow at them as he eased down onto his seat on the bench. "That was easier than trying to carry three."

"I don't mind sharing." Fieran balanced the plate on his knee so that she could easily reach it.

"Well, you know, you and Merrik could share, and I could have a plate to myself." Pip already missed the warmth of Fieran's arm around her shoulders.

Fieran and Merrik shared a look, then both of them shook their heads emphatically, almost in sync. "No."

"Fine. I'll share with Fieran. If I have to." She laughed and inspected the items piled on the plate. Merrik had picked out a good variety of items.

For this event, the elves seemed to be going all out in providing a taste of elven culture for their human allies, from the traditional elven entertainment to a selection of traditional elven desserts to the elven juices to drink. Many of the desserts involved things like berries, molasses, or honey that was sourced from Tarenhiel's forests and woodland meadows. Since elves used fires for cooking as little as possible, most of the treats featured pastries that only took minimal baking. Some, like the molasses twists, didn't need baking at all.

Pip blinked, her throat unexpectedly tightening. This was a taste of home. Of the western rail terminal at the edge of Tarenhiel where she'd grown up. How she missed it. Missed her parents, even though she'd seen them only a handful of weeks ago.

Next to her, Mak shifted before he nudged her gently. When she looked up at him, his eyes were searching. As if he could read the sudden surge of homesickness twisting her chest.

She forced a smile and mouthed *I'm fine.*

And she was. She might be homesick, but she also didn't want to be anywhere else.

Within a few minutes, the elven flutes finished with a flourish. The elven announcer stepped onto the stage and proclaimed the next ballad that would be performed.

Fieran stiffened, his hand pausing partway to his mouth with one of the desserts. On his other side, Merrik's face washed even more pale.

The title of the ballad finally registered, and Pip gasped. "Why would they perform that one, of all stories? That hardly seems fitting as an entertainment for a morale boost."

"What? What's the ballad about?" Lije leaned around Merrik to better face them.

Rothilion's expression had tightened. "It is a history that chronicles all the past warriors of the magic of the ancient kings. It tells of their great victories…and their deaths in battle."

"Oh. *Oh.*" Lije's eyes rounded.

Stickyfingers choked on his dessert and coughed. "*Another* tragic ending? Multiple tragic endings? What is with elven stories?"

"Pip's right. It does seem like an odd choice for a morale boost." Lije eyed Fieran.

Rothilion sighed and shook his head. "We elves do not see it that way. This ballad is a stirring story of the warriors of old who made great sacrifices and won even greater victories. It is meant to encourage those watching to a similar sacrifice. But I agree that the choice is…regrettable, given the audience."

On the stage, the dancers were whirling with blue ribbons like magic flowing around them as they portrayed the many warriors who lived before the fall of the elven empire. Within moments, all of them fell but one as they all died in the final battle that ended an empire.

Fieran stared, but he didn't seem to be seeing the stage. "No warrior of the magic of the ancient kings has died of old age in millennia. Oddly enough, my dachasheni's disease likely prolonged his life, since it kept him from battle, even if it killed him in the end. Even my dacha won't have a long life by elven standards because of his elishina with my mama, even if he lives to old age."

If. That little word, the one that acknowledged the frailty of life, hurt like a bullet wound in her chest. Warriors of the magic of the ancient kings seemed destined to die in battle.

Pip reached for his hand and squeezed his fingers. Stirring those watching to honor and sacrifice might be the purpose of this ballad, but for Fieran, it would be a reminder that his dacha could be killed.

On the other side of Fieran, Merrik's face had gone as gray and bleak as Fieran's had. He would be thinking of Adry. Of how she, too, had inherited the seemingly doomed destiny that the ballad before them was celebrating.

As had Fieran.

Pip swallowed, that ache clawing up her throat. She'd already come perilously close to losing him once already. Would he suffer the same end that so many of his ancestors had endured?

On the stage, the lone warrior of the magic of the ancient kings performed feats of acrobatics as the blue ribbons whirled around him in a storm. The ballad spoken by the narrator told of great victories, although Pip noticed a few changes from the last time she'd heard this ballad performed. This version was much more delicate in the way it handled the wars with the trolls, likely to avoid offending any trolls in the audience now that the two peoples had spent the past seventy years repairing their kinship.

"There is one crucial difference now compared to then." Merrik gave a small wave toward the stage, where the dancer pretending to be the previous warrior of the magic of the ancient kings died after rending the Gulmorth Gorge to split Tarenhiel and Kostaria. When the others looked at Merrik, he tilted his head. "For many centuries, there has only ever been one warrior of the magic of the ancient kings at a time. Now there are five."

"And they do not fight alone." Rothilion turned to face Fieran, tipping his head in a nod that was almost a salute. "The whole of the Alliance is behind you."

Pip held tight to Fieran's hand, the sweets she'd eaten churning in her stomach.

Would Fieran, his sister, and his dacha survive the war? Or could victory only be achieved through a sacrificial death?

On the stage, the tone of the ballad changed. An acrobat portraying Fieran's great-grandfather Ellarin whirled onto the stage. Blue ribbons fluttered from his hands, but they were small, not the long bolts the other dancers had wielded. The ballad told of how he'd reigned over hundreds of years of great peace and prosperity for the elves.

When that actor stepped from the stage with a dignified exit rather than the dramatic death of the others, a new warrior stepped onto the stage, this one with blond hair and a storm of blue ribbons whirling around him as he moved. He held two swords in his hands alongside all the ribbons.

Fieran slouched deeper in his chair, as if he was hoping everyone would forget he was there. He leaned closer to her, whispering in her ear, "Dacha would really hate this."

She could imagine. His dacha didn't seem the type to enjoy watching a dramatized version of his past battles play out like this.

And then, more dancers with blue ribbons joined the one portraying Prince Farrendel, including one with red hair—long as if the elves didn't know how to show him as anything else.

Pip straightened. This was definitely new. The last time she'd seen this performance, it had ended with Prince Farrendel. A great victory over the trolls, but a warrior still standing alone. This time the ballad ended with the magic of the ancient kings reborn in a family standing together.

Next to her, Fieran stiffened, his eyes widening. Down the line, the other flyboys and flygirls gaped from him to the actor portraying him.

Pip squeezed his hand, then leaned her head on his shoulder once again.

Perhaps Fieran's ending wouldn't be like that of previous warriors of the magic of the ancient kings. He had a family at his side.

And he had Pip. Her magic. Merrik. The whole squadron.

She wouldn't let him ever fight alone.

SEVEN

Rain drummed on the mansion's roof, a low rumble of thunder announcing more thunderstorms on the horizon. The breeze that swept through the open double doors that led onto a brick patio and garden behind the manor held the damp chill of the coming autumn.

Fieran sprawled on a plush, overstuffed chair facing the open doors, staring at the rain and enjoying a few rare minutes when he didn't have anything to do or anywhere to be.

The rest of the flyboys lounged about the mansion in a similar fashion. Some napped. Some read books. Others played cards or board games. At a desk, Tiny was industriously writing a rather lengthy letter to his girlfriend back in Defense City.

Lije, Stickyfingers, and Aylia had somehow roped Rothilion into a game of cards. Despite the fact that they were still teaching Rothilion the rules, he appeared to be winning.

Several of the flyboys had stumbled across some lawn games in a closet, and they'd turned the marble-floored foyer into a game area. The crash of a heavy ball knocking over pins reverberated at intervals while cheering and hooting accompanied the noisy games. Surprisingly, a bunch of the elven pilots had joined in with the games, creating a racket right alongside the humans.

Heaving a sigh, Merrik eased onto the chair next to Fieran and stretched out his boots before him, his left foot propped on his right prosthetic foot. The pant leg over his prosthetic glowed slightly green, showing he was using his magic.

"Tired?" Fieran eyed Merrik, taking in the slightly darker smudges under his eyes.

"Weather fronts make my ankles ache." Merrik spoke without opening his eyes. "It kept me awake last night."

"Ankles?" Fieran emphasized the plural in Merrik's statement.

"Yeah. It is annoying enough when the ankle I still have aches. It, at least, has an excuse." Merrik grimaced without looking at Fieran. "But it is especially aggravating when the ankle I do not have decides to hurt."

Fieran wasn't sure what to say to that. Merrik spoke so matter-of-factly with an edge of humor that indicated he didn't want the compassion that welled within Fieran's chest.

And yet Fieran couldn't come up with anything humorous to say in reply. It was one thing for Merrik to joke about his lack of a leg, but Fieran still wasn't sure when it was appropriate for him to joke about it or when Merrik wanted him to do so.

When Fieran's silence lingered too long, Merrik lifted his head and met Fieran's gaze. "It is just a few aches, and they are infrequent. Often, wearing my prosthetic the next day and using my magic to move my foot makes the phantom pain go away, as my magical senses tell my brain I am feeling my leg. If it gets worse, I will go to the healer."

Fieran nodded and cleared his throat. "Good. Uh, good."

Merrik sighed, reached over, and lightly punched Fieran's shoulder. "I am fine. And I can now predict when storms are coming."

"That's convenient. Especially for an aeroplane pilot." This time Fieran actually managed a note of humor.

"Exactly." Merrik settled back in his chair, closing his eyes again.

For a few moments, the two of them sat in silence, the rain beating a steady rhythm over their heads.

Then Merrik grinned and gestured at the roof. "I am so glad you dragged me into the Flying Corps. If you had not, we likely would have been in the infantry, languishing in the flooding trenches right about now. Instead, we get to lounge about a mansion and have a day off when it rains."

"It is more pleasant." Fieran slid farther down in his chair, enjoying the comfortable cushioning. Then he tilted his head to better face Merrik, searching his expression as he added, "Although, if you had been in the infantry, you might not have lost your leg."

Merrik snorted and shook his head without looking at Fieran. "Doubtful. I would have followed you or Adry into battle, one of you would have inevitably done something reckless, and I would have gotten my leg blown off anyway. Except instead of crashing into the airfield conveniently close to the hospital, I would have been lying in the mud of the battlefield far from help where I likely would have bled out."

Fieran knew exactly what that felt like. He'd only survived because he'd been able to keep himself alive with his magic.

"Still, you would have been fighting at Adry's side."

Merrik barked a laugh. "That would have been disastrous for our relationship. I would not have been able to resist hovering and worrying, and she would have resented the smothering. It is better that we fight this war together, but in our own places."

"Instead I'm the one who gets the full dose of your good sense."

"Can you deny that you need it?" Merrik raised an eyebrow.

"Nope." Fieran settled back in his chair, but his gaze remained on Merrik. "You're okay. You're truly okay."

There was a note of peace in Merrik's tone and in his face that hadn't been there even a few weeks ago.

"Yeah, I think I am." This time, Merrik's sigh was more contentment than exhaustion. He slouched deeper in his chair, his eyes closed, his hands folded across his chest.

Some days would still be harder than others. But Fieran could see the way his friend had pieced himself back together. He would be all right. And on the days when he wasn't, Adry would be there for him, as would Fieran.

The distant sound of ringing broke the silence. Fieran groaned, gathered himself, and forced himself to his feet. "I had better see who that is."

Leaving Merrik to his lounging, Fieran picked his way between the groups of elven and human pilots as he crossed the parlor. In the foyer, he had to dodge the various lawn games that were very much not meant to be played indoors.

After hurrying down the corridor, he stepped into his office and picked up the telephone. "The forest sings at the birth of day."

"The shy moon retreats." The voice on the other end finished the other part of that week's recognition code.

Taking inspiration from the elven entertainment the other day, the recognition codes had been lines from elven poetry, although something was lost in the translation to Escarlish. "General Julien Ardon and General Laesornysh have requested that Major Laesornysh, Capt. Loiatir, Capt. Rothilion, and Capt. Detmuk-Inawenys join them in General Ardon's office at headquarters."

Here in the depths of the house, Fieran didn't have a window to glare at the rain, but he could still hear it pounding on the roof. Did the truck even have a canvas top? "We'll be there shortly."

Fieran sighed as he hung up the telephone. So much for a leisurely rainy day off.

"WHY WOULD I be included in this meeting?"

Fieran glanced down at Pip where she was clinging painfully tightly to his hand. The two of them huddled beneath the shield she held over their heads. "I don't know."

Rothilion and Merrik trailed after them beneath the edge of the shield to stay dry as the four of them sloshed through the puddles on the cobblestone road, crossing the street from where he'd parked the truck.

Uncle Julien's office was on the first floor of the townhouse he'd taken over, and Fieran led the way in that direction. The MPs at the door let them in without too much hassle, and soon the four of them were standing in the foyer, their boots leaving puddles on the tiled floor.

Multiple voices resonated from a room deeper within the townhouse. Who else was there with Dacha and Uncle Julien?

Uncle Iyrinder stood just outside of a door in the corridor

to their right. His gaze went first to Merrik before he motioned to them.

Apparently they were to head right in. Fieran led the way down the corridor, then into the office.

Dacha had planted himself with his back to the wall, his swords resting against his back, his hands gripping the back of one of the chairs. Uncle Julien lounged behind the desk, a grin framed by his beard.

But across from them stood a man with auburn hair, eyes that looked blue in the current light, and a laugh that filled the room.

Pip squeaked, her steps faltering, as her gaze landed on Uncle Edmund and she realized Dacha and Uncle Julien weren't the only ones in the room.

"Uncle Edmund!" Fieran let go of Pip's hand to step into Uncle Edmund's hug.

"Fieran." Uncle Edmund slapped Fieran's back, finished the hug, and turned to Pip. "It is a pleasure to meet you, Pippak."

Pip's eyes widened still further. "You know who I am?"

"Of course I know who you are." Uncle Edmund grinned, his eyes sparkling in that way that held secrets. "I was on the diplomatic mission to Dalorbor with your parents. They are quite proud of you and your brother and happy to talk about you."

"But you wouldn't have known about..." Fieran reached for Pip's hand again, clasping it.

"That was a surprise on my return." Yet somehow Uncle Edmund's tone didn't sound as surprised as he should have. "I returned before they did, as my part in the diplomacy was complete by then."

"Diplomacy?" Dacha raised his eyebrow at Uncle Edmund.

"Yes, diplomacy. That's all it was this time. Well, mostly." Uncle Edmund's grin was accompanied by a hint of a shrug. "It isn't my fault Dalorbor doesn't know to be wary when I show up to a diplomatic meeting."

Pip glanced from Uncle Edmund to Fieran, her brow wrinkled. This conversation would make far less sense if one didn't know exactly what Uncle Edmund did with his time.

Fieran leaned closer to her. "Uncle Edmund is Escarland's head spy."

On the surface, Uncle Edmund seemed much like Fieran's mother: gregarious, personable, friendly. But that hid the devious layers beneath.

Her eyes widened. "Am I cleared to know that? Isn't that some kind of national secret?"

"Somewhat. Mongavaria knows, so it isn't exactly a very well-kept secret. And there's my last name. I'm not exactly hiding my job from anyone who knows elvish." Uncle Edmund shrugged and waved as if it wasn't a big deal. "But if you didn't mention it to your dwarven relatives, I'd appreciate it. They might start re-examining every move I made while on the diplomatic trip, and that might make our new treaty more shaky."

"I won't say anything." Pip swallowed, nodding, before she leaned closer to Fieran and whispered, "I had wondered about the last name, but I didn't think a real spy would just say he was a spy in his name. I thought it must be some kind of inside joke or something."

Fieran grinned as he whispered back, "That's Uncle Edmund for you."

Uncle Edmund's and Aunt Jalissa's chosen last name *Ispamir* meant *Spy Prince* in elvish.

Merrik and then Adry strode through the doorway, though Fieran wasn't sure when his sister had arrived.

Rothilion remained at the door across from Uncle Iyrinder, as if he didn't feel fully welcome inside the room.

"Uncle Edmund!" Adry released Merrik's hand to hug Uncle Edmund. "When did you get back?"

"A few weeks ago." Uncle Edmund returned her hug.

Uncle Julien straightened and stood. "Now that everyone's here, we can head to the planning office for the meeting."

"Meeting?" Fieran glanced between all of them.

"Yes. The one on how to end the war." Uncle Edmund's grin vanished as he turned and headed for the door.

EIGHT

Fieran wedged himself against the wall with Pip on one side, Merrik on the other. Adry leaned against Merrik while Dacha and Uncle Iyrinder pressed into the corner as if trying to disappear in the crowded room. Rothilion had taken up the station on the other side of Pip, and Fieran appreciated the way he helped shield Pip from all the jostling.

The various generals and other higher-ups bumped and bustled to find room around the table. Troll and elf generals wedged side by side in the space while Pip's Uncle Thortrad took up station next to the table and refused to budge, no matter the polite pushing and shoving.

Since this room had once been the grand dining room in the largest townhouse on the square, a table dominated the center of the room. Yet instead of the steaming dishes of a feast, a mess of maps and photographs spread across it.

Uncle Julien took the position at the head of the table with Uncle Edmund at his side. Aunt Vriska wasn't there since she was leading one of the troll armies on the front lines, as were King Rharreth and Rhohen since it was their week at the front. Nor was Uncle Weylind there, as he remained in Aldon, last Fieran had heard.

After sweeping a glance over the room, Uncle Julien gave a nod and spoke in a voice that easily carried over the noise of chattering men. "Silence, everyone." He waited a moment for everyone to quiet before he gestured to Uncle Edmund. "Give your full attention to my brother Prince Edmund Ispamir."

Uncle Edmund stepped slightly forward. "Let's start with a small history lesson. Seventy years ago, Mongavaria began their aggression against the Alliance Kingdoms. Realizing that they would need a way to combat Prince Farrendel, they began experimenting with magical ways to shield weapons from the magic of the ancient kings. Back then, their attempts were rather futile. In the years since, they continued this pursuit and eventually stumbled on a new magic. Months ago, Mongavaria unveiled this unknown magic, deflecting the magic of the ancient kings to protect their aeroplanes. This magic grew progressively stronger until it culminated in those machines that took down the Wall."

That was a polite way to put it, even if Uncle Edmund tilted his head toward Fieran's dacha. As if any of them could forget that those machines had nearly drained Dacha of his magic.

A low murmur swept the room. Dacha's expression turned even more hard, his arms crossed tightly across his chest.

"Thanks to the efforts of the Half-Breed Squadron in securing aeroplanes for experts to study and to a squad of dwarves in capturing damaged machines, the Alliance's top magicians, magical engineers, scientists, and elven and troll magical experts have been studying that unknown magic."

Uncle Edmund waved in the general direction where Fieran and Pip stood against the wall before he nodded to Thortrad Detmuk.

Fieran clasped Pip's hand, hiding their hands between their bodies where the others in the room couldn't see. Pip squeezed his fingers in return.

"And?" One of the troll generals flexed her crossed arms. "Stop tip-tapping around. What's the verdict?"

Fieran worked to suppress his smile. Trust a troll to say what everyone else was probably thinking.

"As many have suspected, it's ogre magic." Uncle Edmund pressed his hands to the table as he stared at the crowd in the room.

Fieran sucked in a breath, then released it slowly. Ogre magic wasn't too surprising, after all. What else could that mysterious magic have been?

But Fieran had never heard that ogre magic was strong enough to deflect or take the magic of the ancient kings. He hadn't thought any force in the entire world could do either of those things. Except for Pip's magic.

In the corner, Dacha's expression never flickered. Perhaps Uncle Lance had shared this hypothesis with him at some point.

"It took far longer than expected to confirm it." Uncle Edmund grimaced and shook his head. "Even though Escarland shares a border with Groyria, the ogres are very elusive. Even when some of them do cross the border to trade, they never do magic where Escarlish citizens can see or sense. They don't even do magic near their own borders."

"Nor do any of the living elves remember a time when they had contact with ogre magic." One of the elven generals scowled as well, her long black hair braided at the sides.

"Our archivists are still searching our records for additional information."

"Lance Marion had to track down an old colleague who had moved to southern Escarland. This colleague had some contact with a friend who was half-ogre. This contact could finally confirm that the magic is ogre magic." Uncle Edmund's voice lowered. "But the magic used on the aeroplanes and machines wasn't just ogre magic. It had somehow been tainted with human magic. Almost as if a human magician had wielded the ogre magic."

"That should not be possible." The elven general straightened, even as others around the room murmured to those next to them.

Pip's fingers squeezed tighter on Fieran's.

"No, it shouldn't. But somehow, that's what is happening." Uncle Edmund's tone turned even more grim.

Uncle Julien swept another hard glance around the room. "Which begs the question: just what is Mongavaria doing to the ogres?"

Fieran swallowed as he shared a look, first with Pip, then with Merrik. Once they returned to the mansion and told him, Lije would be especially worried. He came from a small town in Escarland near the border with Groyria, and he'd actually known a few ogres before joining the army.

"This might be indelicate, but do we know the ogres are doing this against their will?" One of the human generals glanced around the table. "They've been resistant to working with us. Perhaps they made some deal with Mongavaria, and they are willingly melding their magic with human magic?"

Uncle Edmund shook his head. "Our scouts have seen Mongavarian soldiers rounding up the ogres—men, women, and children—and holding them in large camps in eastern

Groyria. If the ogres are working with Mongavaria, it's only because their families are threatened. It isn't willingly."

A grim silence fell over the room.

"The conditions in the camps aren't great, but our scouts haven't witnessed any mass executions." Uncle Edmund let that linger a moment before he continued, "Our scouts haven't, however, been able to make contact with the ogres, and any villages they've found have been deserted. If there are any ogres still free and resisting Mongavaria, we haven't been able to find them. But at least that means Mongavaria hasn't been able to find them either."

"When Mongavaria invaded Groyria this spring, there had been a great deal of discussion on whether we should go to war to protect Groyria, even though they had not asked for our help nor do we have a treaty with them." Uncle Julien sighed and shook his head, something like regret in his deep brown eyes. "But Mongavaria's bombing of Bridgetown forestalled any response we might have made. That was likely their intention in attacking us when they did. It drew our focus away from what was unfolding in Groyria, and until now we haven't been in the military position to turn our attention toward the crisis there."

Another shifting and murmuring swept the room.

To enter Groyria without the ogres' request, even to aid them against Mongavaria, would essentially be an invasion, trampling over Groyria's national sovereignty.

Yet in standing by, what had the Alliance allowed to happen to the ogres?

Still, what else could the Alliance have done? From the moment Mongavaria attacked Fort Linder and Bridgetown, the Alliance had been fighting an all-out war along a front stretching from the southern tip of the Whitehurst Mountains, along the Hydalla River, and all the way to the northern seas around Dar Goranth. All their resources had been dedicated to fighting the war there, and splitting their focus more than they already had might have led to a defeat.

War strategy was cold. It had to be. It was a calculation of how best to spend the lives that would be lost, and if the objectives would be worth the cost.

"Our scouts witnessed certain ogres being taken from the camps and transported into Mongavaria, but until recently we were unable to determine where in Mongavaria they were being taken." Uncle Edmund gave a weary shrug. "Our spying efforts in Mongavaria were focused on other things up until now, such as discovering the Mongavarian strategic and tactical plans for the war. Now that we know the ogres are playing a far larger role than believed, we are combing through all our past intercepted messages, pilfered documents, and scouts' reports to see what was missed."

One of the male troll generals muttered something unflattering about spies loudly enough for the whole room to hear.

Uncle Edmund pressed his mouth into a tight line as his shoulders seemed to heave in a sigh, as if this was a conversation he'd had several times over already.

"Thanks to the hard work of the Intelligence Offices in all three kingdoms, we partially broke the Mongavarian naval code and had warning that there was an attack headed for Dar Goranth." Uncle Julien held the troll general's gaze. "Mongavaria changed their codes after that, and through more hard work by many teams of people, we broke the naval code again recently, resulting in a large-scale victory by our navy that has crippled the Mongavarian naval forces. The Intelligence Offices have been invaluable, but they have also had a lot on their desks in this war."

The troll general finally looked away, his gaze dropping away from Uncle Julien's.

"Our efforts to break Mongavaria's army codes have been similar." Uncle Edmund's expression had relaxed out of its tight strain. "We have partially or mostly broken it several times, only for them to change it. They had made a change recently so we'd had no warning about their attack on the Wall. Yet when Mongavaria debuted those machines, that was a stroke of luck for us."

"Luck?" Dacha muttered under his breath. The word wouldn't have carried to Uncle Edmund or Uncle Julien, but Fieran glanced in Dacha's direction.

He couldn't help but agree with his dacha's unamused tone. He wouldn't classify the Wall coming down and Dacha nearly dying as *luck.*

But Uncle Edmund was just a touch crazy like that.

"We knew their code word for those machines in their past codes. We just didn't know exactly what that word referred to up until then." Uncle Edmund gestured more animatedly as he spoke. "But in the aftermath of the Wall coming down, we knew exactly what the code words were referring to. Not only did we break their current army code, but we were also able to trace the source of the machines. Consequently, we know that nearly all of the ones Mongavaria had manufactured up to that point had been destroyed. We know which airships are currently in dry dock waiting for machines to be installed. And by tracing shipments of the machines and collaborating with an agent we have deeply embedded in Mongavaria, we were able to find the source of the machines. They're manufactured in the town of Kilriden."

A few of the human generals nodded, the light of recognition in their eyes.

But Fieran had never heard of that particular Mongavarian town. Was it somewhere important?

"A scouting mission was immediately authorized." Uncle Julien was pointing at something on the table. Possibly a map of Mongavaria, if Fieran were to guess. "Kilriden is in the heavily fortified industrial corridor in the center of Mongavaria, within the Empress Defensive Line, and, worse, it's between Mongavaria's Pamfrey Army Base and Aerodrome and inland of the Ontocotee Naval Base. It's one of the most heavily protected and patrolled sections of the kingdom."

Yep, that was important, all right. Thanks to spending that week supporting the invasion forces pouring through the Barringstall Pass and the Engleston Gap, Fieran had some grasp of the Alliance strategy for the invasion.

The Alliance could have added a fourth invasion along that border—counting the main invasion from Fort Defense—through the southern Cartmer Gorge. But that invasion would have crashed right into that heavily fortified chunk of kingdom Uncle Julien just described.

Instead, the decision had been made to merely hold the border at the Cartmer Gorge and focus on the three northern invasions. They'd bypass the Pamfrey Army Base and the Ontocotee Naval Base, cutting those forces off from the rest of the kingdom instead of engaging them. If those forces didn't surrender when the rest of the kingdom did, they could be dealt with at that time.

Based on the nods around the table, the generals gathered here knew all of that as well. They likely knew far more than Fieran did.

"While we have risked a few scouting flights over the naval and army bases, we haven't pushed into the interior between them." Uncle Julien reached a hand behind him. An aide stepped forward and put a manila folder in his hand. He placed the folder on the table. "Until now. A Kostarian airship made a daring, high altitude scouting run over Kilriden and snapped a few photographs. Unfortunately, the height makes details in the photographs difficult to discern, but we can make out enough. Paired with the information the Intelligence Offices have gathered, we can make some good deductions."

Uncle Edmund reached past Uncle Julien, slid a photograph out of the folder, and held it up, turning it to show those around the table. "This is Kilriden. As you can see, there is a large industrial complex along with a railway hub."

"So we bomb it." An Escarlish general shrugged. "Should have bombed it already."

"As we all know, our bombing efforts have been minimally effective so far." Uncle Julien shook his head on a sigh. "It is an annoyance and has slowed production at some of their factories, especially the locations we've been able to hit enough times to be disruptive. But we currently don't have bombs big enough, or aeroplanes large enough to carry them, to permanently shut down this facility."

The Escarlish general shot a glance at the corner where Dacha stood. "Then lift the restrictions on the magic of the ancient kings. A bomb built with that magic would obliterate it in one strike."

"No." Dacha's tone was steel, ringing sharp and slashing across the room. "Unleashing such a power without the control of a wielder would destroy indiscriminately."

The Escarlish general snorted, all but rolling his eyes. "That's what bombs do. It doesn't matter if they're filled with explosives or magic. Magic would just do it on a larger scale. Whatever line you're squeamish about, we've already crossed it."

"You do not understand the terror you are asking to unleash." Dacha held the general's gaze with his unflinching silver-blue eyes. "The magic of the ancient kings is meant to be wielded by a warrior. Its power is too great otherwise. While I am alive, I will never allow my magic or my children's magic to be used in such a way."

The elven generals, at least, were nodding their agreement. With the way the magic of the ancient kings was held up as near sacred, they would be reluctant to see it twisted into bombs.

"And you don't seem to understand that not using every means at our disposal will cost lives. How many Alliance soldiers—humans, elves, and trolls—will you sacrifice for your scruples?" The general was leaning forward now, as if preparing to march over to Dacha to confront him face-to-face. "It very well could cost your life or the lives of your children if these machines aren't stopped."

Dacha remained unmoved, staring back without answering as if he didn't feel a response was even needed.

Fieran shifted, not entirely sure where he fell on this debate.

On the one hand, he had seen the horrors of this war. If they could create a weapon with enough power to win the war and spare the lives of the Alliance soldiers who would be killed otherwise, shouldn't they do it?

Yet he also intimately knew the power of the magic of the ancient kings. He'd grown up on the stories of the fall of the elven empire. The ancient kings wielding this magic had become too great, too powerful, too arrogant. In the battle that followed, warrior had fought warrior, and the clash of the magic had been so great that the land itself had been scorched and devoid of life across most of what was now Escarland and Mongavaria. While plants, animals, and people had eventually returned, there was a reason those kingdoms still lacked the lush, dense forests of Tarenhiel.

The whirling ribbons and graceful movements of that elven troupe had been far too beautiful when they'd portrayed this part of the story, not fully capturing the horror of what had happened back then.

"Regardless of our stances on this particular issue, gentlemen, that decision isn't up to us." Uncle Julien's voice remained almost mild, even as it was firm enough to cut through the debate. "The ban on creating bombs using the magic of the ancient kings was written into the treaty holding the Alliance together when Kostaria joined. It is not something anyone in this room can change."

Creating weapons powered by the magic of the ancient kings was all right, such as powering aeroplanes, as long as there was a person in control of that weapon. That was deemed no different than a warrior wielding the magic. Using the magic to power shields was also allowed.

But bombs were explicitly banned, as was twisting the magic in any way to create a weapon. Fieran had heard something about Uncle Lance creating a bomb with Dacha's magic once, and that was the reason for the ban.

The Escarlish general shifted and looked away from Dacha, but, given the clench to his jaw, he didn't seem too happy.

"Beyond the ban, it likely wouldn't be advisable to drop any bomb containing magic on this factory." Uncle Julien gestured to the photograph that Uncle Edmund still held, although he'd lowered it during the debate. "It's filled with magic-stealing machines. A magical bomb would likely only fuel them, not destroy them."

"Nor is the factory the main threat." Uncle Edmund retrieved another photograph from the folder and held it up. "This is a secret facility a few miles outside of Kilriden. The Mongavarians call it Ludin."

The elven generals around the table reared back. Beside Pip and Fieran, Rothilion went pale.

Several of the humans shifted, and one of the generals, not the belligerent one, glanced from the elves to Uncle Edmund. "Isn't that a Mongavarian folk hero?"

"Hero." A male elf general spat the word. "He captured elves, tortured them, and cut off their hair and the tips of their pointed ears in order to degrade them."

Now Fieran placed the name. Ludin had been a human living in what was now Mongavaria at the time of the fall of the elven empire. He'd led one of the human resistance groups, but he was so extreme that even other humans despised him as too radical.

"Yes, he was rather horrible, but in recent decades the story has been heralded by Mongavarian propaganda as a shining example of human ingenuity and grit in throwing off their elven oppressors." Uncle Edmund tapped the photograph. "And in this case, his name is rather appropriate for this place. From what my agents in Mongavaria can gather, experiments are being conducted on ogres with the purpose of bringing down the elves—Prince Farrendel and his offspring in particular—and the Alliance along with them."

Fieran swallowed, and Pip leaned into him as if seeking comfort. Around the table, a somber quiet descended once again.

That had always been the Mongavarian goal in this war. They wanted an empire—an empire of humans, specifically —to rival the one created by the elves so long ago. They'd conquered all the kingdoms along the ocean to the south, as well as Groyria.

But Escarland and the rest of the Alliance had always stood between them and expanding farther west. Seventy years ago, Mongavaria had hoped Escarland, as a fellow human kingdom, would willingly join their budding empire in order to form an alliance against the elves and trolls. Fieran had even heard something about a marriage of alliance with either his mother or with his Uncle Julien.

Instead, Escarland had chosen to ally themselves with the elves and trolls against their fellow humans in Mongavaria. Seventy years ago, that had been seen as an affront. Now the most extreme of Mongavarian propaganda portrayed it as unnatural, even a betrayal of humanity.

"What is the exact nature of these experiments?" The black-haired elven female general's voice was low and grim.

"Unfortunately, I haven't been able to obtain the exact details." Uncle Edmund's jaw worked. "There is only one Mongavarian general overseeing the Ludin facility, and all telephone and radio communications between him and the facility are in vague and coded terms. He reports nearly everything to the empress verbally so there is very little in writing for us to find in her office. The general's office is in a heavily guarded complex, which my agents haven't been able to infiltrate yet."

"But due to our experiences with the results, we can assume they are stealing the ogre's magic somehow." Uncle Julien shrugged. "The exact method doesn't change the fact that this is a threat. These experiments are the reason Mongavaria dared start this war. They believe they finally have the means to combat the magic of the ancient kings. And if these experiments are left unchecked, they very well could be right."

That gained a series of grim nods from around the table.

One Escarlish colonel was eyeing Uncle Edmund. "You have access to the empress's office?"

"Yes. If it comes across her desk, I get a copy." Uncle Edmund shrugged, as if seeing everything that the enemy leader saw was no big deal. "That's why she's learned to be cautious about her paperwork, especially since she hasn't figured out who my agent is."

The Escarlish colonel nodded with a new respectful light in his eyes. Several others seemed far more ready to believe whatever Uncle Edmund told them, now that they realized the scope of his sources.

"From what I've gathered, Mongavaria has been abducting ogres for years." Uncle Edmund pulled another photograph from the stack, but he didn't hold it up yet. "Ever since their conquest of Groyria, they've been conducting these experiments on a larger, more industrial scale. The analysts in the Intelligence Office have estimated that at least a hundred, perhaps several hundred, ogres have been brought from Groyria to the Ludin facility. That number is expected to increase dramatically in the next few months, if this facility isn't shut down."

Uncle Edmund held up a new photograph. It must have been an enlarged portion of an original photograph since it was especially blurry. But from what Fieran could see between the shoulders of all the gathered generals, it appeared to show several long buildings with black dots clustered around them. People, perhaps?

"Then there's this." Uncle Edmund held up another somewhat blurry photograph, this one of what appeared to be a giant pit with more tiny black shapes inside. "It's hard to make out details, but the analysts and the observers on the airship that conducted the scouting mission agree that this is a mass grave."

Fieran's stomach lurched. A mass grave was only needed if there was mass death.

"Are they killing off the ogres?" An Escarlish general frowned and gestured at the photograph. "Is all of this—the Ludin facility, the camps in Groyria—some plot by Mongavaria to exterminate the ogres? Perhaps that sounds absurdly melodramatic and overblown, but Mongavarian rhetoric about the elves and trolls has indicated that they have an extreme discrimination against non-humans."

"I wouldn't put that past them at some point, and I shudder to think what they would do to the elves, trolls, and dwarves if they won this war." Uncle Edmund's jaw flexed, his eyes holding a dark kind of anger. "But at this time it appears the deaths are a byproduct of the experiments. A byproduct they are not in a hurry to fix. The conditions in the holding camps in Groyria are decent enough that it seems Mongavaria needs their lab rats alive and well."

Beside Fieran, Pip's breathing had turned ragged. Fieran turned to her, partially sheltering her from the rest of the room. "Are you all right?"

"Just trying not to be sick. That's awful." Pip pressed her face against his arm, her shoulders giving a slight shudder.

Fieran rubbed her back, holding her close for a moment. He'd thought he'd lost his ability to be horrified at the things people could do to each other. But nope, it seemed there were levels of horror still to be reached.

A long, heavy silence fell across the meeting room.

Fieran's magic crackled in his chest, but there was nothing he could do with it here. The enemy was far away, and all he could do was hold Pip close by his arm around her shoulders and hope his uncles had come up with a plan for ending this.

The belligerent Escarlish general cleared his throat. "While this is all...grim, does this change anything? As awful as this is for the ogres, our current strategy will likely end the war sooner rather than later. After all, we have Mongavaria on the run, and our advantage will only increase as winter sets in, thanks to the troll ice magic we have on our side. If we win the war, we will also, in essence, liberate the ogres at the same time."

"We need to shut down this facility to prevent Mongavaria from making more of those magic-stealing machines." Uncle Julien tapped the map on the table once again. "Mongavaria intends to fortify the Empress Line with those machines, negating our magical advantage. That would halt our advance, if not turn it back altogether. We could find ourselves fighting a war in a bloody stalemate. Our invasion has only made such incredible progress these past few weeks because Mongavaria has been strategically falling back in a delaying action and making only minimal use of those machines while they further reinforce the place where they actually intend to take a stand. Don't mistake our gains these past weeks for victory. This war is far from won."

That sent a murmur around the room. These generals—the Escarlish ones in particular—apparently didn't like to be told that their seemingly inexorable march into Mongavaria wasn't as victorious as it seemed right now.

But the elven and troll generals were nodding, severe lines on their faces. With their long lives, those generals were the ones who had actually fought wars before. They likely remembered all too well the stalemate of a hundred years of war between the elves and trolls.

"In addition, our warriors of the magic of the ancient kings are currently at a significant risk, as are our warriors with magic of any kind. If we lose them, we lose this war." Uncle Julien's jaw was hard beneath his thick beard as he stared at the generals. "Simply put, we can't win the war until we get rid of those machines."

Fieran wasn't about to argue with that. He'd experienced the power of just one of those machines firsthand and had seen what a whole bunch of them had done to Dacha. Until those machines were eliminated, the Alliance couldn't unleash the full force of its magical power to win the war.

"I say we bomb the Ludin facility to put it out of action for a while." That Escarlish general jabbed a hand at the photographs Uncle Edmund had set on the table. "A few ogres might be killed, but they will die anyway in the Mongavarian experiments."

That sounded cold, but that general's first priority was Escarland and Escarlish lives. From his point of view, his suggestion made perfect sense.

Even if Fieran hoped that wasn't what his uncles actually planned to do.

"As we mentioned, bombing is still mostly ineffective." Uncle Julien fished a photograph from the folder and handed it to Uncle Edmund, although neither revealed it yet. "It takes numerous and near continuous bombing raids to put a factory or facility out of action, and with the Pamfrey Aerodrome putting up a stiff resistance, such a campaign would be dangerous and drawn out. Nor could we guarantee that we would hit a vital enough section of the Ludin facility to cripple it."

"And there's this." Uncle Edmund held up the photograph. It was even more blurry than the previous one, but it appeared to show a large yard where a faint symbol had been formed in whatever gray surface created the flat landscape.

Fieran swallowed and met first Merrik's gaze, then Rothilion's on his other side, even as one of the generals said, "Is that the Escarlish Flying Corps wings?"

Merrik had a grim set to his jaw while Rothilion flexed his fingers. Yet there was a glint of hope in their gazes as well.

That same hope twisted in Fieran's chest. Could Pretty Face be there? Was this why he hadn't been able to escape back to the Alliance?

"We believe so, yes." Uncle Edmund's gaze lifted past the pack of generals at the table to meet Fieran's across the room.

So this was why Fieran had been included in this meeting. This had something to do with the Flying Corps, and Fieran was the ranking officer in the area.

"Several months ago, a shipload of Alliance prisoners was taken from the main prisoner of war camp outside of Landri." Uncle Edmund shifted his gaze away from Fieran and back to the men around the table. "The paper trail is hazy, but our best guess is that they were taken to the Ontocotee Naval Base and from there to Ludin. They are likely intended to be laborers of some sort. The reconnaissance photographs show what appears to be a factory on the site— likely manufacturing the Mongavarian version of a magical power cell to hold the stolen ogre magic. All the elves at the prisoner of war camp were included in this transfer."

"Are they going to experiment on elves now?" the male elf general sputtered, his face going white beneath his already pale silver complexion.

"It is a possibility, yes." Uncle Edmund's voice had a catch in it.

Fieran shifted, sneaking a glance at Dacha before taking in the other elves. All the elves in this room were now very motivated to shut down Ludin.

As was Fieran. If Pretty Face was there, then Fieran would do whatever it took to rescue him.

Yes, Pretty Face might be at the larger prisoner of war camp near Landri. Those Escarlish Flying Corps wings could have been done by any number of flyboys who had crashed in Mongavaria since the war began. Still…there was just something about it that Fieran couldn't shake.

"If you are saying we can't bomb this facility because our people are there, are you suggesting we launch a ground strike against it?" The blustering Escarlish general broke the moment. "Thousands would die in that case. Are a handful of ogres and a few of our own men worth the cost it would take to spare them? Even an ineffective bombing campaign would be better than that. The losses to the Flying Corps, and to the Alliance prisoners of war, would be far more manageable."

Fieran used to think that generals should be like his Uncle Julien and Aunt Vriska. Good warriors who held to a strict code of honor.

But perhaps effective generals were also those who were rather awful people. It took a certain level of cold ruthlessness to send men into battle and keep sending them to their deaths until the battle was won.

Even if this Escarlish general had a point, Fieran didn't have to like him or like his suggestions.

"No, I agree that any kind of ground strike against this facility prior to the end of the war would be inadvisable." Uncle Julien shook his head. "It's in a too heavily fortified area of the kingdom, and any attempt would just dangerously split our forces and focus."

"What about a small infiltration force? Possibly from the Cartmer Gorge or landed from the ocean?" another general suggested.

"The fields surrounding the Ludin facility are too well-guarded with hidden bunkers, and the Mongavarians would likely kill all the Alliance prisoners before we got there." Uncle Julien held up another series of photographs, showing bunkers and strong points in the area around Ludin. "Even if we were willing to sacrifice the prisoners for the greater objective of shutting down the experiments, an attack with a small group would need a warrior of the magic of the ancient kings to succeed, but any use of the magic of the ancient kings would need to be limited around Ludin until it was securely in our hands. The chance of actually succeeding would be very low."

"What about parachuting from an airship or aeroplane?" Fieran hadn't even realized he'd spoken out loud until all eyes in the room swung to him, the general directly in front of him whirling around, as if they'd forgotten he and his friends were even in the room. At their gaping looks, Fieran shrugged. "Just a thought. If you got an airship over Ludin once, perhaps you can do it again."

"We considered it." Uncle Julien nodded to Fieran. "But the height the airship traveled was far too high for a safe parachute jump. And while the army and navy have been conducting experiments with parachutes and parachute designs, our technology isn't there yet. We wouldn't have a way to guarantee a force would actually land in Ludin. They'd probably be shot out of the sky long before reaching the ground."

Fieran sighed. It had been a thought. But Uncle Julien was right. They hadn't even figured out how to include parachutes in the cockpits of aeroplanes so that pilots could jump out of a crashing aeroplane and possibly survive. Trying it on some kind of dangerous mission was still impossible. Maybe someday, but not now.

"How are we going to take it out?" The loud Escarlish general appeared ready to punch someone in frustration. "So far, all you've done is convince us that taking it out is necessary, only to prove that doing so is impossible."

"We get sneaky." Uncle Edmund's smile was more sharp danger than mirth. "We have come up with a plan that will not only take out Ludin but also end the war."

That created a flurry of comments and questions around the room.

Fieran was all for doing something to end the war quicker. He'd already witnessed too much death. He'd lost his cousin Myles. Lost members of his squadron. Lost Pretty Face to either captivity or death.

It was beyond time for this war to end.

Yet what could Uncle Edmund and Uncle Julien have come up with that would possibly accomplish both goals?

"I'm afraid we can't share too many details as this mission is top secret." Uncle Edmund swept a glance around the room, that edge still in his eyes. "But it will involve two of our warriors of the ancient kings venturing into Mongavaria, leaving you to proceed with the invasion with the remaining two warriors."

"That will severely hamper our efforts!"

"What if they're killed?"

"Or, worse, captured? If Mongavaria gets their hands on them…"

Fieran glanced at Adry and Dacha. Of course Dacha would be one of the warriors going into Mongavaria, leaving either Adry or Fieran as the second since Rhohen was too young for such a mission. Some clenching in Fieran's chest told him he would be the one sent with Dacha. By the way Pip gripped his hand in a vice, she knew it too.

"This mission has been carefully calculated and planned in conjunction with an attack by our naval forces." Uncle Julien gave each general assembled there a hard stare. "It is a risk, but the time to strike is now. Yes, we could continue as we are, forging across Mongavaria foot by foot. We would win eventually, but we would pave every mile of Mongavaria with our blood."

Uncle Julien had the room in the grip of his voice, his fervor wrapping around each of them. The generals around the table were leaning closer, the trolls with clenched fists and savage grins, the Escarlish with brutal resolve to the sets of their chins, and the elves with that finely honed edge like swords about to strike.

"As you pointed out"—here Uncle Julien nodded to the bellicose Escarlish general—"our greatest weapon is the magic of the ancient kings. If we can't drop a bomb with that magic on Mongavaria, then the next best thing we can do is drop them"—Uncle Julien waved to where Dacha, Adry, and Fieran stood along the wall—"and let them do what they do best: end the war."

"In that case, why didn't we just do that months ago and save ourselves all the trouble of fighting this war?" The Escarlish general seemed determined to remain pugnacious.

"At the start of this war, we only had one seasoned warrior with the magic of the ancient kings. The next generation of warriors did not yet have the battle experience or magical stamina necessary to fight as full-fledged warriors as they can now." Uncle Julien remained just as unflinching as the general he faced. "Nor was Mongavaria ready to surrender back then. We were facing an equally matched opponent with nearly identical industrialized capacity and food production. If anything, their army was the more experienced and battle-hardened after their years of conquest. If we had sent in a warrior, assuming we could do so given we didn't yet have control of the skies or the seas as we do now, it would have only strengthened their resolve instead of making them break."

Fieran felt the truth of that to his bones. It would have been nice if Dacha could have just marched on Landri and ended all of this before it had truly begun.

But that would have just reinforced the Mongavarian propaganda about the dangers of the elves. They would have doubled down on their efforts to exploit the ogres and build those machines.

At the start of this war, Mongavaria hadn't been able to invade Escarland because of Dacha's magic. But the Alliance hadn't been militarily strong enough to invade Mongavaria either. They'd been equally matched in that.

It had taken this war with all its defeats and victories, death and carnage, for the Alliance to fight its way to the military edge it had now.

"We have gained this opportunity to end the war thanks to all the blood we've already shed and the sacrifices we've already made. Let's not waste it." Uncle Julien pounded a fist on the table. "We are going to give Mongavaria everything we've got. We will hit hard, and we will be unrelenting. We need to have Mongavaria on its knees when our warriors go for the throat. They won't surrender to anything less than that. This is a gamble, but if it succeeds, the war will end in mere weeks rather than months or even years from now."

The generals weren't raucous enlisted men to meet that statement with something as undignified as cheers. But there were fervent murmurs, firm nods, and a few more fists pounded on the table.

Fieran gripped Pip's hand and held Merrik's gaze, seeing the same determination mirrored there. Whatever his uncles' plan, whatever it took to end this war, they'd do it.

NINE

Fieran's ears were still buzzing with his uncle's words, and he couldn't manage to take in the brief discussion that followed before Uncle Julien dismissed everyone.

Fieran pushed from the wall to move, but Uncle Iyrinder reached out a hand, stopping him. When Fieran glanced at him, Uncle Iyrinder gave him a shake of the head.

Between them, Merrik's jaw was working, as if he'd realized something that Fieran hadn't yet managed to put together.

The generals gave Fieran and his friends a variety of looks as they filed from the room. A few were curious while others were more hostile, as if they were wondering why this handful of captains and a major would be entitled to stay and hear the details of a secret mission when they, the generals actually running this war, were kept mostly in the dark.

Once the last of the generals had left the room, closing the door behind him, Dacha strode forward, regarding Uncle

Julien with a steely glare. "I do not like this plan. You are sending one of my children into Mongavaria."

Apparently he had no problem with being sent himself, just that either Fieran or Adry were going with him.

"I don't particularly like it either." Uncle Julien pressed both hands to the table, a hint of weariness in the line of his shoulders. "But you heard our alternatives. I don't like the other choices even more."

Dacha's jaw worked, as if he wanted to object but couldn't.

Perhaps that had been part of the point of that meeting, to prove to Dacha that the plan Fieran's uncles were about to unveil was the only viable option.

Fieran squeezed Pip's fingers before he released her hand and strode closer to the table. She crept behind him, her steps tentative.

"I don't like it either. And you should have heard the lecture Weylind gave me when he heard the plan." Uncle Edmund held Dacha's gaze. "But I understand. My daughter has been facing this danger for two years already. The sooner we end this war, the safer all our children will be."

Dacha sighed and the set of his shoulders relaxed somewhat. "I still do not like it."

Uncle Edmund held Dacha's gaze for another moment before he turned to face the rest of them, beckoning them forward.

Merrik, Adry, and Rothilion caught up with Fieran and Pip, and they took the spots around the table that the generals had occupied earlier. Dacha and Uncle Iyrinder slipped into the final places next to Uncle Julien.

Uncle Edmund pointed at a spot on the map along the defensive Empress Line. "There's an airship dock here that we've been saving to bomb for a special occasion. Word has reached me that they will be getting a shipment of those machines to install on the airships in a week. That gives us a small window where a large number of airships will be docked in one place and won't have those machines yet. In case of a raid by the Half-Breed Squadron, the airships are under orders to take off and scatter to avoid being easily taken out by Fieran."

He wasn't sure if he should be flattered that the Mongavarians had contingencies specifically for him. But considering how many airships he'd taken down, it was valid.

"The Half-Breed Squadron will attack the airship docks." Uncle Julien tapped the aerodrome on the map before moving his finger to point at another spot farther south. "Another squadron of fighters and bombers will attack the railyard here to attempt to prevent those machines ever reaching any of the airships. If we are especially fortunate on our timing, we'll hit the train transporting the machines."

"Either way, during the chaos of the bombing, we'll hijack one of the airships." Uncle Edmund spoke as if hijacking enemy aircraft was no big deal. "They'll be lightly staffed while at dock, and we'll get it off the ground before the crew has the chance to return. Those left behind won't think anything of it, since the orders to flee include leaving anyone behind who can't get on board before the airship takes off. We'll fly the airship to Ludin, using the Mongavarian codes to get past the aerial blockade, and rescue the prisoners."

"Once the facility is secure and the prisoners rescued, they will be escorted back to Escarland, either in the airship or on the ground as necessary." Uncle Julien waved his hand at the spread of photographs. "Farrendel and Edmund will continue on to the Mongavarian capital, where they will do what is necessary to end this war. I'm afraid I can't tell even you what that particular part of the plan involves, but I'm in contact with the navy to arrange help in that regard."

Rothilion cleared his throat, glancing around at all of them. "While I have no wish to be the voice of cold reason, would it not make more sense for General Laesornysh to head straight for Landri and end the war sooner without the detour to the Ludin facility? The ogres and prisoners would essentially be rescued by the end of the war. Or they could be rescued by the other warrior of the magic of the ancient kings sent on the mission."

"It's quite possible that Mongavaria won't even consider surrender until that last hope of fighting off the Alliance is snatched away." Uncle Julien tilted his head in a respectful nod to Rothilion. Uncle Julien wasn't one to discount someone's input, even if they were a far lower rank than he was. "Thus, I would like two warriors of the magic of the ancient kings to take on the facility to be absolutely sure it is secured as quickly as possible, especially given the danger of using magic around those machines."

Fieran nodded, sharing a glance with Adry. Uncle Julien and Uncle Edmund hoped that, with two warriors, they'd be able to overwhelm the machines if their magic should get caught by one. That was how Dacha and Fieran had destroyed the machines they'd faced previously.

"Nor would the ogres and prisoners necessarily be freed by the end of the war." Uncle Edmund heaved a sigh, shaking his head. "I've received reports that the political situation in Mongavaria is growing shaky. There's every chance that Mongavaria will implode if they surrender. At the very least, the Mongavarian army stationed around Ludin may hold out long after a surrender is announced. They might even use the prisoners of war as hostages against us. Besides that, it's too much of a risk to leave the ogres and that experimental research unsecured when Mongavaria surrenders. There's too great a chance it will fall into the wrong hands, and if that happens, we'll find ourselves battling rogue elements with nothing to lose and the ability to counteract our greatest strength."

That didn't sound like a great option either. It was bad enough having those machines in Mongavarian hands. But the established government at least provided some measure of control over the use of them. There was no telling what someone could do if they didn't care what chaos they caused.

Rothilion nodded. "I thank you for the clarification."

"And Pretty Face might be there." Fieran wasn't sure if he was speaking to himself or to the others, but both Rothilion and Merrik nodded. Pip squeezed Fieran's fingers.

Merrik turned to Uncle Edmund, gesturing from himself to the rest of them. "And who will be going on this mission?"

Fieran tensed, waiting for his uncle's answer. He and his friends must be involved in some way, if his uncles had gathered them all here to go over this plan. He didn't think they'd get such a thorough briefing if their only contribution was leading the bombing raid.

"Farrendel, Fieran, Pippak, and me." Uncle Edmund waved to each of them as if to make sure there was no mistake in whom he was referring to.

"Pip?" Fieran started at the same time as Pip yelped, "Me?"

"Yes." Uncle Edmund's gaze rested on Pip. "You have experience with both magic-powered and gas-powered engines, which will be necessary to keep the hijacked airship flying. Not to mention, your shielding magic will make you a more powerful addition to the team than any other mere mechanic. On the trip back to Escarland, you and Fieran can hold a constant shield while still allowing the other to rest. And you're all but immune to the magic of the ancient kings so that in a fight, I will be the only one Fieran and Farrendel have to worry about accidentally incinerating."

"No, not Pip." Fieran stepped in front of her, as if to protect her from his uncle's schemes. He wasn't doubting Pip's courage or magic in the least.

But he agreed with his dacha. He didn't like this plan. At all.

Pip rested a hand on his arm. "I'm officially in the army now. They actually can order me to do this."

"But they won't." Fieran held Uncle Edmund's gaze for a moment before he looked at Uncle Julien, who would likely be the more sympathetic of the two. "She's not a warrior. She's a mechanic. If she doesn't want to do this, she won't be forced."

"No, she won't." Uncle Julien's voice was low, but his gaze was unwavering.

"None of you will be forced into this." Uncle Edmund nodded to Fieran before gesturing between Dacha and himself. "Your dacha and I will be going regardless, of course. Fieran and Pip, your participation is strictly voluntary."

Fieran half-turned to meet Pip's gaze. He didn't want her to come along and experience that kind of danger. He'd been determined to do whatever it took to end the war, but risking Pip's life on a crazy mission wasn't what he'd had in mind.

But this was her decision, and he wouldn't make it for her. She wasn't a child who needed choices made for her about what danger she could handle.

No, she was a capable woman who had faced bombs and battles. Her magic was strong, and her courage even stronger.

Pip's gaze dropped for just a moment, her shoulders hunching as if to make herself smaller. She was silent for several moments before her posture straightened. Her eyes flashed back up to meet his with an iron determination. She reached out and gripped his hand again. "If you're going, then I'm going."

Pip would stick by his side no matter which choice he made. He clasped her hand, nodded, and turned to face his uncles again.

Dacha's gaze and jaw were hard, his arms crossed over his chest. He was likely hoping Fieran would decide to stay here.

Yet this was everything Fieran had dreamed about as a child. Going into battle and glory at his dacha's side, a warrior worthy of the Laesornysh name.

Now he knew there was no glory in battle. War held nothing but death and destruction. But he was still Laesornysh, and he still longed to go into battle at his dacha's side. He knew deep within his soul that, together, he and his dacha could end this war.

Fieran glanced over his shoulder first at Rothilion, then at Merrik. His childhood dreams might spur him to go, but his duty and loyalty to his squadron grounded him to stay. He couldn't leave his squadron behind. More than his magic, they were the source of his strength. The reason he'd made it this far in the war. He couldn't abandon them now.

But Pretty Face might be a prisoner at that facility. If Fieran went, he could rescue him and finally bring him home. Did Fieran's duty lie with the one he'd lost or with the many he'd leave behind?

"The squadron will be all right." Rothilion tipped his head. "I will look after them."

"Due to the shielding wires invented by Capt. Detmuk-Inawenys, the squadrons will still have the benefit of your magic to protect them." Uncle Julien spoke up, as if he understood the source of Fieran's hesitation.

Fieran shook his head and gave Pip a fake glare. "Told you that you'd make me obsolete."

"I might have thought twice about it if I'd realized it would free you to be sent off into danger in Mongavaria," Pip muttered with a glance toward his uncles.

"But speaking about the Half-Breed Squadron..." Uncle Julien's tone had Fieran turning his attention back to him. Uncle Julien held up a folded piece of paper. "Capt. Rothilion, you have a choice as well. If Fieran should take the mission to Mongavaria, you would be the new captain of the squadron. However, I'm working with the navy on a top-secret project that will coincide with the mission into Mongavaria. We are looking to recruit six of the top elven pilots for this project, and, if you agree, I'd like you to lead those elves."

Rothilion glanced from Fieran to the paper in Uncle Julien's hand. "And this project...will it assist with Laesornysh's mission into Mongavaria?"

"Yes. It will help ensure the end of the war." Uncle Julien continued to hold out the piece of paper. "I'm afraid you won't be told more than that until you report to Sylmare to prepare for your mission. If you agree, you'll leave in two days."

Fieran's throat closed. All of them had choices, choices that would split the Half-Breed Squadron apart. It would be what was best to win the war, but that didn't mean he couldn't mourn it.

Rothilion stepped forward and, with a deliberate motion, took the paper from Uncle Julien's hand. "Then I accept."

"Good." Uncle Julien nodded, picked up a second folded paper, and held it out to Merrik. "Then, should Fieran accept the mission, you would be the captain of the Half-Breed Squadron."

Merrik took a step back, his eyes widening. As if he'd never thought such a duty would fall to him.

And it never would, if Fieran stayed here.

That settled deep within his heart, making his decision for him with a sense of right certainty.

"Then you'd better take that paper, Merrik. Because I'm going with my dacha into Mongavaria." Fieran couldn't believe those words were coming out of his mouth.

But instead of twisting nerves, a peace filled him. This was what he was meant to do. He and Pip, together.

Pip's fingers tightened on his, but she didn't flinch away. If anything, she stood taller.

His hand trembling slightly, Merrik took the paper from Uncle Julien, opening it and staring at the words on the page as if he couldn't believe it.

Adry hugged him around the waist, grinning as she murmured into his ear.

Pip leaned into Fieran's shoulder. "Mak is going to hate this."

TEN

"No. Absolutely not."

Pip perched on her workbench, swinging her legs, as she faced her brother. Sitting on the workbench put her more level with his face so that she didn't have to crane her neck to stare him down. "I'm going."

The words twisted everything inside her from the pit of her stomach all the way into the burning in her throat. But she wasn't going to back down. There was no way she was staying here, waiting and wondering, while Fieran went off into the depths of Mongavaria.

Even if the thought of going on a crazy, dangerous mission like this scared her like nothing else ever had.

Mak paced—stalked in fury, more like—across the space in front of her workbench. "You're not a warrior. What are the generals thinking, sending you off into Mongavaria like this?"

"They needed a mechanic." Pip shrugged and nudged one of her wrenches. At least she'd gotten permission to tell Mak some of the details, even if he couldn't know all of it. It wasn't like the Half-Breed Squadron and their mechanics wouldn't notice when Pip, Fieran, and Rothilion left.

"Then send one of the airship mechanics along. For that matter, why isn't an airship pilot going instead of Fieran?" Mak jabbed a hand in the direction of the mansion. "Surely that would make more sense than sending the two of you."

"None of the airship pilots or mechanics have magic like Fieran's or like mine." Pip raised her hand and created a small sphere over her palm.

"If they want a mechanic with magic, then I should be the one to go." Mak crossed his arms and glared at her.

"You know it isn't the same." Pip expanded her sphere. "Assuming we can neutralize those magic-stealing machines, Fieran and I are just about invincible when we're together."

"Then I'll come too." Mak took a step forward, standing squarely in front of her.

A part of her desperately wished he could. He was her big brother. Stepping into the unknown would be far less daunting with him at her side.

And yet it was time she forged this path on her own. For too long, she'd been stuck in a rut, not moving forward, not taking chances, because she'd been too scared to leave home.

She couldn't go back to being the same girl who had gotten up the courage to go to Escarland for university, only to return home and work the same job she always had for several more decades because she hadn't dared pursue her real dream.

She wanted a life at Fieran's side, even if that meant fighting in the depths of Mongavaria. He was worth it because he would fight at her side just as hard as she would at his.

"You can't just invite yourself along on this mission. Not

this time." Pip braced her hands on either side of herself on the workbench.

Not to mention, Mak wasn't invulnerable to Prince Farrendel's magic the way she and Fieran were. Anyone not impervious to his power would be a liability during whatever battle they might face to take the Ludin facility.

"Pip, I can't—"

"No." Pip gave his chest a shove with the flat of her hand. "No, don't go all protective big brother on me. I know this is hard. I'm not particularly thrilled with the idea of marching into Mongavaria either. But I *have* to do this. And I can't go unless I know that you'll be here, looking after the squadron."

As beyond terrified as she was by this mission, she couldn't shake the deep conviction that she had to go. It wasn't just because of Fieran either. She'd seen so much and done so much because of this war.

Somewhere out there in Mongavaria, there were people who needed to be rescued. Perhaps even a friend who needed her and Fieran. She couldn't be a coward, not when her magic could make all the difference.

Mak's shoulders slumped, his gaze dropping for the first time. "I never would have encouraged you to leave home if I thought this was where we'd end up."

"It likely wouldn't have made that much difference." Pip shrugged, letting another sphere form on her palm. "My magic was bound to get the attention of the higher-ups one way or another. There is no one else who can do what I can."

"No, there isn't." Mak finally uncrossed his arms before he stepped forward and wrapped her in a hug. "Just stay safe, Pipsqueak."

"I'll do my best." Pip embraced him back, holding tightly, her throat closing. "And you stay safe as well. The aerodrome will be a more dangerous place once all of us are gone and can't shield it during attacks."

"I'll be fine." Mak released her and took a step back. He stood there for a moment, an awkward silence falling between them.

Pip flapped a hand at him. "Go on. I don't leave for a couple of days, and both of us have work to do."

Mak sighed before he smiled, the expression still strained. He turned and strolled away, likely to find the first aeroplane on his checklist that was in need of repairs.

Fieran stepped into sight as he entered the barn, his swords strapped across his back. He halted by Mak, and the two of them exchanged a few words in a low tone too quiet for Pip to hear.

Not that she needed to hear it. Whatever he said, it was likely some version of *Keep my sister safe or else*.

Fieran nodded, clapped Mak on the shoulder, and strode past him, headed for Pip. When he reached the workbench, he shoved a few tools aside and boosted himself to sit next to her on the wooden surface. "Mak seems to have taken the news as well as could be expected."

"Yeah. He's worried, but he knows this is something I need to do." Pip picked up one of her wrenches, turning it over to keep her hands busy.

Fieran sighed and nodded, as if he was struggling with the same thing. After a moment, he drew one of his swords, resting it across his lap as if he too needed something to fiddle with.

Yet as the silence lingered between them, Pip glanced up at him, searching his face. "No practice this morning?"

"No." Fieran turned his sword over in his hands so that the flat was up, then the single, dulled blade. "They weren't up for practice. Dacha needed time alone, and Adry is with Merrik."

Understandable. Even though both Merrik and Adry would remain here, the burden of being Laesornysh would fall squarely on her shoulders once Prince Farrendel left. Pip couldn't imagine facing war quite like that. Even on this mission, she wouldn't be expected to fight. She was going for her mechanical skills and ability to create defensive shields.

Pip leaned her head against Fieran's shoulder, drawing on his warmth and strength. "Are you all right?"

Fieran released a long breath as he stared down at the sword in his hands. "Yeah. It's just…going to be hard to leave the squadron behind."

"Yes, it is." She blinked at the pressure of that fast-approaching parting. She'd started this war with the flyboys. For some reason, she'd thought she'd end the war with them as well.

Perhaps they still would. Depending on how long it took them to return with the former prisoners, she and Fieran might be able to rejoin the squadron in time to be there when Prince Edmund and Prince Farrendel did whatever they planned to do to end the war.

After taking a deep breath, Fieran lifted the sword he was holding. "Do you know one of the dwarves who could put a proper edge on my swords? They're dwarven-made, but they're dull-edged practice swords, barely more than the toys that my first wooden training swords were. I think for this mission that I'm going to need my swords to be proper weapons. Like Dacha's."

In other words, he needed to fully become Laesornysh, an elven warrior who carried deadly blades capable of tasting blood.

Pip swallowed and nodded without lifting her head from his shoulder. "Yes, Draenelynn probably could, and if she can't, her mentor is also here. She's training to be a warrior bladesmith, someone highly valued by the dwarves."

When she peeked up at him, he was grimacing. Probably at the thought of having to ask Rhohen's girlfriend for a favor.

But after a moment, he held the sword out between them. "So…do I just…or should you…"

Pip laughed, straightened, and held out her hand. "I can ask her. Cousin-to-cousin."

Fieran rested the sword across his lap and unbuckled the sheaths and remaining sword from his back. Once he shrugged free, he sheathed the sword and handed both of them to Pip.

Pip swallowed as she wrapped her fingers around his swords. There was a strange finality in the gesture. When he held those swords again, they would be lethal in a way they never had before.

He would be Laesornysh. His dacha's son.

And she could only hope the Fieran she'd fallen in love with would remain beneath the warrior he would become.

As the gray after the sunset descended around the mansion, Pip sat on the front step of the mansion, staring at the line of trees, parked aeroplanes, and makeshift airfield that stretched before her.

What had she been thinking when she agreed to go on that mission into Mongavaria? She wasn't a warrior. She'd nearly fallen apart on that small incursion to retrieve those machines. How could she possibly face a deadly secret mission into the very heart of the enemy empire?

This was crazy.

She knew exactly what she'd been thinking. That she couldn't let Fieran go off alone. She couldn't stay behind for weeks on end, wondering if he was still alive. More, she had to be at his side to ensure that he didn't do something reckless and get himself killed since Merrik was staying behind.

Yet despite her show of determination with her brother, her stomach twisted into painful knots. How was she going to do this?

With the crunch of boots on the gravel, Fieran strolled along the line of aeroplanes before he halted next to her. He lowered himself to sit on the stone step next to her, close enough that their shoulders brushed. "Are you all right?"

"Just second-guessing a few life decisions." Pip leaned against him, needing to be held close.

Fieran wrapped his arm around her shoulders, tugging her closer. "You don't have to go. My dacha and uncles won't force you if you decide you don't want to do this."

She squeezed her eyes shut and searched her heart for long moments. Did she want to back out? Just tell everyone that it was too much. That she just wasn't brave enough.

It was so tempting. The words hovered on the tip of her tongue, a sense of relief filling her at the thought of not going.

With the last shreds of her courage, she swallowed back the words. When she finally spoke, she whispered, "But you're still going, aren't you?"

Fieran hesitated before he released a long breath. "Yes. If this could destroy those machines before any more of my family is put at risk, then I have to go. And if Pretty Face is there..."

"Then we can't leave him there." Pip clenched her fists in her lap, even as some of the knots in her stomach loosened.

Losing Pretty Face had hit their group of friends hard. If there was a chance he was still alive, that she and Fieran could rescue him, then they'd have to take it.

"No, we can't." Fieran tightened his arm around her shoulders for a moment.

"Then that's it. I'm going." The words were flat as they came out of her mouth, but a sense of peace, far sharper than the relief of a moment ago, washed through her.

Staying here would be the easy thing. But if this war had taught her anything, it was that she had to face the hard things in life.

"In that case…" Fieran released his grip on her shoulder, stood, and held out his hand. "Come on. We're going to fly."

"What?" She stared at his hand, trying to comprehend his words.

"The first time you fly in an aeroplane shouldn't be on this mission." Fieran waggled his fingers, his hand still between them. "I'm going to take you on a flight tonight."

Even as she placed her hand in his, she shook her head. "Do you have permission to do this?"

"I'm a major. I gave myself permission." Fieran grinned as he hauled her to her feet.

Pip shook her head and fell into step with him as they strode down the gravel drive toward the shapes of the aeroplanes parked at the edge of the dark airfield.

But as they halted beside one of them, the fading light fell on the elf ear surrounded by hair-flames and blue bolts of magic.

"Uh, Fieran." Pip gripped his arm and gestured to the aeroplane. "That's your aeroplane. Not one of the two-seaters."

"Well, *some* mechanic grounded the two-seaters in order to make sure they had a full refit before their upcoming mission." Fieran bumped into her, raising his eyebrows as he glanced down at her.

Oh, right. That would be her.

"But there's only one seat." Pip pointed at the aeroplane ahead of them.

"Then it's a good thing you're nicely travel-sized." Fieran grinned before he grabbed the chocks holding the wheels in place, setting them to one side. He leapt onto the toe step, swung into the cockpit with easy movements, and settled into his seat, still grinning. "Come on."

This might be the craziest thing she'd ever done. Pip gripped one of the wing struts and stuck her toe in the step, her knee halfway to her chin. With a heave, she boosted herself up.

Fieran gripped her hand to steady her as she scrambled, stumbled, and tumbled into the cockpit. For a moment, the two of them were all awkward limbs as they tried to find a way to sit so that Fieran could still reach the rudder bar and the control stick.

She eventually found herself sitting on his lap with her legs tucked to one side of his. She hadn't snuggled quite this much with him since those moments after they'd learned his cousin Myles had been killed. Both of his arms were looped around her as he flicked the switch to turn on the engine.

The whining whir of the propeller and the hum of the engine filled the air, breaking the stillness of the night.

"This cockpit isn't designed for two people." Pip tucked her arms tighter to her sides as she tried not to elbow him in the stomach.

"But we fit." Fieran nudged one of her knees slightly

more out of his way so that he could get a better grip on the control column.

The aeroplane vibrated as the engine spun up, already rolling forward since the wheels weren't chocked.

Fieran tugged a flight cap into his head before he handed her a second one. "Sorry. You won't be able to plug into the radio since there is only one spot. But this will keep your ears warm."

This might be a reckless whim, but Fieran had put some thought into this at least. She tugged the cap onto her head, then pulled on the set of goggles he handed her. "No other flight gear?"

"I think we'll stay warm enough, wedged as we are in the cockpit." Fieran waggled his eyebrows at her, his grin lopsided. "Besides, we won't be up that long."

Fieran steered the aeroplane out of the line of trees and waved to one of the ground crew who was standing by. As the aeroplane rolled to the end of the airfield, two rows of elven lights flared to life on either side, marking where the airstrip lay.

Pip gripped the front of his uniform shirt and tried not to squeal as the aeroplane gained momentum, shaking and shuddering and bouncing. They were hurtling so fast, the wind blasting against her face in a way that made it hard to breathe.

Then the world grew light, and Pip was shoved against Fieran. The aeroplane's wings caught the wind, and then the ground was falling away.

Pip couldn't stop her squeal this time. It was far too disconcerting to watch the ground disappear while she wasn't even belted into this rickety aeroplane.

And, yes, it felt rickety, even if she was the mechanic in charge of maintaining it.

The aeroplane muscled its way higher into the sky, the propeller whipping the air, the engine humming with power.

"Look up." Fieran all but shouted into her ear to be heard over the noise of wind, engine, and propeller.

She tilted her head back and gaped upward at the dome of early evening stars arching overhead.

As the aeroplane leveled out, she relaxed, easing her grip on Fieran's shirt. Held within his arms, she felt safe despite her somewhat precarious position perched on his lap.

The stars glowed overhead while the lights of the mansion and the headquarters town speckled the land below. In the distance, more lights reflected off the distant Hydalla River as boats traveled the waters and towns bustled next to its banks.

Pip peered over the side, taking in the dark landscape spreading far below. She'd flown once before on that training trip on an airship, but this was far more visceral. The airship was a fortress, but the aeroplane was strangely lonely. Just the two of them in a small contraption with the huge world and even larger sky all around.

She could see why Fieran loved this so much. The lone warrior fighting in the sky would appeal to him.

Pip rested her head on his shoulder. "I'm scared."

"Of flying?" Fieran wrapped an arm around her waist, piloting the aeroplane with only one hand.

"No." She half-turned as best she could so that she could wrap both arms around him. "I'm scared of the mission. About what's going to happen to the squadron while we're gone. I'm scared that this war will never end, and I'll have to watch it slowly consume everything and everyone I care about."

"We aren't going to let that happen." Fieran's arm tightened around her, holding her close even as he eased the aeroplane into a gentle turn. "We're going to go on that mission. We'll rescue Pretty Face and any other prisoners held at that facility. My dacha and Uncle Edmund will end the war. And the two of us will have the peace to keeping falling in love."

That sounded good to her. Especially when Fieran gently pressed a kiss to the top of her hair.

She would have tipped her head up to kiss him, but she didn't want to distract him while he was flying.

Peace. It sounded like such an elusive dream, even though they'd been at peace not that long ago. This war hadn't even been happening for a full year, and yet it felt like it was all she'd ever known.

But that wasn't true. She'd gotten a taste of what peace could feel like while Fieran had been recovering at Aldon and during that meal when she'd introduced Fieran to her parents.

Was it time to let herself dream of what the future could look like after the war?

ELEVEN

Fieran strolled between the groups of elves and humans as they lounged about the parlor and foyer of the mansion. He occasionally stopped by one of the groups to talk before moving on, never staying for too long.

They'd had many parties over the months they'd been a squadron. But this one beat all the previous ones. Perhaps it was the impending losses—the coming fracturing of the squadron—that had all of them savoring the night more than ever before.

To one side of the foyer, Stickyfingers was snorting soda out his nose as Lije pounded his back. Pip was leaning out of the splash zone as Mak tossed a towel at Stickyfingers. Tiny had gotten a care package from his girlfriend, and he was passing out the donuts she'd made, doling them out in pieces so everyone got a bite. Aylia led some of the elven pilots in singing a song that was as raucous and loud as an elven song ever got.

A group of both human and elven pilots were setting up some kind of contraption around the grand staircase, and

Pip and Mak were supervising them when they weren't making sure Stickyfingers didn't choke.

Stepping into the somewhat quieter parlor, Fieran leaned against the wall next to where Rothilion had stationed himself well out of the chaos. "Are you going to miss this?"

Rothilion opened his mouth, closed it, then sighed. "I want to say *no*, but strangely I fear I will."

"We've gotten under your skin." Fieran elbowed Rothilion's arm.

"Like a fungus." Rothilion gave Fieran a flat look, although he couldn't quite hide the slight twitch fighting to break into a smile.

Fieran snorted and shook his head. "But you don't know what you'd do without us."

"No." Rothilion settled more firmly against the wall behind him.

Fieran let the silence lengthen for a moment before he spoke again, the smile dropping from his face. "Stay safe doing whatever my uncles will have you doing. It's going to be dangerous."

"No more dangerous than your mission into Mongavaria." Rothilion's eyes searched Fieran's face.

"I'll be with Pip and my dacha. We'll have enough magical power along to destroy an army if necessary." Fieran rolled his shoulders in an attempt at a nonchalant shrug, although he didn't think he was fooling Rothilion.

"Still, take care of Pip and yourself." Rothilion reached out and clasped Fieran's shoulder. "We will meet again once this war is over."

"I have no doubt." Fieran clasped Rothilion's shoulder in return. "Take care, Saranthyr."

"And you, Fieran." Rothilion nodded to Fieran before he dropped his hand.

Stickyfingers appeared in the parlor doorway, a few wet splotches on the front of his uniform shirt the only indication of his soda-spewing. "All right, everyone! Time for the show!"

Fieran pushed away from the wall and gestured from Rothilion to the crowd of pilots heading for the door to the foyer. "Now if you think I'm going to let you keep hiding in the corner…"

Rothilion sighed and shoved away from the wall. "Fine. I suppose I will have peace and quiet on my flight in the morning."

"That's the spirit." Fieran fell into step with Rothilion, making sure he wasn't about to back out.

The two of them stepped into the foyer, only to be ushered to a line of the cushioned chairs that had been lined up facing the grand staircase. Pip took the other seat next to Fieran while Merrik was ushered to the final seat, a footstool placed in front of him with an extra flourish, as if the flyboy were presenting it to the king.

Another flyboy had a towel over an arm and a tray in hand as he formally offered each of them a glass of the finest vintage of soda found in the latest supply shipment. Apparently this was what Stickyfingers had been taste-testing.

All the lights were dimmed except for those that had been turned to focus on the grand staircase and the area immediately in front of it.

One of the flyboys, who had a resonant voice, stepped to a landing where the two wings of the staircase met. "Give your attention to this, the first performance by the Half-Breed Players."

"We agreed to be the Half-Breed Acting Troupe!" one of the other flyboys called out from somewhere just out of sight.

"No, I thought we were the—"

"Ahem." The flyboy making the announcement shot a look over his shoulder. "It doesn't matter. We're getting started."

The others fell silent.

One of the male elven pilots who had a similarly deep voice joined the flyboy on the landing. "Behold, the story of the Half-Breed Squadron."

With that, the two announcers retreated farther up the two wings of the stairs until they were nearly out of sight.

Around each side of the staircase, the human flyboys and elven pilots marched forward, dressed in their uniforms. While the elf and human narrated the story, the two halves of the squadron pantomimed flying and training in a clumsy version of the acting-dancing of that elven entertainment troupe.

Rothilion gave a satisfied sigh as he stretched out his feet in a more comfortable sprawl than Fieran usually saw from him. "It appears my work here is done. Your humans have gained a taste for culture."

Before them, the narrators reached the part where the two halves of the squadron arrived in Dar Goranth, which apparently everyone had decided to portray as a collision. Flyboys and elves ran into each other, some stumbling and falling down. It was chaotic and messy, the two sides turning away from each other with huffs, crossed arms, and noses in the air.

Rothilion gave a small groan and pinched the bridge of his nose. "Never mind."

For some reason, the sight had Fieran reaching for Pip's hand, holding her fingers tight. The squadron had come so far since those early days. The ragtag, disjointed Flights had melded into what was now the finest squadron in the Alliance.

And now he would be leaving them.

Rothilion would leave first, flying out bright and early tomorrow morning. Fieran and Pip would leave a few days after that to head into the danger of the skies over Mongavaria.

Fieran glanced over Pip's head to where Merrik sat, a slight smile on his face, his gaze focused on the stumbling attempts of the flyboys to match the graceful elven movements. At least Fieran was leaving the squadron in good hands. If Merrik could keep Fieran more or less out of trouble growing up, then surely he could keep the squadron safe and in line.

The squadron told the story of the Battle of Dar Goranth, then the battles over Fort Defense. When Fieran and Merrik crashed, two of the flyboys went so far as to tumble down a few stairs to represent crashing.

Then there was his triumphant return. The introduction of the flygirls to their numbers. Merrik's return. The Wall coming down.

For their grand finale, the elves climbed on the shoulders of the flyboys, all of them gripping each other's arms until they formed the semblance of an aeroplane.

Fieran grinned and clapped while Pip gave a cheer beside him. Rothilion's and Merrik's clapping was less raucous but both of them were smiling broadly.

He would miss this squadron fiercely while he was in Mongavaria. But he had to go. For them.

Fieran strolled between the parked aeroplanes, resting a hand on a fuselage here, tracing the line of a wing there. The artwork emblazoned on the aeroplanes was as individual as each of the pilots who flew them.

This was a farewell, of sorts. A moment to linger among the aeroplanes, surrounded by the twinkle of fireflies dancing among the mechanisms of war, as the quiet of the evening settled into his soul.

Boots crunched behind him before Merrik strode from the gray of the deepening night and halted beside him.

Fieran rested his hand against his aeroplane's fuselage, his palm resting on the elf ear painted there. "I never thought we'd end the war like this. You going one way, me another. I thought I'd end this at your side."

Merrik shook his head, staring off into the night. "I always knew it would be like this. You were destined to outgrow me and the squadron. You are Laesornysh. The squadron was just your stepping stone to become a warrior capable of fighting at your dacha's side."

"The squadron *is* my strength." Fieran nudged Merrik with his elbow. "I wouldn't be Laesornysh without all of you."

He wouldn't have become the warrior he was now without the Half-Breed Squadron. They were the ones who had followed him into battle time after time. They had pulled off his plans, no matter how crazy. His magic wouldn't have been half as potent if he hadn't been wielding it with the help of his squadron.

"No. But it is time for you to *be* Laesornysh as you were always meant to be." Merrik finally turned to Fieran and clasped his shoulders. "That is not a bad thing. The Alliance needs its next generation of Laesornysh warriors. You and

Adry will be the ones to win the war. I am just glad I got to be a small part of it."

"Merrik..." Fieran clasped Merrik's shoulders in return, giving him a small shake. "Do you know what finally made me decide to go on this mission to Mongavaria?"

Merrik huffed and rolled his eyes, dropping his hands from Fieran's shoulders. "No. Despite our long years of friendship, I have not yet learned to read your mind."

"Just as well. The number of far crazier plans I think about then discard before settling on a plan that is merely a normal-level of crazy would drive you into insanity." Fieran grinned as he, too, dropped his hands and instead lounged against the aeroplane behind him.

Merrik tilted his head back as if searching the stars for patience and good sense. "Spare me, I beg you."

Fieran chuckled, letting the conversation pause for a moment, before he spoke again. "I took this mission because I need to get out of your way. It's beyond time you stepped out of my shadow to become the captain of the Half-Breed Squadron that *you* were always meant to be."

"Fieran..." Merrik straightened, shaking his head as his gaze dropped. "I cannot be the captain you are."

"No. You will be a far better captain than I ever was." Fieran lightly punched Merrik's arm. "You actually have sense. I know the squadron will be in good hands."

"You're leaving intimidating wings to fill." Merrik's shoulders hunched as if under the weight of the responsibility that would soon fall to him. "And with the way the Alliance generals are planning to push hard in the next few weeks..."

Fieran swallowed. Adry and Merrik would bear the brunt of that fighting. Any day now, the invasion push would reach the Empress Line and face far fiercer fighting than any they'd encountered in Mongavaria so far.

And Adry would no longer have Dacha at her side.

Merrik slumped even more, his hands in his pockets. "I do not know if I am enough. If I am whole enough. I have barely learned to walk again. I do not know if I can be what the squadron needs me to be. What Adry will need me to be."

Fieran rested his hand on Merrik's shoulder again, but for a long moment, he didn't speak. This wasn't a time for quick, thoughtless words but for thinking everything through before he opened his mouth. "You will be strong for the squadron, and the squadron will be strong for you. You won't be doing this alone."

Merrik released a shuddering breath, but he raised his head, his shoulders straightening.

"You will have a hard-fought battle ahead of you. But you will protect my sister and the squadron, and they will protect you." Fieran gave Merrik a slight slap on the back. "You will be a great captain. I'm only sad that I won't be here to see it."

If he was here, then Merrik would never have this opportunity to step forward. Without being prompted, Merrik likely wouldn't put himself into such a leadership position.

But he would be good at it. Excellent, even.

"Linshi." After a moment, Merrik's smile returned, even if it still had a melancholy tilt.

Together, the two of them kept a peaceful vigil, even as the night grew deeper and the stars burned brighter overhead.

TWELVE

Fieran sat in the second seat of the aeroplane, tapping his fingers against his legs since he didn't have anything to do with his hands. He held two large packs of supplies on his lap while his swords—now lethally sharpened by Pip's cousin—rested across his back.

Darkness closed around the aeroplane, the chill even more pronounced this high up. Fieran wore his flight jacket, cap, and goggles, but he had to wiggle his toes in his regular army boots to keep them warm, despite the wool socks he wore. He would need the stiffer soles of his regular boots rather than the soft leather flight boots, which would lack traction.

Merrik sat in the front pilot seat, guiding the aeroplane through the sky by the instruments lit with a blue elven light.

Across the sky, more faint blue lights marked where the rest of the squadron flew, lights that would be covered if the squadron spotted enemy aeroplanes.

In the darkness, Fieran couldn't see the other two-seaters

where Pip, Dacha, and Uncle Edmund were riding, those aeroplanes piloted by Lije, Aylia, and Stickyfingers.

Merrik's head moved as he checked the instruments. His voice echoed in Fieran's ears through the radio built into his cap. "Half-Breed, we are five miles out. Prepare to go into battle formation."

Fieran was now tapping his fingers and his feet. It was strange to sit here without a control column in his hand or a rudder bar at his feet, simply a passenger while someone else commanded his squadron.

At least that someone else was Merrik. He had no doubt that Merrik would take care of the squadron and command it well.

Fieran leaned forward and pulled the receiver sewn into the flaps of his flight cap away from his face so that the radio wouldn't pick up his next words. He reached out and gripped Merrik's shoulder. "Merrik, I…"

For a moment, his words failed him, a lump clogging his throat. What could he say at this moment?

In some ways, he and Merrik had already said everything that needed to be said before they'd ever climbed into the aeroplane for this mission. Fieran had said his goodbyes to Mak, Lije, Stickyfingers, Aylia, Tiny, and the rest of the squadron. What else was there to say?

Merrik half-turned in his seat, his face mostly hidden behind the goggles and his flight cap. He gave a nod, as if he didn't think any more words were needed.

Perhaps they weren't.

But Fieran couldn't help but speak them anyway. He squeezed Merrik's shoulder. "Take care of my sister."

Merrik gripped the control column in one hand as he pulled the flap of his flight cap away from his mouth as well, raising his voice to be heard over the rush of the wind and hum of the engine. "You know I will."

"Yes, but she will need you more than ever, now that she will be fighting alone." Fieran couldn't put as much meaning into his voice since he had to shout. But perhaps Merrik would hear what he wasn't saying anyway. The way he was stepping back, acknowledging the place that belonged to Merrik in Adry's life.

"Not entirely alone. She will have Rhohen." The flight cap didn't hide Merrik's lopsided smile.

"Don't remind me." If Fieran thought about the fact that Adry would be fighting this war with only Rhohen as magical backup, he might demand that Merrik turn this aeroplane around.

Merrik nodded again, more solemnly this time. "I'll take care of her."

"And take care of the squadron." Fieran gave Merrik's shoulder a slight shake. "Be the legendary leader I know you can be."

"Legendary." Merrik snorted. "That has always been more your thing than mine. I will settle for unassumingly competent."

"You're greater than you think you are." Fieran dropped his hand as the low lights of the airship base came into view ahead. Airships hovered in the sky, keeping guard, while airship upon airship lined up at docks near the ground, waiting for refits or supplies. "I think you'll make a few legends for yourself whether you want to or not."

"That is not as comforting as you think it is." Merrik reached around to hold out his hand over his shoulder. "Stay safe. Do not do anything too reckless. I am counting on Pip to get both of you back more or less in one piece."

Fieran took Merrik's hand and gave a firm shake. This

was it. Moments from now, they'd part, likely until the end of the war, depending on how long it took Fieran and Pip to fight their way across Mongavaria after rescuing the prisoners.

Withdrawing his hand, Merrik faced forward again, tugging the flaps of his flight cap back into place as a burst of chatter filled the radio.

The aeroplanes of the Half-Breed Squadron swept into a formation of two columns, preparing to attack the guarding airships.

Fieran listened to the orders given back and forth over the radio, the sounds of the fighters going into battle. He was strangely detached instead of being at the heart of the action like he usually was.

Merrik directed his two-seater toward the front of the formation, and Aylia mirrored his movements until their two aeroplanes flew side by side.

Fieran glanced over at the other aeroplane, his dacha so bundled underneath flight cap, coat, and goggles that even his distinctive hair wasn't visible. His dacha's goggles swung in his direction, and Fieran gave a small wave.

Dacha nodded back before his magic sprang around his fingertips.

Fieran, too, drew on his magic, letting it pour from his chest to crackle around his hands. He reached over the side of the aeroplane and shoved his magic outward, stretching for the other aeroplanes.

Dacha did the same so that all aeroplanes were covered with each of them only using a portion of their magic.

The large guns below boomed, and the airborne airships turned toward them, their guns barking as well. The bullets burst against the dual shields of Dacha's and Fieran's magic, the fire from the ground as useless as always.

Fieran peered through the gunfire, blue magic, and smoke, searching the airships. He didn't see any with a network of wires and a machine dangling below, nor could he feel any tugs on his magic. Hopefully Uncle Edmund's information was accurate, and the machines hadn't been delivered to this aerodrome yet.

If everything went well tonight, this aerodrome would be in tatters by morning, and the shipment of machines would be derailed by the mission of the squadron of fighters and bombers flying out of one of the aerodromes farther south in Escarland.

"Half-Breed, let us attack with everything we have." Merrik shot another glance over his shoulder. "One last time with Laesornysh on board."

"For Laesornysh!" The shout echoed through the radio as the rest of the squadron swept in behind Merrik and Aylia.

Fieran grinned as he let his magic build within his chest. He pressed the talk button built into the side of the aeroplane next to the spot where the wire from his flight cap plugged in. "For the Half-Breed Squadron!"

"For the Half-Breed Squadron!" the voices on the radio shouted.

As Merrik bore down on the first airship in line, Fieran unleashed the magic building in his chest and cast a bolt filled with power straight at it.

This airship didn't yet have that deflecting magic placed on it, and the outer dirigible layer vaporized in a moment. Explosions burst within it, and it tilted downward in a groan of metal.

More blue magic engulfed a second airship, consuming it.

Merrik pointed the aeroplane between the two crashing

airships, leading the Half-Breed Squadron into the center of the airship line.

Fieran poured his magic over the airships, sending wreck after wreck plunging toward the aerodrome below. Several of the airships tied to the docks caught on fire or crumpled as wreckage crashed into them. What wasn't hit by wreckage, the squadron destroyed as they swept low over their targets before dropping their small incendiary bombs.

He'd forgotten just how easy it was to destroy a fleet that wasn't protected by that deflecting magic or magic-stealing machines. Especially with his dacha doing half of the destroying.

At the far side of the aerodrome, Merrik wheeled the aeroplane around, losing altitude as he did so.

Once he leveled out of the turn, Fieran unbuckled his lap belt and wiggled about the confined space to pull one pack onto his back over his swords and situate the other across his chest.

Aylia and Stickyfingers executed their turns as well, maneuvering so that they were ahead of Merrik. Lije, with Pip in his second seat, followed Merrik and Fieran.

"Captain, Prince Edmund has requested that we target the final airship in line to the south. It appears to be taking longer to get into the sky than the others." Sticky's voice crackled over the radio. He and Uncle Edmund were flying in an older two-seater that didn't have radio wires rigged for the second seat.

Merrik tilted the aeroplane to give them a better view of the aerodrome. Most of the middle of the aerodrome had been devastated. Fires burned in many of the buildings, and even as Fieran watched, one of the warehouses went up in a massive ball of fire. To either side, the undamaged airships were slowly rising into the air with the ones at the farthest end of the line seemingly waiting for those closer to the destruction to get off first.

"I agree. That one will work well." Merrik swerved the aeroplane's tilt into a turn. "Half-Breed, we're making a low pass over the airships to the south for our drop-off."

The flyboys and flygirls acknowledged, and the squadron closed into a tighter formation around the two-seaters.

Something both painful and somehow fiercely warm filled Fieran's chest, watching the way his squadron skillfully flew between the crashing airships and bursts of explosions. They'd come such a long way since those first days of training at Fort Linder.

And now he was going to have to leave them behind.

The lead aeroplanes of his squadron dove among the docked airships, firing their machine guns at the dirigibles.

Under the cover of the distraction of the whole squadron flying low and close, Aylia swung toward their chosen airship. She must have cut out her engine because her aeroplane slowed. At the last moment, she flipped the aeroplane on its side as it drifted almost lazily up and over the top of the airship.

A figure dropped from the rear seat, landing in a crouch as lightly as a cat, despite the pack on his back.

Aylia's aeroplane put on a burst of speed as she likely turned her engine back on. She regained control just before it would have plummeted toward the airship. As she sped away, she triggered her machine gun a couple of times, shooting well away from the target airship, so that it wasn't so obvious that this particular airship wasn't being shot at.

Even as Dacha headed for the hatch, Stickyfingers pulled the same maneuver as Aylia, cutting out his engine and drifting over the top of the airship. Uncle Edmund dropped from the second seat, landing more heavily than Dacha had, but he still came up from his roll and got to his feet without issues.

As Dacha cut off his magic, the aeroplanes that had been protected by it switched on their built-in shields. The blue glow surrounding them disappeared for only a heartbeat before reappearing. While the individual shields didn't provide the network through the sky that the direct power from Fieran or Dacha did, the Mongavarians likely wouldn't be able to tell that Fieran and Dacha were no longer with the squadron.

It would soon be Fieran's turn. He pushed the talk button for the radio. "Happy flying, Half-Breed Squadron. I look forward to toasting to victory with all of you in a few weeks."

"Take care of yourself and Pip." Lije's voice had a hitch to it.

"And bring back Pretty Face." Sticky's voice wobbled even more than Lije's had.

Fieran's throat closed. He wasn't sure how he was going to leap from this aeroplane and leave all of them to fight this war without him.

But then Merrik was nearing the airship and turning off the engine.

Fieran thought about muttering a last farewell into the radio, but everything had already been said. He unplugged the cord and crouched on the seat, bracing himself with a hand on either side of the fuselage.

The two-seater bore down on the airship, even with its engine off. As they neared, Merrik skimmed within feet of the airship, then tilted the aeroplane's nose upward, stalling the aeroplane only yards above the airship so that Fieran could make his leap.

There was only time for a brief clasp to Merrik's shoulder. Then Fieran leapt from the aeroplane. He fell for a heartbeat before his feet touched the surface of the dirigible. He immediately turned his momentum into a roll, made awkward by the packs strapped on both his chest and back.

He came up onto one knee, glancing skyward just as the aeroplane engine roared back to life. Merrik poured on the power, one of his wings clearing the side of the dirigible by mere inches before his aeroplane regained enough control for him to pull up.

And then he was disappearing into the clouds of smoke and fire wreathing the aerodrome, one aeroplane among the many buzzing around the airships, leaving Fieran standing alone on the top of the airship.

PIP'S HEART hammered so hard it throbbed through her whole body from her temple to her throat to her wrists.

How in all the dwarven kingdoms was she going to leap out of a moving aeroplane? Sure, Lije was going to all but stall it so that it would be briefly stationary above the airship, but still. This was absolutely insane.

And she didn't even have a pack weighing her down. Fieran had offered to take both of their packs so that she could jump unhindered.

Merrik's voice crackled over the radio. "Fieran is away."

Pip swallowed, her heart somehow racketing up. Was it possible for a heart to pound right out of one's chest?

Lije twisted in his seat. "Look after our major for us, will you?"

"Yeah. Don't let him do anything too crazy," Stickyfingers piped up over the radio as he piloted his aeroplane to fly above theirs.

"I'll try. But you know Fieran." The radio banter helped ease the pounding in her chest somewhat, even as emotion gripped her throat in a stranglehold. How was she going to leave her flyboys?

She reached up to touch the wrench necklace Fieran had given her, only to find the space empty. Right. She'd left behind both the necklace from Fieran and the wooden train from Mak, pressing them into Mak's hand as they'd said their goodbyes. She hadn't wanted to risk losing either of those items while in Mongavaria.

Still, her fingers felt empty without that necklace to fiddle with.

"Coming in for drop-off." Lije swung his aeroplane downward toward the airship. "Ready, Pip?"

"Not really." Pip's hands shook so hard that it took her four tries to lift the latch to free her lap belt.

She was going to be sick. And probably pass out. Why had she thought she could do this?

Lije's aeroplane skimmed close to the airship. She yanked out the radio cord and struggled to get her shaky legs beneath her in preparation for jumping out.

Fieran stood on the top of the airship. He opened his arms toward her, as if he planned to catch her.

The aeroplane slowed, then almost seemed to pause, hanging in the air for a breathless moment.

"Now, Pip!" Lije called over his shoulder.

Pip locked eyes with Fieran and leapt.

She fell through the empty air, and she couldn't help the shriek that tore from her.

Then she plowed into Fieran, the force knocking both of

them to the dirigible's roof. Fieran's arms held her tight as they rolled before they were yanked to an abrupt stop.

Fieran gave a grunt. "Can you climb up?"

She lifted her head from where she'd had her face pressed into his chest. He was hanging from one arm as he gripped one of the ropes strung over the airship. Their roll had taken them perilously close to tumbling all the way over the sloped side.

Her pounding heart swooped deep into the pit of her stomach. Somehow she reached up, boosting herself off his shoulder, and gripped the rope with both hands. Slowly, she hauled herself upward, trying not to kick Fieran in the face as she scrambled upward.

Once she was safely on the flat part of the airship's top, she reached down to help Fieran. He didn't take her hand and instead pulled himself upward hand over hand, despite the weight of two packs dangling from him. When he scrambled onto the walkway running along the spine of the airship, he rolled to his back, his torso propped partially upright thanks to the pack, and gulped in a few deep breaths.

After a moment, Fieran climbed to his feet and held out his hand. "We need to get below."

Pip nodded, took his hand, and let him pull her to her feet. When she was standing, Fieran didn't drop her hand, but instead clasped her fingers. She held his hand tightly, probably too tightly, but he didn't flinch.

Above them, the aeroplanes dodged and fired. Airships groaned as they burned while the few remaining airships worked to get into the air and scatter.

Fieran tugged Pip along the spine of the airship until they reached a hatch, which had been left open. Fieran went down first, barely squeezing through with both packs, and Pip followed.

As the two of them reached a platform amid the gas bags holding up the airship, Pip leaned closer and whispered, "I can take my pack now. Or I probably should take both packs. If we run into trouble, it would be better if you were free to move."

"I got them." Fieran shrugged, glanced over the platform, then climbed down the next ladder. "Besides, Dacha and Uncle Edmund have had several minutes to get ahead of us. If there is anyone left alive in here, I'd be surprised."

True. Pip followed him down the ladder. Prince Farrendel and Prince Edmund had gone first for just that reason. Their job had been to clear the airship of the few people who might have managed to climb aboard in the chaos. Since no one on the ground could know this airship had been taken, they needed to either kill or capture anyone they found.

Harsh, yes, and she tried not to think about it too much. But war was harsh.

Pip remained tucked behind Fieran as the two of them navigated their way through the ladders, passages, and corridors that made up the gas balloons and gondola of the airship. In many ways, the interior of the Mongavarian airship was almost identical to that of the Alliance ones, except for the louder rumble of the steam-powered engines that vibrated through the whole ship in the way that the quieter, magically-powered engines in the Alliance airships didn't.

When they reached the airship's bridge, it was deserted, although there was a spot of blood near the wheel used for controlling the rudders.

"I hope you can figure out the engine controls." Fieran

released her hand and hurried to the front of the bridge. He flipped a few switches, then shoved a lever forward.

Pip jogged to where a few levers controlled engine speed. Hopefully this really would control the engines and not just communicate with the engine room.

She shoved the lever to full speed, satisfied when a louder rumble and vibration filled the airship. It was working.

"Releasing the mooring lines," Fieran announced a moment before he shoved several levers all at once.

The airship jerked upward so quickly that Pip stumbled and would have fallen if she hadn't grabbed hold of the control station ahead of her.

Glancing over her shoulder, she caught one last look at the aeroplanes of the Half-Breed Squadron glowing blue in the golden-orange fires of the burning aerodrome before Fieran turned the wheel and pointed the airship into the darkness, heading south.

THIRTEEN

Fieran rolled out of the bunk where he'd finally fallen asleep sometime in the early hours of the morning.

The stolen airship was now many miles to the south, flying over the long stretches of farm fields that made up the center of the Mongavarian heartland. If Fieran had plotted their course correctly, then they were sticking to a line in the sky inside of the Empress Line that would avoid Mongavarian internal defenses, army bases, or aerodromes.

After washing up as best he could in the little fold-out sink, Fieran picked through his pack to find a fresh set of clothes. They'd been wrapped around a leather case padded with moss, which held six vials of elven juice infused with healing magic. The healing magic wouldn't be strong enough to heal a mortal wound, but it would speed the healing along and prevent infection if any of them were injured.

Once dressed, he made his way out of the small cabin he'd claimed as his.

The cabin opened into a narrow hallway with a small

wardroom across the way. In the wardroom, two tables with benches on either side provided a mess for the officers to hang out. Other cabins opened off this same narrow hallway, and Dacha, Uncle Edmund, and Pip had found rooms there as well. It had seemed natural to stick together, especially since these rooms were conveniently close to the bridge or pilot house or whatever it was called on an airship.

No one else was in the mess room, so Fieran looked through the cupboards until he found a can of pears. He opened it, found a fork, and ate the pears right out of the can. Not the best breakfast, but it was something to tide him over until he could find the time to locate the galley and get a better breakfast.

Making his way to the bridge, he stepped inside to find Uncle Edmund still at the helm. His uncle released the wheel long enough to race back across the bridge to move the speed dial a hair. As he ran back to the wheel, he glanced over his shoulder at Fieran. "Glad to see you're up. I think I kept us on course, but you'll want to double-check my calculations. It's rough trying to fly this thing by yourself."

"This was your plan." Fieran paused by the chart table, his gaze flicking over the maps and calculations. Everything looked correct, at least at a quick glance.

Figuring out if they were where they thought they were would be more complicated. It wasn't like he would automatically recognize whatever towns and villages they were flying over the way he would the Escarlish towns. He'd have to do some measurements of the sun or stars and run some calculations to be completely certain.

"I can take the wheel now, if you'd like to get some sleep." Fieran halted next to Uncle Edmund and reached for the wheel. Another quick glance over the controls indicated that everything seemed in order.

"Sleep sounds rather good." Uncle Edmund grinned and stepped away from the wheel. "Have you eaten?"

"I had a can of pears." Fieran closed his fingers over the wheel. A surge of something primal and exhilarating coursed through him. He loved flying his aeroplane. He loved the breeze in his hair and the air below his wings.

But there was something about holding the wheel of a ship and piloting it through the sky. It was like he was one of the adventurers who sailed the seas in wooden ships in days of old.

Uncle Edmund slapped him lightly on the back. "Then I'll get you a proper breakfast before I hit the bunk."

"Thanks. Have you seen either Pip or Dacha this morning?" Fieran adjusted the airship's course half a degree.

"Your dacha was here earlier. I think he planned to inspect the engines." Uncle Edmund headed toward the door. "I haven't seen Pip yet."

With that, he disappeared into the corridor, leaving Fieran alone.

Fieran left the wheel and inspected the various knobs and dials more closely. He adjusted a few things, but he couldn't leave the wheel for long without the airship drifting off course.

This airship wasn't designed to be run by four people. It was impossible to maintain everything on the ship. Nearly impossible just to keep the engines running and the airship more or less on course.

But it wasn't like they cared if the ship fell apart around them, as long as it didn't blow up or crash before they reached their destination, rescued the prisoners, and got everyone back to Escarland.

PIP MADE her way through the corridors of the airship, chewing the last of the breakfast of toast and apples she'd made for herself in the galley.

While she wanted to head for the bridge where Fieran was likely piloting the ship even now, it was her duty to see to the engines. After all, she was here because she was a mechanic.

As she neared the aft end of the airship, the rumble of the engines turned into a roar that vibrated through the metal causeways beneath her feet and reverberated into her bones.

She stuffed the elven moss earplugs she'd brought into her ears, muffling the sound, before she stepped into the engine room, its cavernous space laced with layers of catwalks.

The engines were huge compared to the Alliance magically-powered ones. Here, coal-burning boilers heated steam to power the massive drive shafts for the propellers or air screws as they were called for an airship. Everything smelled of heated metal, grease, and coal while the heat here was well over a hundred degrees.

And yet this was all familiar. The trains that crossed the Afristani plains were steam-powered rather than magically-powered, and these engines were similar enough that Pip could read the gauges and decipher what she was seeing in the maze of wiring, pipes, and mechanics.

A pair of booted feet stuck out from beneath one of the blocks of pistons and gears. Pip's heart leapt into her throat. Was that a dead body? Or one of the enemy mechanics still alive and too deep in the ship to realize his airship had been hijacked?

Pip cast about. She needed a wrench. A hammer. Some kind of weapon.

Then she glanced at her hands. What was she thinking?

She had magic. She could just shield herself. She drew on her magic, placing a small shield around herself as she called, "Hello?"

The boots moved. Then a figure wiggled out from beneath the engine and sat up.

Not a dead body. Not an enemy either.

Pip bit down on her squeal, her breath seizing in her chest.

Prince Farrendel Laesornysh was sitting on the catwalk staring at her, goggles over his eyes, his hair loosely tied back to keep it out of his way. Dark smears of coal dust smudged his clothes and face. He pushed the goggles up, revealing his silver-blue eyes focused squarely on her.

Breathe. She needed to breathe. She could do this. She had to do this. He was Fieran's dacha. And there were only the four of them on this airship. She needed to act normal around him.

"Um, I…" She sucked in a deep breath and dropped her magical shield. "I wanted to check the engines. Because I'm the mechanic. Not that I mind that you're here. I…"

This was awkward. So awkward. If only magic could turn her invisible.

Prince Farrendel stared at her for a long moment before he blinked and made a stilted motion toward the engine. Like her, he raised his voice when he spoke. "I wanted to check the engines too."

"Ah. Good." Pip shifted from foot to foot as he remained where he was, not moving.

There was something in his posture. In the tension of the line of his shoulders. He reminded her of Tryndar. Or, rather, Tryndar had inherited those mannerisms from him.

She liked Tryndar. Surely she could have a normal conversation with Fieran's and Tryndar's dacha.

"I...uh...wondered if there was a way we could power the engines with magic. Or make the coal distribution automatic." Pip made her own stiff gesture toward the engines. "I don't want to spend our whole trip shoveling coal."

"Indeed. My thoughts as well." Prince Farrendel turned back toward the engine, picking up one of the wrenches. "It does not appear that we can rig these engines to run on magic."

"Is the wiring the problem? Or a place to hold the magic?" Pip crept closer and held up her hand. "My magic can reinforce inferior metal to be able to work with the magic of the ancient kings."

"I considered that." Prince Farrendel slid beneath the engine again. "Still I do not believe it would be possible to convert the engines from burning coal to running on magic without significant time and energy. I believe an automatic distribution system might be more achievable with what we have. But please have a look for yourself. You might be able to come up with a solution that I cannot."

Anyone else might have said those last two lines sarcastically. But Prince Farrendel's words held nothing but a genuine invitation to join him in tinkering with the engines.

"Maybe. But you have far more experience with magical engines than I have." Pip climbed onto the catwalk above the engines and lowered herself onto her stomach to peer into the inner workings.

Something inside her eased. A mechanical project. She could handle that.

FIERAN GRIPPED THE WHEEL, scanning the sky through the wide windows lining the pilot house of the gondola. He hadn't seen anything but birds sharing the sky with them, but he kept the airship at a high elevation to prevent being spotted from the ground.

His stomach rumbled yet again, and he glanced around. Breakfast had been a long time ago, and it was now approaching time for a late lunch.

Could he lash the wheel into place so that he could get food? How much would the airship drift if he just let it fly itself for a while?

Uncle Edmund's plan had merits, but trying to fly this thing with only four people was proving a challenge.

"I brought lunch. I see no one has relieved you yet." Uncle Edmund strode into the pilot house with a tray in both hands.

"I haven't seen Dacha or Pip at all today." Fieran stepped away from the wheel to relinquish it to Uncle Edmund. "But the engines have made some weird sounds and cut out briefly here and there throughout the morning. So I'm guessing Pip, at least, is tinkering with them."

"That would explain the jolt that woke me up." Uncle Edmund set the tray on the map table before he took the wheel. "Eat, then see about catching a few hours of sleep if you can."

"Thanks." Fieran grabbed one of the plates from the tray. After giving Uncle Edmund a few notes on their heading, the wind speed, and their location, Fieran strolled from the room.

He ate the sandwich as he worked his way through the airship, stuffing the last bite in his mouth as he reached the kitchens. Raiding the cupboards, he prepared two more sandwiches—one with just ham and butter and the other with every sandwich topping he could find—located another tray, and set out once again.

He peeked out the windows as he worked his way along the inner corridor, but he couldn't spot his dacha on the catwalk ringing the outside of the airship. Oh, well. If he didn't find Dacha by the time he reached Pip in the engine room, he'd just eat the sandwich himself, even if it was rather plain.

At least the engine room wasn't hard to locate. All catwalks and corridors led there eventually if he kept going toward the stern. Not to mention that the reverberating roar pounding through the airship was a beacon.

He stepped into the engine room, the noise assaulting his ears. He should have thought to put in his moss earplugs.

"Pip." Even shouting, he could barely hear his own voice over the noise.

No answer.

Not too surprising. She probably couldn't hear him any more than he could hear her.

He wandered deeper into the labyrinthine engine room, ducking under pipes and around the line of large boilers that heated the steam for turning the drive shafts.

Near the wall that divided the coal storage from the engine room, he found Pip perched on top of a contraption, sweat dribbling in rivulets through the coal dust and grease smeared across her face.

Dacha lay underneath the contraption, holding a piece into the place as Pip worked her hands into the center, using her magic to attach it.

Fieran halted, staring. Pip and Dacha were here. Working together. And Pip wasn't frozen in terror. Was this a hallucination from staring at the sky too long?

He cleared his throat. "I...brought lunch."

"Linshi." Pip tilted her head. "You can set it down over

there. I'll grab the sandwich once we have this piece secured."

"And after we have had a chance to wash up." Dacha shifted the piece of metal slightly, giving Pip a better angle for attaching it. "Eating with our fingers now would be highly unsanitary."

"Exactly. All this coal and grease can't be healthy." Pip's mouth went lopsided as she stretched her arm a few inches farther to continue melding the metal. "Could you fetch me a ratchet with a three-eighths socket? There's one bolt I need to finish tightening after we get this in place."

"Could you also fetch that metal panel?" Dacha pointed with his foot at a piece of metal sheeting leaning against the wall. "That needs to go on next."

Dacha and Pip were bonding. He couldn't believe it.

Fieran set the plate with the sandwiches down on the floor, stepped around it, and found the toolbox to search for Pip's ratchet. It took him far too long to concentrate enough to locate first the ratchet, then the correct socket.

Grabbing the metal panel, he approached the contraption, handing the tools to Pip and setting the metal next to Dacha on the floor. "What are you building?"

"An automatic distribution system for coal so that we don't have to be constantly shoveling." Pip took the wrench and climbed farther onto the contraption to tighten a bolt holding a bundle of wires in place. "It was your dacha's idea to use the temperature of the boilers to regulate the coal distribution."

"It was Pip's experience with trains that made the design feasible." Dacha took the panel and started wedging it into place.

Fieran studied the contraption more closely, following the various parts and pieces.

At one end, a system of shovels on a track scooped coal through the hatch that led into the coal bunker next to the engine room. The coal was then dumped into a series of metal chutes with gates that were opened and closed based on those temperature sensors. Each of the chutes led to one of the boilers, feeding the insatiable fires.

"I assume the two of you have taken into account the risk of fire traveling from the boilers to the coal bunker?" Fieran stepped back to wait for the next request for a tool or part from either Pip or Dacha.

"We're going to rig a way to open and shut the hatches on the boilers as part of the system." Pip reached through the contraption to secure the next metal panel in place.

"But there is an increased risk of fire due to the automation instead of shoveling manually." Dacha shifted as he held the panel in place over his head. "As long as we do not engage in battle, the risk is marginal."

"And if we get into battle, we'll have other problems to worry about." Fieran nodded and leaned against a section of pipe that wasn't scorching, ready to be Pip's and Dacha's tool-fetcher if it meant he could watch them bond like this.

FOURTEEN

Fieran carried a tray laden with the food he had scrounged from the galley, a red-and-white-checked tablecloth looped over his arm. The food wasn't anything fancy: some kind of canned meat with gravy that he'd dumped into a pot to heat, mixed vegetables also from a can, and a box of powdered potatoes that he'd managed to make unpowdered with judicious use of water and heat. It was hardly tasty, but it would be filling.

He stepped onto the bridge where Dacha was at the wheel. Uncle Edmund stood out on the walkway, taking a few star readings, before he returned to the bridge, going straight to the chart table and scribbling notes in the log book. Only once that was done did he glance up. "Looks like we're still on course. And food is here."

"Food might be a generous word." Fieran headed for the back of the bridge, where he found enough space to set down the tray and lay out the tablecloth on the floor. "The options are limited without spending more significant time in the galley."

"If we'd wanted better food, I guess I should have

included a cook on the mission." Uncle Edmund made one last note in the log before he headed across the pilot house and sank onto the edge of the tablecloth across from Fieran. He swept a glance over the spread. "Actually, this doesn't look half-bad. Though your dacha will likely disagree."

At the wheel, Dacha gave a rolling elven shrug of his shoulders. "It will be better than some of the unpalatable meals I have consumed before."

"Well, yes, it's not hard to be better than army food." Fieran spooned some of the slightly too watery mashed potatoes onto a plate. When he topped the mashed potatoes with the meat and gravy, it almost looked palatable.

Dacha made a noncommittal noise as he remained behind the wheel.

The door to the pilot house opened again, and Pip shoved her way inside, toting a long pole with metal plates on either end. Her hair was still wet, her clothes now clean. "The automatic coal distribution chutes seem to be functioning as designed. I grabbed this while in the engine room. I can rig it to hold the wheel in place."

"A good solution." Dacha stepped to the side, keeping one hand on the wheel to hold it steady.

Pip didn't even freeze as she crossed the room to the wheel. Planting one end of the metal pole on the floor, she wedged the other end against the metal wheel. She then used her magic to fuse the pole into place so that it wouldn't move.

Dacha released the wheel, but neither he nor Pip retreated for a few seconds as they eyed the wheel and pole holding it in place. Then Dacha gave a nod. "That will work well."

"Someone will still need to make adjustments occasionally, but we won't be as tied to the wheel as we were." Pip nodded before she turned and crossed the pilot house. She sat on the side of the tablecloth next to Fieran, casting a glance over the food. "This looks good."

The army had certainly downgraded their definitions of food.

Pip scooped the mashed potatoes onto her plate before she topped it with the meat as Fieran had done.

Dacha took the final spot on the tablecloth, folding his legs as he sat in a cross-legged position common among the elves. He eyed Fieran's, Pip's, and Uncle Edmund's plates, his nose wrinkling slightly. He claimed portions of the meat, potatoes, and vegetables and organized them so that they weren't touching, a feat considering both the meat and the potatoes were so watery that they wanted to flow together.

For several minutes, they ate in silence, the rumble of the engines vibrating through the metal beneath them and the blue Mongavarian skies passing outside the banks of windows.

It was a strangely peaceful moment, picnicking on the floor high in the air, despite the fact that it was an enemy airship flying in hostile skies.

Uncle Edmund set his empty plate aside and leaned back on his hands. When he spoke, he spoke the language Escarland shared with Mongavaria but with a Mongavarian accent. "All right, Fieran and Pip. Since the two of you are going to be on your own once we liberate Ludin, you need to practice your Mongavarian accent just in case. So let's hear it."

Fieran shared a look with Pip before he attempted the accent. "How does this sound?"

"Rough, but you might get there with practice." Uncle Edmund still sounded identical to those Mongavarian soldiers Fieran had heard after his crash.

Pip's face twisted as she took longer than he had to make her attempt. When she did, her words were a mangle, still too accented with elvish to get anywhere near Mongavarian. "I do not think I can manage it."

Uncle Edmund laughed and shook his head, switching back to his normal Escarlish accent as easily as changing his shoes. "No. It would probably be best if you let Fieran do the talking."

"He is rather good at it. The talking part." Pip elbowed him.

Fieran grinned back.

Dacha shook his head, giving Pip a slight smile. "I cannot manage another accent either. Even after all these years, I have not perfected my Escarlish accent."

"My Escarlish still has an elvish accent too." Pip smiled back at Dacha with only a trace of her former hesitancy. "But my dwarvish is good. Probably because I grew up speaking it with my muka."

Uncle Edmund nodded sagely. "It is your native language as much as elvish."

Fieran finished his last bite of meat and potatoes, set aside his plate, and eyed Uncle Edmund. "Now that we're out here, is there anything you can tell us about the Mongavarian countryside where we'll be?"

Uncle Edmund's grin turned lopsided. "I've never been this far south in Mongavaria. Officially, I've only been to Mongavaria once, and that was to visit the capital city of Landri."

"You should tell them the story." Dacha shifted so that his back was to the wall. "Much of our current war is rooted in the events of back then."

"All right. But fair warning, you might hear a few details you didn't know before." Uncle Edmund shared a look with

Dacha before he turned to Fieran and Pip. "It all started when your Uncle Julien chose an arranged marriage to your Aunt Vriska over a marriage of alliance with Princess Bella of Mongavaria."

"Your uncle nearly married the current empress of Mongavaria?" Pip glanced at Fieran, her eyes wide.

"From what I've heard, the offered marriage was more a trick than a true gesture of peace." Fieran gave a shrug. He couldn't imagine Uncle Julien married to anyone else besides Aunt Vriska. The two of them were deeply in love and a powerful team.

"It was. Princess Bella took a whole trunkful of poison on her visit. She didn't get the chance to use it, but poisons are something of a hobby for the Mongavarian royalty." Uncle Edmund stretched his feet out. "My part of the whole thing started when Jalissa and I left for a diplomatic visit to Mongavaria days after our wedding."

Fieran settled into a more comfortable position with his back to the post for the speed control, draped an arm around Pip's shoulders, and listened to the only somewhat familiar tale of his aunt and uncle's adventures in Mongavaria.

"And then you *drank* the poison?" Pip gaped at Prince Edmund.

He was as crazy as a songbird stuck in a mine shaft. If she'd realized that, she might have hesitated a lot longer about her decision to come along on this mission.

Prince Edmund shrugged. "I was reasonably sure Jalissa and I were developing a heart bond, and I calculated that we had a good chance of getting across the border before I died. But if I hadn't drunk the poison, the Mongavarian crown prince would have seen to it that I was disposed of in a different way, considering that I was the only witness to his murder of his father. Our only chance was for me to drink the poison so that the crown prince would relax his guard on us enough to let us escape."

Crazy. Absolutely crazy. Also scarily coldly calculating.

Pip eyed Prince Edmund where he sat there, relaxed and lounging, a grin on his face as he spoke about poisons and nearly dying. He certainly didn't look like a calculating mastermind with his easy grin and twinkling eyes that reminded her of Fieran.

At least once they reached the facility, she would be headed back to Escarland with Fieran, and crazy Prince Edmund would be Prince Farrendel's problem as they set out to do whatever they were going to do to end the war.

Prince Edmund further cemented his status as mad genius as he finished the story of his and Princess Jalissa's flight across Mongavaria, which involved stowing away on trains, money won from gambling, and horse stealing.

Once Prince Edmund wrapped up the tale, he went over a few more notes about the Mongavarian countryside that they ought to know in case something happened. The conversation eventually worked its way from the serious to more light-hearted topics until Prince Farrendel declared that he should head for bed since he had the final watch.

Prince Edmund took the middle watch, giving Fieran the first watch. Before Pip could offer to help, Prince Edmund had gathered the empty dishes and disappeared out the door, saying he would take care of the dishes before heading to bed.

Prince Farrendel gave Pip, then Fieran one last rather parental warning look before he followed Prince Edmund out, leaving Pip alone with Fieran.

"Here. I'll disconnect this so you can actually steer and correct our heading if we've drifted." Pip hurried to the wheel, using her magic to disconnect the pole.

"Keep that handy. It would be nice to be able to prop that up and wander the skywalk occasionally during my watch." Fieran checked the chart table, poked his head outside, and glanced at the charts again before he finally strode to the wheel. After a moment, he grinned and held one hand out to her. "Would you like to steer? It isn't right that you're the only one of us who doesn't know how to fly this thing."

"I think it's more I don't have the navigational skills to take a watch by myself. Piloting can't be that hard." Still, she gripped the wheel as Fieran took half a step back, giving her space. The wheel was so tall that the top of it was level with her nose. "Besides, I don't mind the excuse not to take a watch. I'm here for the engines, after all."

"Engines that you rigged to run without supervision for the most part." Fieran's warm breath brushed her hair as he stationed himself behind her, his hands resting lightly over hers on the wheel in a semi-embrace.

Pip resisted the urge to lean back against him, even though it was incredibly hard to focus on adjusting the wheel against the air currents shoving at the airship. "Give me enough time, and I'll have this whole airship rigged to run by itself. Just you wait."

"Always making me obsolete." Fieran's chuckle was far too close, making the hair on the back of her neck prickle.

She flushed as Fieran trailed a light kiss on her cheek, then her neck. One of his hands dropped off hers to rest on her waist instead. A part of her—a large part of her—wanted to lean into him. Forget steering. Forget the mission.

Instead, she shook her head slightly. "You're distracting me. Not to mention, you're the one officially on watch."

Fieran's sigh was hot against her neck a moment before he pulled back, putting a cold layer of space between them. "Fine, fine. No kissing and no distracting."

"At least while we're on watch." Pip wasn't sure why she was clarifying that. While they were on this mission, they were pretty much always on duty, needing to be alert rather than distracted.

With a light laugh, he returned his hand to its place over hers on the wheel. "We? I seem to recall this watch is mine."

"Yes, but I think I might as well stay up with you. Keep you awake and help run the airship and all that." Pip wiggled her fingers beneath his on the wheel. "It will probably take a few hours to teach me how to fly an airship."

"True, true." Fieran nudged her left hand slightly to prompt her to turn the wheel a fraction. "Although you are doing a good job of flying it already."

"Steering is easy. Steering in the right direction is the hard part." She nudged the wheel back the other way at his prompting. "Although, I'm a little curious why your Uncle Edmund knows how to fly an airship. Surely he didn't learn in the three days we had before leaving."

"I've learned not to question how Uncle Edmund knows things." Fieran laughed, his shrug bumping his arms against hers. "I assume he learns how to drive, fly, or pilot any new vehicle, just in case he needs to hijack something while spying. After all, he and my uncles put this plan together way too quickly for it not to have already been some kind of plan Uncle Edmund had brewing in the back of his mind."

"After hearing his stories tonight, I'd believe it." Pip laughed, letting herself lean slightly against Fieran as she stood in the circle of his arms.

"That's Uncle Edmund for you." Fieran tightened his grip over her hands on the wheel, taking over the bulk of the steering. "I always knew I never could get away with anything growing up. Even if I somehow hid it from my parents—which was difficult enough already—my Uncle Edmund was bound to know about it."

"Again, doesn't surprise me." Pip leaned even more against him, no longer even pretending to steer the airship. Semi-snuggling with Fieran—in a very non-distracting kind of way, of course—was better.

For a moment, they lapsed into silence. Outside the large windows, the stars gleamed so brightly they were visible even through the slight reflection from the low lights in the pilot house.

When Fieran broke the silence, his voice was a low, almost somber murmur. "Do you remember our first airship flight?"

"Of course." Pip told herself sternly that letting go of the wheel to instead wrap her arms around Fieran would definitely cross the line into distraction. "I was already falling for you then."

"As I was with you." Fieran's breath brushed her hair, but he didn't cross the line by kissing her. Instead, he cleared his throat. "Do you remember that discussion we had about last names?"

"Yes." Pip found herself swallowing, something in her chest twisting at the tension growing between them.

"How would you feel about a change to your last name eventually?" Fieran's voice sounded slightly strangled, as if he was feeling the same tension she was.

Pip stilled, her heart hammering. Was he asking what she thought he was asking? "Is that…is that a proposal?"

She wasn't sure if she wanted it to be. Yes, she wanted to marry Fieran. And an impulsive proposal while they were headed toward danger was just the sort of thing he'd do. She'd say yes, if he was asking.

But a part of her also wanted the full experience. A properly romantic proposal, the elven traditional gifts to ask for the family's blessing, all of it.

Behind her, Fieran froze too. "No. Is that all right? I just thought…there are a few things we should talk about. Before we get there."

Pip's breath whooshed out. "No, I mean, yes. I mean, don't take this the wrong way, but I was hoping it wasn't. Because you're right. There are things we need to talk about."

Up until now, they hadn't talked much about the serious things. While their intentions were serious, they'd simply enjoyed courting, getting to know each other more deeply as people without pressuring each other to move the step beyond that.

But now Fieran was inching across an unspoken line, testing if she was ready for taking the step in their relationship where they started talking about a future that was dreamed together.

"Good." Fieran's voice turned low, soft against her hair. "And just so you know, when the time comes, there isn't going to be any question about whether or not I'm proposing. You'll know."

Pip forced herself to laugh, struggling to keep herself from tensing. "I'll keep that in mind."

"Now about last names…" Fieran's tone warmed, holding the memory of their last discussion of last names all those months ago on a different airship in distant skies. "It's not as straightforward as you'd think it would be, is it?"

"No." This time, Pip's low laugh was more genuine as

she shook her head. With their three heritages in the mix, they were working with three different naming conventions. "It's a mess, isn't it? While humans generally go by the man's last name, dwarves go by the clan name. But the couple can choose to join either clan and take on either clan name."

"Since I don't have a dwarven clan, would that automatically make us Clan Detmuk?" Fieran shifted as he braced himself as the airship tilted under a gust of wind.

"Kind of. Unless we moved to Mt. Detmuk to live, we wouldn't be officially joining the clan. But like you said, you don't have a dwarven clan, so we could be considered a part of the clan the way my parents are." Leaning into Fieran to brace herself, Pip shrugged before she glanced over her shoulder at Fieran. "Between the two of us, our elven heritage is the majority. Perhaps we should follow the elven naming convention."

"What convention?" Fieran barked a laugh, his fingers flexing on the wheel. "For a people who are normally quite strict on rules, propriety, and tradition, the elves have devolved into chaos over the change from titles to last names."

"True." Pip shook her head with another laugh. "I've heard many elves just keep their own names or come up with a new family name altogether. Others just keep tacking on names as if collecting them."

"Perhaps that's what you should do." Fieran leaned closer to speak in her ear. "Pippak Detmuk Inawenys Laesornysh."

"That *would* be a mouthful." Pip couldn't imagine going around with *that* as her legal name. "But maybe just Pippak Detmuk Laesornysh? I'd like to keep my link to my dwarven clan and that way I'd still have my dwarven and elven heritages combined. But I'd be claiming a link to you and…"

And she wasn't sure what else to say, her face heating as her words trailed off.

"I like the sound of it." His tone lowered still further. "It's a mouthful I'd share with you, if you wanted. I'd take on the Detmuk part, if that's what you'd want."

She tugged her hands free of the wheel so that she could turn in the circle of his arms, placing her back to the wheel. She needed to face him for this discussion.

His gaze had been focused above her head, staring at the windows to the stars beyond, but as she turned, his eyes dropped to meet hers.

She rested a hand on his cheek. "Don't take this the wrong way, but you're Laesornysh through and through, and I'd never want to change that. I'd like to keep Detmuk for myself, and maybe it could be an option for our children if they wanted to embrace their dwarven heritage, but you're Laesornysh. Our children will likely be Laesornysh, or a rather interesting version of it depending on how your magic mixes with mine."

A slow smile spread across Fieran's face. "You said *children*."

She had, hadn't she? Well, if they were going to open up discussions about what a future together might look like, then she was going all in. "Yep, I did. What do you think? Three? Four?"

"Sounds good to me." Fieran grinned down at her before he glanced up, turning the wheel slightly as the deck shifted beneath their feet with a strong gust. His grin vanished a moment later. "Once the war ends, where would you want to go? What would you want to do? I can probably get a post in the Flying Corps reserves in Aldon if you wanted to work at the AMPC. Or I'm sure the Alliance will be expanding their aerodromes. They might even set up one near the western rail terminal, if you wanted to return to your home there. I'll follow you wherever you want to go, and I'll support whatever dreams you want to pursue, Pip."

She swallowed, dropping her gaze away from his to stare instead at the star-filled windows.

For the past few months, it had been hard to envision the future when the war seemed to be all there was. All consuming. Never ending.

But now they were very likely staring at the end, if Fieran's dacha and uncle had anything to say about it. And if the stories were to be believed, ending wars was their specialty.

She could go anywhere. Do anything.

She could return home. To the peace and quiet of her childhood home at the far western rail terminal. She could go back to fixing trains and…and…

Fieran would hate it out there. He'd go insane with boredom within a month or two.

And, truthfully, so would she. She'd outgrown her life there and, despite how the thought filled her chest with a hollowed out sense of mourning, she wasn't going to go back, except to visit her parents.

Would she have left all those months ago if she'd known that she would never return to live there again? Yet she wouldn't trade the life she had now to go back. She wouldn't want to miss out on falling in love with Fieran. Or on making all the new friends she had in the squadron.

Yes, she'd lost a piece of herself. But she'd gained far more than she'd lost.

"I don't want to go back to the western rail terminal. Not to stay, anyway. I'd like to visit, of course." Pip drew in a deep breath and forced herself to meet his gaze. "I'd like to stay with the squadron for as long as there is a Half-Breed Squadron. They won't disband or reassign anyone right away, not until everyone is sure whatever peace treaty ends the war is going to last."

Fieran's smile was wide, gleaming in the depth of his eyes. "I'd like that."

"I know." Pip wrapped her arms lightly around his waist. "You belong with the squadron. And I'm content where I'm at. But eventually…"

"Eventually the humans will retire. Or the Alliance will downsize the Flying Corps. Or they'll promote me to the point I'm stuck behind a desk…" Fieran took one of his hands off the wheel to rest lightly on the small of her back.

"And when that happens, I'd like to finally take a position at the AMPC. It's where I was always meant to be, I think, even if I hadn't had the courage to take that step before now." Pip swayed closer to him. It was far too tempting to rest her head against his chest. "I really liked working there while you were recovering in Aldon. It felt like home."

"I'm glad." Fieran's grip on her tightened, as if he wanted to tug her fully into an embrace. "And you know whatever job you get at the AMPC someday will be entirely because of you and your talents. Nothing at all to do with me."

"I know." Pip felt the confidence of that all the way to her bones. She'd earned a place there if she wanted it.

"The moment you're discharged from the army, Uncle Lance will be waiting with a pen and a hiring contract." Fieran's light laugh reverberated in his chest.

"If he can remember the day." Pip grinned, remembering how absentminded the inventor would get.

"You know him well." Fieran's laugh deepened. "In that case, Louise would be there to make sure you were hired."

"Yes, she would." Pip would love having Louise for a sister someday.

Fieran's breath washed against her as he pressed a light kiss to her hair. "There's a good chance you might be able to stay with the squadron and work at the AMPC. The army will remain stationed at the border for a while. But probably sooner than you think, they'll go back to peacetime status. There's a good chance I'd end up stationed in Aldon or even downgraded to reserve status where I would be free to travel between Estyra and Aldon as needed."

"That sounds really nice." Pip gave in and leaned against Fieran.

If she closed her eyes, she could picture it. Fieran still flying with the squadron. Her working with the AMPC during the week and hanging out with the flyboys in the evenings once everyone was off duty.

It was a future so tangible she could taste it, sweet as the donuts Tiny's girlfriend made.

They just needed to end the war to actually make it happen.

FIFTEEN

On their fourth morning, Fieran blinked awake at the sunlight splashing into his cabin through the porthole.

The past three days had been nearly blissful. Lazily drifting over the Mongavarian countryside, occasionally changing direction to avoid Mongavarian patrols, aerodromes, and army bases. Each evening, he and Pip would stay up late talking through his watch and dreaming about what a future together after the war might look like until Uncle Edmund arrived to take up his watch and the two of them drifted to their bunks to get some sleep. Each day, Pip spent a lot of time tinkering on the engines and the other mechanical parts of the ship, often with Dacha, and each day she and Dacha grew less stilted with each other. More than once, he'd caught them having an actual conversation as they talked over a mechanical problem they were trying to solve.

Fieran washed, dressed, and made his way down the passageway, stepping onto the bridge.

Dacha stood behind the wheel as the morning sunlight

beamed bright through the bridge windows and glinted on the strands of his silver-blond hair. He glanced over his shoulder and nodded to Fieran. "Good morning, sason."

"Morning." Fieran drifted toward the chart table and checked their location. Everything seemed to be in order.

Dacha waved a hand to the bank of dials and gauges in front of the wheel. "We appear to be losing altitude, and I cannot seem to make us regain it."

Fieran grimaced and headed for the dials, checking the altitude gauge. "I suspected as much last night, but I was hoping I was wrong. I'm not an experienced airship pilot so for the first couple of days, I didn't think anything of the fact that we kept losing altitude. I could adjust the heat to the balloons and raise us again. But now even that isn't working without raising the heat to dangerous levels."

"What's that about dangerous levels?" Pip strode into the pilot house carrying a tray piled with bread and hardboiled eggs for breakfast.

"Heating the gas balloons more to regain altitude." Fieran tapped the glass top of the altitude dial. "Any ideas why we'd be slowly losing altitude?"

Pip set the tray on the corner of the chart table and crossed the room to join him, her mouth pinched in a flat line. "There could be a small puncture in one of the gas balloons. Or possibly multiple of the balloons. Despite how careful everyone was, this airship might have been hit by some small pieces of shrapnel. Or there could be a leak in the steam pipes that run through the dirigible, causing some of the balloon not to get enough heat to provide lift."

The Mongavarian airships were designed with two main methods of lift. Most of the gas balloons were filled with helium while a few near the bow and stern held regular air.

For quick descents, these gas balloons were emptied, and for an ascent, they were refilled.

The air in the balloons and within the dirigible's outer skin could also be heated using the steam pipes running between the balloons. More steam, more heat, and the airship rose. Cut off the steam, and the gas cooled, lowering the airship. This was better for smaller adjustments.

"The steam pressure gauge seems to be all right, but I'm not sure how accurate the gauges are here." Pip nudged Fieran aside to take the primary spot before all the dials. "And if there was a leak in the steam, then we probably would have noticed. So I'm leaning toward a leak in the gas balloons."

"Can it be fixed?" Dacha's grip on the wheel had turned white-knuckled, even if his overall expression hadn't changed.

"I might be able to track down the holes, but it could take a while. If I ever find them. If the holes are small, they will be nearly impossible to find in the miles of canvas gas balloons up there." Pip shook her head and turned from the gauges to face them. "And even if I find the leaks, it's a multi-person job to patch them. There's a reason that maintaining the gas balloons takes a whole crew."

"The good news is that we aren't losing altitude fast enough to jeopardize getting to Ludin." Fieran grimaced again and turned to better face both Pip and Dacha. "But unless we fix the leak, this airship won't be able to carry the rescued prisoners for long, if at all."

Pip frowned and pointed upward. "There are rumors that Mongavaria has gotten desperate enough to start using hydrogen in their gas balloons despite the risk. Helium is rare, and you've destroyed a lot of their airships."

Right. That meant any leak could potentially be pouring

flammable gas into the dirigible where any spark or static could set it off. The gas balloons themselves were magically coated to prevent such things normally.

With a swallow, Fieran stuffed his magic deep within his chest. Best not to take any chances.

Dacha's hard expression cracked with a grimace of his own. "This airship is sounding like an inadvisable risk of death."

Uncle Edmund strolled into the pilot house, halting and glancing around at each of them. "I missed most of that. Which inadvisable risk of death are we talking about?"

"The airship slowly sinking. And, quite possibly, becoming a giant bomb filled with hydrogen gas." Fieran shrugged and crossed his arms. "So...is attempting to find that leak the priority?"

Uncle Edmund halted by the chart table, then shook his head. "Perhaps it would be worth spending a few hours searching for the leak, but we're nearing where my contacts reported strengthened Mongavarian air patrols. I'd like everyone on the bridge in case we run into trouble."

Fieran shared a look with Pip.

She nodded back. "Fieran and I can spend this morning looking for the leak."

Hopefully they could find it and patch it before any other trouble found them. Otherwise, they were sailing with a bomb strapped over their heads.

PIP CLAMBERED through the hatch onto the catwalk inside the dirigible. She rolled to her feet, getting out of the way as Fieran climbed up after her.

She peered around the inside of the dirigible. "Where should we start?"

"Maybe over there?" Fieran pointed upward and toward the stern. "Does that part seem a bit brighter than elsewhere?"

"Yes, it does." As if sunlight was shining through a hole in the outer skin of the airship. Pip set off down the catwalk in that direction. Even though she was walking normally, her boots rang against the metal, the sound echoing hollowly in the cavernous space formed by the airship's outer skin. Fieran's bootsteps, too, reverberated far too loudly.

It was eerily quiet and empty in here. On the airship she'd flown on before, this section had been bustling with activity. An airship was supposed to be alive with men and women, not this shell so stripped of life.

It was almost sad, even if this was an enemy airship. But if all went well, she and Fieran would fill this airship to the brim with rescued ogres and Alliance pilots. It wouldn't feel so dead then.

The two of them climbed up several ladders, went down a few catwalks, and finally reached the upper balloons in the stern section.

"Well, there's part of the problem." Fieran gestured to the gashes ripped in the outer skin. None of the slices were that long, but there was a whole series of them, as if an explosion had blown shrapnel through the side.

The outer skin acted like its own air balloon, warmed and pressurized when all the hatches were dogged closed. While it wasn't as crucial as the inner balloons, every little bit of lift made a difference.

Since the catwalk ran close to the side, Pip reached out and touched one of the tears. "We wouldn't have noticed in the chaos of the hijacking. Nor could your dacha and uncle

Edmund have seen them in the dark when they did their sweep looking for any enemy sailors left up here."

Nor had she noticed either Fieran or his dacha disappearing to exercise on top of the airship. All of them had been far too busy, and when either of them had exercised, they'd run and leapt on the catwalks surrounding the gondola where they could be fetched easily if needed.

"At least there shouldn't be too much risk of blowing up from hydrogen." Fieran also poked at one of the holes. "It should have mostly vented out the rips."

"Still, it's a concern." Pip positioned herself beside one of the rips then turned toward the inside, squinting as she tried to follow the possible trajectory of the shrapnel.

The balloon directly in front of her appeared somewhat more spongy than it should. And the thick canvas was peppered with blackened spots that were probably holes. The balloons on either side and below, too, looked like they might have been damaged.

Fieran leaned against one of the metal ribs next to her, his mouth pressed into a line. "That's a lot of holes to patch."

Pip could only nod as she took it in. "Do you have any idea how one goes about patching airship inner balloons?"

"Nope. Not a clue."

Fieran gripped the end of the rope, bracing himself against the rails of the catwalk, as he held Pip suspended in the air above one of the air balloons. She was spreading the waxy substance over the tear she'd sewn shut.

After some searching, they'd found the maintenance closest where thick thread, needles, jars of a waxy goo, safety harnesses, and rope had been stored. Even better, there had been a training manual tucked onto a shelf, which included instructions on patching air balloons.

The two of them had sewn and patched the rips they could reach from the catwalks. But when it came to the ones where someone needed to be harnessed up, it made more sense for Pip to be the one dangling in the air. While she probably could hold Fieran, if properly rigged and secured, it was safer this way.

"And...that should do it." Pip wiped her greasy hand on a rag she had tucked into a pocket.

As Fieran began lowering her back to the catwalk, the airship gave a shudder, slowing enough that Pip swayed on the end of the rope with the change in speed.

Pip's feet landed on the catwalk. "We're slowing."

"Yeah. We'd better get back to the pilot house." Fieran took the jar of wax and other patching items from her. He glanced around before setting them down on the edge of the catwalk with a shrug. There was no reason to take the time to put stuff away now.

Pip wiggled out of the harness and dropped it to the catwalk, kicking it aside.

The two of them hurried back through the maze of catwalks and ladders and dropped through the hatch into the gondola.

Fieran glanced through the windows as they hurried down the corridor. Halfway to the pilot house, he halted so abruptly that Pip ran into his back. He pointed at the porthole. "Look."

The dark shape of an airship was gliding into view, coming from ahead of them.

"We'd better hurry." Pip gave him a light shove against his back.

Fieran broke into a jog. He took the time to duck into his

room and grabbed his swords from where they lay on his bunk. Swords would do little good against airships, but he felt better as the weight of the sheaths settled across his shoulders. Still buckling the straps, he burst into the pilot house.

Dacha was at the wheel, his knuckles white, his swords strapped across his back as well. Uncle Edmund wasn't in sight, but his muttering could be heard coming from the radio room just off the pilot house, along with a rhythmic beeping and tapping sound.

The wide windows provided a panoramic view of the clear blue sky around them and the three Mongavarian airships facing them. One remained directly ahead of them while the other two were slowly positioning themselves to either side. All three had metal boxes and wires dangling from the undersides.

"I can take the wheel." Fieran skidded to a halt next to Dacha, gripping the wheel even before Dacha had fully let it go.

"Your uncle claims he has the code needed to safely pass them." Dacha paced a few feet away to the levers set in the floor that controlled the airship's ascent and descent. "The air balloons?"

"Patched as best we could, but we didn't have time to find the compressed air canisters to refill them." Fieran flexed his fingers on the wheel, his heart pounding harder in his chest. While he trusted Uncle Edmund and his information, he wasn't all that comfortable staring down the guns of three enemy airships. No matter that they would think they were looking at one of their own.

If something went wrong, would Fieran and Dacha dare fight back? Could the two of them take out three machines before they were too drained of magic?

Pip halted at the station at the rear of the pilot house beside the engine controls, and she was currently checking all the dials. Her fingers trembled slightly as she adjusted one of the levers.

Fieran would have gone to her to reassure her and hold her, telling her it was all right. But he couldn't leave the wheel. Right now, they both had to be army officers facing a possible battle rather than boyfriend and girlfriend.

A string of elven swear words rang from inside the radio room. Uncle Edmund raised his voice. "They're suspicious. Apparently the codes were changed in the past few days. I'm trying to convince them that we've been traveling in radio silence since fleeing the Alliance bombing."

Another flurry of taps and beeps burst from the radio room. If Fieran had paid more attention in the class on the older telegraph system, perhaps he would have understood what was being sent back and forth. Then again, this was all in code and likely in a slightly different system than the one Escarland had used.

Uncle Edmund muttered another string of elven curses as he ran from the radio room and disappeared out of sight toward some of the unused cabins. He raced into sight a moment later, tugging a Mongavarian uniform shirt on over his other clothes, the uniform trousers loose around his waist.

"Edmund." Dacha's tone held a warning as he shot a look at him.

"Sorry, sorry. I know, little ears and all that. No time." Uncle Edmund dashed out the door onto the outer catwalk.

Fieran shared a look with Pip. Neither of them were exactly what one would call "little ears" anymore, and the fact that he recognized all those words showed exactly the type of education he'd gotten in the army.

No, he was far more concerned about whatever had Uncle Edmund dashing about and donning a Mongavarian uniform.

Uncle Edmund stood on the catwalk, taking down a set of the signal flags. He waved them in a pattern, similar to the orange signal flags that they'd originally used in the Flying Corps before installing radios.

The airship ahead of them slowly turned, presenting its broadside of machine guns toward them. The other two airships were now on either side of them, perfectly positioned to blast them with the full might of their guns as well.

"I don't think they're buying it." Fieran gripped the wheel tighter. "Dacha, can we overwhelm those machines without getting knocked out?"

"Possibly." Dacha braced himself against the front panel of levers and gauges, prepared for battle. "But I would not wish to put it to the test."

"Perhaps if we kept our magic contained within this airship?" Fieran gestured toward the airship facing them. "Those machines need to get close to or touch the magic to latch on to it. At least, the one I faced before did."

"We cannot assume they have not made improvements since then." Dacha nudged one of the levers so that their airship began drifting slightly downward, subtly putting the gondola below the line of fire.

Uncle Edmund sprinted back inside, using the edge of the door to fling himself around the corner and into the radio room. "They aren't buying it."

"Will they fire on us?"

"Maybe. This seems to be a no-fly zone for anyone who isn't authorized to be here." Uncle Edmund sent off another blistering set of taps. "They're under orders to fire on anyone who tries to enter, even their own ships."

"Should we turn around?" Fieran found he was already, almost subconsciously, putting pressure on the wheel in preparation. "We can try getting past at night or at a different spot."

"Not sure they'll let us leave." Uncle Edmund's voice was tight, grim. "They're—"

A boom rang out as the airship blocking their way fired one of their largest artillery pieces.

"Incoming!" Uncle Edmund shouted, even as he kept tapping on the radio. Perhaps he was sending a string of Mongavarian curses, still trying to pretend they were a Mongavarian airship wrongfully fired upon.

The shell clipped the top of the gondola and tore into the dirigible above their heads. Fieran ducked, his magic leaping to his fingertips even if he didn't unleash it yet.

The airships on either side opened up with their machine guns, tearing into the dirigible above their heads.

"Edmund?" Dacha raised a hand, his magic lacing around his fingers. "Should I unleash my magic?"

"Not yet. The moment they see your magic, they'll know we aren't who I've been saying we are." Uncle Edmund's tapping had ramped up to a furious pace. "There's a chance I can get them to call off their attack."

The two airships swerved toward them, their guns blazing. The large artillery gun in the airship ahead of them boomed yet again.

One of the side windows shattered. Fieran ducked behind the wheel as Dacha crouched below the protection of the metal side.

Pip gave a short shriek, and Fieran swiveled on the balls of his feet to look toward her. "Pip?"

"I'm fine." She crouched below the engine controls, but she was left with little protection, her back to the windows.

More windows shattered, glass bursting inward, as bullets pinged off the walls over their heads.

"I do not think they believe you." Dacha raised his hand, his magic crackling around him. It coated the inside of the bridge, and more machine gun bullets incinerated against it.

An explosion shook the whole airship, bucking the deck beneath Fieran's feet so violently that he was flung forward, the metal wheel digging into his ribs.

Pip gave another shriek as she clung to the engine controls. Still gripping the metal stand, she tilted her head upward. "I think that was a boiler. The readings from boiler two are off, and it's showing elevated temperatures in the engine room."

"The coal bunkers will catch fire." Dacha slammed one of the levers, venting more air from the balloons. The deck tilted even more steeply beneath their feet, and Fieran had to brace himself more firmly against the wheel.

The three airships still pounded away at them, showing not a shred of mercy.

Uncle Edmund dashed out of the radio room, gripping various gauges and edges of control stations to keep himself from sliding on the slick, steeply tilted floor. He halted next to Pip at the engine controls. "Do you have enough engine power to give us some headway? Fieran will need some steering control to crash this safely."

Crash. Fieran hadn't let himself think the word. But hearing it sent his heart hammering in his ears, his gut twisting. His fingers would have trembled, if he hadn't been gripping the wheel so tightly.

There was a whooshing sound, something between an explosion and a roaring wind. The airship hung for a moment before its descent turned into a dive.

Pip screamed as her feet fell out from under her.

"Pip!" Fieran tried to push away from the wheel, but he couldn't move quickly with the force pressing him forward. Beside him, Dacha crouched with one foot on the deck and one on the front panel, which was rapidly becoming the floor.

Uncle Edmund grabbed Pip's arm, his other hand clutching one of the levers on the engine control panel. With a grunt, he pulled her upward so that both of them were dangling semi-securely from the engine controls.

Wind blasted through the openings where the windows had once been, the ground rushing toward them far too fast.

Everything whirled and tilted. Wind roaring. Explosions shaking the airship's frame. Nothing but ground outside the windows.

"Fieran!" Pip's voice ripped his gaze upward.

He met her eyes, his hand reaching for her even though he couldn't stretch far enough. "Your magic! We need a shield!"

Her magic flickered into a globe around them, shimmering and looking all too flimsy compared to the ground rising to meet them.

Dacha released his magic and pulled himself along the front console.

And then everything was imploding and crumpling and the last thing Fieran knew before the world went black was his dacha's arms wrapping around him.

SIXTEEN

Everything hurt. Her mouth was gummy. Her brain banged against her skull.

She cracked her eyes open. The world was fire and smoke and twisted metal.

Figures picked their way through the debris. "There are two more over here!"

Then a person was standing over her, kneeling, pressing a chemical-smelling rag to her face. And she was fading back into the darkness once more.

Pip groaned and shifted. She seemed to be lying on something hard and metal, her arms twisted at an awkward angle as something unyielding dug into her wrists. Her head pounded like a ball-peen hammer was rapping at her skull.

"That's it. Take it easy. Crashing isn't fun." A voice was talking in a soothing tone.

She groaned again and blinked her gritty eyes, squinting as she struggled to focus.

She was in the cargo bed of a military truck. The floor and sides were metal while canvas was stretched on metal ribbing above her head. Her hands were shackled to a rail at the front of the cargo space.

Prince Edmund sat with his back to the front of the cargo bed, his arms twisted to the side since they, too, were shackled to the rail. His clothes, both the Mongavarian uniform and the Escarlish clothing beneath, were ripped, blackened, and begrimed. But he didn't appear to have any cuts or gashes. He regarded her with a searching look. "Are you all right?"

"I think so." When she pulled herself into a sitting position, her head pounded, her muscles ached, but nothing screamed with intense pain. "Just a horrible headache."

"Getting knocked out from the crash, then sedated will do that." Prince Edmund rolled his head on his neck, as if trying to work out kinks. "But it doesn't appear either of us was hurt worse than that. Thanks to your magic, no doubt."

Pip nodded, as she performed a more thorough assessment of herself. Both feet were working. As were her legs. All her fingers moved, and breathing didn't hurt. All in all, she was in far better shape than she had a right to be after falling from the sky.

She glanced around, but she and Prince Edmund were alone. "Where are Fieran and Prince Farrendel?"

"I don't know. I woke up only a few minutes before you did." Prince Edmund shifted again, as if trying to find a more comfortable position with his hands shackled.

"Then...should I..." Pip gave a small tug on the shackles. They were metal. She could easily release both herself and Prince Edmund. "We can—"

"Not in Escarlish," Prince Edmund cut in, speaking in dwarvish with only a trace of an accent. "I'm guessing none of the Mongavarians will know this language. They might have a few soldiers who learned elvish over the past seventy years, but likely not dwarvish."

"You speak dwarvish?" Pip replied in the same language, gaping at Fieran's uncle. No wonder he'd been a part of the diplomatic mission to Dalorbor. If she were to guess, he hadn't let her family know he spoke the language.

"It seemed prudent to learn." Prince Edmund shrugged. "I have a knack for languages, and thanks to my heart bond, I have plenty of time to make a hobby out of it. How's my accent?"

"I can tell you aren't a native dwarf, but I wouldn't necessarily pick you out as Escarlish just from your accent." Pip gave a shrug of her own, which rattled the shackles.

"I'll have to keep working on it, then. I haven't had any dwarves to practice with." Prince Edmund lifted his hands, making his own shackles clank. "As to your question, yes, you might as well remove our shackles so we can talk more comfortably."

She'd been thinking more on the lines of escaping rather than talking. But talking through a plan was probably wise instead of just diving out the back canvas flaps, running pell-mell in a random direction, and hoping for the best.

Easing her magic into the shackles, she gently opened the metal so that she could free her wrists. Something told her that she shouldn't destroy the shackles too much, in case she and Prince Edmund wanted to put them back on, for some unknown reason.

After taking just a moment to rub her wrists and shake out her arms, she reached over and freed Prince Edmund's hands as well. "So…what's our plan?"

"Farrendel does not take to captivity very well." Prince Edmund rubbed his wrists and settled into a more comfortable sitting position. "As we haven't heard any explosions and screaming, I'm guessing Farrendel and Fieran either aren't here or are still unconscious. We can't make a move until we've discovered which it is."

Right. If they were here but unconscious, it would be up to her and Prince Edmund to rescue them as part of their escape plan.

"All right." Pip swallowed and hugged her knees, despite the stiffness in her muscles and bones. "And if they aren't here, then we escape?"

"Not necessarily." Prince Edmund held up two fingers, pointing to the first finger with his other hand. "We have two options. We can escape, but then we'll spend the next days and possibly weeks on the run in a foreign kingdom. Trust me, it's terribly uncomfortable. No food. No supplies. Nothing but the clothes on our backs and whatever we manage to steal along the way."

That did sound rather unpleasant. Her chest twisted. She wasn't cut out for this. She was a mechanic, not a spy used to being hunted. "And our other option?"

"We stay where we're at." Pointing at his second finger, Prince Edmund said it as if it was perfectly logical to remain captured when one could escape. "The Mongavarians will nicely provide us with transportation to wherever they're taking us. We'll be fed, probably given blankets at night, and hopefully they'll treat you reasonably well."

"Me? Not you?" Pip dug her fingers into the grimy fabric of her trousers.

"I'm the most wanted man in all of Mongavaria. I don't think treating me nicely will be on their priority list." Prince Edmund was far too nonchalant about that.

"More wanted than Prince Farrendel or Fieran?" Pip hugged her knees tighter.

"By the basic soldier on the ground? Probably not. By the Mongavarian empress? Oh, yeah." Prince Edmund gave another rolling, elven-style shrug. "Which is why I'm reasonably sure they'll take us to Landri. She'll want to oversee my execution herself."

"So we'll escape before then?" Pip eyed Prince Edmund. Surely he had escape somewhere in his plans.

"No, not unless Farrendel and Fieran are here somewhere. I won't leave Farrendel captured if I can help it." Prince Edmund met her gaze. "But if they aren't here, then Landri is exactly where we need to be. We'll just have to be clever about it. It's where Farrendel will head once he gets free of wherever he is, and we'll have help arriving in about a week and a half."

That mysterious second half of the plan. The part she and Fieran hadn't been told. It seemed that she would find herself tagging along with crazy Prince Edmund.

"We have one big advantage." Prince Edmund nodded his head toward her. "They clearly don't know about your magic."

That was true. They'd locked her up in a metal box with metal shackles.

"Do you think they realize I have magic?" Pip gestured at their surroundings, the canvas stretched tight over the metal ribs arching overhead.

"I doubt it. Yes, being shackled like this would make it difficult for your average elf warrior to escape." Prince Edmund stretched his legs out in front of him. "But we've also been left alone, without a guard. They're pretty confident in our inability to escape. Something tells me they wouldn't be so confident if they thought you had magic of any kind."

"So I probably should keep my ears hidden." Pip reached

up, ensuring that her straggling and frizzing hair covered her ears. "Strange they didn't check."

"Likely a subconscious oversight. You don't exactly look like your typical elf warrior." Prince Edmund sighed and leaned his head against the canvas stretched tight across the front of the cargo bed. "The good news is they're going to underestimate you. The bad news is, if they don't think you have magic, then they probably assume you're one of my spies."

"That would explain why they have divided us up like this." Pip shifted, trying to find a more comfortable spot. Her head was still aching, and, despite how much time she'd been unconscious, she still wanted sleep. "The two with magic together, and the two spies together."

"Yes. At least, we can only hope they are together and just in another truck in this same convoy." Prince Edmund held out his arm. "I know we don't know each other that well yet, but you can lean against me if you wish. It will likely be hours before we stop."

It was a fatherly gesture, and after several days in an airship with only the four of them, he felt almost like he was an uncle to her.

Pip leaned her head onto his shoulder, sighing at how good it felt to rest. She let her eyes fall closed. "Do you think they're still alive?"

"I believe so. Your magic protected the two of us from serious injury. It should've done the same for them." Prince Edmund shifted slightly, as if to get her head into a more comfortable position on his arm. "I'm communicating with Jalissa in our heart bond. The heart bond doesn't lend itself to true telepathy, but with some time, I should be able to communicate the gist of what happened. At the very least, Jalissa knows I'm still alive and that something went wrong.

I'm trying to prompt her to talk to Essie, who will know if Farrendel is still alive. We should be able to get some idea of what is happening eventually."

"That's good." Pip found her body relaxing as she drifted toward sleep.

THE JOLT of the truck stopping woke her. Pip bolted upright, blinking for a moment as she tried to process where she was and what was happening.

Prince Edmund moved first, shoving his wrists into the shackles.

Pip molded the metal back into place before she scooted to her original spot. Fumbling, she worked her wrists into the shackles and eased the metal into place.

Not a moment too soon. The canvas flaps at the back of the truck were flung aside, revealing three Mongavarian soldiers standing there.

One of them pointed a gun in her and Prince Edmund's direction while the other two climbed into the truck bed.

It wasn't particularly good form, considering the man with the gun would risk hitting one of his fellow soldiers if a scuffle broke out.

But Pip didn't resist as the soldier unlocked her shackles, freed the chain from the rail, and reshackled her hands in front of her. He yanked her to her feet and dragged her across the truck bed. He jumped down first, then pulled her after him. She landed with a stumble and nearly went down to her knees. Only the man's grip on her arm kept her upright.

Prince Edmund didn't resist either as he was similarly unshackled and dragged from the truck, though his hands were secured behind his back. A sign that the Mongavarians considered him the greater threat.

As she got her feet beneath her, Pip finally took a good look around.

The line of trucks was parked on the side of a dirt road beside a recently cut hay field, the hay still in rows waiting to be baled.

A Mongavarian officer was talking with a man in farmer's garb in front of a ramshackle farmhouse, the barn behind it in better shape. Other Mongavarian soldiers were in the process of setting up some kind of camp in the field complete with tents and campfires.

As she was hauled farther from the trucks, she glanced over her shoulder, taking in the soldiers unloading supplies. But none of them were dragging a second set of prisoners from any of the vehicles.

Pip shared a look with Prince Edmund. If Fieran and Prince Farrendel weren't here, then where were they?

SEVENTEEN

Pinpricks of pain dotted his chest, the first sensation in the hazy sea he drifted on.

"…waking up."

"…sedate again?"

"No need. It will not matter…"

Fieran clawed toward wakefulness. Some sense was prickling along his skin, telling him he needed to wake up. He let just a hint of his magic flow through his veins, burning away whatever sedative they'd used on him all the quicker.

"Turn on the machine."

There was the click of a switch. A whirring noise.

Then agony stabbed downward through those points of pain and clawed deep and sharp within his chest, as if determined to rip his heart out of his body.

No, not his heart. His magic.

His magic lurched within him, wanting to attack. But some deep-seated instinct told him to cling to his magic, pulling it back and locking it within his chest. It was *his* magic. This thing couldn't have it.

But that pain was still digging and clawing like a cat caught beneath his ribs.

Fieran snapped his eyes open. Brightness blared down at him. He blinked rapidly, gasping in pain and grappling to keep hold of his magic.

The brightness solidified into lights set directly above him, the rest of the room a stark white. Even the two men standing on either side of him wore white lab coats, white caps, and white masks tied over their faces. Even their gloves were white, although one was stained with fresh, red blood.

"He's awake." The white-garbed man on the right looked at the other rather than at Fieran.

"Ramp up the power." The man on the left said the words with an utterly flat, unbothered voice.

The other man leapt to obey the orders, pushing a lever forward on a machine next to him.

A large cable of wire extended from that machine, suspended over where Fieran lay, before branching into many smaller wires directly above him. These were stabbed into various points on his chest, taped into place like hypodermic needles transfusing blood.

Except these wires were trying to take instead of give.

The machine whirred louder, and the digging increased, as if that strange something was trying to carve Fieran's magic out of his chest.

He bit down on a cry of pain, arching his back as he fought to hold his magic inside of himself. He was pinned down, restraints tight around his wrists, ankles, and even a strap across his upper chest. The cold metal of a surgical table pressed against his bare back.

This was just like that magic-stealing machine he'd fought under that airship, except this machine wasn't trying to take magic he'd already unleashed. No, it was trying to steal the very essence of his power straight from his body.

And if it succeeded, he'd never survive it.

He glanced around, searching for any way he could escape, and his gaze caught on a figure lying on the next table over.

Dacha was still unconscious, his eyes closed and his hair trailing over the side of the table. Strapped down at his wrists, ankles, and across his shoulders, he'd been stripped of his clothes except for his underwear, and a mess of wires was attached to his chest. But the machine next to him was dark, not yet on.

No. Dacha couldn't die too. Fieran wouldn't let it happen.

"Dacha." Fieran's voice was a croak between his groans of pain. He struggled to hold on to his magic, as if in a tug-of-war with the machine trying to tear it from him.

"He's still fighting us. The machine can't get a grip on his magic." The man on the right shifted, fiddling with the dials and levers on the machine next to him.

The man on the left turned to a tray, then picked up a scalpel. He inspected it for just a moment before, without any kind of flicker in his eyes to signal his intent, he swiped that scalpel across Fieran's ribs.

Fieran cried out and yanked on the restraints, his magic lashing out to protect him. The machine snatched his magic, sucking it along the wires, greedily tearing it from him. Something shredded within him, and he *screamed*.

One of Dacha's fingers twitched, but he didn't wake.

"I told you it would work." The man's voice was no longer merely flat. Instead, a self-satisfied note rang in his tone. "Even the magic of the great elven warriors is no match for our invention."

The other man glanced from Fieran to the dials on the machine, as if worried the magic would be too much.

Fieran gritted his teeth around another scream. That was it. His magic was too much. His only chance—Dacha's only chance—was for Fieran to stop fighting and give the machine everything it wanted.

With as deep a breath as he could manage past the agony, he released his magic and instead shoved it outward with a yell. "Dacha!"

The wires glowed white-blue with the force of his magic, the machine whining instead of whirring.

On the other table, Dacha stirred, his head tilting. But his eyes remained closed.

"He's waking up!"

"Get the sedative!"

"More power!"

The shouts blurred with the pain and the fiery light of his magic. The smell of lightning filled the air, punctuated by the acrid scent of burning metal.

The men in the white coats were lunging, one toward Dacha with needle in hand and the one with the scalpel toward Fieran. He raised the scalpel, as if he intended to slit Fieran's throat before he destroyed their machine and them with it.

With another scream, Fieran shouted with all the trust and terror of a child whose father had never let him down. "Dacha!"

Dacha's eyes snapped open. He swept a single glance around the room, his gaze locking on the men in white lab coats. "Get your hands off my son."

His magic erupted in a searingly white blaze of power, so bright Fieran had to squeeze his eyes shut against it.

There were two screams, both ending abruptly.

The machine beside Fieran exploded, sending shards of metal throughout the room. Fieran gasped at the relief as the clawing ended, even though pain remained. His magical senses felt raw and scorched and *wrong*.

He blinked rapidly, gasping and shuddering. Sometime in the past few seconds, he must have sliced through the restraints with his magic since they fell off him, severed.

Then Dacha was at his side, ripping what was left of the scorched and blackened wires from his chest. "Sason. Fieran. Are you all right?" His other hand pressed to the gash across Fieran's abdomen.

Fieran moaned at the rush of pain from the pressure. "I'm okay. I'm okay." He started to push himself onto an elbow, but a wave of dizziness swept from his head, stabbed in his chest, and sent his stomach lurching. "Not okay. Gonna barf."

He barely had the presence of mind to lean over the opposite side of the table from where Dacha stood before he vomited onto the floor. He gagged and heaved for several moments until nothing more would come up.

Even when he managed to get his gag reflex under control, his stomach still churned with nausea.

He pressed a hand over his wound and lay back down on the table, catching his breath.

Easing closer to the table again, Dacha rested a hand on Fieran's forehead. "You do not look well, sason."

"I'm fine." He wasn't fine. Something was deeply wrong with his magic in a way he couldn't describe. But he felt it in the ache in his chest, the painful hitch every time he breathed, in the wooziness that wouldn't go away. He started to push himself onto an elbow again. "We need to move. Someone must have heard that."

"Even if they did, I do not think screams and loud noises

are unusual coming from this room. We have time." Dacha moved his hand from Fieran's forehead to the gash, his hands somewhat shaky. "We need to tend this before we go anywhere. I will see if I can find bandages."

As Dacha turned to move away, Fieran gripped his wrist, stopping him. His stomach churned even worse, but he worked to get his thoughts in order. "No. No, bandages and stitches won't be enough." He didn't want to say the next part. But he could feel how deep his wound was, and he had been fighting this war too long not to know what they'd face the moment they stepped from this room. "You're going to have to cauterize it."

"No." Dacha's tone was short, sharp, as was the shake of his head. "No. I will fetch bandages."

Fieran didn't release his dacha's wrist, holding him there. "We don't know what we'll face once we leave this room, but odds are we'll have a fight on our hands. I can't go around leaving a blood trail, and I'll just tear open stitches. No, you'll need to cauterize it. I'd do it myself, but I can't burn myself with my own magic. It has to be you."

Dacha was still shaking his head. "No."

"Please, Dacha." Fieran waited until Dacha finally met his gaze, holding it. "We need to get out of here and find Pip. And Uncle Edmund. I can't worry about reopening a wound while rescuing her."

Dacha's shoulders sagged, his head hanging for a moment. He gave a shuddering exhale, and when he lifted his head, his expression had gone blank and hard. Magic laced one of his fingers as he sliced off the end of the leather strap that had been around Fieran's wrist. He held it out to Fieran. "Bite this."

Fieran took the leather, stuck it in his mouth, and bit down, bracing himself. This time there would be no healing magic. No numbing morphine. Whatever sedative that remained in his system would burn away.

All in all, the next few minutes would be highly unpleasant. Hopefully not as unpleasant as the previous few minutes had been, but he couldn't guarantee that.

Dacha gripped Fieran's hand and leaned an elbow onto Fieran's chest, effectively pinning him down. Magic wreathed the fingers of his other hand, which he held poised over Fieran's wound.

He gave one deep breath, his muscles tensing, his grip tightening on Fieran's hand. But he hesitated, just holding his hand a few inches above the gash.

Fieran squeezed Dacha's hand and spoke as best he could around the leather strap. "I trust you, Dacha. It's all right."

Dacha drew in another deep breath, his jaw working. Then he pressed his magic-wreathed fingers onto Fieran's wound.

Blinding, burning pain tore across Fieran's stomach, and he screamed around the leather even as he clamped his teeth on it. He arched against Dacha's arm, and Dacha leaned even more weight onto him to keep him in place.

His magic jolted within his chest, rising to defend him. Yet even that sent a secondary flare of pain through him, swirling with more nausea and dizziness.

Then Dacha cut off his magic. He remained frozen as he was, his shoulders hunched, his breathing ragged.

Fieran slumped on the table, also gasping for breath as he tried to conquer his lurching stomach. His head pounded painfully at the temples while a lingering ache remained in his chest and across the wound.

After another moment of catching his breath, he turned his head and spat out the leather. "I always wondered what that would feel like. Being burned with the magic of the ancient kings. Haven't you? Wondered, I mean."

Dacha pushed away, swiveling so that Fieran couldn't see his face. But his tone was hard, his shoulders stiff. "No."

That was Dacha's *Do not ask; I will not tell you* tone.

Fieran snapped his mouth shut on the rest of his chatter and breathed deeply, still trying to settle his stomach.

Dacha moved across the room toward the white cupboards and stainless-steel countertops that filled two of the walls. He opened and shut cupboards and drawers. "I will see if I can find bandages."

Fieran eased first onto an elbow, then all the way upright so that he was sitting on the steel surgical table. Like Dacha, he wore only his olive-green army-issue undershorts. The gash across his stomach was an angry red slash, but it wasn't bleeding anymore. He was, however, still dribbling small rivulets of blood from the various pokes on his chest. "And maybe some clothes while you're at it."

Dacha halted, glanced down at himself, and sighed. "Why is it that every time I am captured, my captors insist on taking my clothes? The trolls, at least, left me the dignity of trousers."

Fieran grimaced and swung his legs, working some of the stiffness out of them before he tried standing. "With the way we were laid out like frogs for dissection, I'm just glad they even left us our undershorts."

Dacha made a noncommittal noise in the back of his throat as he went back to searching the cupboards.

Fieran pointed to where the two white-coated men lay still and very dead on the white-tiled floor. "I suppose we could always take their clothes."

Glancing over his shoulder, Dacha grimaced, shook his head, and turned back to the cupboard he was searching.

"Yeah, I agree. I'd rather make this escape under-dressed." Fieran scowled down at the two dead men. Books and moving pictures made it sound so simple to merely take a dead man's clothes for making escapes like this, but death was a rather messy affair. He was as reluctant as his dacha to put on some dead man's soiled clothing.

Dacha gave a triumphant grunt before he pulled some-thing from a cupboard. He tossed one of the folded white lab coats at Fieran.

Fieran caught it, nearly tipping over as a wave of dizzi-ness washed over him. He had to press a hand onto the surgical table beside him to steady himself for a moment before he could shake out the lab coat and shrug it on.

It didn't have any buttons or a belt to close it, but it was better than nothing.

Dacha pulled on his own white lab coat before he returned to looking through the cupboards and drawers.

"Where do you think we are?" Fieran eased to his feet, keeping a hand on the surgical table to steady himself. The room still tilted somewhat, his stomach churning with nausea. But he stayed upright and didn't pass out, so that was something.

"Based on the presence of those machines, I suspect we are at the Ludin facility." Dacha halted beside a notebook on the steel countertop, pausing from his perusal to wave a hand at the now smoking, blackened, and shattered husks of the machines. "Edmund suspected there were experiments being done to the ogres."

Fieran grimaced and resisted the urge to shudder as he took in this room. Drains set in the floor gave away just how prepared this room was to handle blood and gore while the straps on the surgical tables indicated that the people were alive when experimented on, as he and Dacha had been.

One side of the room must have been a large window, perhaps for honored guests to stand and watch the experiments being conducted. The viewing window had been shattered in the magical explosion, shards of glass littering the floor. If there had been anyone in the room beyond, they were now lying dead on the floor out of sight.

The last wall held only a thick steel door, windowless and locked. Even if there was a guard, no one was getting in until that door was unlocked.

Another churn whirled through his head and down into his stomach. He pushed away from the surgical table, only to have his knees nearly give out beneath him. He gripped the table again, steadying himself. "Pip. Do you think they'll experiment on her? We need to get to her before they hurt her."

Dacha remained where he was, so he must not have seen how close Fieran had come to falling. Instead, he cocked his head for a moment, his eyes going distant in that way they did when he was communicating with Mama in the heart bond. "Your macha seems particularly relieved I am awake. I get the sense she has been in contact with Jalissa, and that Edmund has been awake longer than we have. I will need to confirm once we are no longer in the middle of escaping. But I think Edmund and Pip are safe enough at the moment. We should look after ourselves first rather than act in haste."

"Good. That's good." This time when Fieran pushed away from the surgical table, he didn't fall over. He shuffled across the room, the tiles cold beneath his bare feet. He reached the opposite end of the cupboards from Dacha. "Weren't we an almost two days' drive from Ludin when we crashed?"

"Yes. We were likely kept sedated while being transported here." Dacha's words were somewhat absent as he paged through the notebook.

A shiver ran down Fieran's spine, and for a moment he couldn't move enough to open the first cupboard.

He'd lost a day of memory when he'd crashed last time and been drugged out of his mind. But back then, he'd known he'd been safe the whole time.

It was an entirely different feeling, one that shook him deep to his core, to think about being kept unconscious while in the hands of his enemies. They'd taken his clothes, strapped him to a table, and intended to take his magic all without him waking. If he hadn't woken when he had—likely due to them underestimating how quickly he'd burn through the sedative thanks to his magic—then he very well could have died without ever regaining consciousness.

He forced himself to move, opening a cupboard and staring at the contents for several long moments before he could process what he was seeing.

Rows upon rows of empty glass jars were lined up, along with racks of empty test tubes. He slowly bent and opened the cupboard below. This one held what looked like rough facsimiles of the magical power cells used by the Alliance. The design wasn't as refined as the ones for holding the magic of the ancient kings, but such things had been around for nearly a century for storing magic from human magicians.

Closing both of the cupboard doors, he moved to the next section over, where open shelving held more glass jars, except these were filled with a faintly yellow liquid. Most of the jars held ears that were rounded like a human's yet the skin was a mottled green tinged faintly brown in places. A few other jars held pointed ears with skin the silvery tone of the elves.

Fieran's stomach lurched again, and this time he couldn't blame it on his continued nausea. "Someone was a little too inspired by the story of Ludin."

Dacha glanced over his shoulder again, not a flicker of disgust or surprise breaking the hard look in his eyes, before he turned back to the notebook. "The penmanship is atrocious, but it seems they experimented with taking magic."

Fieran rubbed at the pinpricks of drying blood on his chest. His magic still felt *off*. "I gathered as much. Does it say how it's possible to steal magic right from someone's body?"

"Something about a type of ogre magic, but I would need to study this more." Dacha closed the notebook and slid it into one of the large pockets on the front of the lab coat. At Fieran's look, he rolled his shoulders in a hint of a shrug. "While I do not wish to preserve or study such technology or methods, we will need proof of what kind of experiments they were conducting here."

Right. Fieran returned to searching the cupboards, drawers, and shelves. Between the two of them, he and Dacha found a few more notebooks filled with notes on the experiments. These they took, along with a jar of salve and bandages they finally located. Whether the medical supplies were there in case the "scientists" were hurt or for "experiments" that they didn't want to kill off so quickly, Fieran didn't know and didn't want to know.

Fieran filled his wound with salve and wrapped it securely. While cauterizing it with Dacha's magic had both prevented more bleeding and thoroughly sterilized the gash, the salve would aid in healing, and the bandage would keep it clean while they fought their way out of wherever they currently were.

Dacha dabbed some of the salve on each of the small poke marks on his chest, as did Fieran.

Then they were ready to venture out of this room, figure out exactly what they faced, and rescue the others.

Fieran pressed his back to the wall as Dacha unlocked and cracked the door open. After a moment, Dacha opened the door wider and motioned for Fieran to follow.

Padding barefoot in Dacha's footsteps, Fieran crept out the door into a hallway. The white floor tiles ran here too, but the walls were painted a basic gray. Several more doors were set into the hallway while additional doors blocked both ends.

After glancing both ways, Dacha headed toward the right. He pressed his ear to the door to the next room before he opened the door.

The room must have been empty since he opened the door the rest of the way, stepping inside.

Fieran followed, taking the door from Dacha and making sure it closed softly instead of slamming closed.

This room held shelves upon shelves of magical power cells, these filled with a variety of colors of magic.

But there was something about the sense of the magic in this room. As Fieran walked along the shelves, occasionally placing his hand on a power cell, he could feel the *aliveness* of the magic held within. These held more than magic willingly stored by the wielder. This was the very essence of a person's magic contained within glass and steel instead of a living body.

Another steel table sat in the center of this room while the stainless steel countertops here held microscopes and even more notebooks.

A familiar, semi-scorched pack lay on the center table. Beside it, two sets of swords gleamed in the overhead lights, the blades unmarred where they lay beside the sheaths.

Dacha strode straight for the table and picked up his

swords, holding them for a long moment as if drawing strength from them.

Fieran crossed the room at a slower pace, pausing to glance at his swords before he opened the pack. Inside lay all four cases with the glass vials of juice laced with healing magic. Sticky stains and glass shards showed that several of the vials had broken in the crash, but the moss padding had preserved most of them. "It looks like they collected anything with even a hint of magic from the wreckage. Perhaps they planned to study these."

Dacha paused in buckling on his sword sheaths, the leather straps looking rather ludicrous over the white lab coat. "Drink one of those."

"We might need the magic for later." Fieran didn't reach for one of the jars. What if Pip or Uncle Edmund were hurt worse than he was?

Dacha drew one out and pressed it into Fieran's hands. "Drink. You will need your strength for rescuing her."

Well, he couldn't refute that logic.

He struggled to twist the lid and break the seal, but finally he got it off. He took a sip, the sweet raspberry flavor coating his tongue, and the soothing warmth of the healing magic filtered into him. It wasn't as strong as a direct healing, but it finally took the edge off the dizziness and pain.

He drank about half of the jar before he twisted the lid back on. He might as well make it last as long as possible. He placed the jar back in the case before he reached for his swords. "Do you see any of the packs with our clothes?"

"Unfortunately, no." After grabbing the pack, Dacha moved away from the table toward the countertops. Once there, he stuffed more of the notebooks into the pack without taking the time to look through them this time. Once done, he shrugged the pack on over his swords and the lab coat.

Fieran managed to get his swords buckled onto his back, the leather rubbing across the wounds in his chest. He tried to shift the lab coat to prevent chafing as best he could, but it was never meant to be worn underneath swords. Or as one's only stitch of clothing besides underwear.

The two of them set out again, checking each of the doors and the rooms behind them. They found a room filled with records, and the door at the far end of the hallway led to a morgue where a body was laid out on the table in the middle of a dissection.

The body was that of a male who had been starved before he died. His skin was a patchy green with a faint brown tint. His ears were rounded but his head was completely bald. Instead of hair, a few black lines of ink twisted over his skin in some sort of design.

An ogre. The first Fieran had ever seen. And proof that ogres were held here, somewhere.

He and Dacha tiptoed back down the hallway the other way and paused before the door at the end of the hallway. Voices came from the other side, but they were faint. Likely not right outside the door.

Dacha opened the door and led the way into the hallway on the other side. A room opened into what appeared to be a headquarters of some kind. The voices were louder now as several men discussed the latest shipment of some sort. Stairs to their right led upward.

With a tilt of his head, Dacha crept up the stairs, and Fieran followed.

They passed another level of what appeared to be quarters for the now-dead scientists and their staff. A few people slept or moved about in their rooms, but Dacha and Fieran were able to find enough unoccupied rooms to raid the closets and obtain clothing. Fieran had never thought to be thankful for something as basic as a shirt and trousers before.

The stairs ended at the roof, and Dacha crouched as he crossed the roof to the low wall surrounding it.

Fieran followed, kneeling next to his dacha and peering over the wall. The early afternoon sunlight beamed down on him, extra hot here on the exposed rooftop.

They seemed to be in some kind of complex formed of concrete buildings. The next building was a military barracks with men in gray-blue Mongavarian uniforms strolling in and out.

More soldiers strode along the various barbed wire fences dividing the parts of the complex and stood on the watchtowers at various points.

More buildings, separated from this one by a fence, belched smoke and rang with the sounds of factory work while several more concrete barracks buildings lay farther beyond the factory.

It took Fieran another few long minutes of study to recognize the layout. "I saw this in Uncle Edmund's photographs. We're definitely at the Ludin facility."

"Indeed." Dacha pointed, although he kept his hand and arm below the edge of the low wall to prevent it from being seen. "If there are ogres or Alliance prisoners held here, they will be over there."

Fieran squinted into the sunlight, trying to pick out the figures moving around the factory and barracks. "What's the plan now?"

"The prisoners are our priority." Dacha tilted his head in that direction before he met and held Fieran's gaze, his eyes searching, his jaw hard. "There are only two of us. We do not have the manpower to take prisoners of our own and see to the well-being of those we rescue."

Fieran swallowed and nodded. Perhaps at the beginning of this war, he might have been surprised at what his dacha was telling him. Appalled, even.

But he understood better now. Agreed, even.

It wasn't like this had ever not been the plan. Even if the four of them had reached Ludin in the airship, they always would have had to unleash merciless death on the Mongavarian guards in order to prioritize the safety of the rescued prisoners.

But with only the two of them and no convenient airship out of there, they would have to be even more ruthless, even more swift, about it.

"All right." Fieran faced the facility once again. "How do we divide this up?"

"I will take out the guards on the perimeter and in the bunkers in the surrounding fields." Dacha kept his hand low as he gestured. "You need to head straight to the communications shack there, take it out before they can get a message out, and then secure the captives before the Mongavarians can begin killing them. We can worry about anyone left after that."

A sound plan. Fieran probably should mention the lingering pain in his chest and his uncertainty about his magic. But he didn't. Right now, he just needed to shove the pain aside and do what needed to be done.

EIGHTEEN

Fieran crouched in the shadow of the communications building, out of sight of the patrolling guards and the two men stationed inside.

The sense of Dacha's magic flared, traveling in a circle around the facility even though it was inching along the ground, out of sight.

Fieran tensed, reaching into the painful part of his chest for his own magic. Fresh agony stabbed at his heart and into his temples, but he drew on his magic anyway, preparing to unleash it.

As soon as Dacha's magic encircled the whole facility, it burst into life, rising into a wall of magic cutting Ludin off from the rest of the world.

That was the signal.

Fieran leapt to his feet, threw himself into the radio shed, and unleashed his magic. Pain nearly sent him to his knees, his vision nearly blinded with both white and black flashes, but he swept his magic over the room anyway. Bolts of power blasted through the two men, then the radio. Equipment went up in bursts of sparks and the stench of scorched metal.

He cut off his magic, stumbled to the side, and gagged, trying hard not to vomit up the healing-magic-laced juice. His whole body shook, a chill sweeping through him.

Something was seriously wrong with him. Perhaps it would be best if he didn't use his magic, if he could help it.

Once he got a hold of himself again, he divested the two men of their sidearms, rifles, and ammunition, stuffing what he could carry into the pockets of his purloined pants. He slung the rifles over his shoulders where they bumped against his swords.

Outside, there was shouting and shooting. The whole place was devolving into chaos.

With a deep breath and a grip on one of the rifles, Fieran darted from the shack.

As two soldiers swung their guns toward him, he fired, once, twice, and both men fell, dead.

This was his mother's training, honed by the army. His dacha might have spent years teaching them to fight with their magic, but Mama had made sure all of them could hit what they aimed at when they had a gun in their hands. While Fieran had done most of his fighting with his elven magic, he could fight like a human when necessary.

He forced his shaking legs into a jog across the compound. A few more soldiers fired on him, but most of the soldiers were too distracted by Dacha's display of power as he took out the surrounding bunkers and dug-in machine gun nests to notice Fieran.

He had to use his magic again at the barbed wire fence to take out the guards manning the towers. Even using his magic that much nearly sent him to his knees.

Staggering forward, he wrenched the gate open wide

enough for him to slip inside. One of the rifles dangling from his shoulders caught on the gate, and he was yanked backward for a moment before he could free it.

Taking a guess at where the prisoners would be, he headed for the large factory building and shoved the door open, gun in hand.

Inside, a cavernous space was held up by pylons of concrete. Manufacturing machines ran from belt drives and gears mounted near the ceiling, all of it connected to the steam-powered boiler walled off by an iron grate at the far end. All the noise obscured the commotion from outside.

Several Mongavarian soldiers aimed rifles at a knot of thin, half-starved men wearing the ragged olive-green uniforms of the Escarlish Army. One man had his hands tied to an iron girder overhead, the back of his uniform shirt torn and dotted with fresh red blood. A Mongavarian soldier held a long cane and seemed to be in the middle of administrating some kind of cruel punishment.

Fieran shot him before he could raise the cane again.

As the other Mongavarians swung their guns toward him, Fieran had to draw on his magic again, the pain of it blurring his vision so much that he didn't dare shoot. Instead, he lashed out with his magic.

This time he couldn't help it. He found himself on his knees, his bones aching from hitting the concrete floor. It was all he could do to keep the contents of his stomach where they belonged, even as his head swirled and each breath felt like there was something jagged and sharp stuck inside his chest.

He was vaguely aware of the rescued Alliance soldiers diving on the dead bodies, divesting them of their weapons. One soldier cut the other one down from the girder, pulling his arm over his shoulder.

Fieran gathered himself, pushed to his feet, and staggered to them. "Is everyone all right?"

The one who had been strung up pushed off his fellow soldier, saying something in a low tone Fieran couldn't hear. Then, strangely, the soldier grinned, stepped forward, and hugged Fieran, giving him a slap on the back for good measure. "Fieran! I knew you'd come! Didn't I tell you, boys, that Laesornysh wouldn't leave us here?"

That voice. It was roughened and tired, but still so familiar.

"Pretty Face?" Fieran pulled out of his hug and studied the man facing him. He was gaunt, his cheekbones stark against his hollow eyes. He was shaved completely bald, the pencil mustache gone. His ragged clothes hung on his frame while he stooped slightly as if he didn't have the strength to stand upright.

But his grin was still wide, the look in his brown eyes still very much alive and determined. "Not so much a pretty face now, but, yes, it's me." His gaze swept over Fieran. "You don't look so good either. I was expecting you to come at the head of the army or leading a bombing run. Not..."

"Not get captured and bust out from the inside?" Fieran grinned back, not protesting when Pretty Face took one of his arms over his shoulders. He probably shouldn't be leaning on a man who was half-starved and half-beaten, but Pretty Face seemed to be leaning on him as much as he was on Pretty Face.

"Yeah, that wasn't the plan I was expecting you to go with, but I should've realized you'd pick the unconventional route." Pretty Face turned the two of them to face the rest of the captured soldiers. "All right, everyone. This is what we've been preparing for. Everyone got their weapons?"

The men brandished a variety of weapons, from

wrenches and pieces of metal that appeared to have been sharpened into blades to guns they'd taken from the dead Mongavarians.

One of the soldiers stepped forward. "We're with you, Jim."

"Jim?" Fieran eyed Pretty Face.

"My name is James, you know." Pretty Face gave a shrug, then winced as if the movement hurt. "Jim seemed to fit better here than Pretty Face."

Right. Fieran had gotten so used to calling Pretty Face by his nickname that he'd all but forgotten that he had a real name. As the seventh son of a wastrel lord, Pretty Face had spent his time in the army distancing himself from his father and avoiding connections with him, including his name.

Pretty Face's grin dropped as he started toward the door. "But enough catching up. We have to rescue the others."

The other Alliance soldiers surged past Fieran and Pretty Face, brandishing their weapons and racing for the door. Fieran staggered along with Pretty Face, the two of them stepping back into the sunlight as the rest of the men pounced on the few remaining Mongavarian soldiers.

Pretty Face—Jim—tugged him toward the farthest and largest concrete building. A large padlock threaded through the bolt holding the steel door shut, and Fieran gritted his teeth as he used another thread of his magic to break it.

Pretty Face hauled the door open, releasing a gust of fetid air reeking of excrement and other rank odors.

Dropping Fieran's arm, Pretty Face hurried inside without so much as a heartbeat's hesitation.

Fieran followed more slowly, his eyes adjusting to the near pitch-black inside the building. He could just make out what appeared to be an aisle down the center. On either side, barred doors blocked off rooms. No, not rooms. That was too generous a word. These were more like cages or animal stalls.

Fieran tottered a few steps farther into the building. People were packed into each of the cages as if they were animals. Men and women with the rounded ears and mottled green skin of the ogres. They stared back at Fieran with wide eyes, none of them speaking.

Pretty Face had halted by one of the cages, and he reached through the bars, holding the hand of a young ogre woman standing near the cage door. "We'll have you out of here in just a moment. You'll be free."

Fieran opened his mouth, only to close it again as bile rose in his throat.

He turned on his heel, dashed back the way he'd come, and stumbled outside into the fresh air and blue sky. This time, he couldn't swallow it down. He fell to his hands and knees and vomited onto the dirt.

Fieran sprawled with his back to the wall and his legs stretched out across the hallway, too exhausted and sick to move, even as people continued bustling back and forth in front of him, stepping over his legs. He probably should move more out of the way, but he couldn't find the energy.

With the facility secure, Fieran and Pretty Face—mostly Pretty Face—had organized the rescued soldiers and ogres. Those in better shape had been sent to the mess to prepare food. Others were tending those in worse shape, settling them into beds here in the barracks for the Mongavarian soldiers where there were actual beds and clean clothes. Still others were rotating through the showers, washing off the weeks and months of captivity.

Fieran had helped where he could until he finally collapsed here in one of the hallways of the officers' quarters.

But the worst part—even worse than the gnawing pain in his chest and continued dizziness—was the incontrovertible fact. Pip wasn't there. Neither she nor Uncle Edmund were anywhere in this facility.

A murmur came from somewhere down the hall a moment before Dacha strode into view. He still wore the baggy trousers and gray-blue uniform shirt, but they were now spattered with blood. He must have had to take a few Mongavarian soldiers down at close quarters.

After seeing the conditions the ogres had been held in, Fieran didn't feel any remorse at wiping out the entire complement of enemy soldiers here.

When Dacha's gaze landed on Fieran, his forehead scrunched, and he broke into a jog. He fell to his knees next to Fieran, his eyes darting over him. "You do not look well, sason."

"Don't feel so great." There was no point in lying, now that they'd liberated Ludin.

Dacha nudged Fieran's shirt up, then tugged back the bandage. "Your wound does not appear infected."

"Didn't think so." Nothing was going to survive getting blasted by Dacha's magic, not even the things that would cause his wound to become infected. Fieran squeezed his eyes shut, resting his head against the wall behind him.

Footsteps came closer, then someone else knelt at Fieran's other side. "You were hooked up to the machine, weren't you?"

Fieran tilted his head and opened his eyes, finding Pretty Face next to him. It was still a shock, seeing Pretty Face so unrecognizably gaunt and bald.

Behind Pretty Face, two ogre women, one about Pretty Face's age and one elderly, stood with near identical impassive expressions. They both were as bald as Pretty Face, but the green skin of their heads was inked with designs. The older one even had inked designs stretching down both of her arms as well.

Fieran gave a short nod. "Yes. We both were, but only mine was turned on."

The elderly ogre moved to stand in front of Fieran as Dacha shifted out of her way. She knelt, her dark brown eyes locked with his. She spoke in a creaky voice in her language, but the other younger ogre woman translated the words. "We of the O'gresha have the ability to interact with magic itself. For some, that manifests in the ability to deflect magic. But for others, we can reach into a person and touch the very heart of their magic."

"That's the magic in those machines, isn't it?" Fieran broke eye contact with the elderly ogre woman to glance up at Pretty Face. "You had already crashed by then, but the Mongavarians used a bunch of these magic-stealing machines to take down the Wall."

"We heard about the Wall coming down." Pretty Face's jaw worked. "The Mongavarians were rather jubilant their invention had worked, and they doubled down on their efforts here."

The younger ogre woman spoke in a low tone, likely translating the conversation. As she finished, the elderly woman's eyes flashed, her posture stiffening. When she spoke again, her voice held an extra snap to it, one that the younger ogre woman matched as she translated into Escarlish. "Yes, that is our magic, but it was stolen and twisted. Several years ago, the empire of Mongavaria began probing our borders and capturing some of our people. They soon realized the ways our magic could be exploited, and they set out to do just that."

"That was the reason for the invasion of Groyria earlier this year." Dacha gave a slight nod, his eyes flinty. He spoke in Escarlish rather than elvish. "Mongavaria needed to begin exploiting your people on a broader scale. They needed your magic to combat mine."

There was a pause as the younger woman translated. Then the older ogre woman gave a short, sharp nod, the eyes she turned on Dacha just as flinty as his. "My people's magic has long been exploited. Humans have done so. The elves did so, in an age so long ago even the elves have forgotten. We can detect magic in the young and control the magic of those newly come into their power. That is our true purpose."

Something like that would, indeed, be powerful. An ogre with that magic could find out what type of magic a person would have while he or she was still a baby. The ogres could keep magic in check in a way few others could.

Dacha tipped his head to the elderly ogre. "I am sorry for what has been done to your people."

The ogre nodded back, something in her eyes softening.

Time to turn the conversation back to the machine and what was happening with Fieran. Not that all this history wasn't fascinating, but Fieran couldn't appreciate it as much as he probably should while he was swallowing down his nausea and trying not to pass out with pain every time he breathed. "So all that to say, is there something you can do to fix whatever is going on with my magic?"

The younger ogre woman straightened and spoke, her words her own instead of translated. "Of course she can. My grandmother's magic is strong. So strong that they put her on the machine several times, and they never could take her magic from her. She fought it off."

Fieran gaped at the elderly woman in front of him. That was impressive. He knew better than anyone just how powerful that machine was when it came to clawing out magic.

The elderly woman gestured to him, and the younger ogre woman translated, "Unbutton your shirt."

Fieran worked to unbutton his borrowed shirt with shaking fingers. When he gave her a nod, the elderly woman placed her hand on his chest, right at the same spot where the dots of dried blood marked where he'd been hooked to the machine.

Her hand didn't glow or do anything else to indicate that she was using magic. Yet he felt the moment her magic reached deep within him, grasping that aching place inside him.

He cried out, lurching away from her as his magic rose inside him in a stab of pain.

Dacha's hand gripped his shoulder, holding him steady. Yet his dacha also tensed, as if poised to defend Fieran from the ogre woman if she did anything to him.

The ogre woman's magic retreated for a moment, although her hand remained on Fieran's chest. "You are strong. The machine did not take your magic. But your magic is now dislocated within you, like a shoulder that is out of joint. You have experienced great pain in using it, yes?"

"Yes." Fieran nodded, struggling to draw in a deep breath to settle his whirling head and churning stomach.

Dacha's fingers tightened to near painful on Fieran's shoulder. "Can you help him?"

"Indeed. I will move his magic back into place." The ogre

woman turned to Fieran, her granddaughter translating for her. "But it would be best if you refrained from using your magic for at least three days—a week would be better—to allow your magic to resettle back into its proper place in your body."

A new bolt of fear and dread jolted through his stomach and increased the pain in his chest.

A week without using his magic—there was no way his dacha would let him use his magic before that—while they were here in enemy territory.

Dacha flexed his fingers on Fieran's shoulder and cleared his throat. Even then, his voice was rough. "Will he have any long-term effects from using his magic while it was dislocated? My dachasheni died of a disease of the magic."

"No, I don't believe he will suffer any ill effects. But if he had not used his magic, then he would have needed only a day or two for his magic to resettle rather than a week."

Good to know he wasn't dying because of this—well, he was pretty sure he would die eventually if his magic was left as it was. But this ogre woman seemed pretty confident in what she was talking about.

Would refraining from using his magic for a week put Dacha in danger? Or Pip, wherever she was?

"Enough talking about it. Please just fix it." Fieran gritted his teeth and pressed himself more firmly against the wall behind him.

The elderly ogre woman glanced from Dacha to Pretty Face, her words translated into Escarlish by her granddaughter. "Hold him still. This will hurt."

Dacha changed his grip on Fieran's shoulder to pinning him against the wall. With his free hand, he pinned Fieran's hand to the floor. Pretty Face matched Dacha on the other side, his grip on Fieran's shoulder and arm much less firm than Dacha's.

Fieran squeezed his eyes shut, bracing himself. "I don't know why everyone always warns that stuff is going to hurt. Of course it's going to hurt. It doesn't really make—"

Her magic stabbed into his chest, clutched his magic, and *shoved*.

Fieran screamed and thrashed against the hands holding him. With the ogre magic so firmly wrapped around his, he didn't even have to try to hold his magic back. It was incapable of rising to defend him.

Then the foreign magic released his, retreating from his body. He slumped against the wall, and when he gulped in a deep, gasping breath, it didn't hurt. Sure, there was a faint ache, but it felt the same as the ache of healing magic working on a bone or the ache of a muscle after a good workout. The good kind of ache instead of the tearing pain of before.

"Okay, yes, that hurt." Fieran peeled his eyes open, working up the energy to grin. The dizziness, nausea, and pain in his chest were gone. He was still deeply exhausted in a way he hadn't been since he'd been recovering from his crash. "But that helped. I don't feel like I want to barf anymore."

Dacha immediately released him, rocking back on his heels.

Pretty Face patted his shoulder once before letting go. "There's the Capt. Laesornysh I know."

"It's Maj. Laesornysh now, actually." Fieran drew in one last, deep breath and thought he might have the energy to sit up somewhat straighter. "Although it is hard to tell right now. I'm rather out of uniform."

"I've missed a lot while away." Pretty Face's smile turned

somewhat strained, his eyes going hollow again. "But before you tell me all about it, you should get some rest."

"We should get moving. There's no telling how long it will take the Mongavarians to notice this facility isn't responding." Fieran braced himself against the wall as he tried to totter to his feet.

Dacha took his arm over his shoulder and pulled him the rest of the way upright. "You need rest, sason. Nor are you the only one. We have enough time. Rest for an hour, then we can meet to discuss our plan."

"And you…" The younger ogre woman pulled Pretty Face to his feet, pulling his arm over her shoulder. "Your back needs tending."

"Yes, ma'am." Pretty Face leaned against her, a gentle smile on his face that Fieran had never seen before.

Had Pretty Face…fallen for someone? Not just the surface-level flirting Fieran had seen from him before, but actual falling in love?

Now wasn't the time to ask. But he and Pretty Face were really going to need to have a talk, either here or once they were all safe in Escarland.

NINETEEN

Fieran stood next to the table in the officer's mess, crowded between his dacha and Pretty Face. Many of the rescued Alliance officers packed into the room as well as several ogres, including the elderly ogre woman and her granddaughter. They stood beside Pretty Face with a younger male ogre on the other side of them.

Dacha glanced around the room, swaying backward for a moment as if intimidated by so many people. Yet he was the most senior officer by far. Making decisions fell to him.

Fieran swept a glance around the room as well. It was hard to tell since all the Alliance officers now wore Mongavarian uniforms, but he might be the second highest ranked officer there. Most of those he did recognize—a few pilots from the other squadrons at Fort Defense who had gone down in Mongavaria over the past few months—were lieutenants.

With a deep breath, Dacha finally seemed to gather himself enough to speak. "Who is the senior officer among those imprisoned here?"

Pretty Face came to attention. "That would be me, sir. We

had a captain here a few weeks ago, but he was shot trying to escape."

Fieran swallowed, clenching his fists.

"How many Alliance officers were killed here?" Dacha's tone remained low.

"I'm not sure. Several were shot trying to escape. And any captured elves or trolls were put right on the machine the moment they arrived and killed." Pretty Face clenched and unclenched his fists at his side. "There are mass graves to the north side of the fence."

"Before we leave, we will want to secure any records we can find that detail that information." Dacha rested a hand on the stack of notebooks he'd set on the table, the ones he'd taken from the laboratories. "When the war ends, we will need proof of what happened here."

Pretty Face nodded. "Yes, sir."

Dacha spread out a map they'd found in the commander's office onto the table, using the notebooks to hold it open. "We are here. The original plan was for Fieran and Pip to make a run for the border either in our hijacked airship or with a convoy of trucks, protecting it with their combined magic."

"I'm not leaving Mongavaria without Pip." Fieran crossed his arms. He didn't want his dacha to get any ideas of sending Fieran to safety along with the former captives.

Besides, Fieran couldn't use his magic. He wouldn't be much help at the moment.

"Of course." Dacha glanced over his shoulder at him. "And I am not letting you out of my sight. As long as you are with me, there will be no reason for you to use your magic."

Oh, right. There was that too.

Pretty Face gave a slight shrug. "We will just have to make do without magic on our run to the border."

As determined as he was to rescue Pip, Fieran's stomach still sank at the thought of sending Pretty Face off without magical protection. The last time Pretty Face had tried for the border, he hadn't made it.

Two of the other Alliance officers shared a look before one cleared his throat. "We have made an inventory of all the weapons and ammunition here. We'll be well armed, and there are enough trucks for everyone, if we don't mind close quarters. We also took all the Mongavarian identification papers and money we could find. We might be able to bribe or bluff our way past low-ranking soldiers, at least."

"And we'll have the ogres' magic to help, if they are willing." Pretty Face glanced at the young ogre woman next to him.

She straightened her shoulders. "You'll have our help for the first while. But we will be headed home."

Pretty Face shook his head, still holding her gaze. "No. Groyria is still occupied territory. If you return to your homes, you will just be captured again. Please. Come to Escarland. Accept sanctuary for your people until your homeland can be liberated. Don't place them back into danger."

Dacha glanced at the young woman before he focused on the elderly ogre woman. "I am Prince Farrendel of both Tarenhiel and Escarland. I can promise you sanctuary on behalf of both of those kingdoms, and I will provide you with a letter of guarantee to present to the border guards and to my brother-in-law, King Averett of Escarland. Ask to speak with him directly. He is an honorable man who will treat you fairly."

The elderly ogre listened as the younger ogre woman

translated. Once the younger ogre finished, the old woman held Dacha's gaze for another long moment before she spoke. "Will you grant me a portion of magic as the guarantee of your word and that I can present to your Escarlish guards and king as proof?"

Dacha hesitated for a moment before he called up a few tendrils of his magic. He held out his hand to her. "If you can hold it, then you are welcome to it."

The elderly ogre woman reached out and almost seemed to gather Dacha's magic as if it were strands of hair rather than power. It disappeared into her skin, vanishing from sight. Something in her expression changed as she regarded Dacha, as if she had learned a great deal about him from the feel of his magic. "Very well, elf prince. I will trust in your word on behalf of my people."

The younger ogre woman's jaw worked, but she turned to Pretty Face. "It seems we will be traveling with you to your kingdom after all."

"It's the best way to keep your people safe." Pretty Face's hands twitched, as if he barely stopped himself from reaching out to her. Instead, he turned back to the table and pointed at the map. "I was thinking about making a run slightly southwest to the Cartmer Gorge. The fighting should be less intense there than farther north near the Engleston Gap, correct?"

"Yes." Fieran pointed to the gorge on the map. "But you'll need to be careful that you aren't caught in the crossfire or by a bombing run."

"Dressed as we are, we're just as likely to get shot by the Escarlish soldiers guarding the border as by the Mongavarian Army." One of the officers plucked at the Mongavarian uniform he wore.

"Perhaps we can wash our old uniforms while on the

road." Another one grimaced down at himself. "We could get shot as spies at the moment."

"As opposed to what the Mongavarians would do to us as escaping Alliance prisoners?" Pretty Face raised his eyebrows at the two men.

The other two shared a look and shrugged.

"Regardless, you'll want to approach the border carefully." Fieran didn't want to imagine these rescued captives surviving all they had, just to be killed by friendly fire.

"Maybe when we get closer to the border, we'll paint the Flying Corps symbol on top of the trucks." Pretty Face gave another shrug.

"So you're the one responsible for that." Fieran clapped Pretty Face on the shoulder. "That EFC symbol was the reason we realized there were Alliance prisoners here in addition to captured ogres."

"I'm glad it worked." Pretty Face's smile faded.

Dacha traced a line on the map again. "Fieran and I will take one of the trucks and make for Landri. I have reason to believe that Prince Edmund and Pip are being taken there. It should take us about a week. While I cannot elaborate more, there is a plan in place for ending the war once we arrive."

If Fieran's reckoning of the days was correct, they had about a week until whatever plan Dacha and Uncle Edmund had come up with for ending the war was supposed to go down. The one that involved Rothilion's mysterious mission.

The elderly ogre turned to the two younger ogres beside her. The three of them conversed for a moment before the young male ogre stepped forward. Like the others, his head was entirely bald with black designs standing out against mottled green skin. "I'll be going with you."

Dacha raised his eyebrows, shaking his head.

The elderly ogre spoke again, and the young woman

translated for her. "This is my grandson Aaruk. He has the strong ability to deflect magic and, while he cannot interact with the heart of magic as I can, he can sense your son's magic and ensure that it's settling into place as it should. Please, elf prince. You have granted me your magic as safe passage. Allow me to grant you the help of my grandson."

Dacha nodded to her. "Very well. I will accept his help."

Fieran suspected the ogre woman had had his father at the whole *help your son's magic heal* thing.

"Then if that's settled, may I have permission to organize my men for our departure?" Pretty Face came to attention again, facing Dacha.

Dacha nodded. "We will need one of the trucks, one of the guns, three sets of identification papers, and some of the Mongavarian currency. Other than that, take all the weapons, clothing, and food you can find. We can make do with what we can glean on our travels, but you will have many more mouths to feed."

Fieran gaped at his dacha. Was his dacha really suggesting what he thought he was suggesting? *Glean* was a rather polite word for *steal food from the locals*. Yes, that was a time-honored way of feeding invading armies, but Fieran hadn't expected his dacha, of all people, to do it.

Although Dacha could be planning to use the money to purchase food. But since the three of them couldn't fake Mongavarian accents, unless Aaruk had depths Fieran didn't know about, buying anything would be difficult. Hopefully the whole *too haughty to speak to lowly civilians* ruse would get them where they needed to go.

"Very well, but I'll set aside as much food as I think we can spare." Pretty Face's gaze didn't waver, even facing Fieran's dacha. "You'll need to keep moving without taking time for finding food."

"Those with you have been starved long enough." Dacha's voice held a tight, strange note to it. "I will not take food from them."

As subtly as he could, Fieran nudged Pretty Face with an elbow. This wasn't a discussion Pretty Face was going to win. He would be better off just quietly stuffing a bag of food into the truck set aside for Fieran and Dacha rather than arguing about it.

Perhaps Pretty Face realized that because he nodded. "Yes, sir."

"And take these with you as well." Dacha gathered up the notebooks and handed them to Pretty Face. "Along with any other records we can find. Place them directly in the hands of either King Averett or Princess Jalissa. They will know what to do with them."

"Yes, sir." Pretty Face took the notebooks, gripping them to his chest.

One of the other officers rolled up the map, tucking it under an arm.

"I would like all of us to leave in less than an hour." Dacha's tone held a finality, indicating that the meeting was over.

Within a few moments, everyone began to disperse. The young ogre woman moved off, speaking in low tones with her brother. Dacha mumbled something about searching for more records and maps, and some of the other officers shouted over to Pretty Face how they were going to start loading the trucks.

Fieran fell into step with Pretty Face, clapping him on the shoulder as they left the room. "I hate sending you off like this. Again. Make it to the Escarlish border this time, okay?"

"You got it." Pretty Face grinned, though it faded only a moment later. "I only made it about an hour down the road last time. Ran straight into one of the patrols coming to investigate the crash. The next thing I knew, I was shipped here."

Fieran had to squeeze his eyes shut for a moment as that sank in. All that time when he and the others were hoping and waiting for Pretty Face to return, he'd already been caught. He'd already been here, suffering these horrible conditions. "I'm sorry we couldn't get to you sooner. I only found out about this place about a week and a half ago."

"I know. I suspected the Alliance didn't know about it. Or knew about it and didn't dare bomb it." As they stepped outside, Pretty Face gave a harsh laugh, turning his face toward the sky. "We kept hoping you'd bomb it. Every day we'd search the skies, hoping we'd see an Alliance squadron overhead."

Fieran swallowed at the tightness in his throat, hearing what Pretty Face wasn't telling him. A bombing like that would have killed many of the prisoners, and yet those very prisoners hoped for such a death if it meant this facility would be shut down and their suffering would be at an end.

Instead of probing that further, Fieran waved a hand at the factory building, the smokestacks no longer belching smoke. "What did they have you making?"

"The power cells to hold the magic they stole. We tried to sabotage them as best we could, although the Mongavarians would retaliate by beating or shooting some of us if they caught us doing it." Pretty Face's jaw worked, his eyes getting that hollow, haunted look again. "We were trying to save as many ogres as we could. The Mongavarian magicians could wield the deflecting magic once it was ripped from an ogre so one ogre's magic could be used many times before exhausted. But the magic that interacts with the heart of magic could only be used in one machine. One ogre had to die for every machine."

Fieran swallowed, thinking of all the machines that had taken down the Wall. An ogre had died to create each of those machines.

Pretty Face had seen things while held captive. Things Fieran couldn't fully comprehend since he hadn't experienced anything like that.

His dacha likely understood far more than he did. Dacha had, after all, been captured twice by the trolls. Tortured twice by them as well.

Pretty Face's voice roughened still further. "After the Wall came down, we knew we had to do whatever it took to prevent more of those machines from reaching the front lines, even if that meant dying ourselves."

"Thank you. You likely saved Alliance lives, not to mention the lives of the ogres here." Fieran held Pretty Face's gaze as best he could.

Pretty Face nodded, though he looked away to stare at Ludin. "I hope so."

There was nothing else Fieran could say to that. Pretty Face saw all the lives he hadn't been able to save rather than the ones he had.

Time to lighten the conversation. Fieran elbowed Pretty Face lightly as they set out again. "The squadron had one thing right in all our guesses on what you were up to. Was I imagining something between you and a certain ogre lady?"

The look in Pretty Face's eyes warmed, even though he shook his head. "It's hard to explain, if you weren't here. We were just trying to survive. It bonds people. But we both know it isn't something that's going to last. Once this is over, I'll return to the squadron, and Inirth will return to her homeland."

Fieran clapped Pretty Face on the back again, not sure what to say to that. Even if this wasn't something that would last, he found himself strangely proud of Pretty Face. He'd come a long way from the flighty lord's son who flirted with anything in a skirt to a leader here who had fallen for a young woman who didn't fit the conventional Escarlish standards of beauty.

Pretty Face shook himself and started walking again. "Anyway, your turn. What's been happening with the squadron? And Merrik? Have you heard from him?"

"He's getting around well on his prosthetic leg and already back with the squadron. He's leading the squadron at the moment." Fieran had to look away, his throat going a little tight at the thought of Merrik flying into battle without him. "Rothilion is off on a mission so secret even I don't know the details of it."

Fieran gave Pretty Face a few more random tidbits on the squadron, and each one seemed to relax Pretty Face more. As if just hearing about them was bringing him back to who he had been rather than who he'd become to survive this place.

Several of the Alliance officers hurried toward them, one of them calling out for "Jim."

Fieran shook his head. "Still getting used to that."

Pretty Face grinned. "I'd better see to my duties. It's going to take a lot to get all of us out of here in less than an hour."

Fieran slapped his back. "I knew you'd become quite the leader if given the chance. You did well here."

Pretty Face swallowed and nodded before he turned away, heading toward the others.

Since Fieran had slept the entire hour he'd been given to rest, he'd better find the bathhouse and take a quick shower.

This would likely be his last chance for one for the next week. Then he would track down his dacha and see what he wanted him to do before their departure.

A line of ogres waited outside the larger bathhouse for the enlisted men, so Fieran stepped back inside the long quarters for the officers, winding through it until he found the bathhouse attached to the end of the building.

He pushed the door open, then froze.

Dacha stood before one of the sinks, facing the mirror. He gripped a knife in one hand, strands of his silver-blond hair in the other.

Fieran eased forward a step, his tone hesitant. He almost felt like he should take the knife from his dacha's hands before he did something drastic. "Dacha? What are you doing?"

Dacha's shoulders rose and fell in a deep, bracing breath, but his gaze never wavered from his own reflection in the mirror. "You cannot use your magic. Thus we will need to avoid attention and blend in as we travel across Mongavaria. I cannot risk that my elven hair will give us away and force you to use your magic to help defend us."

With that, Dacha sliced the knife through his hair. No hesitation. Not a blink or a flinch.

Fieran lunged forward a step, an inarticulate, horrified noise rising in his throat. But he halted with his hands stretched into the air between him and Dacha, rooted in place.

Dacha dropped the shorn ends of his hair into the sink, grabbed another section of hair, and just as ruthlessly sliced it off.

Fieran lowered his hands to his sides, blinking rapidly at the sight of his dacha cutting off his elven hair, the symbol of his warrior honor, in order to keep Fieran safe.

He'd thought he'd understood the depth of his dacha's love when he'd seen his dacha striding through the fog, having taken on an army for Fieran.

But this...this was the depth of his dacha's love for him. He'd give up this very integral part of himself for Fieran.

Fieran couldn't move, couldn't speak, couldn't do anything but blink at the wetness gathering at the corners of his eyes.

Once the hair had been shortened, Dacha set the knife down and picked up a small set of shears, the kind used for sewing, and trimmed the ends. "How does it look in the back?"

Fieran swallowed and cleared his throat. "There is...the middle needs a trim."

He probably should offer to help with the final trim, since it would be easier for him than for his dacha to do on himself. But Fieran couldn't bring himself to offer to cut his dacha's hair. It felt too wrong, too sacrilegious, despite the fact that Fieran had no problem keeping his own hair short.

Finally, Dacha dropped the last of the trimmed ends in the sink, called on his magic, and incinerated his shorn hair, as if he wasn't going to leave it there for anyone to desecrate. He turned around and faced Fieran, the look in his eyes almost too steady for what he'd just done.

His dacha...looked like him. Or, rather, Fieran looked like his dacha. With their hair cut short in nearly the same style, the similar shape to their jaws, their identical pointed ears, the set of their eyes, grew all the more pronounced. They looked like they could be brothers, given how young his dacha appeared.

He'd been told all his life how much he looked like his dacha. But looking at him now, Fieran felt it in a way he never had before.

FIERAN'S CHEST was tight and aching again, but this time it wasn't due to the dislocation of his magic.

He held one of the power cells with stolen elven magic. Before him, the ogres and Alliance soldiers gathered around the churned earth of the mass graves, many of them also holding magical power cells filled with stolen magic.

The elderly female ogre was speaking in their language. Some kind of funeral rites, if Fieran were to guess. After another few minutes, she moved forward, laid the magical power cell on the ground, and opened the valve to release the magic held within. Since the power cell wasn't hooked up to a machine, the magic surged outward and dissipated into the air and the earth. Because the ogre magic was invisible, Fieran couldn't see it, but he could sense it deep within his chest.

The other ogres stepped forward and did the same, placing the magical power cells on the ground and releasing the stolen magic. Fieran could only guess at how much of that magic belonged to family members and friends who now lay in those mass graves before them.

Once the ogres had finished, Dacha, Fieran, Pretty Face, and many of the Alliance soldiers stepped forward, set the power cells they held on the ground, and released all the non-ogre magic, including elven magic, human magic, and troll magic. The elf and troll magic was likely from pilots or warriors captured in the recent invasion into Mongavaria. But there was no way to tell if the human magic was from Escarlish magicians or possibly Mongavarians. Fieran wouldn't put it past them to have experimented on their own people.

Unless the names of those killed were somewhere in the

records that Pretty Face carried in a bag, there were some buried in those graves who might never be known.

Once the last stolen magic was released back to the earth, Dacha knelt and pressed his hand to the ground. Blue magic burst from him, traveling through the ground in a rush, before it wrapped around the empty magical power cells. Within heartbeats, it had melted the glass and consumed the rest of the parts, reducing the magical power cells to nothing.

More of his magic erupted from the ground in the surrounding fields where Dacha had used his magic before until the entire facility was awash in crackling blue power.

The others turned to face the facility, some of the rescued ogres and prisoners staring with hollow eyes while others had tears trickling down their cheeks.

Fieran flexed his fingers, his magic twinging in his chest at the pummeling feel of so much of his dacha's magic unleashed. It was hard to stand by and merely watch when he longed to add his magic to the destruction of this place.

Dacha's magic crawled up the buildings, threading through the cracks in the concrete blocks. With a clench of Dacha's fist, his magic shattered concrete and incinerated anything else. With a roar, the laboratory collapsed into itself, a cloud of gray dust bursting outward. The officer quarters, enlisted barracks, and the factory followed with reverberating rumbles and clouds of dust.

Dacha slammed his magic into the ground, the explosive force washing over them.

Fieran blinked into the magical blowback, squinting as the breeze cleared the dust. He glanced from what remained to Dacha. "You left a few of the buildings."

"Some need to remain as a testimony to what happened here." Dacha stood and brushed dried grass and dust from the knee of his Mongavarian uniform trousers. "My magic will ensure that no one can destroy what is left to erase what happened."

Fieran took in what remained—the prison barracks, the buildings that held the cages where the ogres had been held, and the barbed wire fences with the guard towers—and nodded.

Pretty Face stared at what was left a moment longer, his jaw working, his eyes both hard and haunted. Then he turned to face everyone and made a motion with his hand. "All right, everyone. Let's load up. We have long miles to drive yet today."

The crowd of ogres and Alliance soldiers set out across the field to the long line of trucks they'd parked on the road outside of the facility. The trucks would be packed. Between trying to transport several hundred people in far fewer trucks than were ideal and all the other supplies also packed into the trucks with the people, they would be heavily loaded.

Fieran fell into step with Pretty Face, pressing a hand against his middle as he stumbled over the uneven ground of the field. Exhaustion weighed on his shoulders again, and he resisted the urge to hunch over. While he felt a lot better, he was still achingly tired even after his rest.

At the trucks, he and Pretty Face paused. Fieran clapped Pretty Face on the shoulder, careful not to hurt Pretty Face's back. "The squadron is going to be happy to see you."

"Assuming I make it across the border this time." Pretty Face's eyes went distant as he stared, seemingly unseeing, at the line of trucks. His shoulders sagged, as if burdened by how many lives were on the line this time.

"You will." Fieran had to believe that. While Pretty Face and the convoy would be a large, visible target, they were well armed, and they only had to survive the two days to the border. Perhaps less, if they drove through the night.

Even as he stood there, Escarlish soldiers carrying guns sat on the back of one of the truck beds, their feet dangling over the end. Prepared to defend the convoy as it made its dash for the border.

Pretty Face shook himself and clapped Fieran on the shoulder as well. "You take care of yourself. Rescue Pip. End the war."

"That's the plan." Fieran dropped his hand and forced himself to take a step away from Pretty Face.

It was time to go.

Pretty Face grinned and gave him a salute. "See you around, Major."

Fieran saluted back. "Take care of yourself, Jim."

With that, he turned away and headed for the last truck in line. It was the smallest of all the trucks, less for hauling cargo and more a simple work truck. The cab was open and connected to the back open cargo area, but the whole thing could be rigged with a low canvas top in case of rain. They'd already stretched it overhead as a sun shelter and to keep themselves as hidden as possible.

Aaruk waited by the truck, leaning against it with his arms crossed and a slight grin on his face. As Fieran approached, Aaruk pushed from the truck.

Fieran stuck out his hand to him. "We haven't had a chance to properly introduce ourselves. I'm Maj. Fieran Laesornysh."

Dacha appeared at Fieran's side. "Prince Farrendel Laesornysh."

"My father," Fieran added.

Aaruk grinned and shook Fieran's hand. "I'm Aaruk of Clan Girakuhr."

"Good to have you along." Fieran glanced along the row of trucks as they rumbled to life. Alliance soldiers gripping weapons clung to the backs and sides of many of the trucks while ogres were squished inside.

The column of trucks rolled forward, trundling down the road.

Dacha strode around the front of their truck. "I will drive. Fieran, get some rest."

Fieran wasn't going to argue with that. He crawled beneath the flap and into the back cargo area. A few supplies were tied along one side while a mattress from one of the beds had been placed on the floor.

He collapsed onto it, biting back a groan at the stab of pain from the gash across his middle. Now that he was no longer in agony from his magic, the pain from the wound was more noticeable.

Dacha climbed into the driver's seat with Aaruk taking the passenger's seat, the truck rocking from their movements.

The engine roared to life, shaking through the whole vehicle in a way that the magically powered engines Fieran was used to didn't.

He pressed a hand over his wound, closed his eyes, and tried to relax.

Wherever Pip was, he was coming. She just needed to hold on for a little while longer.

TWENTY

Pip caught just a glimpse of the elegant white spires of the castle perched on a cliff above the sea before a black hood was shoved over her head. With her hands now shackled behind her back, she lost all sense of balance as she was dragged from the train by two burly Mongavarian soldiers.

At least she could hear Prince Edmund's stumbling footsteps behind her. He occasionally made some joking comment to his guards, reassuring her that they were still together.

After two days in the truck, they'd been transferred to a train for the rest of the journey to Landri. The train's boxcar hadn't been particularly comfortable, but they'd been left mostly alone.

The hood was stifling hot against her face, but the occasional ocean breeze cut through the fabric, giving her a refreshing breath filled with the scents of salt and sea.

The smell brought back memories of Dar Goranth and the storm-tossed northern oceans. How she missed the squadron. Her flyboys. Fieran. A soft bed beneath her instead of cold metal. The safety of an Alliance base instead of being constantly surrounded by enemies.

Each day that passed made it more and more tempting to escape. She could have done it at any point. But she'd stayed because Prince Edmund believed it was the best plan.

With a hood over her head and shackles on her hands, that no longer seemed like such a good option. She and Prince Edmund might very well find themselves hauled before a firing squad. That could even be where they were headed now.

The cold of stone surrounded her, the echoes of the footsteps telling her this was a tunnel of some sort. Perhaps beneath the outer wall of the castle?

After a few minutes, the stone arching over them vanished, although the stone cobbles below her boots remained. A courtyard of some sort.

Hinges creaked as a door was opened. Then Pip was dragged inside a building. She tried to keep track of the turns but lost count within a few minutes.

She could tell when they entered a more lavish section of the building because her footsteps became muffled by soft carpet.

More doors opened, and the echoes told her this was a large space.

She was hauled across the room before she was shoved onto her knees. At least the carpet here was thick and soft, sparing her from bruises.

The hood was yanked off her head, and she blinked at the rush of relatively cold air against her face and the lights beaming down on her.

Next to her, Prince Edmund had also been forced to his knees and the hood removed from his head. He swept a glance around the room before a slow smile broke across his face. "Empress Bella. It's been a while."

Pip faced forward and took in the room more fully. They were in some kind of lavish throne room with a blue carpet below her and walls so papered and gilded that it hurt to look at them in the shine of the electric lights overhead.

Ahead, a dais held a single throne where an old woman sat, bedecked in an extravagant blue dress and glittering jewelry. Three men, whose ages ranged from twenties to seventies, stood beside her, and all of them wore similar clothing and crowns.

The woman on the throne, Empress Bella, was tiny and somewhat hunched, but her long white hair was braided and coiled on her head, all the better to set off her crown. When she smiled, it was strangely sweet and soft. "Not long enough, Prince Edmund."

If Pip had imagined what the elderly empress of Mongavaria would look like, it wasn't this. This woman looked so grandmotherly that she appeared more apt to distribute hugs and cookies than start a war that had killed thousands.

"And who is this? One of your little spy minions who you hoped to plant within my empire?" Empress Bella waved a hand, rings glinting on her fingers.

Pip swallowed and kept her mouth shut. If she spoke, the empress was sure to hear the elvish accent in her Escarlish. As bad as it was to be considered a spy, it would be worse if anyone guessed that Pip had magic.

Prince Edmund shrugged, his smile still lazily nonchalant. "Aren't you going to introduce me to your family?"

He was neatly sidestepping her question about Pip. Pip would be more than happy if Prince Edmund kept the focus of the conversation on himself.

Empress Bella's smile remained that far-too-grandmotherly one as she gestured to either side of her. "Prince Edmund, meet my son, grandson, and great-grandson. My line of succession is well-established."

"Good for you," Prince Edmund drawled with that sarcastic edge.

"Family, this is Prince Edmund. The man who poisoned my grandfather." Empress Bella's smile showed a sharp edge for the first time, something glittering in her perfectly blue eyes.

"Still parroting your father's lies, I see." Prince Edmund's nonchalant look dropped, replaced with something hard. "I didn't kill your grandfather, and you know it. Your father was the one who poisoned him and me. After all, why would I poison myself?"

"Perhaps you are an inept poisoner?" Empress Bella drummed her fingers on the armrest of her throne. "Or you were never poisoned at all. You escaped with rather a lot of energy and agility for someone who claims he was poisoned."

Pip would have been rather confused at this conversation, if Prince Edmund hadn't told them the story of what had happened back then. The roots of this war extended all the way to those events seventy years ago.

Prince Edmund's jaw worked for a moment, as if that rejoinder had actually struck a nerve. His tone turned even harder. "I do wonder. How did your husband die? He passed away quite young, conveniently for you."

"It was indeed a tragedy, losing my dear husband as I did." Empress Bella's tone was so sincere Pip might have believed her, if she hadn't seen the sharp edge to her smile. "But enough of this chitchat. Prince Edmund, you were discovered in my kingdom in a hijacked airship and wearing a Mongavarian uniform. I am well within my rights to have you shot as a spy."

"But you aren't going to do that." Prince Edmund sounded far too sure of that.

"No, I won't. Not yet, anyway." Empress Bella's smile turned even more sharp-edged. "You have far too many valuable secrets in your head, and I'm determined to pry them out of you."

Pip's chest seized. Was the empress implying what Pip thought she was implying?

The empress made a languid motion with her hand. "Take them away."

Pip found that her legs were shaking as the hood was placed over her head again. She was hauled through several more corridors and down a set of stairs. After a jangle of keys, a door opened with a creak, her hands were unshackled, and she was pushed forward.

She stumbled, nearly falling to her knees. She yanked the hood off, tossing it to the ground and spinning around as a large door formed of metal bars was swung shut behind her. The guard gave her a sneer as he twisted the key in the lock, shutting her in.

Or so he thought. The whole front wall of this cell was one giant piece of metal she could manipulate if needed.

She hurried to the front of her cell, gripping the comfortingly solid metal bars as she peered one way, then the other.

The guard retreated down the passageway and climbed a set of stairs until he disappeared through a metal door at the top.

The passageway on the other side ended in a dark corner. The cells on both sides had barred doors while the occasional torch lit the space.

But there was no Prince Edmund.

"Prince Edmund?" Pip whisper-called the word.

No answer. Not even another prisoner calling back to her.

She was alone. Absolutely alone.

PIP PACED BACK and forth across her cell as she tried to decide what to do. Her cell was actually quite spacious at seven feet by ten feet and included a cot with an astonishingly clean straw mattress and wool blanket. The corner out of sight of the door even had a metal sink and a rudimentary toilet rather than the bucket or hole in the ground as she might have expected.

A window set high in the wall peered into the castle courtyard at cobblestone level. It was blocked by bars and glass, of course, but large enough that Pip could wiggle through the opening if she removed the bars and broke the glass.

Should she escape? Try to find Prince Edmund?

Although she had her magic, she was woefully unprepared for escaping an enemy stronghold and hiding out in enemy territory. She couldn't even manage to fake a Mongavarian accent.

There was a clang from the direction of the stairs, and Pip jumped, hurrying to the barred door of her cell.

The door at the top of the stairs opened, and two guards came through, dragging a limp body between them.

Pip gasped and gripped the metal bars to steady herself. That was Prince Edmund. She could only recognize him because of the color of his hair, his head hanging, his boots scraping against the stone floor.

The guards hauled him into the cell across the

passageway from hers, taking the time to chain his hands to the wall instead of merely shoving him inside. With a final kick, the two guards left the cell, locked the door, and retreated up the stairs, the door at the top clanging shut with a grim finality.

Pip waited only another few seconds before she shoved her magic into the bars, yanked them apart wide enough for her to step through, and dashed across the passageway. At the far side, she shoved two of the metal bars aside as easily as she might a strand of yarn and slipped into Prince Edmund's cell.

She crashed to her knees beside him. "Prince Edmund?"

He lay still, his body sprawled in a heap. His face was a bloody mask, rivulets of blood trickling across his skin and dripping onto the front of his shirt.

What should she do? Pip cast about, her heart squeezing.

Prince Edmund's cell held the same cot, sink, and toilet that hers did, although his cell didn't have a window.

She could try to get him on the cot, but she wasn't sure she should move him.

Perhaps washing the blood from his face would be a start. Maybe the water would wake him up.

Jumping to her feet, she dashed to the metal sink. She nearly wet her sleeve before she realized that if she got blood on herself, the guards might notice and question how it got there.

Instead, she used her magic to slice through the end of her shirt. It was long enough that hopefully the guards wouldn't notice that a piece of it had gone missing. Wetting the fabric in the sink, she returned to Prince Edmund's side and dabbed at his face.

Prince Edmund groaned and stirred.

"Lie still. It looks like you took quite the beating." Pip dabbed more blood from a cut across his cheekbone.

One of his eyes flickered open. The other was swollen shut. When he attempted something of a smile, his swollen jaw made the expression more a grimace. "I always wondered how I'd stand up to torture. That always seems to be Farrendel's thing. The enemy takes one look at him and just has to torture him. It always made me wonder if I could take it if I had to."

"If that's an attempt at humor, it isn't funny." Getting tortured was no laughing matter. Pip dabbed at the blood streaming from his nose. "And you don't have to take it. We should escape. I can get us out tonight."

"No, not yet." Prince Edmund pushed himself somewhat more upright, propped against the wall. "I learned a lot about what the Mongavarians know about the Escarlish spying efforts based on the questions they asked me. I'll learn more next time."

Really? He planned to use his torture sessions for *spying*? Pip shook her head as she stood, returned to the sink, and rinsed out the scrap of fabric. "You are even crazier than Fieran."

"I'll take that as a compliment." Prince Edmund wiggled another few inches more upright. But when she returned to his side, he gently grabbed her wrist, halting her ministrations. His one open eye searched her face, his expression returning to something far more somber. "But you're right. It's one thing to risk myself to gain information, but I won't risk you. If it looks like the Mongavarians are going to hurt you in any way, then you need to escape. Don't worry about me. Get yourself out of here. Find a place to hide in the city until help arrives."

"I won't leave you behind." Pip shook her head, her

chest going tight. As tantalizing as escape sounded, she wouldn't abandon Fieran's uncle. Nor could she imagine trying to hide in the city all by herself for a week. She'd never manage it.

"You might have to." Prince Edmund held her gaze rather firmly for a man who could barely sit upright. "Promise me."

"I promise." Pip nearly choked on the words.

It wouldn't come to that. She'd make sure of it. After all, she had iron magic, and she had her shields. When she chose to escape, she'd just have to take Prince Edmund with her.

There came a rattle from the direction of the door at the top of the stairs.

Pip leapt to her feet, heart hammering. Dropping the rag beside Prince Edmund, she leapt through the bars, barely pausing to straighten them, and lunged across the passageway and through the gap in the bars of her own cell. She'd barely put the bars back the way they'd been before the door swung all the way open.

A maid in a black uniform with a crisp white apron and a white cap over her glossy, dark brown hair paused at the top of the stairs, saying something to one of guards about how she would be fine alone.

Yet at the sound of her voice, Prince Edmund straightened, his good eye widening. He began struggling to his feet, using both the wall and the cot to steady himself.

After a moment, the guard shrugged and closed the door after her, leaving the maid to walk down the stairs by herself. She carried a tray that appeared to hold only two cups and two plates with bread.

At the bottom of the stairs, she set the tray on the floor and rushed forward, her voice a hoarse whisper that wouldn't carry. "Dacha!"

Prince Edmund took a step toward the barred door of his cell, that grimace-smile back on his face. "It is good to see you, sena." He used the elven word for *daughter* with the same warm emphasis Prince Farrendel used for *sason*.

Pip remained frozen in place for a moment. This maid was Prince Edmund's daughter? That made her Jayna, the cousin Fieran hadn't seen in two years.

Well, this explained where she'd been all that time.

Jayna gripped the bars of Prince Edmund's cell, as if she desperately wanted to pull the door open to hug her father.

Pip might as well help with this touching family reunion. She pulled open the bars of her own cell again, crossed the space, and reached for the bars of Prince Edmund's door. "Here. Allow me."

Jayna jumped, her deep brown eyes swinging to take in Pip for the first time. But she just nodded her thanks, slipped through the opening Pip created, and stepped into her dacha's hug. Prince Edmund wrapped his arms around his daughter, holding her close and murmuring words that were broken with emotion and too low for Pip to hear.

Pip's throat clogged, and she turned away for a moment, blinking rapidly. How she missed her own dacha. She'd seen him far too briefly when he and Muka had returned from the dwarven mountains.

She just wanted to go home. To the far western rail terminal. To the sounds of the clacking wheels on the tracks, the chug of the trains, the whistles piercing the still night. Mak's hugs, her dacha's quiet strength, her muka's boisterous laughter. All those beautiful, peaceful moments untouched by death and war.

Yet home was so achingly far away. It wasn't even just the physical distance, though that was great.

But Pip herself had changed so much. She wasn't sure if

it was even possible for her to return to the home she longed for.

She had a new home now. One where she was held safe and secure in Fieran's arms. Where she fixed aeroplanes and laughed with her squadron. And, perhaps someday, her home would be brick buildings filled with inventions and magic in Aldon.

But that didn't mean she didn't get a pang of twisting melancholy when she thought of the home that was slipping away from her more every day.

When she dared glance over her shoulder, Prince Edmund was gently breaking the hug. "As glad as I am to see you, the guards will be suspicious if you stay much longer. Can you sneak back tonight?"

Jayna hesitated and looked at Pip. "You must have some kind of iron magic?" When Pip nodded, Jayna pointed toward the other end of the passageway where it turned a corner. "This prison used to be part of the servants' wing before it was converted into a dungeon. They walled off that end of the passageway with a piece of steel. If you could open that…"

Pip nodded again, her throat still too clogged with the emotion of a moment before to speak. She wasn't sure how Prince Edmund and Jayna could be so calm about this after being reunited for the first time in who knew how long.

Although, something told Pip the time they'd been apart was far less than two years.

"Then I'll come that way tonight. If I don't have to go past guards, I can bring more food. And some salve." Jayna gave Prince Edmund one more quick hug before she slipped through the bars again. "I'd better go."

"You…um…got a little something…" Pip motioned to Jayna's front.

Jayna glanced down at herself and grimaced. The front of her apron had several blood spots, thanks to hugging Prince Edmund. "Well, that's not great. Here, take the bread and water, and I can hold the tray to hide my apron."

Pip grabbed the plates with bread from the tray, then the two cups of water. Jayna picked up tray and positioned so that it would hide the stains from the guards. With one last glance at Prince Edmund, she hurried down the passageway, saying loudly in a perfect Mongavarian accent, "Don't complain, Escarlish scum. That's all the food you're going to get."

Pip shook herself, shoved Prince Edmund's water and bread to him, and returned his bars to normal. She had barely gotten herself back into her own cell and straightened the bars before Jayna reached the top of the stairs and called for the guards to let her out.

Once she was gone, the door closed firmly behind her, Pip sat on the floor behind her barred door. "So that's Jayna. I see she's in the family business."

"Yes, she is." Prince Edmund's bruised smile still managed to hold a fond, fatherly warmth. He, too, sat on the floor at the end of the length of his chains, which prevented him from reaching the door.

Pip bit into the piece of bread. The crust was too hard, and the inside had gone dry. Yet while the bread was somewhat stale, it wasn't moldy or otherwise spoiled. When she drank from the glass, the water was clear and tasted fine. "It's sparse, but not what I was expecting for prison food."

"It isn't like the cooks keep watery gruel and spoiled vegetables sitting around just in case they have prisoners who need to be fed something awful." Prince Edmund shrugged, then winced as if the movement hurt. "We'll probably be fed random kitchen scraps of varying quality. Whatever Jayna can bring us will help. We might have to be careful how much we eat, though. The guards might notice if their prisoners get too fat."

"So we're staying?" Pip gnawed off another bite of the bread.

"Can you think of a more comfortable hiding spot? We have private rooms, decent beds, and meals delivered to us each day. Even a convenient and secret way in and out." Prince Edmund set aside what was left of his bread. Perhaps chewing the tough crust hurt too much on his swollen jaw. "All in all, we're strategically placed in the heart of the enemy's palace. As long as they don't turn their torture on you, I don't see any reason why we can't spend a more or less pleasant week here."

Comfortable and pleasant wasn't exactly what Pip would have called it, especially since she doubted this would be the last time Prince Edmund would be beaten, but she could see how this would be somewhat preferable to trying to hide in some squalid hole while being hunted by Mongavarian soldiers.

Something about what he said niggled at her. "Strategically placed?"

Prince Edmund's smile turned into something downright dangerous. "Oh, yes. We might as well put this week to good use. How do you feel about becoming a spy?"

TWENTY-ONE

Fieran woke as the sunset splashed a deep orange against the deeper blue and purple of the evening sky. After stretching, he and Aaruk awkwardly scrambled to exchange places. Aaruk stretched out on the mattress while Fieran settled with a sigh and a hand pressed to his wound into the front passenger seat.

"We should stop to look at that." Dacha gestured briefly at Fieran's side before he returned the hand to the wheel.

"It'll be fine for a while longer. Moving just makes it hurt." Fieran took in the rolling fields on either side of the dirt road, the sight only broken by the occasional farmhouse and barn. "We can tend it when we stop for the night. If we stop. I can drive for a spell if we want to push through the night."

Dacha shook his head. "As much as I want to keep moving, all of us will need our sleep. We have a long trip ahead of us."

That they did. With the miles they needed to travel on unfamiliar roads, it was going to be iffy whether they could reach Landri at the right time.

Sure, Uncle Edmund and Dacha had already planned on making this trip. But Uncle Edmund could pass as a Mongavarian, and they would've had a far easier time of it.

"Have you been able to communicate with Mama more in the heart bond?" Fieran stifled a groan as the truck hit a particularly deep rut. "Is Pip still all right?"

"Yes." Dacha's gaze flicked from the road to Fieran. "She is all right, and she is with your Uncle Edmund."

"I'm not sure if that's a good thing or a bad thing." Fieran grimaced as he leaned his head against the seat. Uncle Edmund would look after Pip as if she was his own daughter. But considering Jayna was likely spying somewhere here in Mongavaria, Uncle Edmund wasn't above encouraging people to sneakiness and danger.

Dacha opened his mouth, sighed, and shook his head. "He will see that she is not hurt."

Fieran should find that comforting. But the longer he sat there, thinking about Pip in the clutches of the enemy and locked away somewhere, the more a tightness clenched his chest and clawed up his throat. What must they be doing to her to keep her captive? "I need to get to her."

Dacha glanced at him, his gaze lingering longer than before. "She will be all right, sason."

"But how do I know?" How would he stop this worry from eating him from the inside out? He would go insane before the week was out at this rate.

"You fell in love with a strong, capable young woman who can look after herself." Dacha met Fieran's gaze briefly before turning his eyes back to the road ahead of them. "Trust her. Trust that she will do what she needs to do to get to you, just as you will do what you need to do to get to her."

Fieran remembered the way his mother had growled *I*

have it handled and all the stories he'd been told over the years of how Mama had fought her way across Kostaria to rescue Dacha from the trolls.

His parents were an example of people who were not just strong together but also strong apart. That was what made them capable allies for each other as they faced whatever was thrown their way.

Fieran loved Pip both for her vulnerability and for her strength. He would have to trust that she was strong enough for whatever she faced in the next week. She had incredible magic and a core of iron when needed. She would be all right.

That didn't mean he wasn't still desperate to get back to her. Perhaps he was the one who was weak without her, not the other way around.

He and Dacha lapsed into silence. The deepening gloom of night closed around them, but Dacha didn't yet turn on the truck's headlamps. The lights of a few distant farmhouses broke the night, and someone might glance out and see the vehicle if they didn't run dark.

After a few more minutes of quiet, Dacha released a long exhale, as if he'd come to some kind of decision. His fingers flexed on the polished wood of the steering wheel. "This morning, you asked if I had ever wondered what it would feel like to be burned by the magic of the ancient kings."

Fieran winced. That had been a joke. An inadvisable one fueled by his wooziness, pain, and semi-sedated state.

Dacha continued speaking, his gaze focused on the darkness outside the windscreen, before Fieran could work up the words to respond. "My dacha had strong magic, but it was plant magic like your Uncle Weylind's. When I came into my magic, he did his best, but he could not hold back my magic when it flared out of my control. He tried to hide it, but I know I burned him. Several times."

Fieran swallowed, bracing himself against the truck door. His whole body tingled with the urge to run, to leap out of the truck, to tell his dacha to stop telling him these things. He didn't want to know. He didn't want the burden of the truth laid on his shoulders to carry. He didn't want to see his dacha's broken pieces rather than the perfect armor of the dacha he'd held up on a pedestal as a child.

But he was an adult now. He saw, with the clarity of an adult, all the ways his dacha's trauma had shaped Fieran's childhood. Fieran might not carry the same scars, but he was still indelibly marked by them, a secondhand trauma he couldn't ignore as much as he wanted to remain in his blissful ignorance.

"Weylind has never confirmed it, but I believe I burned him as well." Dacha's knuckles were white on the steering wheel now, his gaze focused ahead as if he couldn't bring himself to see Fieran's reaction. "So, no, I have never wondered."

What could Fieran say? There were no words, and any words he had were lost in the scrambling panic that screamed at him to plug his ears rather than acknowledge what his dacha was telling him.

Would he still have asked his dacha to cauterize his wound if he'd known the internal wound he'd be reopening?

Yes, probably. It had been what needed to be done, and, as bad as it had been, it had hurt far less than the whole *nearly getting his magic ripped from his body then shoved back into place* thing.

But he would've been far less cavalier about it.

"It isn't that I've wondered, exactly. Just curious. Occasionally. But not…I don't…" Fieran wasn't even sure how to explain. It wasn't like he went around hoping to get burned by the magic of the ancient kings. It was just fleeting, morbid curiosity.

"I am thankful you do not know and must instead wonder." Dacha's grip on the steering wheel eased a fraction, the set of his mouth less strained. "Because I accidentally linked my magic to the elishina, your macha can use my magic. You never had to fear burning anyone because someone who could hold back your magic was always around. We were very deliberate about that."

"I never feared my magic. Not after the first time it broke out of my control." Fieran flexed his fingers in his lap, his magic locked deep inside rather than rising to the surface as he normally would let it.

He'd been terrified the first time he'd come into his magic, and it had lashed wildly out of his control. But the moment his dacha had enfolded Fieran's magic within his, Fieran had sensed the vast, far greater strength found there. He'd never worried after that, secure in the knowledge that his dacha—and his macha with his dacha's magic—would always be there to keep his magic in check while he was still learning.

"As you contemplate getting married and, someday, having children of your own, you will need to consider how to handle the reality of raising a child with the magic of the ancient kings." Dacha's voice went slightly rough, the pink flush to the tips of his ears giving away his discomfort at bringing up these topics.

Fieran's own ears burned, and he shifted in his seat. "Pip is essentially immune to my magic."

"Yes." For the first time in the discussion, Dacha glanced

at him with a hint of a smile playing across his mouth. "She is a good match for you, sason."

Fieran blew out a breath, shaking his head as his own smile returned. "You're just wondering what kind of magical mutants we'll end up with, combining her unique magic with the magic of the ancient kings."

"Yes." Dacha's smile broadened. After a moment he sighed and shook his head. "You are going to make me a dachasheni before I am even two hundred."

"Don't rush things. I'm not even engaged yet." Fieran slouched deeper in his seat, his knees knocking against the wooden dashboard.

"I will not turn two hundred for another twenty-five years yet. That should be more than sufficient time." Dacha's grin betrayed the humor beneath his sternly serious tone.

"If you want grandchildren so much, talk to Merrik and Adry. The way they're going, they're probably going to beat Pip and me to both marriage and kids." Fieran grinned. The thought didn't itch at him the way it had before.

Dacha snorted, a twist of agreement to his smile.

Fieran's smile faded. "Merrik isn't immune to Adry's magic."

While Merrik's plant magic was decently strong, it wasn't nearly as strong as Uncle Weylind's. He didn't have any chance of holding back even the weakest tendrils of the magic of the ancient kings.

"No, he is not." Dacha's smile vanished in a blink, that hardness back in his eyes. "If they should have children with the magic of the ancient kings, they will face more difficulties than you and Pip. But Adry will be able to contain the magic. As can the rest of us. Their children will not be alone."

Not as Dacha had been, he meant.

Still, after hearing what Dacha had gone through—the pain he still carried from the knowledge that he'd burned his father and brother while coming into his magic—Fieran couldn't help the tension tightening his chest.

After a long beat of silence, Dacha shook his head again, a trace of his smile returning. "It will be good to have a generation grow up actually knowing their dachasheni."

Fieran nodded, trying not to think about all the grandparents he'd missed out on knowing.

He'd had his grandmother on his mother's side for his younger years, but she'd been gone by the time Tryndar was born. At least they all still had Machasheni Leyleira, who was Dacha's grandmother, but she was the only elven grandparent they'd had until she and Taranath married a few years ago. Taranath had already been filling the role of dachasheni even before he'd officially become theirs.

Even then, Fieran had grown up with far more family than his dacha had. He, at least, had both parents. He'd had two grandmothers. He had aunts, uncles, and cousins in abundance.

Still, there were gaps in the generations. Missing pieces that couldn't fully be filled.

What would it be like for Fieran's children, growing up with both parents, all their grandparents, aunts, uncles, and cousins, several generations deep?

"Yes, it will be." Fieran glanced at his dacha, still thrown by the sight of him with short hair and wearing a Mongavarian uniform. His parents would make excellent grandparents. Young as they were, they'd likely see their grandchildren, great-grandchildren, and possibly even great-great-grandchildren.

If Dacha survived the war. If they all survived this war.

Fieran would have to make sure he did, despite the fact

that he would sacrifice his soul, his life, and even his hair, for his children. Dacha needed to be there for Ellie, Tryndar, and all the future grandchildren he might have.

Enough serious topics. Fieran shot a grin at his dacha. "Just no more siblings, okay? I don't want any siblings younger than my own children."

Dacha raised his eyebrows. "There was some discussion on whether we wanted five children or seven…"

"Dacha…" Fieran's ears were burning. "Never mind. Forget I brought it up."

Still grinning, Dacha slowed the truck and pulled it off to the side of the road. The truck jounced over a few ruts, but there weren't deep ditches here.

"Wha—" There came a few other indecipherable moans and mutterings from Aaruk as he woke up to the bouncing and bumping.

Dacha pulled the truck behind a stand of trees and scrub brush. "This will do for the night."

They didn't have much to set up for camp. They didn't light a fire since that would be far too visible. The straw mattress remained in the back of the truck, and Fieran managed to convince Aaruk to claim that sleeping spot. The young ogre was still rail thin after his ordeal. He deserved the best bed.

Dacha and Fieran spread their bedrolls—Mongavarian ones they'd scrounged at the facility—underneath the truck where they would be protected from dew.

Once they finished setting up their meager camp, Fieran leaned against one of the truck wheels, his legs stretched out in front of him, as he munched on the cold rations of smoked meat and dried biscuit.

Dacha jumped down from the cargo bed, holding their medical kit, a canteen, and a human-magic-powered torch they'd found at Ludin. He knelt next to Fieran. "We should check on your wound."

Fieran sighed, stuffed the last bite of meat in his mouth, and lifted his shirt, holding it out of the way. With his other hand, he took the torch and positioned it on the running board so that it provided a dim light. He could tend the wound himself, but it would make Dacha feel better to fuss over him.

After untying the bandage and unwrapping the extra from around Fieran's waist, Dacha tugged on the section of bandage directly over the gash.

Fieran sucked in a breath through his gritted teeth. "Ouch, that hurts."

"We should have taken the time to change the bandage more frequently." Dacha sat back on his heels for a moment as he regarded the bandage. "It appears to have dried to the wound."

"Yeah." Fieran released a slow breath and braced himself. "Perhaps you need to just rip it off?"

"That would risk reopening the wound." Dacha uncapped the canteen and dribbled water over the bandage, using the excess bandage to keep the water from simply running off. He gave another tug.

Fieran hissed and pressed his back harder against the wheel behind him. His magic rose in his chest, sending another twinge of pain through him. He tamped down on the magic, gasping at the competing stabs of pain.

Dacha halted. "Are you all right?"

"Fine. I'm fine," Fieran gasped between his clenched teeth. "Don't get your magic half-yanked out of your chest. It's uncomfortable."

"We should check on your magic as well." Dacha braced a hand against the running board of the truck and pushed to his feet.

Aaruk's soft snores echoed from inside the vehicle. After setting up camp and nibbling on a biscuit, he'd collapsed on the mattress and gone right back to sleep.

Fieran reached for Dacha's arm but missed. "Don't…"

Dacha was already climbing into the truck, disappearing past the canvas flap.

Fieran closed his mouth and just breathed for a long moment. It wouldn't do any good to protest that his magic was all right. It just hurt when it tried to lash out. Dacha was too worried to listen, and checking on Fieran's magic was one of Aaruk's main reasons for being on this trip.

Aaruk's snore ended in a snort before his sleepy voice came from the back of the truck. Moments later, Dacha exited, followed by Aaruk.

Still rubbing sleep from his eyes, Aaruk knelt in front of Fieran and held out a hand. "May I?"

Fieran nodded. "Sorry to wake you."

Aaruk shrugged as he placed a hand on Fieran's chest. "I should've thought to check before going back to sleep."

Ogre magic tickled within his chest, and he struggled to keep a hold on his magic so that it didn't lash out painfully once again.

To distract himself from the wiggling discomfort, Fieran forced a smile. "Ogre magic is pretty impressive. I never thought there could be a magic that could overpower the magic of the ancient kings."

Aaruk grinned, even as his gaze went a little distant in that way of someone focusing on their magical senses. "That's because our magic doesn't try to overpower it. It can't. Your magic is too powerful. We, instead, use the power of other magic against itself."

"Ah. That makes sense." Fieran had, after all, been able

to overpower and disintegrate the deflecting magic eventually. But it had been when he hadn't tried to overpower it but instead had used its deflecting power against itself, such as forcing those aeroplanes to the ground or shoving back Mongavaria's tanks.

Dacha was nodding, his eyes contemplative as if he, too, were thinking through the magical theories and ramifications. "I can see why your magic would have been both exploited and feared in ages past. It is remarkable."

"Yes." Aaruk grimaced, although it didn't appear directed at Dacha. "Hiding has become our way of life, so deeply ingrained in our culture that, even when we were under attack by Mongavaria, we didn't reach out to take the hand of friendship the Alliance offered us. There were those of us in the younger generation who wanted to, you know. I've visited Escarland. I believe it's time to come out of hiding and rejoin the wider world again."

"It seems your grandmother might be reconsidering her stance on the Alliance." Fieran breathed a shallow breath past the continued tickle of ogre magic in his chest.

"Perhaps. It was a big deal that she agreed to head for Escarland rather than return to Groyria." Cutting off his magic, Aaruk withdrew his hand and sat back on his heels. "Your magic is settling in nicely. You must have exerted quite the claim on your magic while fighting the machine."

Releasing a breath, Fieran nodded. He'd learned a great deal about his magic this past year, and he likely wouldn't have been able to hold to his magic so tightly if he hadn't come to the place of owning it as *his*. "Thanks."

"Then unless you need something else..." Aaruk stood, making a motion toward the truck.

"Go on. Rest. Linshi." Dacha waved toward the truck in a dismissal.

Aaruk climbed back into the truck, and it rocked on its tires as the ogre got settled.

Fieran smiled at Dacha. "See. I'm fine. I just need rest, that's all. And this bandage changed." He motioned to his wound, where the bandage was still fused.

After another moment of hesitation, Dacha reached for the bandage again. He was able to peel some of it away, but it was still rather stuck.

Sucking in a hiss of pain, Fieran gripped the truck's running board with one hand, his other hand still holding his shirt out of the way. Perhaps he should find another piece of leather to bite.

Dacha sighed and shook his head. "I think I might have to incinerate it with my magic."

"That would probably hurt a lot less than ripping it off." Fieran squeezed his eyes shut and locked his magic deep within his chest. Even better, his dacha's magic would sanitize the wound rather than leaving bits of bandage stuck to it.

The blue of his dacha's magic flared, visible even through Fieran's closed eyelids. When Dacha's magic swept over Fieran's wound, it was a familiar and comforting tingle rather than the burning of that morning, and it eased something both within his chest and in his muscles.

After a moment, the blue magic vanished, and Fieran opened his eyes. He swept a glance over the gash, now free of the bandage, before he met Dacha's gaze.

Dacha's eyes searched his face. "You did not flinch."

"Of course not. I'm not afraid of your magic." Fieran didn't look away, hoping Dacha heard the depth in his words. Dacha had done what he needed to do to help Fieran by cauterizing the gash. That didn't change how Fieran saw his dacha or his magic.

Dacha turned away first, busying himself with cleaning the wound. "It seems to be healing well. If only you could have had more of the healing magic."

The rescued ogres had needed the healing magic more than Fieran had, and they'd divided it up between the worst of the injured.

"The little I had helped, I think." Fieran swallowed back a cry of pain as Dacha touched a wet rag to the gash. He didn't want to disturb Aaruk again nor risk any passersby hearing and coming to investigate. "How long do wounds take to heal without magic?"

"Much, much longer than a few days, I am afraid." Dacha's mouth pressed into a tight line, but he gave a little shrug, as if even he didn't know how long it would be.

He likely didn't. Neither of them had ever recovered from injuries without an elf healer stepping in. Fieran's first aid training in the army had mostly consisted of how to deal with an injury until one could get the wounded person to a healer. There hadn't been much on long-term wound care.

Funny how relative pain could become. After the whole dislocated magic thing and, even before that, crashing and breaking nearly every bone in his body, a little scratch like this was nothing.

Once Dacha had spread a salve, he wrapped a fresh bandage around Fieran's middle.

Fieran let his shirt fall over the bandage again. "I can take first watch. I got a lot of sleep earlier, and I doubt I'll fall asleep for a while yet."

Dacha opened his mouth as if he wanted to protest. But then he sighed and nodded. "I will take the second watch. We will have only two watches tonight."

That made sense. Aaruk needed rest and to regain his strength before they trusted him to stand watch at night.

As much as Pretty Face had trusted Aaruk, he was still a stranger. Neither Dacha nor Fieran would feel comfortable sleeping while he was on watch until they knew him better.

While Dacha returned the medical kit to the truck, then lay down on his bedroll beneath it, Fieran settled in more comfortably against the wheel, trying to ignore the ache in his freshly bandaged wound.

He tilted his face toward the sky, taking in the array of stars twinkling far overhead in the vast darkness.

Could Pip see the stars where she was at? Was she all right?

As Dacha had said, she was strong and capable. He had to trust that she would be fine.

That still didn't make being separated from her while in an enemy kingdom any easier to take.

TWENTY-TWO

After the guards had checked on them for the evening rounds, Pip opened the door of her cell. The bars were getting a bit bent out of shape after she'd manipulated them so often, so she'd spent some time that afternoon fiddling with the locks on the doors to their cells. Thanks to all the lockpicking practice with Stickyfingers, she had a good enough idea of the internal workings to adjust the locks in such a way that the keys still turned, felt, and sounded like they were doing something, but the cell doors didn't actually lock. She'd also used some metal from the bars of her cell to make a key to Prince Edmund's shackles so he could take them on and off at will.

Prince Edmund pushed open the door to his cell. He still hunched slightly, shuffling as he walked, but he appeared better than he had that morning. "Can you do something to the lock on the main door? We don't want them coming in while we're out of our cells."

Pip nodded and tiptoed up the stairs. Her heart hammered as she neared the door at the top. If a guard heard her or happened to open the door at that moment, there would be no hiding that she was out of her cell.

She placed a hand on the door and simply melded the bolt of the lock into place. The key would still go into the lock, but it wouldn't turn.

The guards could probably still break through the door eventually, but the time it would take would give her and Prince Edmund a chance to return to their cells.

She crept back down the stairs to Prince Edmund's side. He grinned and set off at a slow amble down the passageway. "Let's explore our accommodations, shall we?"

"I don't think you quite have the right idea of what it means to be held prisoner." Pip fell into step with him, sticking close in case he appeared in need of support staying upright.

"But my version is much more fun." Prince Edmund grinned as the two of them turned the corner.

Here the passageway was dark, lit only by the torchlight behind them. The doors on the rooms were wooden rather than barred, and when Pip opened one and peered inside, the room still had a bed, table, and other limited furnishings. This corridor would've made rather gloomy servants' quarters, likely only used for the lowest scullery maids. "I think they never got around to turning this section into a dungeon."

"Or they left it for prisoners who they don't want to treat so prisoner-like." Prince Edmund waved back in the direction of their cells. "I'd say it is for prisoners of high rank, but clearly my high rank doesn't count."

"I think their high hatred counts more than your high rank." Pip entered the room and grabbed the stub of candle in a holder that had been left on the table.

"Undoubtedly." Prince Edmund held the door for her.

"I'm actually rather surprised I even have a cell as nice as that. A hole in the ground was more what I was expecting."

Considering the Mongavarians planned to torture him, Pip wasn't going to rejoice too much at their civilized prison cells.

She hurried back around the corner, held the candle up to the nearest torch until it lit, and returned to Prince Edmund.

The two of them peeked into each of the rooms until they reached the panel of metal that blocked the passageway. It seemed to have been welded in place to a frame set into the stone.

While Prince Edmund made himself comfortable in the nicest of the servant rooms, Pip set to work modifying the panel. She could just open a hole in it, but that would mean she would have to manually open and shut it each time Jayna wanted to come through.

Instead, she borrowed more metal from the bars of one of the unused jail cells to create hinges, which she attached to both the metal sheet and the frame. Then she freed the panel from the frame, turning it into a swinging door. Once that was done, she created a hidden latch that could be opened from both sides.

As she was finishing, there was the soft scuff of footsteps from farther down the deserted hallway stretching from the other side of the metal panel.

Pip quickly shut the panel, pressing her back to it as she waited, breathing shallowly. Was that Jayna? Or some other servant wandering the halls this late at night?

Someone rapped a knuckle on the metal. "It's me. Jayna."

Pip lifted the latch on her side and pulled the panel open.

Jayna stood there, still in her black maid uniform, though she had ditched the white apron and cap. Her dark hair remained piled on her head, the sleek sides hiding her ears, while her deep brown eyes twinkled. She held a tray with two plates piled with food and had a bag slung over a shoulder. "I see you made some modifications."

"Yes. When you want in, just lift this here." Pip showed Jayna where she'd hidden the latch to open the secret door.

"You're handy to have around." Jayna grinned as she slipped through the door and closed it softly behind her. "I'm surprised Dacha hasn't recruited you for the Intelligence Office long before now."

"I would have, but I didn't know about her until the war started," Prince Edmund's voice called from one of the rooms just down the hall, although he kept his tone low enough that no one outside of this short stretch of hallway would hear him. "By the time I found out about her, the army was already in a tug-of-war with the AMPC for her. No way was I getting into the middle of that."

"I'm shocked. Something you didn't know about. You're slipping, Dacha." Jayna headed down the passageway.

Pip crept after her, not quite sure how to respond, given that she was standing right there while Prince Edmund and Jayna discussed her.

"She was well hidden at Tarenhiel's western rail terminal. And she stayed invisible enough in her university studies that she didn't catch attention then." Prince Edmund's grin was wide as Jayna and Pip stepped into the small room. He had sprawled on the bed, propping himself up with pillows. "It was quite the spy-level job, staying so out of notice while having such remarkable magic."

"I didn't do it on purpose," Pip muttered, her ears burning at the backhanded praise. She hurriedly took a seat on the one wooden chair in the room, which was pulled up to the table.

After setting the tray on the table and letting the bag fall to the ground, Jayna sat on the edge of the bed and hugged Prince Edmund, even as he wrapped his arms around her. He held her tightly, his voice low and somewhat shaky as he said, "I missed you, sena."

"I missed you and Macha so much," Jayna murmured the words, her eyes squeezed closed as a single tear trickled down her cheek.

Pip looked away. She probably shouldn't be here to witness this.

Instead, she helped herself to one of the plates of food. It seemed to be an assortment of kitchen leftovers, from a few bites of roast beef to potatoes to a jumble of vegetables. It was only lukewarm now, but it still tasted rich and savory.

After a moment, Jayna pulled out of the hug. "What are you doing here, Dacha? And like this? I would've expected you to come in disguise and sneak in, like you did before."

As Pip had suspected. Prince Edmund and Jayna had seen each other at least once in the past two years. But she wasn't going to ask for more details. The less she knew, the better.

"That was the original plan, but that plan crashed and burned rather spectacularly." Prince Edmund was still smiling, as if an airship crash was nothing major.

He proceeded to explain what had happened, and Pip remained quiet as she polished off all the food on her plate.

It hurt, remembering how safe and content she'd been on the airship. Had that really been less than a week ago?

"In about a week, there's a plan in place to end the war. I won't tell either of you more now, just in case you're questioned." Prince Edmund glanced between them, his smile disappearing. "I'll tell you if things are looking dire. But for right now, you'll be safer not knowing. Still, rest assured, help is coming. And Farrendel and Fieran are on their way. We just need to hold tight until they get here."

"I can help with that." Jayna hopped to her feet, retrieved the second plate of food, and passed it to her father. "I can keep bringing leftovers, and I brought medical supplies." She nudged the bag on the floor with her foot.

"I appreciate it, sena." Prince Edmund held Jayna's gaze for a moment, giving her a smile that quickly died. "But you will need to be careful. Very careful. With me here, the guards will be watching to see who tries to make contact with me. If they suspect you have had anything to do with me, they might realize you're an Escarlish spy. Let's hope they don't already have their eye on you because of your visit this afternoon."

"I don't think they will." Jayna dropped her gaze to her hands in her lap. "I just happened to be in the kitchens when the guards came, talking about prisoners. The cook volunteered me to take the tray. But I'll do my best to avoid bringing you food from now on."

"Good. I know it's hard, but you need to stay safe." Prince Edmund's voice held the pain of a father who knew how much danger his daughter was in simply by being here, spying on the enemy. He poked at his food for a moment before he sighed, still not taking a bite. "Which is why I'm hesitant to ask this next bit. It will put you in more danger."

"Whatever it is, I'll do it." Jayna straightened her shoulders. "I can handle it."

"I know you can." Prince Edmund's smile was both warm and proud as he regarded his daughter. But the smile faded just as quickly as it had before. "The worst part is, I won't be able to help you. They're going to be watching me closely, and most likely I won't be in any shape to be sneaking around anywhere."

He would be too injured from torture was what he meant. Pip swallowed, the meal she'd eaten rising in her throat.

Jayna paled, but she nodded, her hands clasped in her lap.

Prince Edmund's gaze swept from Jayna to land on Pip. "Which is why I'm hoping Pip will be willing to help you."

"Me?" Pip straightened on the chair. Why would he want her to help? She wasn't trained as a spy.

"Ah, so you *are* going to recruit her." Despite her pallor, Jayna grinned, first at her dacha, then at Pip.

"Yes. Your magic will get Jayna into places she can't access alone." Prince Edmund held Pip's gaze. "But I won't ask this of you if you aren't willing. You'll be a lot safer if you simply remain here in the dungeons, out of sight and out of mind. If you're caught actively spying here in Mongavaria, you'll be in much greater danger."

She could sit here in the dungeon, relatively safe and comfortable.

But if she did that, she'd always regret it. Right now, Fieran was crossing a country to get to her. The least she could do was step up and do what needed to be done here.

"I'll do it. Whatever it is." Pip sucked in a deep breath, then let it out slowly. She could handle this. She'd walked into battle before. Surely some sneaky spy stuff wouldn't be half as bad as all that.

Prince Edmund gave her a slow nod before he turned his gaze back onto Jayna. "If this plan works and we end the war, we'll need to know who gave what orders and when. We'll need proof of the war crimes Mongavaria committed in Groyria. We'll need to know which Mongavarian generals and officials are somewhat honorable and worth working with, and which ones should not be left in power. You have provided some of this information already, Jayna, but we'll need to start collecting the official Mongavarian files to take with us once we leave here."

Jayna nodded, as if she'd expected as much. "The empress has some of what we'll need in her hidden study. I've kept an eye on it, but I haven't stolen anything yet."

"We can store whatever you steal in here." Prince Edmund waved at the room. "Pip and I can keep an eye on it during the day, and it won't be in your room where you could be caught with it."

Jayna nodded, then bit her lip. "The rest of the information, though…it's in the War Office. I haven't dared try to break in there yet."

"That's where Pip comes in." Prince Edmund gestured past Jayna to Pip.

Pip swallowed. Breaking into the Mongavarian War Office sounded rather dangerous. Just what was she getting herself into?

TWENTY-THREE

As the midday sun beamed down hot and shimmering, Fieran gripped the wheel of the truck as it rumbled down the narrow macadam pavement that had replaced the dirt several miles back. They must be nearing a larger town or crossroads of some type.

Dacha sat in the passenger seat, a map unfolded on his lap, while Aaruk remained out of sight in the back of the truck. All of them wore Mongavarian uniforms with their caps pulled low and, for Dacha and Fieran, covering the tips of their ears.

"I think we should be nearing the town of Highmeadow." The map crinkled as Dacha pointed.

"Do we try to go around?" Fieran peered ahead, but he couldn't see any places to turn within sight.

"I do not think we will have much of a choice but to drive through the town." Dacha frowned as he carefully folded the map. "There are no roads that bypass the town on the map. Perhaps there is a farm track that is not marked, but we would have no way to know if it goes in the direction we wish to go or if it dead-ends at some farmer's field."

"Then it's good we prepared as best we could." Fieran patted his front pocket.

Before leaving Ludin, the former prisoners had gathered all of the identification papers they could find from the various dead Mongavarian officers and soldiers. Fieran, Dacha, and Aaruk had taken the papers that featured pictures closest in look to them. It wasn't like the photographs were that detailed, small and grainy as they were. Then they'd ensured they had Mongavarian uniforms that matched the ranks listed on their identification papers. A forged document with the commander's seal completed their disguise.

It wouldn't hold up once news of the escape spread, but they'd have two days, maybe more, before the boots on the ground got word of what happened.

The road crested a hill, and as the land beyond came into view, Fieran tightened his grip on the wheel.

The buildings of a small town clustered in the valley below. Most of the homes were wood with wood shingles of the style found in many small Escarlish villages. A few bigger brick buildings lined the main street while a large brick factory building, complete with brick chimneys puffing black smoke, loomed to one side.

But what had Fieran nearly slamming on the brakes were the Mongavarian soldiers patrolling a post before the town, a wooden gate blocking the way.

He shared a look with Dacha before he focused forward. He drew in a deep breath, trying to calm his thundering heart. "Aaruk, we're nearing the town and a checkpoint. Stay in the back. Hopefully our papers are good enough that they won't search us."

"You mean the papers your friend forged?" Aaruk's

voice came from the back, but he didn't peek his head into the front.

"Yeah, those." Fieran swallowed and tried to remember everything Uncle Edmund had taught him about speaking in a Mongavarian accent.

But as Uncle Edmund had taught them, if he played this right, he wouldn't have to speak at all.

He slowed, then halted the truck before the board set to block the way.

One of the guards approached Fieran's side of the vehicle while the other remained at his post, his rifle held loosely in his hands rather than aimed at Dacha.

The soldier halted next to Fieran. "Papers?"

Fieran reached into his pocket and pulled out his papers. He handed them over, trying for the haughty look Rothilion had worn when he'd taken over the squadron.

Dacha, too, pulled out his identification papers along with the crisply folded forged document. He handed those to Fieran. With his hair short and his jaw hard, he was doing a far better job of appearing aloof and haughty than Fieran was.

Fieran handed all of the papers over to the soldier.

The soldier didn't do more than give the identification papers a cursory glance. When he unfolded the forged document, his eyes dropped to the seal, then widened. He shoved the whole stack back at Fieran as hastily as if the papers were on fire. "Sorry, sirs. I wouldn't have stopped you if I'd known you were operating on orders for Colonel Haggan."

Fieran tipped his head in a nod toward the man, still giving him that supercilious *I'm too important to even speak with a lowly private* look.

"And, sirs?" The soldier shifted. "I wouldn't stop in town, if I were you. You probably haven't heard, but this village is on lockdown after the riots. No one is supposed to go in or out. You're an exception, of course. So watch to make sure no one tries to hitch a ride."

Fieran gave another, more agreeable nod, as if he was a commander appreciating the warning, as he returned Dacha's papers and stuffed his own back into his pocket.

Then the two soldiers hurried forward and opened the bar blocking their way. Fieran released the brake and drove forward.

Inside, the town was far too quiet and still for the middle of the day. No one was out and about besides the handful of Mongavarian soldiers pacing along the sidewalks, rifles to their shoulders. They saluted as Fieran and Dacha passed, and Fieran had to work hard not to snap an Escarlish salute in return out of habit. He took an extra moment each time, making sure he tipped his hand with the slightly more angled salute the Mongavarians used. He also eased the truck to a greater speed so that he and Dacha were passing the soldiers so quickly that the soldiers wouldn't get a good look at any returning salutes.

A few of the common people peered out of windows, the curtains fluttering back into place, as they passed by.

Near the center of town, some of the shop windows were broken, and a military vehicle had been shoved into an alley, its paint blackened from a fire. There were a few darker brown spots on the sidewalk that could only be dried blood.

Something bad had gone down here. Fieran clamped his mouth shut to keep from asking Dacha what he thought.

At the far side of town, the guards didn't stop them, but instead lifted the bar out of their way. The accommodating guard at the other end must have radioed ahead.

Once they were rolling down the road at a good clip and

well away from town, Fieran released a breath and glanced at Dacha. "That went well."

"Yes." Dacha tapped his fingers on the door handle next to him, his knees bouncing.

"And riots?" If Fieran hadn't been busy driving, he might have been jittery as well.

"It seems the Mongavarian people no longer support the war." Dacha gestured over his shoulder in the direction of the town. "At least, those in that town do not."

"That's good for the Alliance, right?" Fieran glanced from the road to Dacha and back. "They will be much more ready to surrender if the people are rioting instead of rallying in the face of the invasion and increased bombings."

"Perhaps." Dacha gave a small shrug. "We do not know if the riots are a localized thing or something that is occurring across a larger part of Mongavaria. But it will likely make our task harder."

"It will?" Fieran could only see good things if Mongavaria was on the brink of falling apart.

"Yes." Dacha's drumming fingers clenched into a fist. "We were fortunate back there. The Mongavarian government will increase scrutiny and restrict movements. We might not be able to pass as easily next time."

No, they wouldn't. Fieran flexed his fingers on the steering wheel. No matter how hard it was, he would do whatever it took to reach Pip.

THEY'D PARKED the truck inside an abandoned barn next to the bombed-out farmhouse only a mile away from a Mongavarian factory town. The town itself had some damage—collapsed walls and shattered bricks—but the factories themselves were untouched.

Sitting on a hay bale in the barn's loft, Fieran chewed on a piece of stringy smoked beef and glanced through a hole in the wall, keeping watch while Dacha and Aaruk settled onto their bedrolls for the night.

Fieran's gaze landed on the blackened remains of the farmhouse once again.

Had a family been inside when the bomb had fallen? Had the grieving man left his farm, unwilling to stay after losing a wife and children? Or had the whole family been killed in one swift blow, and that was why it was now abandoned?

At the beginning of this war, Fieran had been so horrified when Mongavaria targeted civilians at Bridgetown.

And yet here the Alliance was, killing civilians. Everyone knew bombs weren't accurate. Yet the deaths were considered an acceptable loss to fight the war. By this point, the Alliance had probably killed far more civilians than Mongavaria had at Bridgetown.

Fieran wasn't the only one who had lost his innocent optimism to this war. The whole of the Alliance had lost its innocence. They were now ruthless and bloodied and prepared to cross lines they'd never imagined crossing before.

Fieran hadn't escorted the bombing mission that had destroyed this farmhouse. If he had, the factory would have been far more damaged.

But he had still escorted plenty of bombing raids. He likely had the blood of civilians on his hands as surely as he did soldiers', and he'd carry that for the rest of his life.

Yet he'd seen what Mongavaria had done to the ogres. They'd been keeping them in cages like animals, experimenting on them, killing them as they stole their magic. Those horrors had to be stopped.

Still, he mourned the horrors that were committed in order to stop other horrors. War was awful. Death was awful, even when it happened to an enemy.

Outside, the darkness closed in deeper around the barn. Crickets chirped so loudly in the grass and from the hay that Fieran wasn't sure he would've been able to hear anything above the racket.

Aaruk had the pallet inside the truck, but Dacha had laid out his bedroll on some of the relatively clean hay that had fallen to the barn's floor. He'd fallen asleep, but now he shifted restlessly, his face twisting as if he were in pain. He made a muffled cry as he curled his arms over his head.

Fieran pushed off the hay bale. Dacha had slept restlessly the night before as well, but he'd woken before Fieran had gotten to him.

Fieran climbed down the ladder, grimacing as the movement tugged on his wound. At the barn floor, he pressed a hand over the gash as he limped his way to where Dacha lay.

Dacha thrashed again, his cry louder this time.

Fieran knelt on one knee and reached out a hand. "Da—"

No sooner had Fieran's hand touched Dacha's shoulder than Dacha lashed out with both a fist and his magic.

Fieran toppled backward, barely resisting the instinct to block with his own magic. He deflected Dacha's arm with his own raised one, Dacha's magic passing harmlessly over his head.

Dacha started, then lurched upright. Fieran had only one glimpse of Dacha's wide, panicked eyes before he rolled to his feet, placing his back to Fieran. Dacha braced a hand on the truck's hood, gasping and trembling.

"Dacha?" Fieran remained where he was, not daring to move. He didn't want to startle Dacha any more than he already had.

Dacha shook his head. He heaved a deeper breath, his shoulders rising and falling. When he spoke, he still didn't look at Fieran. "Get some sleep. I will take over watch."

"I've only been on watch an hour." Fieran wasn't sure why he was protesting.

"Fieran." Dacha's tone was sharp, sharper than he usually used when speaking to Fieran or his siblings. "Just...go."

Fieran swallowed and eased to his feet. "All right. I'll get some sleep. Tell Aaruk to wake me for the last watch then."

If Dacha even turned the watch over to Aaruk. The way Dacha was looking now, he might just do something crazy, like stay up all night.

Fieran would just have to drive tomorrow if it looked like Dacha hadn't gotten enough sleep.

Settling down on his bedroll spread out on the hay, Fieran tried to get comfortable. The gash across his abdomen hurt. His magic in his chest faintly ached.

But worse was the gnawing worry in the pit of his stomach. Would Dacha be all right? Or would this trip across Mongavaria break him?

THE SENSE of magic bursting to life yanked Fieran from sleep. He bolted upright, the movement twisting his wound and making him groan and press a hand to it.

Dacha was pacing back and forth in the narrow space between the truck and the barn wall, magic wreathing his hands and arms.

"What's wrong?" Fieran had to clamp down on his own magic before it leapt to his fingertips. "Have we been discovered?"

Dacha shook his head as he spun on a heel and marched away from Fieran. As he did, he pressed one of his hands to his chest, almost as if his heart hurt. At the door of the barn, he whirled again and paced closer to Fieran before he finally spoke. "There is trouble back home. In Aldon. Ellie and Tryndar are in danger."

"What?" Fieran scrambled to his feet, his own magic rising so close to the surface that pain twinged through his chest before he could fully tamp it down.

Dacha stalked away again, his magic still crackling around him. He muttered something under his breath, likely words meant for Mama through the heart bond rather than for Fieran.

Fieran braced himself against the truck's hood. His siblings were in danger, and there was nothing either he or Dacha could do about it all the way over here. "Can you tell what's going on? Does Mama—"

"I do not know!" Dacha snapped the words as he dug his fingers into his shirt over his heart, the other hand burying in the short strands of his hair. When he repeated the words, they were more a whimper than the bite of before. "I do not know."

Aaruk's snores ended in a snort a moment before he poked his head between the seats, peering blearily at them. "What's going on?"

There was no point in trying to sleep more tonight. Fieran pushed away from the truck and knelt to hastily roll up his blankets. "We're going to get moving."

"All right..." Aaruk glanced between him and Dacha, a furrow still between his brows.

Fieran finished packing up his bedroll and moved on to Dacha's. Once done, he tossed both into the back of the truck. "I'll drive. Aaruk, take the passenger seat."

With a glance at Dacha, Aaruk climbed between the seats. Once Dacha had clambered into the back, Fieran settled into the driver's seat. After turning on the engine, he worked the clutch and gears to slowly back the vehicle from the barn.

Dacha sat on the pallet, shoulders and head hunched. Tendrils of magic still wrapped around him but he had regained some control. At least this truck wouldn't be lit up like a beacon of blue fire in the night.

After they reached the road and set out once again, the acetylene headlamps providing some illumination, Aaruk leaned closer to Fieran. "What's going on?"

"Have you heard of the elven elishina? Heart bond?" Fieran glanced at Aaruk before turning his gaze back to the road. The back of his neck prickled with the sense of his dacha's magic.

Aaruk nodded, his eyes widening. "I have heard of it. It's considered a deep mystery of magic even to us who know magic more intimately than most."

"My parents have a very strong elishina. And right now, my dacha is sensing some kind of trouble from my mama." Fieran swallowed and flexed his fingers on the wooden steering wheel. "My youngest siblings are in trouble. They are too young to have come into their magic yet."

Aaruk's jaw hardened, his eyes filled with the haunted memories of what he had endured. "I'm sorry. Mongavaria?"

"Probably. Mongavarian agents have been hassling them for months now." Fieran had to stuff his magic deep within his chest. "They must know Dacha and I are here. That my

Uncle Edmund is here in Mongavaria. They must have seen it as their opportunity to strike."

Surely Ellie and Tryndar would be all right. Dacha wasn't there to help, but Mama could use Dacha's magic. And Louise also had the magic of the ancient kings. She might not be the warrior that Adry or Fieran were, but that didn't mean she wasn't fierce when her family was threatened. The two of them would hunt these Mongavarian agents to the ends of the earth if necessary.

Fieran kept his focus on the road as he drove long into the night.

TWENTY-FOUR

Pip tiptoed down the deserted hall following Jayna, both of them dressed in the black maid uniforms. That way if they were caught, Jayna could make up some reason for them being there. As long as they weren't caught in the empress's study, they'd be fine.

At least hemming the maid's dress had kept Pip busy throughout the day. The sewing wasn't that great, and it was a good thing it was dark right now. Otherwise, anyone would be able to see how crooked both the stitches and the hem were.

Besides sewing, Pip had also rigged up a length of wire she'd made by thinning some of the bars of the cells. The wire ran from Pip's cell, along the ceiling, and attached to the main iron door at the top corner by the hinge where it wouldn't be noticed. With the wire in place, Pip could lock or unlock the dungeon door without ever leaving her cell. Much safer than tiptoeing up and down the stairs, hoping she could get there and back without the door opening.

All of that had helped distract from the hours Prince

Edmund had been gone, only to be returned even more bloody and battered than before.

Jayna held up a hand, and Pip halted. The two of them froze, pressed in the shadow along the wall, while two guards tromped down the connecting corridor. They didn't even look down this side passageway, lulled into inattention by their familiar routine.

Once the sound of the footsteps faded, Jayna peeked around the corner before she led the way down the corridor in the wake of the guards.

Pip's heart thumped in her throat as she crept after Jayna. Her fingers itched for a wrench in her hands, a mechanical project to tinker with. That was her comfortable place. Not all this sneaking and danger.

Jayna halted before a door, glanced around, and motioned to the door. "I've picked this before, but why don't you make a key? Then I'll have an easier time getting in and out in the future."

Pip swallowed and pulled one of the small globs of iron from her pocket. Just like for the wire, she'd thinned several of the bars to arm herself with a pocketful of iron just in case. By the time she was done, there wouldn't be much left of the iron bars in the castle dungeon.

She pressed it and her hand to the door latch. Closing her eyes, she sent her magic into the latch first until she had a good picture in her mind. After that, she sent the iron into the lock, forming it into the space so that it created a key for the door. Once that was done, she unlocked the door, pushed it open, and handed the key to Jayna.

Jayna grinned at her and slipped inside. She held the door open just long enough for Pip to step inside before she closed it softly.

Pip pressed her back to the door as she squinted into the

darkness of the room. Only the light glowing underneath the door and the moonlight outside provided some visibility.

"You make breaking and entering almost too easy." Jayna made her way across the room without any apparent trouble, despite the murky darkness. There was a clicking sound, then a creaking. "But I won't need your skills for this door. The secret study hasn't been a secret since Dacha discovered it nearly seventy years ago."

"If the empress suspects that Prince Edmund knows, wouldn't this be guarded?" Pip inched her way toward the sound of Jayna's voice. As she neared, she discovered that a part of the wall next to the fireplace was cracked open.

"Empress Bella doesn't trust her guards enough to actually share this secret with any of them." Jayna opened it the rest of the way and vanished inside, her voice going slightly muffled. "There are supposed to be guards in the main study and by the outer door, but there seems to be a rather nasty stomach bug going around."

By her tone, that stomach bug was Jayna's fault. She must have slipped something in the guards' food or drink.

Pip stumbled after her, keeping a hand on the fireplace to avoid running into anything.

The fireplace extended into the secret study on the other side, a reassuring solid presence in the pitch blackness.

There was a stirring of the air and another click as Jayna closed the door after her. Then, finally, a light flared.

Jayna held it up, showing that it was a small elven light. "Let's get to work. I'll search the desk if you want to get a start on the file cabinet over there. Pull out anything that looks like it might be useful for the Alliance to have in hand when the war ends."

Pip pulled a second elven light from her pocket—one Jayna had brought for her—and set to work paging through the papers in the file cabinet. The first drawer she searched held nothing but tax reports and other innocuous internal communications. But when she started on the second drawer, it held reports on Mongavarian spying efforts in Escarland. Pip didn't even try to read more to figure out the details. She grabbed whole file folders, setting them in a stack on the floor next to her.

The Mongavarians were sure to notice someone had been in here stealing files the next time they opened this drawer. But it didn't sound like she and Jayna were trying to hide their incursion.

As she glanced at the second set of files, the word *magic* caught her eye. She halted, peering at the paper more closely.

A report of some kind of magical experiments. There weren't that many details, but it seemed to have been compiled by a General Krellian.

"Is General Krellian stationed here in Landri?" Pip withdrew the file of papers.

"Yes. He's one of Mongavaria's top generals. He works in the War Office." Jayna paused where she was perusing some of the letters in one of the desk's drawers. "Why?"

"There's a report from him on magical experiments." Pip added the file to her stack.

"His office is going to be on the top of our list when we break into the War Office." Jayna grinned, sounding far too cheerful. As if she found breaking and entering as fun as Pip found tinkering on a new mechanical project.

Pip swallowed and turned back to the file cabinet. She was swimming way out of her depth.

As the sun pierced the eastern horizon, Fieran's eyes burned after driving all night. He followed the road more by instinct than conscious thought. The road ahead curved to follow the lay of the land between two rolling hills.

When the road exited the other side and joined another, larger road, Fieran slammed on the brakes hard enough to send the pallet sliding in the back and Aaruk scrambling to brace himself in the front seat.

The road before them was clogged with trucks, horses, carts, and people on foot, all the people and vehicles laden with bags and crates and furniture.

Aaruk slumped low in the front seat, holding up a gloved hand to hide the side of his face even as he pulled the uniform cap low. "What's going on?"

"They're Mongavarian citizens fleeing the front." Fieran let the truck idle, watching the people shuffle past. "This is going to make things complicated."

Should he try to find another route? Was there another route or would all the roads from here to Landri be as jammed as this one? It would only get worse as Adry and the army pushed farther into Mongavaria.

"What do we do now?" Aaruk was scrunched so low in the seat he would barely be visible over the dashboard.

"Go forward, I guess." Fieran let the truck roll forward once again. "You'd better get in the back. Slouching like that is suspicious."

Aaruk pushed from his seat, keeping low as he crawled into the back of the truck. After a few minutes, Dacha slid into the front passenger seat with a weary sigh.

As Fieran eased the truck onto the main road, the crowd shuffled and parted, creating some space for the military truck driven by someone wearing a Mongavarian uniform. That still didn't give Fieran space to do more than roll slowly forward with the flow of traffic, but he was at least on the main road.

"How are Ellie and Tryndar?" Fieran risked peeling his eyes away from the road long enough to glance at his dacha where he was slumped beside him. When Fieran returned his gaze to the road, he had to slam on the brakes again to avoid hitting the rear end of the mule in front of the truck's bumper.

He really shouldn't be driving right now. His reactions were seriously impeded by his lack of sleep. But Dacha wasn't in much better shape.

"Safe. Or still in danger." Dacha sighed and scrubbed a hand over his face. "It was a long night, and what is coming through the elishina is jumbled."

It must still be bad, if Dacha couldn't fully interpret Mama's emotions.

Fieran flexed his fingers on the steering wheel. While worry still tightened his chest and twisted his gut, the long night of it—both for his siblings and for Pip—and the exhaustion because of it dampened the sensation somewhat. Surely with both Mama and Louise looking out for them, his siblings would be all right.

After all, Fieran had seen the rifle Mama kept over the door and heard the fierceness in her tone. Nor would he discount Louise. She was, after all, a wielder of the magic of the ancient kings, the daughter of a long line of warriors and trained by the Laesornysh.

Whoever was endangering Ellie and Tryndar had no idea who they were messing with.

"If you can find somewhere safe to stop, we should rest for a few hours." Dacha leaned his head against the back of his seat, briefly closing his eyes before the bray of a donkey had him jerking upright again.

Fieran stared with gritty eyes at the sea of displaced humanity clogging the road and spilling onto the surrounding fields before them. "I'm not sure that's going to be possible."

FIERAN TRUDGED ALONG THE ROAD, a pack on his back, both his wound and his feet aching. His stomach rumbled, but he resisted the urge to complain about the lack of food. With each breath, he choked on the dust being kicked up by the people, animals, and vehicles walking, clopping, and rattling around them.

Aaruk shuffled along beside Fieran, gloves on his hands and dirt rubbed over his face to disguise his green skin. Dacha, too, had smeared dirt on his face to hide the silvery paleness of his complexion.

Not that anyone came too close or looked at them too closely. The benefit to the gray-blue uniforms they wore was that the regular citizens on the road gave them as wide a berth as they could manage on the crowded road.

Dacha marched just ahead at a ruthless pace, his jaw set and his eyes hard. He'd relaxed somewhat once he finally received confirmation from Mama that Ellie and Tryndar were safe.

But now that relief had turned into a flinty anger that was driving him onward, Fieran and Aaruk with him.

They'd run out of fuel for the truck miles back and made the decision to abandon it. They'd packed their bags, hidden their swords in the packs and bedrolls as best they could, and set out.

Unfortunately, they hadn't been able to steal any food. There had been nothing left to steal, even if they'd wanted to, after the hordes of displaced people had passed by. Instead, they had to make do with the sparse supplies they'd taken from Ludin.

Dacha and Aaruk marched along the road as if eating only one tiny meal a day wasn't a big deal. Dacha, especially, didn't seem to even notice the lack of meals, walking at an unflagging pace as if he was running on pure elfness.

Fieran's stomach growled again, louder this time. Dacha glanced over his shoulder, shooting Fieran a look as if he thought he was drawing too much attention to himself.

As if Fieran could stop his stomach from rumbling. Worse, he couldn't even protest since none of them dared talk while so surrounded by other people.

All this walking and rationing wouldn't do any good if they didn't get their hands on more transportation. They'd never reach Landri in time at this rate, nor would their food last.

Yet finding new transportation was proving difficult. Any farm horses that hadn't been confiscated by the army were either already stolen or well-hidden. Same for trucks and motorcars.

After another two miles of walking, a village came into sight. It, too, had several factories on the outskirts, although these hadn't been touched by bombing.

At least the town didn't have any guards blocking the road, but the horde of people were flocking onto the streets, likely as eager as Fieran was to get their hands on food.

As he, Dacha, and Aaruk entered the town, the townsfolk bustling down the road gave them a wide berth, glancing at them before looking away quickly. At least their active avoidance of making eye contact meant that they weren't looking at them too closely. All they saw were the uniforms.

Something smacked into Fieran's shoulders and spattered into the side of his face. He jumped, barely keeping a hold of his magic, as he whirled to face his attacker. At least his magic hadn't hurt when it crackled against his control.

"Swine!"

"Empress's dogs!"

There were a few more shouts with increasingly vulgar words. Another tomato came from somewhere out of the crowd to splatter against Aaruk's back.

Dacha shoved Fieran behind him, his fists clenched, as a rock the size of an egg flew past Fieran's shoulder.

Would the crowd notice the faint hint of magic curling around Dacha's fingers?

They needed to get out of here. Fieran grabbed Dacha's sleeve, then Aaruk's arm, and dragged the two of them down the sidewalk. Dacha resisted a moment before he turned and jogged at Fieran's side. Aaruk stumbled, his shoulders hunched around his ears.

Shouts, tomatoes, and more rocks flew at them, chasing them down the road.

A dark alley opened between two of the buildings, and Fieran ducked into it, hauling Aaruk after him. Dacha followed at his heels, glancing over his shoulder as if prepared to halt and hold off the angry crowd if necessary.

The alley ended at an even smaller alley between these shops and the row of houses on the next street over. Fieran darted to the right, then down another alley, until he, Dacha, and Aaruk were crouched beside a pile of trash in a dark corner.

The three of them remained as they were, not moving, their panting loud in the close stillness of the alley, for several long minutes.

Fieran released a long breath and pressed a hand to his side. That had hurt. At least he didn't see any blood seeping through his shirt to indicate that he had opened the wound. "I don't think we were followed."

"I think our disguises worked too well." Dacha grimaced as he swiped a piece of tomato from his cheek.

Aaruk rubbed at a spot on the back of his shoulder. Likely a place where he'd been hit by a rock. "I'll say."

The distant sound of shouting grew louder. Was the rioting crowd coming this way? Would they go down this alley? With so many people packed into this town, a riot could turn quite deadly.

"Psst."

The voice had Dacha jumping to place himself in front of Fieran again. Fieran had to lean around him to spot the older woman peeking her head out a door farther down the alley.

She motioned to them, waving them toward her.

Fieran's breath caught in his chest. How much had she heard? Even if she hadn't overheard the words, just their cadence and sound would give away that the three of them were not Mongavarian soldiers.

What was riskier? That she thought she was helping three Mongavarian soldiers? Or that she realized they weren't Mongavarian soldiers?

The sounds in the street grew louder, echoing down the alley. The woman made the waving motion again, this time with more frantic force.

Fieran shared a look with Aaruk before he pressed a hand to Dacha's back and gave him a push forward. "I think we should follow her. At the very least, it will get us off the street. If she plans to betray us, we can overpower her."

Not that Fieran really wanted to tie up an old woman, but taking her out and using her house as a hiding spot would be safer than remaining here.

Dacha sighed, nodded, and crept down the alley toward

the woman's door. She moved out of the way, holding the door open and ushering the three of them inside.

Once Aaruk, the last in line, crossed her threshold, she shut the door, bolting it behind them. She hurried to tug heavy curtains closed, leaving the small kitchen where they stood in a dimly lit gloom.

"Now." The woman planted her hands on her hips and glanced between them. "Who wants to explain what an elf and an ogre are doing in Mongavaria?"

TWENTY-FIVE

Her heart hammering from her chest into her throat, Pip followed Jayna down a corridor of the palace in broad daylight. Both of them wore the black maid dresses with pristine white aprons and white cap. Between the cap and the way she'd pinned her curly hair into a bun, the tips of her ears were hidden.

Jayna explained the various duties that needed to be done in each of the rooms they passed, as if she really was showing a new maid around. A few of the maids even stopped to talk with them, and Jayna easily stepped in. Pip, of course, couldn't reply to any questions, otherwise her elvish accent would give her away.

Down in the dungeon, she'd left a stack of pillows under the blankets to make it look like she was still there. As she'd been sleeping most of the days away anyway, given how long she was up each night, the guards wouldn't think much of it. Besides, the Mongavarians were focused on Prince Edmund and the secrets he had in his head. As long as he remained in the dungeon, they wouldn't check Pip's cell.

Still, it felt incredibly dangerous to just walk around Landri Palace like this. It was far too bold and brave.

Yet this was the life Jayna had been living for the past two years. A humble maid by day. A spy at night. Although, she could speak Mongavarian like she belonged and her ears were only vaguely pointed.

"And this is the royal wing. Always knock and ensure the chambers are empty before cleaning. We are not to disturb the royal family." Jayna pointed her duster at the rooms as they passed. Each door was made of heavily carved dark wood of the type that Mak and Pip's dacha would probably appreciate.

One of the doors opened, and a young man stepped out. He wore a deep blue shirt with a black jacket. His black boots reached his knees while his brown hair was lightly tousled.

Jayna came to an abrupt halt before she dipped into a deep curtsy, holding the pose with her head down.

Pip hurried to copy her movements, thankful that her elven grace hid any awkwardness.

The young man glanced over them with barely a pause, as if they were part of the furniture of the hallway, before he set out down the corridor.

Once he turned the corner, Jayna straightened. Pip did as well and stepped closer, keeping her voice at a whisper. "Who was that?"

"Prince Ryland. He's in line for the throne, after his brother, father, and grandfather." Jayna's eyes lingered on the empty end of the hallway for a moment before she shook herself. "We need to keep moving."

The two of them continued winding their way through the palace until they arrived at its lower reaches. Jayna neatly got herself assigned to fetching new stockings for the youngest Mongavarian princess, Prince Ryland's younger sibling, from town.

The next thing Pip knew, the two of them were strolling across a courtyard and out a side gate of the palace.

A stiff sea breeze whipped at Pip's skirt, and she pressed one hand to her skirts, the other to the cap on her head. Behind her, the ocean spread out in layers from sandy-brown at the beach to turquoise to deep blue in the distance. White foam topped the waves as they crashed against the cliffs below the palace in a rhythmic susurration.

Before Pip and Jayna, the path joined the main road that led into the city. To their left, a huge harbor bustled with ships and noise, from cargo ships entering the docks to lines of iron warships lined up in a sheltered spot beneath the large armaments guarding the harbor's entrance. Several of the iron warships patrolled across the harbor's mouth.

To their other side, seagrass led to a stretch of sandy beach. At this time of day, the beach was filled with people, likely the rich of the city who had the leisure to spend the sunny late summer day lounging by the seashore instead of working.

The city directly before them must be the wealthy part of Landri, given the clean streets, broad brick streets, and stately stone buildings rising on either side, a sharp contrast to the dark smudge of coal smoke that lingered on the other side of the harbor.

At the very base of the causeway before the road entered the city proper, a huge sprawl of stone buildings was hemmed in by a tall stone wall topped with barbed wire.

As they passed the huge iron gate set in the wall, Jayna tilted her head in that direction. "The War Office is in there, along with all other governmental offices."

Pip risked a brief glance as they passed. The gate blocked

off a broad avenue that led to a complex of stone buildings. Men in Mongavarian uniforms guarded the gate, patrolled between the buildings, and stood before each of the doors.

They were going to break into *there*? She swallowed and faced forward. Was Jayna absolutely crazy? There was no way just the two of them could sneak into that heavily guarded area.

Jayna's stride remained the same brisk but nonchalant pace as she led the way deeper between shops, taking the time to retrieve the requested stockings, until they ended up on a street of townhouses. She leaned closer to Pip. "The gardens of these homes back up against the wall surrounding the government buildings."

Jayna paused by one of the homes, giving the street such a casual glance that it didn't seem unusual, and strolled up the drive. Pip hurried to keep up, resisting the urge to glance around.

At the end of the drive, Jayna darted around a hedge until they were next to a door to the carriage house. Jayna motioned to the door. "The lord who lives in this townhouse is currently staying at his country estate with his family. There is only a small staff keeping the house running. We can hide in here until it gets dark."

Pip unlocked the door with her magic, and the two of them slipped inside.

The carriage house was dim and dusty, the middle empty except for the muddy tracks of a motorcar left on the concrete floor. A few stalls lined one wall, but all of them were devoid of horses.

Jayna led the way to one of the stalls that was half-filled with miscellaneous junk, from a broken end table to what appeared to be parts for the motorcar. She settled into a seat on the old straw. "Now we wait."

Pip sat next to her, placing her back to the wooden wall of the stall. Perhaps while they waited, she could get her thundering heartbeat under control.

DARKNESS CLOAKED their movements as Pip and Jayna crept out of the carriage house and into the townhouse's back garden. They were now dressed in dark gray trousers and gray shirts that Jayna had stashed in the bushes sometime earlier in the week. To complete the look, they had their hair pinned up out of sight beneath knit caps and dark kerchiefs pulled up over their noses and mouths so that only their eyes were visible.

They had a couple of hours until the moon rose, and the clouds overhead hid the stars, giving them a window to sneak into the government buildings in near pitch blackness.

Pip's breath was hot against her face beneath the kerchief, and her hands shook as she and Jayna neared the back wall. Could she do this?

Someone had to. Fieran and Prince Farrendel were coming. They'd end the war. And this information would be necessary to ensure that the Alliance didn't leave a problem in the Mongavarian Empire that they'd have to solve with yet another war down the road.

Jayna pressed her back to the wall. She motioned upward before whispering, "I can get us up and over the wall, but there are glass shards and barbed wire at the top. Can you get us over that?"

Pip nodded, realized how dark it was, and swallowed to clear her throat. "Yes, I can."

Jayna reached out and pressed a hand to the ivy twining

over a lattice arbor. A hint of green glowed around her fingers and vanished into the plant.

The ivy on the nearby arbor moved, slithering over the ground until it twined up first Jayna's legs, then Pip's.

Pip resisted the urge to shiver or move as the vine wrapped itself securely around her waist.

Moments later, the vine climbed the wall, inching upward over the cracks and crevices and taking Pip and Jayna with it. Jayna's face was twisted, her eyes focused, as she gripped a part of the vine, still pouring her magic into it.

As they reached the top of the wall, Jayna halted the vine's growth and glanced at Pip.

Pip took in the jagged pieces of glass embedded into the concrete at the top, along with the rolls of barbed wire. With a deep breath, she reached out and touched the wire, pouring her magic into it. Within minutes, she had changed the coils of wire so that they formed a smooth arch instead of running along the top in sharp spikes.

Jayna grew the vines so that they ran over the wires and hoisted both herself and Pip up and over the top. Pip lifted her feet so that they didn't drag on the sharp glass.

On the other side, Jayna lowered them back to the ground.

Pip exhaled a sigh as her feet touched the solid ground once again, bracing herself against the beautifully solid wall behind her.

The vines retracted from around her waist, but Jayna left them still dangling over the wall. She pointed at it, breathing slightly more heavily as if using all that magic was tiring. "This will be our primary escape route."

"Are you all right?" Pip eyed her.

Jayna shrugged. "I have plant magic, but I'm not that

strong. I can get us back out, but using too much magic will exhaust me."

Pip nodded. If they got into trouble and had to fight their way out, magical protection would be her job. "Do you need a moment to rest?"

"No, I'm all set." Jayna flashed a grin. "Now for the fun part."

None of this was the fun part, but Pip didn't waste the breath to comment. She crept after Jayna as she led the way across the stretch of lawn and toward the shadows behind one of the stone edifices looming against the darkness.

Even at this time of night, many of the windows remained lit. Government never truly slept.

Jayna padded from one shadow to the next, glancing at the various buildings until she reached one near the center of the complex. Halting beneath a dark window, she gestured upward at it. "Can you give us a boost?"

Pip created a shield beneath their feet, lifting them upward the three feet they needed for Jayna to reach the bottom of the window.

Pressing her hand against the wooden sash, Jayna eased some of her magic into it. A moment later, she wiggled her fingers beneath the lower window and boosted it upward, the lock remaining where it was at the bottom.

She crawled inside, and Pip followed, sticking her head through the opening, hanging by her waist for a moment before she wiggled the rest of the way inside. She released her shield once she was safely inside the darkness of what appeared to be some kind of office.

"Now we just need to locate General Krellian's office." Jayna tiptoed to the door, pressing her ear to it for a moment. "Or wherever they are keeping the records. They could be in a bank of file cabinets in a basement."

Great. Pip's skin already crawled with the need to get out of there. They were going to be caught for sure if they had to wander through this building for too long.

Jayna cracked the door open, peeked out, and led the way into the hallway. When she turned back to Pip, she pointed, her eyes crinkled as if she was grinning.

Pip glanced around, not sure what Jayna had seen, until Jayna leaned forward and tapped something on the door.

Oh. A brass plaque. It conveniently had the name of the Mongavarian officer who used this office. Even better, it had a symbol to denote which branch of the military he served. This office belonged to a colonel in the navy.

This would make finding General Krellian's office easier.

Jayna set out down the hallway, Pip tiptoeing after her. They had to duck into other offices a couple of times as people strolled the corridor, but no one paused as if they'd seen or heard anything suspicious.

The corridor ended in a grand foyer done in wood paneling with an oak staircase rising to the second floor. Military flags hung above the doorways for the various corridors, denoting which military branch occupied each.

"Handy of them to make this building so easy to navigate." Jayna grinned and headed across the way toward the hallway underneath what Pip assumed was the Mongavarian army's flag. Unlike Jayna, she certainly didn't recognize which flags belonged to which service.

This corridor had even more bustle than the previous one. Pip and Jayna had to duck into empty offices several times to avoid being seen.

Finally, they reached General Krellian's office. It remained dark, as were the offices around it.

Pip used her magic to open the door, then she and Jayna slipped inside.

As they had in the empress's study, Jayna took the desk while Pip perused the file cabinets.

The stuff contained in these files had her stomach churning. The men stationed in Groyria. The ogre villages wiped out.

And then a file had her pausing. It was all here in black-and-white, stark numbers. A systematic rounding up of the ogres and holding them in various internment camps in Groyria near the border before group upon group was taken to the Ludin facility in southern Mongavaria for magical experimentation.

Pip closed the file and grabbed the whole thing. She pulled out a few more files before she turned to look for Jayna.

Jayna stood by the desk, a piece of paper gripped in her hands. As if sensing Pip's look, she half-turned to her, the paper trembling. No, her fingers were trembling as they clutched it. "This…this is a report that they captured Uncle Farrendel and Fieran. General Krellian gave the order to take their magic."

"But they didn't succeed. Your dacha said they were both fine." Pip hugged the files to her chest, her heart thumping harder again.

She'd been trusting what Prince Edmund had told her. But what if he was mistaken? After all, he was getting news of Fieran and Prince Farrendel from his heart bond with Princess Jalissa who was talking to Princess Elspeth who was communicating with Prince Farrendel through their heart bond. It was a rather convoluted method of communication back and forth. Could something have been missed?

"They probably are." Jayna sucked in a breath, her shoulders shuddering for a moment, before she straightened. "I don't see any reports confirming that their magic has been taken. So that's a good thing. Let's grab this stuff and get out of here."

That sounded good by Pip. They'd already stayed long enough as it was.

After gathering a few more files and papers, she and Jayna stuffed it all in a leather satchel they found stashed under the desk.

Then the two of them sneaked into the corridor and back the way they'd come, dodging patrols and various military men going about their late night duties.

At the hallway they'd been in before, Jayna glanced at each of the doors.

One of the doors down the corridor opened, and a slim man in a Mongavarian uniform stepped out. His gaze flashed directly to Jayna and Pip standing there in their nondescript gray clothing.

Pip squeaked and jumped, her heart racing, as she clutched the satchel with all the incriminating papers to her chest.

Jayna ducked her head, grimaced, and shoved the door open. "That's done it." She all but shoved Pip into the room.

Pip stumbled but somehow managed to get her feet underneath her enough to scramble across the room. At the window, she grabbed the sash, swung her feet out, and dropped to the ground. The satchel banged against her, but she kept hold of it.

Jayna landed next to her. "Come on."

The two of them raced through the buildings toward the wall. In the office behind them, the man shouted, raising the alarm.

They just had to get out of the complex, then they could disappear into the city streets.

More shouting rang out behind them. Then a gunshot cracked against the night.

Pip bit down on her squeal of fright and ran faster at Jayna's heels. She didn't dare use her magic. Not yet, anyway. At this point, the Mongavarians didn't know a person with her kind of magic existed. At least, they didn't know she was in Mongavaria.

But if they saw her magic, realized what she could do, and started putting the pieces together…

Then she and Prince Edmund would be in a lot of trouble.

At the wall, Jayna grasped the vine, her green magic blasting into it with such force that the whole thing glowed green for a moment.

The vine snatched Pip off the ground with such speed that her breath was squeezed out of her. She gasped as she was yanked upward, and it was all she could do to cling to the satchel and try to catch her breath.

"There they are!" The shout rang out just as they crested the top of the wall. For a moment, they hung, suspended and silhouetted against the night sky.

A gunshot rang out just as Pip was being yanked downward again. Pain sliced across her upper arm, and this time she cried out, slapping a hand to the spot.

Then she was below the wall, even as more gunshots blasted into the quietness of the night, the bullets zipping high overhead.

Her feet touched the ground in the relative safety on the other side of the wall. The vine released her before it slumped, already brown and dying.

"How badly are you hit?" Jayna appeared in front of her, her gaze searching.

"Not…not bad. I don't think." She was shaking as if

caught by an extreme chill. Something hot squeezed between the fingers she had pressed over her upper arm.

Jayna's gaze settled there as she tugged the handkerchief off her face. "Let me see."

Pip gritted her teeth and lifted her hand. Her arm burned, and just shifting it enough for Jayna to get a better look had tears gathering at the corners of her eyes.

Jayna stepped closer and peered at Pip's arm. "I think it is just a graze. But we can't take time to deal with it now. We have to get moving."

Then with a swift, almost ruthless movement, she wrapped the handkerchief around Pip's arm and tied it tightly.

Pip kept her mouth shut around her cry of pain, forcing herself to take off her own handkerchief and hand it to Jayna.

Jayna tied that one around her arm too before she took the satchel from Pip. "Come on."

The two of them briefly ducked into the carriage house, grabbed the bundles they'd made of their maid uniforms, then set out through the back garden of the next house over.

Thanks to all the commotion, lights were turning on in the townhouses, and people were peering out windows and opening doors to see what was going on.

Jayna kept them going through the back gardens until they reached an alley just as motorcars screeched around the corner of the main street, men shouting orders.

Pip stumbled in Jayna's wake, following her lead as they ran through the streets of Landri. At one point they even used the train tracks to cut through a neighborhood without being seen.

Eventually, they found a sheltered spot near the castle where they changed back into their uniforms. The black fabric hid the blood that was still seeping through the two layers of handkerchiefs and dribbling down Pip's arm. Instead of heading for the door they'd gone out of, Jayna led them to a sheltered spot where she used her plant magic to lift them up and over a garden balustrade.

When the two of them finally stumbled their way through their back door into the dungeon and into the room they'd turned into their headquarters, Prince Edmund took one look at them and pushed off the bed where he'd been lounging. "What happened?"

"We were seen leaving. Pip was shot." Jayna collapsed onto a chair, breathing hard, her face washed in a gray pallor.

"How bad?" Prince Edmund's gaze focused on Pip as he shuffled toward her.

Pip's legs wobbled, and she somehow tottered her way forward. "Just a graze. That's what Jayna said."

"Let's take a look." Prince Edmund stepped out of her way and motioned her to sit at the edge of the bed.

Pip's head felt kind of light. She sank onto the edge of the bed and, shakily, pulled up her sleeve. It was so sticky with blood that her fumbling fingers struggled to grasp it.

"May I?" Prince Edmund reached for her sleeve but stopped short before touching it.

Pip nodded and dropped her hand, far too tired to wrestle with the fabric.

Despite the bruises swelling his fingers, Prince Edmund's touch was gentle as he rolled up her sleeve and peeled off the handkerchiefs.

Pip peeked down at her arm. A deep gash cut across the top of her arm, blood welling, flesh gaping.

Her stomach churned, black spots dancing before her

eyes, and she had to look away before she threw up or fainted.

"You'll need stitches." Prince Edmund grimaced and glanced down at his hands. "Jayna, I'm afraid you'll have to do it. My fingers are in no shape for such delicate work."

Stitches. In her arm. Pip's head swirled even more. She'd been hurt before. One couldn't work in mechanics without getting a few nasty gashes. But there had always been an elf healer on hand to patch her up quickly afterward.

"There's a suture kit in there. I just need a moment." Jayna gave a halfhearted twitch of her hand in the direction of the bag of medical supplies on the floor. Her face was still far too pale, her voice slightly breathy as she still gasped for air.

"Are you all right?" Prince Edmund tensed, as if he wasn't sure if Pip or Jayna needed him more.

"I'm fine. I just used a lot of my magic tonight." Jayna gripped the satchel, her jaw working and her eyes pained. "I'm sure they saw my plant magic. They'll know an elf broke into their War Office."

Prince Edmund went still for a moment, his eyes going distant as he absorbed that. "They'll blame me. I'm the only one they know of here with ties to the elves."

"I'm sorry, Dacha. They'll…they'll…" Jayna's voice broke as tears welled up in her deep brown eyes and spilled down her cheeks.

Prince Edmund crossed the room and pulled Jayna into a hug. "It will be all right, sena."

"No, it won't. They'll torture you even worse. All because I messed up." Jayna pressed her face against her father's shoulder.

"You didn't mess up." Pip forced herself to pick up one of the handkerchiefs again and pressed it to her wound. Her head was swirling, but she tried to concentrate. "That man just opened the door at the wrong moment and saw us."

"I should have been more cautious. I should have heard his footsteps. Something." Jayna's voice was a broken murmur between semi-silent tears.

"Shh, sena." Prince Edmund rubbed a hand up and down her back. "That could have happened to anyone. Even me. Don't blame yourself. We'll just adjust our plan and go from here."

After a moment, Jayna sniffed her way into conquering her tears, and she lifted her head.

Prince Edmund took a step back, although he still gripped her shoulders in the elven-style hug. "Whatever happens in the next couple of days, don't react. Don't come to check on me. Understand? You need to stay away so that they don't suspect you. Take the papers we've stashed here and hide them elsewhere. Not in your room. Don't tell me where you've hidden them, got it?" He glanced over his shoulder at Pip. "Did they see your magic?"

"No. I didn't use it. I didn't want to give away that I had it." That seemed rather foolish now that she was clutching a handkerchief to a bullet wound while blood dripped through her fingers.

Prince Edmund nodded. "That's one surprise we still have up our sleeve, at least."

"But they might know they hit one of us. I cried out." Pip couldn't help the tremble that traveled down her spine and into her fingers.

"Not ideal, but not something to worry about." Prince Edmund tottered back to the bed and sank onto it next to Pip. "We'll stitch your wound, and you'll have to do your best to pretend you aren't hurt. Hopefully they won't suspect you. We only need to hold out a couple more days."

Pip swallowed and hunched more on the bed. Those handful of days until whatever big plan went down seemed so far away. How badly would Prince Edmund be tortured? Would the Mongavarians torture her too? She'd never hold up. She'd tell them everything.

And what if Fieran and Prince Farrendel didn't arrive like they were supposed to? Would Prince Edmund's big plan work then?

After a few more minutes, Jayna pushed to her feet and dug out the suture kit.

Prince Edmund glanced at Pip, his gaze searching her face. "I would offer to let you hold my hand, but I fear my fingers would never hold up. But you are welcome to lean against my shoulder, if you wish."

Pip nodded, scooted a little closer, and leaned against his shoulder. He wasn't her dacha, but he was doing a good job of stepping in as an uncle.

Jayna sat on Pip's other side near her wounded arm. After rolling up Pip's sleeve out of the way, she set to work cleaning the gash.

Pip clamped her teeth around a whimper and squeezed her eyes shut. That hurt. A lot. And Jayna hadn't even started on the stitching yet.

Prince Edmund wrapped an arm around her shoulders. It would have seemed entirely for comfort, but he rested his hand on her elbow below her wound, holding her arm in place so that she didn't move.

A tear trickled down Pip's face, and she didn't reach up with her free hand to swipe it away. It wouldn't matter. She'd probably cry lots more before this was over.

She just wanted Fieran. She wanted *him* to hold her close while her gash was stitched up. She wanted to cry into his shirt and feel safe again. She just had to know he was all right.

And if he wasn't and the Mongavarians had done to him what they'd been doing to the ogres? She wasn't sure how she would survive it.

TWENTY-SIX

Fieran tensed, his hands clenched at his sides. Should he reach for his sword? Bolt out the door? She was just one old woman, yet she could cause a lot of trouble if she called the Mongavarian authorities.

Yet she was currently hiding them from the rioting crowd. Surely that counted for something.

Dacha stepped forward, placing himself between the old woman and Fieran. He didn't unleash his magic. Yet.

The old woman swept another glance over them before she shook her head and gestured to the table. "I can see it is a long story. Why don't we get comfortable? We're going to be here a while if you wish to wait out the riot."

As long as they kept this woman in sight, she wouldn't be able to call the authorities or otherwise betray them. If anything, they were more a danger to her than she was to them.

Fieran stepped around Dacha and slid into a seat at the small table that dominated the center of the kitchen. Aaruk followed his example, taking the seat to Fieran's right. After giving Dacha a long look, the old woman sat across from

Fieran, leaving the final seat with its back to the door for Dacha, if he should decide to sit.

With another glance at Dacha, who had taken a spot next to the door where he could both watch them and guard the door, Fieran faced the old woman. It seemed explaining would be up to him. "We were on a mission to rescue ogres who were being held at and experimented on at a facility in southern Mongavaria."

The old woman's gaze shot from Fieran to Aaruk.

Aaruk crossed his arms, his smile disappearing into a hardened look. "It's true. My cousin was killed. His magic was ripped out of his chest."

Fieran swallowed, his chest aching in the memory of that sensation. This was the first time Aaruk had talked about what he'd experienced.

"I'm sorry." The old woman ducked her head, releasing a heavy sigh. "Not everyone supports the empress's Mongavaria. I've lost the kingdom I once knew."

Aaruk tipped his head, although his hard expression didn't ease.

Fieran cleared his throat. "We rescued the ogres and Alliance prisoners-of-war. They made a dash for the border. However, two of our friends were captured and brought to Landri. We're on our way there to rescue them."

He wasn't going to explain that they were hoping to end the war or that there were more detailed plans. She might sound sincere, but he wouldn't trust her that much.

The old woman gave a nod. "I see. If you'll trust me, you're welcome to spend the night here. I will see that you are slipped out of the village in the morning."

Fieran glanced from the old woman to Dacha. While he was inclined to take the woman up on her offer, he'd trust Dacha's instincts more than his own.

After a moment, Dacha gave a slight nod.

"Thank you for your hospitality." Fieran held the woman's gaze. "We'll gladly stay the night."

FIERAN CLIMBED down from the back of the cart, his legs and rear end aching from the miles of jolting and bouncing over the rough road. Due to the crush on the main road, she'd taken them down winding back roads, little more than two ruts through the rolling fields, until they were now in a deserted stretch with nothing but fields of rustling, drying corn on either side of them.

Dacha and Aaruk climbed down after him with Aaruk rubbing his rear end. Dacha's expression twisted just briefly, his only acknowledgment of the discomfort.

The old woman turned her borrowed horse and cart around, the cart covered with a canvas that no longer hid anything but the cart's emptiness. She halted the cart next to the three of them, her gaze sweeping over them. "Please end the war. For the sake of the true Mongavaria."

All Fieran could do was nod in return. None of them had mentioned that goal, but perhaps she had sensed it.

Then she flicked the reins, and the cart horse set out once again, plodding down the road toward the village they'd left far behind.

Once she was gone, leaving the three of them standing in the road, Fieran turned to Dacha. "Where to now?"

They'd had a good night of sleep and their first decent meals in several days. But while the woman had spared some of her food to provide a good supper and breakfast, she hadn't had anything else to give them for their travels.

Dacha reached into a front pocket of the Mongavarian

uniform and pulled out their much-folded and abused map. Stepping off to the side of the road, he held up the map. "We are here, I believe."

It had been rather difficult to tell where they were going when they had been meandering through endless fields and tiny paths.

Glancing at the map, Fieran took in the miles they had to go, his stomach sinking. "At this rate, we are not going to arrive in Landri on time."

Walking was taking too long. Even if they stole another truck, it would be difficult to arrive in time, thanks to all of the displaced Mongavarian citizens filling the roads and pouring into the towns, severely slowing any travel.

He peered closer at the map, grinned, and pointed. "There. That's how we'll get to Landri."

Dacha raised his eyebrows. "Are you sure?"

"We hijacked an airship. Hijacking an aeroplane should be far easier." Fieran's grin stretched wide across his face. Inside his chest, his magic burned, eager to leap to his fingertips. No pain accompanied the inner crackle of his magic, and that buoyed him still further.

His magic was healing, and he was going to fly again.

DARKNESS SHROUDED the outskirts of the Swenson Aerodrome while only a few low red lights inside one of the hangars provided light. The other three hangars were dark, and giant holes were punched in the roof of the nearest one, steel ribbing visible. Piles of wreckage were heaped against one of the other hangars while the whole area was pock-marked with craters. Another destroyed building was still smoking.

At least the Alliance Flying Corps bombing had been rather effective here.

The fear of more bombing worked in their favor as Fieran, Dacha, and Aaruk crept through the surrounding field and dodged the various patrolling guards, whose only sources of light were shielded lanterns. If the place had been well-lit, they would've had a much harder time infiltrating the aerodrome.

They'd already had a hard enough time hiking across the rolling hills of Mongavaria for the past several days, avoiding the crowded roads and villages. It had been a long hike with very little food, an aching wound because he didn't have access to an elven healer, and nothing but a bed on the ground to look forward to each evening. If Fieran had wanted to be that footsore and hungry, he would have joined the infantry.

But now, a single row of aeroplanes were parked beside the airfield, just waiting for him to steal one and finally fly once more.

Fieran darted between the aeroplanes, peering at each one. He needed to find an aircraft that had at least three seats. A fighter or scout with only one or two seats wouldn't fit all of them.

As he went down the line, his stomach sank. At this point, he'd take an aeroplane that was even somewhat functional. While it was gratifying to see how shot up and destroyed these aeroplanes were, it was rather inconvenient for their hijacking plan.

At the end of the row, he finally located four aeroplanes with three seats. They appeared to be some kind of scout aeroplane or small bomber with two seats facing forward in a cockpit with a third to the rear manning a machine gun. They must have been new or transferred from somewhere else recently since they were in much better shape than the rest of the aeroplanes.

"I think one of these will work," Fieran whispered and rested a hand on the side of the nearest aeroplane. "Let me check the fuel levels before we pick one."

They wouldn't have a chance to refuel, even if he knew how to do that. He had to make sure whatever aeroplane they picked wouldn't just conk out on them.

Annoying fuel-burning engines. He couldn't wait to get back to the Alliance with magic-powered engines.

He climbed into each of the aeroplanes, checking what he guessed was the fuel gauge. Two of the aeroplanes were completely full while the other two only had half tanks.

Fieran chose the aeroplane with a full tank that was farthest down the line and motioned for Dacha and Aaruk to join him. Once they'd crept to him, he whispered, "We'll take this one."

Dacha peered around before he knelt. "Get it. I will start the distraction."

"I can help if you wish." Fieran held up his hand, although he didn't unleash his magic. "It has been nearly a week."

"No, not yet. Rest your magic for one more night." Dacha laid his hand on the ground. "I can handle a small distraction alone."

He hadn't expected anything else. Fieran motioned to Aaruk. "Take the rear seat."

Aaruk nodded and clambered into the aeroplane, settling into the rear-facing seat. Fieran found the toe step on the side and settled into the unfamiliar pilot seat. Thankfully, the pilots had left their flight caps and goggles in the aeroplane, and Fieran tugged them on, though he left the goggles on his forehead for the moment.

He swept a glance over the gauges. They had a few not installed on Alliance aeroplanes, including the fuel gauge, and far more switches.

After a few moments, he located the switch that he thought would turn the two engines on, but he didn't flip it yet.

Blue bolts flared around Dacha's hand and burst into the ground. They shot off into multiple directions, rushing through the ground and reaching for various points in the aerodrome.

A building to the far side of the hangars exploded in a flash of blue giving way to orange. More blue magic climbed over many of the parked aeroplanes before they exploded in balls of fire.

A siren alarm rang out over the sounds of shouting and anti-aeroplane guns barking out toward the sky.

As Fieran had hoped when he and Dacha had discussed this plan. The Mongavarians assumed this attack was coming from the air. In the darkness, they wouldn't have been able to see any aeroplanes in the sky, and with how quiet Alliance aeroplanes were compared to the roar of the Mongavarian engines, they wouldn't think it strange that they hadn't heard them.

Men came running in their direction, and Dacha cut off his magic. He stood, poised, although he didn't climb into the aeroplane just yet. He would need to take out any of the Mongavarians who seemed inclined to take this aeroplane.

Pilots reached the section of aeroplanes that Dacha had left untouched, and engines roared to life.

Fieran waited another few seconds before he flipped the switch.

Nothing happened but a clicking sound.

Was this the wrong switch? He'd never tried to start a Mongavarian engine before.

He peered at the Mongavarians starting their aeroplanes. There seemed to be someone spinning the propeller before the engine roared to life.

"Dacha," Fieran hissed and gestured at the front of the aeroplane.

For a moment, Dacha glanced from him to the other aeroplanes before he nodded and headed for the front of the aeroplane. He gripped one of the blades and tugged it downward.

The engine gave a little shudder, but it didn't fully catch.

Dacha grabbed a blade again and gave it another quick tug downward.

This time, the engine caught with a shaking rumble. Dacha leapt back as the propeller spun into motion, quickly whirling into a blur.

Fieran grinned at the feeling of an aeroplane coming to life around him again. It had been less than two weeks since he'd last flown an aeroplane, but how he'd missed it.

Several of the aeroplanes that had first spun up were moving forward, headed for the airfield.

After another moment, Dacha grabbed the wheel chocks, tossed them aside, and jumped onto the aeroplane as it rolled forward. He sank into the seat behind Fieran as Fieran steered the aeroplane into line with the others.

In the darkness, no one gave them a second glance, not even the men at the end of the airfield who waved each aeroplane forward once the previous one had successfully taken off.

When it was their turn, Fieran spun the engine all the way up. These fuel-powered engines felt sluggish compared to the quick-responding magically-powered engines. The rumble was so loud that his ears hurt with it even with the slight muffling provided by the flight cap.

At least the feel of the rudder bar on his feet and the control column in his hands was familiar, although there was no talk button. After all, there was no radio. He would have said the cockpit was silent without all the familiar radio chatter, but the engine noise far made up for the lack.

The aeroplane rumbled down the airfield, jouncing and bouncing like a sluggish, drunken turtle. The end of the airfield rushed ever closer, marked only by men holding lanterns.

Finally—*finally*—the aeroplane's wings caught the air, dragging the aeroplane from the ground. Fieran tugged the nose upward, willing the aeroplane to claw its way into the sky. It rose slowly, both engines choking the air with exhaust. Hot oil splashed back into his face, and he tugged his goggles down to protect his eyes.

The other aeroplanes ahead of them were only black shapes against the dark sky. In the confusion of the scramble, none of them even got close or seemed to think anything of it as Fieran turned his aeroplane in a different direction, pointing its nose toward Landri.

Toward Pip.

TWENTY-SEVEN

Pip swiped at the tears running down her face.

The screams and shouts of pain had finally stopped, although she wasn't sure if that was a good thing or a bad thing. Were they done torturing Prince Edmund? Or had he died?

Guards had come for Prince Edmund first thing that morning, dragging him from his cell and out of his dungeon before either of them had even been served their paltry breakfast of hard bread.

The screams hadn't started until early afternoon.

The iron door at the top of the stairs clanged open. Guards marched through, dragging a limp and bloody body between them.

Pip pressed her hands over her mouth to stifle her gasp as she huddled on her cot.

The guards didn't so much as glance at her as they opened Prince Edmund's cell and dumped him inside. They didn't even bother with the shackles this time, as if they knew the spy prince was too incapacitated to need the secondary level of security.

No sooner had the upper door closed than Pip shoved her power through the wire, locking the door behind the guards so that they couldn't get back in. Then she pushed open the door to her cell, keeping her injured arm tucked close to her body, and ran across the corridor. "Prince Edmund?"

He didn't stir. Not when she opened the door to his cell. Not when she knelt next to him. Not even when she rested a hand on his shoulder.

"Prince Edmund." She tightened her grip on his shoulder, but she didn't dare even give him a shake. How badly was he injured this time?

She dragged the blanket from his bed and lumped it underneath his head. Once she'd done what she could to make him comfortable, she hurried from the cell and fetched the medical kit from the room around the corner.

She couldn't do anything like stitch his wounds that would give away to the Mongavarians that someone had been here. But she dabbed away the blood with scraps of cloth and spreading salve over wounds where the Mongavarians wouldn't see.

Prince Edmund didn't stir the entire time. He occasionally groaned in pain, but that was all.

As she was finishing up, the door at the top of the stairs rattled. Then there came a banging as a guard tried to open it.

Pip leapt to her feet, her heart hammering. Pain shot through her injured arm at the sudden movement, and she gritted her teeth. Grabbing all the medical supplies, she dashed from Prince Edmund's cell, ran down the hall for the spare room, and stuffed all the items under the bed. It was the only thing she could think to do with them.

The banging was growing worse. Before too much

longer, the guards would grab an acetylene torch and a crowbar to get the door open.

She returned the lock on Prince Edmund's cell to normal before she returned to her cell and did the same. Once she had taken another moment to get her breathing under control, she sent her magic down the wire to unlock the door.

She didn't wait to see the result. She sank onto her cot and pulled her blanket around her to hide any blood on her clothes.

There came a massive bang accompanied by the ringing of metal on stone. Someone swore.

Footsteps pounded against the stairs before several guards came into view. Yet they didn't reach for either cell door. They merely stood to the side at attention.

After a moment, softer footsteps scuffed on the stone. Empress Bella herself swept into sight, a golden dress swathed around her petite figure. One of the men Pip had seen standing beside the empress on the dais—likely her son, the emperor-to-be based on his age—strode behind her.

Empress Bella faced Prince Edmund's cell, her mouth twisting in an expression that was somewhere between disgust and satisfaction. "Guard, wake him up."

A soldier stepped into view carrying a bucket. He splashed the water over Prince Edmund's still form.

He groaned and finally shifted, his eyes cracking open before falling shut.

"Prince Edmund." Empress Bella's far-too-grandmotherly tone sent shivers over Pip's skin.

Prince Edmund's eyes flickered open again. He gave a weak laugh between bloodied lips. "I see you came to gloat."

Empress Bella pressed her mouth into a tight line, a flash of anger in her eyes. "I see you are still unwilling to tell us what we want to know. But perhaps your little spy will be more willing to talk."

Little spy? Had they caught Jayna? Pip clutched the blanket tighter around herself, her heart pounding.

Prince Edmund rolled onto his side, reaching for the bars to pull himself somewhat upright. "No. She has nothing to do with this."

Yet instead of pulling Jayna from the shadows, Empress Bella waved her hand toward Pip's cell. Two of the guards moved in her direction.

Right. They thought Pip was one of Prince Edmund's spies. Well, she kind of was, now.

One of the guards opened the door and stood back while the other stomped into her cell. She cringed away from him, her heart in her throat, her mind racing. Was this the point she was supposed to flee? Should she simply pretend she was a terrified, powerless girl? Not that the *terrified* part would take a lot of pretending.

The guard grabbed her upper arm, right where she'd been wounded. She cried out as he dragged her to her feet.

Empress Bella's gaze sharpened, and the crown prince took a step forward, his eyes narrowing. "Mother, wasn't one of the spies shot?"

"Yes." Empress Bella stepped forward as Pip was hauled from the cell. The empress's gaze swept over Pip, her mouth twisting, before she reached out and yanked up Pip's sleeve, revealing the bandage around her upper arm. "Two spies broke into the War Office. And here are two spies in my dungeon. One with a bullet wound."

"The use of elven magic must have been him." The crown prince jabbed a hand at Prince Edmund. "One of those infernal elf heart bonds."

Pip swallowed, avoiding the empress's gaze and instead

meeting Prince Edmund's. Seeking what, she didn't know. It wasn't like he could reassure her that their carefully constructed mining tunnel of deception wasn't about to come crashing down on their heads.

Prince Edmund's eyes were wide—at least as wide as they would go with his face swelling—before he schooled his expression back into that more languid neutral.

"Search their cells. I want to know how they got out and where they've hidden the paperwork they stole. I want guards stationed here at all times. They are never to be out of sight." Empress Bella swept one last glance over Pip, her gaze dismissive, before she turned to Prince Edmund. "Regardless of what we find, enjoy your final night alive. You and your spy will be executed by firing squad in the morning."

With that, Empress Bella spun on a heel and swept down the corridor with all the speed of the ninety-year-old grandmother that she was. At the stairs, she had to lean on her son's arm to climb upward.

Pip's legs were shaking, her heart pounding, as she tried to take in those words *executed by firing squad*.

The words didn't have time to settle before she was hustled off to a new cell, this time on the side of the passageway without windows. A maid was called—not Jayna—who thoroughly searched Pip to make sure she didn't have anything hidden on her person.

Prince Edmund was moved to a new cell as well next to her instead of across the way as before. He, too, was searched, and they found some wire and a lockpick he had on him.

Then guards turned the dungeon inside out, including searching the rooms around the corner. They found the medical supplies she had stashed under the bed, as well as a few other things Jayna had fetched for them.

At least the guards assumed that Prince Edmund and Pip had gotten out with his lockpicks and that the two of them had been the ones sneaking out somehow and taking those items. Thankfully, the guards didn't seem to suspect that they'd had someone else inside the castle helping them.

But they still could get suspicious. Especially since they didn't find any papers in the dungeon. After all, Jayna had stashed those somewhere, and not even Prince Edmund knew where.

At last, the bulk of the guards left with only two soldiers remaining behind, one staring into each of their cells. It seemed the empress had been very literal about Pip and Prince Edmund never being out of sight.

Pip pulled the rather musty blanket of this new cell around her shoulders and tried to ignore the weight of the guard's stare on her. She wouldn't sleep that night while under constant watch like this.

Would the guards allow them to talk? She had to swallow several times before she could get her dry mouth and constricting throat to work. When she finally spoke, she used dwarvish so that the guards couldn't understand. "Is this the time to escape?"

The guard outside of her cell kicked his boot against the metal bars. "No talking. Especially not that jibberish."

"Not yet." Prince Edmund also spoke in dwarvish. He lay on his cot where the guards had dumped him. "We might as well enjoy Mongavaria's hospitality for one more night."

The guard in front of his cell kicked his door. "As he said. No talking."

"But...tomorrow..." She couldn't even say it out loud.

Prince Edmund tilted his head toward her, raising his eyebrows as much as he could with all the cuts and bruises on his face. "They can't actually execute you by firing squad. You can shield yourself. And hopefully me, if it comes to that."

He really shouldn't sound so cavalier about execution. Yes, she could shield herself from bullets. They would be nothing after the bombs and crashing airships and everything else she'd shielded herself from throughout this war.

But she still couldn't stop the words from echoing in her head anyway. She couldn't be quite so unworried about *execution* as he was.

"And if they have one of those magic-stealing machines?" Pip could barely get the words out past the fear squeezing her throat and chest.

"Then we hope our rescue arrives in time." Prince Edmund settled back as if getting more comfortable on his cot. "And hope my daughter has enough sense to stay away tonight."

"That's it. Don't make me come in there." The guard before Prince Edmund's cell brandished his rifle, as if he was prepared to beat Prince Edmund with it if he said another word.

Pip swallowed and forced herself to lie down with her back to the guard. Her fingers shook as she clutched the blanket around her.

She wanted to get out of here. Away from dungeons and executions and danger.

Was Fieran on his way? Would he arrive tomorrow morning as planned? Or were she and Prince Edmund on their own?

TWENTY-EIGHT

Fieran guided the Mongavarian aeroplane toward the pink dawn blazing around the horizon ahead, reflecting off the sparkling waves of the ocean. He flexed his cold fingers on the control stick and wiggled his toes within his boots. While he was flying lower than he normally would for combat, it was still chilly in the air without proper gear.

Against the blush of dawn, the white spires of a castle glowed with the same pink, its graceful silhouette rising on a bluff high above the crashing waves. A city sprawled down the bluffs and around the harbor formed by a large river mouth. The forms of large ships barely crested the far horizon, out of sight of land but visible here from the sky.

"There it is. Landri." Fieran had to turn his head to shout to Dacha.

Dacha gave a nod before he turned and shouted over his shoulder to Aaruk.

Fieran scanned the ground spreading out before them. He needed a long straight and flat field or road to land. But this close to the city, farms and manor plots were broken into small sections rather than large fields ideal for landing. The main street followed the curves of the river with the rest of the roads branching outward in less than straight lines.

There. At the very edge of the city itself, the road straightened enough to give him a place to land. It was hard to tell at this height, but he was pretty sure the space between the brick buildings was wide enough for the wings. At least the traffic on the road was minimal, given the early hour.

Fieran circled lower to line the nose up on the road.

Dacha leaned forward and gripped Fieran's shoulder. "That road was not designed for an aeroplane landing. Nor does it appear spacious enough for such maneuvers."

"I think we'll fit. Probably. This landing might be a little interesting." Fieran gripped the control stick more firmly, feeling the way the two fuel-powered engines shuddered through the Mongavarian aeroplane.

"As long as it *is* a landing." Dacha's tone was acerbic, and someone who didn't know him wouldn't have heard the trace of his humor. "You are making a habit of crashing."

"The airship wasn't my fault." Fieran circled one more time, the aeroplane so low that the handful of early risers below were pausing and looking up, shading their eyes.

At least the large guns surrounding the city hadn't yet been trained on him. He was in a Mongavarian aeroplane, after all. Perhaps they assumed his aeroplane was in distress and that was why he was doing something as crazy as landing on a city street.

The aeroplane sank lower, and he feathered the engines to as little power as he could without them entirely cutting out. The tops of the buildings appeared only inches below his wheels, as if he was about to clip them.

The straight street opened before him, and he eased the

aeroplane lower, the wings only feet away from the build-ings on either side.

Ahead, people dove out of the way, likely screaming, although he couldn't hear them over the roar of the engines. Horses reared as people dragged their carriages to a halt while vehicles swerved to get out of the street, clearing the way before him.

The right wings clipped an awning, and the whole aero-plane crabbed in that direction. Fieran gave one last burst of power and yanked on the rudder and ailerons to straighten the aeroplane out before it could crash into the buildings.

Then the wheels touched down on the cobblestones, bouncing and hurtling forward at a blazing speed. He switched off both engines and hung on. The tail of the aero-plane thudded onto the road, the tailskid screeching.

He'd landed on cobblestones once before. But back then, the upward curve of the Alliance Bridge had eventually brought him to a stop.

Here the road was flat and, if anything, had a downward slope. Unlike the miles he had on the bridge, there was only a limited length before a sharp curve essentially ended the runway in a brick building.

Dacha gripped Fieran's shoulder, his fingers tight and near bruising.

Fieran braced himself, flaring the ailerons to do whatever he could to slow the aeroplane. What he wouldn't give for a little bit of elven plant magic to catch the wheels and halt their careening flyer.

The aeroplane hurtled down the street, rushing closer, closer, closer, toward a head-on crash with a solid brick building.

His magic crackled against his hold in his chest, and he had to swallow back the whoop of exhilaration that built inside him. He might have matured throughout this war, but there was still something about being at the brink of death that made him feel so very alive.

Ahead, the smaller shops turned into grander edifices, the street lined with tall lampposts instead of the small lamps attached to the buildings themselves.

Fieran braced himself as best he could. "We're going to—"

Both sets of wings struck the iron posts of the first set of gaslamps. The impact jarred the whole aeroplane, flinging Fieran forward so swiftly that he bashed his forehead against the leather padding on the edge of the cockpit.

The tips of the wings ripped and splintered, letting the aeroplane roll forward. But by the time the splintered ends of the wings ran up against the next set of lampposts, the aeroplane had slowed to the point that this second impact halted it entirely.

Fieran straightened, peeled his fingers out of their death grip on the control stick, and rubbed his forehead. He'd likely get a bruise, but there wasn't any blood. "Is everyone all right?"

Dacha released his death grip on Fieran's shoulder. "Yes. But that was a near thing."

Fieran just nodded as he peered around them. The few people out and about were gaping at the aeroplane now wedged across their otherwise quiet street. A carriage came around the far corner, the horses trotting smartly, before the driver jerked back on the reins.

Dacha yanked off his flight cap and goggles, grabbed his swords, and leapt down from the aeroplane, landing gracefully in the street. With a glance at the gaping crowd, he released a flicker of his magic, sweeping it around him.

Those few people who hadn't had the sense to run

screaming at the sight of an aeroplane landing in the middle of the street *now* took off running and screaming in terror.

Subtle surprise was out. Though, that had probably been out from the moment Fieran ditched an aeroplane in the road.

Fieran peeled off his own flight cap and goggles. Grabbing his swords from where they had been tucked next to him, he scrambled down from the aeroplane with Aaruk following.

Dacha had set his swords on the lower wing and was shrugging out of the Mongavarian uniform coat, leaving behind only the plain gray shirt beneath. At Fieran's look, he gave a rolling shrug. "I do not wish to go into this battle dressed as the enemy."

"Good call." Fieran set his swords next to Dacha's on the wing and began divesting himself of his own Mongavarian uniform coat. It had served its purpose in getting them across the empire, but now it was time to fight under his true allegiance, even if he didn't have an Alliance uniform to put on instead. The plain gray shirt and the blue-gray uniform pants would have to do.

At least they had plenty of time. The street was now utterly deserted.

Dacha gave a sigh and reached to touch his shortened hair. "The last time I ended a war, I also had short hair."

Fieran paused, his gaze shooting to Dacha. While he'd heard, vaguely, that the trolls had cut Dacha's hair, he somehow had never put it together that Dacha had short hair during the events in the stories he'd heard growing up.

Dacha met Fieran's gaze, holding it a moment before his disconsolate look disappeared into something else. A tilt of a smile banished the frown while a glint sparked in his eyes. "But it is just as well this time, I believe."

Fieran straightened his shoulders and held his gaze. With their short hair, similar features, and identical swords, they were a matched set. More clearly father and son. Two of the warriors Laesornysh.

Grinning, Fieran tapped the tip of one of his own pointed ears. "At least the short hair makes our ears more obvious."

"That it does." Dacha picked up his swords, slung them over his shoulders, and buckled them in place.

Fieran matched Dacha's movements, also buckling his own swords into their familiar place across his back.

Dacha reached out and gripped Fieran's shoulders, holding his gaze once again. "Short hair or long, sason, we are elven warriors, and we will end this war as elves."

If Dacha's short hair didn't make him less of an elven warrior, then Fieran's short hair didn't lessen him either.

"Yes, we will." He straightened as he faced his dacha, the weight of that knowledge settling deep within him. He was human. And he was elf. And neither of those things made him less. He was capable and worthy of ending this war at his dacha's side.

Dacha's returning smile glinted in his eyes for a moment before the smile faded. "How is your magic?"

After a week of not using it, his magic simmered hot and eager beneath his skin. "It's been a week. My magic is fine."

"It is." Aaruk stepped forward and held out a hand. "I can check again if it would make you feel better."

Dacha's flat look was answer enough. Fieran sighed and unbuttoned the first few buttons of his shirt, standing patiently while Aaruk went through the now familiar routine of pressing a hand over the now nearly healed spots where the machine had been hooked to him.

Aaruk had no sooner brushed his magic against Fieran's than he yanked his hand back with a hiss, shaking his fingers. "Yeah, he's fine. I think he will be in far more danger if he doesn't use his magic soon and expend some of it."

Dacha made a noise in the back of his throat, his deep frown remaining.

"See, I'm fine." Fieran hurried to rebutton his shirt. "Where are we headed?"

Dacha waved his hand at the street ahead of them. "Landri Castle and the empire's governmental offices are near the ocean on this side of the river. We will head there. Hopefully Edmund and Pippak are being held in one of those places. If not, then we will force someone to tell us where they are."

Now that sounded especially good to Fieran.

The three of them marched down the street in silence for several moments before Fieran glanced at his dacha again. "What happens if we come up against one of those magic-stealing machines again? Do you think the two of us can take one out without passing out?"

"Oh, don't worry about those." Aaruk gave a shrug when both Fieran and Dacha looked to him. He held up his hand. "Deflecting magic, remember?"

"If you can deflect the magic-stealing magic, then how was ogre deflecting magic taken to use on their aeroplanes?" Fieran shot Aaruk a glance before he swept his gaze over the street ahead of them, looking for threats.

"One, the magic's purpose isn't for stealing other magic. That's what those scientists twisted it to do." Aaruk's mouth pressed into a tight line, his eyes flashing. "I can deflect the twisted magic coming from these machines. But that machine hooked up directly to your body was something else entirely."

With a nod, Fieran clamped his mouth shut. He'd experienced that difference firsthand. The machine under the airship had latched onto his magic, draining it, but it hadn't been carving the very essence of his magic out of his chest.

The tromping of boots, too rhythmic to be anything but a squad of Mongavarian soldiers marching double time, echoed from somewhere around the far corner.

Fieran glanced at Dacha, even as he reached over his shoulders for his swords. "So what's the plan?"

Dacha faced the street and drew his swords, letting his magic twine over his hands and down the length of the blades. A smile, both grim and strangely glinting, creased his face. "We destroy stuff until they surrender."

For a moment, Fieran could only blink at his dacha. Then he grinned as he drew his own swords. When he released his magic, it crackled down his blades and pooled around him on the street. There wasn't so much as a hint of pain in his chest.

While Fieran couldn't see it, Aaruk must have been using his magic because Fieran's magic skated away from the ogre when it got too close, the taste of that familiar now-not-unknown magic filling his magical senses, although the wielded version was much stronger and deeper than the false and twisted version he'd encountered before.

As Fieran joined his dacha facing the distant, oncoming Mongavarian soldiers, he flexed his fingers on his swords, readying himself. "Was this always the plan when you and Uncle Edmund were going to be here on your own?"

"No. Your uncle's plan was a lot more subtle. It involved far more sneaking and far fewer explosions." As if growing tired of waiting for the enemy to come to him, Dacha stalked down the street once again, his magic crackling around his feet. "This is my version of the plan."

"I like your plan." Fieran hurried to catch up. "I knew

my tendency for explosions didn't come from my human side."

Dacha's grin was feral, blue light dancing in the depths of his eyes. Behind them, Dacha's magic reached their abandoned aeroplane, and it went up in a concussive explosion. "No, it did not."

Fieran smirked back and let his magic burst more powerfully from his fingertips and down his swords. Time to rescue Pip and end this war.

TWENTY-NINE

Pip jerked awake from a light, restless doze at the sound of boots tromping down the stairs. By the time she rolled upright, blinking at the weak light of dawn filtering through the windows across the way, a dozen guards had marched into the passageway. Six of them headed for Prince Edmund's cell while the other six faced hers.

Across the way, Prince Edmund struggled to push himself onto his elbows.

Pip forced herself to let go of the blanket as the guards unlocked the door to her cell. "Now?"

"Not yet." Prince Edmund answered her dwarvish with the same language.

How long did he want her to wait until she revealed her magic? Was he going to wait until they were facing down the guns of the firing squad?

Probably. He was Fieran's uncle, after all. She now knew where Fieran had gotten his flare for the dramatic.

Pip stood and didn't resist as four of the guards entered

her cell. They shackled her hands in front of her before shoving her into the passageway.

The guards shackled Prince Edmund's hands before they dragged him from his cell. He seemed to be struggling to walk, his legs unable to hold him. She wasn't sure how much was an act and how much of his weakness was real.

The two of them were marched up the stairs and through several corridors before they were hauled through a door into the courtyard that Pip had seen through the window of her original dungeon cell.

She and Prince Edmund were dragged to a spot where several buildings created a sheltered spot near the outer wall.

There, another dozen soldiers were loading their rifles as they stood behind a wall created by a double layer of straw bales. Likely to absorb any ricochets off the stone wall.

Pip swallowed and staggered closer to the guards dragging Prince Edmund. "Now?"

"Not yet," Prince Edmund murmured, hanging nearly limp in the grip of the guards.

The guards hauled Pip and Prince Edmund to a spot in front of the outer wall of the castle. When the guards released Prince Edmund, he crumpled to the ground. One of the guards gave a huff, dragged Prince Edmund back to his feet, and shifted him to where a ring was set into the wall, likely for hitching a horse, back when horses were the primary transportation. He shackled the prince's hands to it.

Prince Edmund gripped it, his legs still wobbling and sagging beneath him as he propped himself up against the wall.

Pip's hands, too, were shackled to another metal ring. The guards probably thought that more secure than tying her to a wooden post, but she breathed a tiny sigh of relief.

Only a tiny one. It was hard to feel too relieved or confident while staring down a line of rifles.

"Do you want a blindfold?" The guard next to Pip held out a black cloth.

Pip swallowed yet again, trying to get her voice to work. "No." The word was a mere squeak of breath. She gave a shake of her head to reinforce her refusal.

She wasn't particularly brave. Her heart hammered harder as she faced the line of soldiers with their rifles, although those guns weren't yet pointed in her direction. Even knowing she could shield herself with her magic, she could barely breathe past the fear squeezing her chest.

But she needed to be able to see when it was time to escape, and she didn't want to fumble around with trying to get a blindfold off.

Prince Edmund, too, shook his head, refusing a blindfold.

The guards retreated, leaving her and Prince Edmund standing alone in front of the wall.

Pip cleared her throat, her heart so loud she wasn't sure she would even be able to hear his answer. "Now?"

Almost unbelievably, Prince Edmund's mouth curved with a hint of a smile. "Not yet."

How much longer would he wait? The sun was rising, the soldiers were ready, and she and the prince were standing with their backs to a wall. Any longer, and the firing squad would start shooting. Surely that would be pushing the dramatics too far, even for Prince Edmund.

More footsteps rang in the stillness of the early morning a moment before another group of guards rounded the corner of the buildings. In their center, Empress Bella minced along, leaning on the arm of her son.

Of course the empress wouldn't miss the execution.

She'd want to be here to witness the death of her spy nemesis.

This must have been what Prince Edmund was waiting for. Pip shifted from one foot to the other. "Now?"

"Almost..." Prince Edmund's gaze sharpened, and he straightened somewhat. "Can you cast a shield around us and around the Mongavarian crown prince?"

Pip eyed the distance. It was harder creating a shield that wasn't directly over herself, but in this case, the distance was short enough that she could do it. Besides, these were two tiny shields. Nothing compared to the large shields to hold off bombs. "Yes, I can. Over the empress, too?"

The empress sucked in a breath, her mouth opening as if she was going to start some kind of gloating speech.

"No, just the crown prince. She'd be too much of a hassle to take along, I think." Prince Edmund didn't even seem to notice the men who were lining up, their rifles pressed to their shoulders, their elbows resting on the straw bales in front of them. Instead, he glared at Empress Bella, his grin sharp. "Now."

Pip reached into her chest and let her magic, finally, flare outward. A shield flashed around her and Prince Edmund. She had to concentrate harder to create a second shield around the crown prince, essentially imprisoning him in place.

The soldiers in front of them shouted. Several of them lowered their rifles and fired, the bullets pinging off her shield and ricocheting back into the courtyard. The guards surrounding the empress hustled her away, even while the guards who were supposed to be protecting their prince bumped and slapped Pip's shield, trying to free him.

Then the soldier at the end of the line reached down and

fumbled with something. Something whirred to life before it latched onto Pip's magic and *tugged.*

She cried out, stumbling, although the shackle attached to the ring in the wall pulled her up short. "They got...it's..."

Prince Edmund swore in elvish and rattled the shackle on his hands. "Can you get us free?"

Her magic was draining, as if sucked down a deep mountain shaft. The shield around the Mongavarian crown prince dropped, and his guards grabbed his arms, hustling him away as quickly as they could.

Gritting her teeth, Pip poured more magic into the shield before her and Prince Edmund. If that dropped, she'd die. The soldiers facing her wouldn't hesitate.

Creating a tendril of magic that the machine hadn't latched onto yet, she shoved it into her shackles, not trying for any subtlety in preserving the metal. Instead, she ripped the shackles off as the metal flexed and parted.

With shaking steps, black spots dancing across her vision, she stumbled to Prince Edmund, gathered another wisp of her magic, and yanked the shackles from his hand.

But that was all she could tear away from the relentless pull of the machine greedily gobbling up her magic. She pressed a hand to the stone wall, trying to draw strength from its solidness, as she held her shield in place with every last scrap of resolve.

Thanks to the draw of the machine, her shield had been pulled forward, its leading edge now covering the straw bales and across the front of the machine. Parts of it were becoming filmy rather than a strong shimmer.

Prince Edmund shoved away from the wall, half-scrambling, half-crawling across the cobblestones until he fell against the straw bales. The top bale toppled to the side, revealing the machine that had been hidden, the extending wires invisible in the cracks of the cobbles.

The soldiers on the other side of her shield beat at it with their rifle butts, only inches from Prince Edmund's head. Any moment now, and one of them would break through her weakening magic.

With a cry—of pain or determination or perhaps both, Pip couldn't tell—Prince Edmund slammed what was left of his shackles into the part of the machine on their side of the shield. He did it again, then a third time.

Something shattered. The machine gave a shredding, grinding noise, giving Prince Edmund just enough time to roll to the side behind the protecting straw bales before it exploded. The nearest straw bale burst into a cloud of golden stalks while the soldiers behind the machine went down with screams of pain.

Pip gasped as her magic snapped back into her grip with a painful lash across her senses. Her knees hit the cobblestones with another sharp rap of pain.

"Are you all right?" Prince Edmund grimaced as he shakily pushed onto his elbows.

"Fine, fine." Pip gasped in a shuddering breath, trying to gather herself.

Somewhere in the distance, something exploded, the cobbles vibrating beneath her fingers. The crackling taste of both Fieran's and Prince Farrendel's magic washed through the air, sparking against her magical senses.

Fieran was here. He was coming for her.

That thought galvanized her, flowing into her chest and outward through her limbs. She shoved more magic into her shield, even as she staggered back to her feet. Her knees throbbed, but she was otherwise unhurt. She'd lost a bunch of her magic, but she still had enough curling in her chest for what she needed to do.

Halfway across the courtyard, the crown prince was still being hustled away in the clutches of his guards, their progress slowed by the soldiers pouring into the courtyard from all directions, running toward this far corner.

Pip reached out, her brain struggling to compartmentalize the two streams of magic, and blasted a shield around the crown prince. At that distance, she couldn't create a more fiddly, exact shield so she caught the crown prince's guards and a number of soldiers in the shield as well. But it would do until she could get closer.

Hurrying forward, she knelt beside Prince Edmund. "Fieran and Prince Farrendel are here."

She couldn't help the grin that crossed her face. Fieran was here. Everything was going to be all right.

"That would explain it." Prince Edmund smirked as another explosion roared, breaking the stillness of the morning. He gripped the straw bales next to him and tried to get his legs beneath him.

Pip grabbed him under the arm and pulled, heaving him to his feet.

Prince Edmund pushed away from the bales, and his legs promptly gave out beneath him. "Well, that's going to make escaping somewhat slow."

"I was hoping you were mostly pretending." Pip propped herself beneath Prince Edmund's arm, grunting as his weight settled heavily across her shoulders. Oof, he was heavy. Gritting her teeth, she took a step, telling herself that she was a dwarf. She wasn't going to collapse under his weight.

"Nope, not pretending. Wish I was." Prince Edmund

gripped his shackles with one hand as he shuffled a step forward. "Ready to get out of here?"

"More than ready," Pip gasped between panting breaths. She could do this.

Fieran was out there somewhere, and she was finally headed his way.

CHAPTER

THIRTY

Fieran stalked at his dacha's side, his swords gripped in his hands, their blades red with the blood of the few Mongavarian soldiers who'd dared still attack.

His magic sparked against Dacha's, and yet even as they sizzled against each other, they also twined together, a blaze of blue bolts shimmering through the air and coating the ground as far as Fieran could see in any direction.

This was his magic fully unleashed, and he let it travel outward as it wished with only the barest hint of control. When his magic touched people or buildings, he left them alone. But any hint of gunpowder he exploded, any weapon he melted, and any military machine he consumed.

To his left, grand houses rose high above the street. On his other side, the road ran along the river, its broad rippling waters separating them from the far bank, which contained the industrial heart of Landri. The merchant ships and factories were giving way to warships and warehouses filled with military material.

Fieran shot out a hand, sending his magic sizzling and hissing over the surface of the river to climb over the first of the warships resting at anchor. This one was a small coastal cruiser, tiny compared to the massive battleships he'd seen at Dar Goranth.

He swept his magic over the ship and into the passageways. When his magic encountered people, he let it zap rather than incinerate, herding the sailors from the ship. Men scurried into sight before they either dove into the river, swimming as fast as they could away from the ship, or raced down the gangplank onto the dock, dashing away into the morning.

Once the ship was clear of people, he let his magic penetrate to the heart of the cordite magazine in the center of the ship.

With a powerful boom, the ship exploded in a ball of flames and shrapnel that pummeled into his magic. He incinerated the smaller pieces while deflecting the larger section back towards the explosion.

"I have the next one." Dacha grinned, that wild light in his eyes, as he flung his own magic across the river. It swarmed over the next ship in line, a nearly identical cruiser. Mere minutes later, men poured from the ship like rats before the ship went up in a fireball.

Already, the men on the next few ships over, having seen the destruction coming their way, fled even before the magic reached their ships.

Over and over again throughout this war, he and Dacha had proved that they could kill in great quantities. But today, they would show Mongavaria that they were so powerful they didn't need to kill to win the victory. They could do it, instead, with a mere wave of their hands and a storm of magic.

Beyond the line of warships, the edge of Fieran's expanding magic flowed into the warehouses, encountering the sense of gunpowder and metal. He closed his magic around it, blowing it up in an inferno that shook the ground and rose in a black and orange cloud high above the city. Closer to him, he sent more of his magic leaping over Dacha's to cascade over the next warship.

More explosions roared at the edge of the city. Dacha's magic must have found some of the gun emplacements that surrounded it.

The unrelenting explosions thundered in the air, punctuated by heaving shudders through the ground. Clouds of acrid smoke hung heavy and low over the city while the wailing screams of thousands of terrified people keened on the breeze.

At the beginning of the war, Fieran could never have marched at his dacha's side like this, matching him magic for magic. Before, he'd been an undisciplined boy wielding his magic clumsily. Now, he was a hardened warrior, honed by war and embracing his magic in a way he never had before.

With shouted orders, the tromping of boots, and the creaking of a wheeled artillery gun, a line of Mongavarian soldiers arrayed themselves across the road in front of Dacha, Fieran, and Aaruk.

Dacha flicked a hand at them, his magic slamming into the artillery gun and tossing it backward. Fieran reached out with his magic and gripped each of the rifles in the soldiers' hands, melting them even as the soldiers yelped and dropped them. Aaruk hung back, staying out of Fieran's and Dacha's way.

Most of the soldiers broke formation and ran. Only a handful pulled out knives or bayonets and dashed forward, as if they thought they could take on two elven warriors with nothing but tiny blades.

With his magic so fully unleashed, there was too much

magic to drag back to confront the soldiers. Instead, Fieran stepped forward in line with Dacha, leaving plenty of space between them, and raised his swords even as his dacha raised his. Their blades already winked red in the morning light.

Just because he wasn't setting out to cause a bloodbath this morning didn't mean he'd avoid a fight when he was forced to it.

A soldier ran at him, and Fieran knocked the bayonet out of the way with one sword while the other swiped a red line across the man's throat. He leapt over the falling body to strike at the next soldier, almost subconsciously shifting to the side to give his dacha more room for his own whirling strike.

They were two of the warriors Laesornysh, unleashing death with the deadly dance of their elven blades. All those years of training, all those mornings spent with a sword in his hand and his dacha's voice pushing him toward discipline, it had all been for this. The moment he fought at his dacha's side.

Fieran stabbed his sword through the last soldier facing him and yanked it out again.

Dacha stepped over the last of the dead bodies, his jaw hard, and stalked up the cobblestone street, rising in a steep hill before them. Fieran fell into step with him, Aaruk hurrying in their wake.

With barely a thought, Fieran sent his magic through more of the warships. One by one, they exploded. A few of the ships seemed to be frantically getting underway, trying to escape before they were destroyed at their moorings like the others.

Then he and Dacha crested the hill, and there Landri Castle stood, a jewel of white stone on picturesque cliffs above the crashing waves of an ocean glittering in the rising sun.

Below the castle, the broad mouth of the harbor was clogged with warships, both those fleeing the destruction and those guarding the entrance. Two hulking shapes of gun emplacements loomed on either side of the harbor, further preventing entrance to Mongavaria's enemies.

High above, airships drifted over the ocean, further guarding the castle and the city from intrusion from the sea. Several airships had turned, heading inland, as if they were trying to decide if they should bomb their own city in an attempt to take out Fieran and Dacha. As of yet, they hadn't unleashed their bombs, nor did they have those magic-stealing machines.

"There it is." Fieran gripped his bloody swords in his hands.

"Yes." Dacha gestured with one of his swords, his magic sweeping ahead of them. "Landri Castle, and that should be the governmental offices."

A large complex of stone buildings dominated the left side of the street, sitting just at the base of the hill from the causeway that led upward to the castle. A high wall with barbed wire at the top surrounded the buildings, and the guards at the gates lowered their guns, preparing to fire.

As fun as blowing up a bunch of stuff was, the whole point was to end the war. And they could only do that if someone with the authority to do so surrendered on Mongavaria's behalf.

Not to mention, he needed that same someone to tell him where Pip was.

Fieran and Dacha strode down the gentle slope, Aaruk behind them, until they reached a spot directly in front of the broad gates of the government buildings. The guards on the wall opened fire, the machine guns juddering in their grips.

Dacha incinerated the bullets with a dismissive wave of his hand. "I will clear the buildings and force the occupants to face us. Do the same for the castle."

Fieran turned slightly so that he half-faced away from Dacha, trusting that his dacha would guard his back. He blasted another wave of his magic toward the castle, and a smattering of gun emplacements around the castle boomed their attempt to defend their monarchs.

Catching the shells with his magic, he slung them into the river mouth where they exploded with gouts of water spraying high into the air. He then latched on to each of the guns, melting the metal even as he touched off the stashes of ammunition.

Then his magic swarmed over the castle walls, wreathing the shining white towers with crackling blue magic.

Somewhere in the castle's courtyard, his magic brushed against another magic, happily leaping over the wonderfully familiar power.

"Pip!" Fieran shouted her name into the fury of his magic, even though she was too far away for her to hear him.

"What was that, sason?"

Fieran glanced over his shoulder and grinned at Dacha. "Pip's here! She's alive! She's using her magic."

Hopefully that was a good thing. And if it wasn't, Fieran would destroy anyone trying to hurt her.

Pip hauled Prince Edmund forward, even as she forcibly drew the Mongavarian crown prince closer to them with her imprisoning shield. The crown prince and his guards stumbled as they dug in their heels, but they couldn't resist the strength of her magic.

Once they were close enough, she placed a smaller shield around just the crown prince and shoved outward, pushing the guards away from the prince. The guards beat at her shield with the butts of their guns and stabbed at it with their bayonets, but her shield didn't budge.

Taking a few more steps closer, she dragged the other shield backward until she could merge the two shields.

Prince Edmund let go of his grip on Pip and stumbled toward the crown prince, all but falling the last few feet into their prisoner. Prince Edmund held up the manacles that had been on his wrists. "I wouldn't advise attempting to resist. You've seen what she can do."

The crown prince glared from Prince Edmund to Pip and back. But he didn't resist as Prince Edmund grabbed his arms and shackled his hands behind his back, assisted by Pip re-forming the shackles into their proper shape.

As soon as he finished, Prince Edmund's knees buckled, and he caught himself by his grip on the crown prince.

Pip hauled Prince Edmund's arm across her shoulders again, propping herself beneath him. Her back and shoulders ached from his weight, but she forced herself forward.

The crown prince whirled, his shoulders tensing as if he was contemplating trying to lash out at them in some way, even with his hands behind his back.

Pip shoved a shield into place between them, turning her single shield into two domes once again, although she kept them attached this time.

Cursing, the crown prince stumbled back, calling Pip—and women in general—a number of unflattering things.

"That's what you get for taking one look at a tiny woman

like me and assuming she couldn't be a threat." Pip was rather done with this crown prince, his family, and his castle. She'd had more than enough of their hospitality.

"Rather hypocritical of them." Prince Edmund sounded far too cheerful for a man who couldn't walk on his own right now. "Considering they are ruled by a woman. The Mongavarian soldiers who captured us really should have realized that you are a far greater threat than I am."

"Hardly." Pip staggered forward a few steps, already breathing hard. Between carrying most of Prince Edmund's weight and holding two shields in place with her magic, she had to grit her teeth and dig into the depths of her dwarven strength and elven endurance.

This escape was turning out to be rather disagreeable. Especially since she was literally carrying the bulk of it solely on her shoulders. Still, she muscled through it. Fieran was here, and she was going to get to him no matter what it took.

Ahead, soldiers packed the courtyard, their rifles aimed in her direction. Several of the large guns on the castle wall top were now trained down at them while soldiers manned three machine guns in a line stretching across the castle gates.

Prince Edmund's arm tightened around her shoulders, sending a fresh stab of pain through the bullet wound in her upper arm. At her flinch, he released his grip, as if remembering the wound. "I'm sorry. Will you be all right, facing all of this?"

Drawing in a deep breath, her knees wobbling, Pip tightened her grip on the back of Prince Edmund's shirt and straightened her shoulders as much as she could beneath his weight. "I've held off bombings. This shouldn't be anything too difficult. Besides, are they really going to open fire when we have him?"

She nudged the shield with the crown prince over a few feet so that the man stood more squarely in the path of all those guns.

"True. If they open fire, hoping to break your shield, then they'll be giving up their crown prince as lost." Prince Edmund lowered his voice, and she wasn't fully sure he was still talking to her when he added, "We can only hope his mother actually has a scrap of feeling in her body and doesn't sacrifice him. She has plenty more heirs, after all. Far younger, more promising heirs."

Pip grimaced and shoved both shields forward. Capturing the heir to the Mongavarian throne wouldn't do much to force a surrender if the empress was willing to simply sacrifice him to the cause.

Ahead of her, the crown prince's face had washed nearly as pale as the strands of white in his gray hair. Despite the fact that he could likely hear the discussion they were having in Escarlish, he didn't comment. Perhaps he, too, had no idea how disposable he was to the Mongavarian throne when it came down to it.

There was no way out of this but through.

Step by step, Pip crossed the courtyard, hauling Prince Edmund, the crown prince, and her two shields with her.

For the first few yards, the soldiers held their fire, as if everyone, even their commanders, weren't sure what to do. Then there was a shouted order, and the soldiers hurriedly affixed their bayonets to the ends of their rifles. With another order, the horde of them rushed forward. They swung their rifles downward, stabbing at Pip's shield with their bayonets.

Pip gritted her teeth and shoved more magic into the

shields. The bayonets bent when they came into contact with her magic and bounced off.

She forged onward, pushing and shoving the soldiers aside with her shields as if they were a herd of cattle and she was the cattle catcher on the front of a train.

The crackling sense of Fieran's magic grew closer, even as more explosions tore through the air and vibrated into the ground beneath her feet. The men manning the guns on the wall top were peering outward now, hurrying to swing their guns back over the wall once again instead of at her.

Fieran was right there. She could sense it. She just had to get to him.

A blaze of blue magic swept over the wall and washed over the men assembled around her. Soldiers yelped and howled, dropping their guns and shaking their hands as if burned. The guns on the wall tops exploded.

But where the magic touched her shields, it danced and twined through her magic with the same alacrity it always had, bolstering her power.

Grinning, her heart lifting, Pip lurched the last few yards. The men at the machine guns threw themselves out of her way, even as the machine guns ahead of her exploded, clearing her path.

Only the massive gates of the castle barred her from Fieran. Large wooden locking bars had been set into their brackets on either side, three of them in total, holding the gates shut. She would never be able to lift those by herself, and doing it individually with her magic would take longer than she had the patience for at the moment.

She shifted the shields so that they covered her back. Since she was going to need both hands for this, she lifted Prince Edmund's arm from her shoulder and propped him against the remains of one of the machine guns.

"Sorry, I need both hands free. Watch him." She jabbed a hand at the crown prince, who had pressed a hand against the stone wall beside the gate, his legs shaking so badly that he looked about as unsteady as Prince Edmund.

Prince Edmund hugged the machine gun wreckage, a hint of a smirk playing across his bruised and battered face. "Gladly."

With that done, Pip faced the massive wood and iron gates rising before her and dug deep within her magic, letting it build within her chest. While she had always wielded her iron magic like an elf, it was time to think like a dwarf.

Closing her eyes, she stomped her feet, setting up a rhythm even as she grounded herself with the solidness of the stones beneath her boots. She hummed along with the rhythm, even as she pictured what she wanted to do with her magic.

Inside her, the magic built and grew, shaping and forming, until her chest ached with it, her mouth tasting of iron.

With a shout, she shoved both hands forward even as she thrust her magic in its purest form at those blasted gates that were the only thing standing between her and Fieran.

Ripped from their hinges, the gates blew outward under the force of her magical shield, tumbling and toppling onto the causeway. The stone arch over the gates exploded with the force of her shield and a whole portion of the walls on either side of the gates tumbled outward and collapsed under the sheer power she'd unleashed.

Oops. She hadn't meant to be quite so destructive. All she'd wanted to do was break the locking bars and shove the gates open. Instead, she'd absolutely destroyed them.

In the haze of the slowly settling dust and debris, two warriors of the magic of the ancient kings stood in the maelstrom of their combined magic, bloody blades in their hands. Magic dripped down their swords and poured from their bodies onto the cobblestones below, as if they were more magic than man.

Yet the magic only highlighted the red of Fieran's hair and the wild grin on his face as his gaze met hers over the distance between them.

"Go on." Prince Edmund had struggled to his feet and was using a gun barrel as a cane. He limped over to where the Mongavarian crown prince was cowering against the wall and pulled out a knife. When he'd gotten a knife, she didn't know. "I've got him."

Taking one more moment to make sure she had Prince Edmund and the crown prince securely ensconced in a shield, Pip turned and ran toward Fieran.

THIRTY-ONE

The moment Fieran saw her, framed in the wreckage of the destruction she'd wrought with the dust in the air glittering around her in the light of his magic, he caught his breath and fell all the more in love with her. How could he do anything else when she stood there, petite and strong and wielding magic capable of blowing a castle door off?

Then she was running toward him, and he was still so love-stunned that he forgot he probably should run toward her too until she was only a few feet away. He shook off his paralysis in time to drop his swords, take two steps to her, and sweep her into his arms just as she threw herself into his embrace.

He held her tightly, burying his face against her hair, and that knot in the pit of his stomach finally eased.

She was safe, and they were together.

And then they were kissing. Little breathless kisses punctuated by just as breathless words between.

"You blew off the castle gates!"

"I know!" Her squeal ended in a kiss. "And you're blowing up…everything else!"

"Isn't it great?" Another kiss. "I love you."

"Good. I love you too." Pip's words were a murmur before she kissed him, this one less frantic and more lingering.

He kissed her back, wrapping both arms around her as he held her tightly against him, her arms around his neck, her hands in his hair.

The rolling roar of an explosion shook the ground beneath Fieran's feet. Right. This probably wasn't the optimal time to get lost in kissing his girlfriend.

Fieran pulled back as she did and set her on her feet, a twinge of pain flaring in his side from the healing gash. He pressed a hand to the spot as Pip grimaced and gripped a hand over her upper arm. He gestured to her. "Are you all right?"

"I was shot. Long story." Pip pointed at his side. "You?"

"Sliced open by a mad scientist. Another long story." Fieran tried not to think too much about the whole *I was shot* thing. She was standing and didn't look like she was in a great deal of pain. Besides, they had other things to deal with. Such as ending the war.

When Fieran straightened, he turned to face Dacha. Inside of the high wall before them, people were flooding out of the government offices, running toward the front gate as they were chased by fizzling bolts of Dacha's magic.

Dacha nodded a greeting to Pip before he looked at Fieran, not even having to say anything.

"Sorry, sorry. I'll get on that." He glanced at Pip. "I'm supposed to be chasing the Mongavarian royal family out of their castle so we can force them to surrender."

"If it helps, we've already captured the crown prince." Pip grinned and motioned back to the castle.

Two figures were picking their way down the slope inside of one of Pip's shields, one appearing to be leaning on the other for support. Strangely as they grew closer, it became apparent that Uncle Edmund was the one barely able to stand while his prisoner, the crown prince, was the one holding him up and hauling him forward. Although, the knife Uncle Edmund held to the crown prince's ribs must have provided sufficient motivation for the man to cooperate.

"That *is* helpful." Fieran grinned at Pip before he retrieved his swords and focused more fully on his magic once again. His magic worked deeper into the castle, crackling down corridors, sparking against anyone he found to encourage them to flee.

As figures poured through the ruins of the castle gates, Uncle Edmund halted next to Pip, his gray-haired prisoner still holding him up. "Your timing is impeccable."

Dacha flicked a glance at him. "You do not look well, shashon."

"I thought I looked rather well for a week of torture." Uncle Edmund grinned. At least, Fieran assumed that was the expression his uncle was attempting. "Your hair is short."

"It was necessary and voluntary." Dacha nudged the crowd of people gathering outside of the governmental offices closer.

"Voluntary? I'll have to hear that story once we've finished here." Uncle Edmund's grotesque grin widened as a new, resounding boom—a naval gun rather than an explosion—echoed from behind them. "Our reinforcements have arrived."

Fieran glanced over his shoulder, then spun around to better take in the sight of a column of Alliance warships, led by a heavy cruiser, as they charged into the mouth of the harbor. The lead ship fired its huge guns nearly point-blank at one of the Mongavarian ships that was trying to get underway. Other ships in the column fired on the outer defenses of the harbor, where the men had been so distracted by Fieran's and Dacha's magical display within the harbor that they hadn't been paying attention to incoming threats from outside of it.

With the familiar whining whir, six aeroplanes with the red, gray, and green circles of the Alliance painted on their wings swarmed the airships. As the lead aeroplane turned to strafe an airship, the elf ear emblazoned over a tree became visible on the side of the nose.

Rothilion. Fieran whooped and sent a burst of his magic skyward. He didn't think Rothilion would even see him, but the aeroplane waggled its wings before it zoomed over the airship and dropped several bombs. The airship exploded with gouts of flames.

How had Rothilion and the other aeroplanes gotten here? Fieran hadn't heard of the Alliance developing aeroplane-launching airships like Mongavaria had. But this mission *was* top secret.

With the Alliance Navy and Flying Corps destroying whatever Fieran and his dacha hadn't already blown up, Fieran turned back to the gathering of Mongavarian government officials.

An old woman with white-gray hair picked her way down the castle's causeway, leaning on the arm of a middle-aged man. He bore somewhat of a resemblance to the older gentleman Pip and Uncle Edmund had captured, making him likely also in line for the Mongavarian throne. Probably the crown prince's son.

The woman halted before them, barely taller than Pip and filled to the brim with both affronted dignity and an intense spite as she glared from Dacha to Fieran to Uncle Edmund.

"Empress Bella." Uncle Edmund took a step forward, pushing away from the shackled man. "I am prepared to accept Mongavaria's surrender."

"I will never surrender to you." The empress spat the words, her gaze flicking over Uncle Edmund, dismissing him. When her gaze landed on Dacha, her mouth curled slightly. "And especially not to you or your *half-breed* spawn. The age of elves is long over. It's time for humans to rise and take our rightful empire."

Dacha's hard gaze didn't change as, in the distance, something exploded.

She wielded the disgust in her tone like a weapon, but her intended blow didn't strike. It couldn't, not after the way Fieran had spent this war embracing his dual heritage.

He could tell her he was stronger because he was a half-breed, and the Alliance was stronger because they weren't just humans. There was so much wrong with her words. With her thinking. But he wasn't going to convince her.

Fieran was so done with that prejudice. It was something they were still fighting within the Alliance. The elves had it, as demonstrated by Capt. Rothilion's family. The trolls had it. The humans had it. It wasn't right, no matter where it appeared.

But to wage a war that had cost tens of thousands of lives because of that prejudice? That was a level of hatred Fieran couldn't begin to comprehend.

Behind Prince Edmund, the crown prince drew himself

straighter, although he didn't wear dignity quite as well as his mother did. Having his hands shackled behind his back didn't help. Yet he spoke with a haughty assertiveness. "Mongavaria will never surrender to the likes of the Alliance."

The words and the twin looks of hatred burning in the eyes of the empress and her son ignited something deep within Fieran's chest. He hadn't fought for months, shed so much blood his soul was stained with it, lost friends and family, crashed, watched his best friend come back after losing a leg, crossed half of Mongavaria, and exploded all this armament only to be told *no*.

He was absolutely done with all of this. The war ended *now*.

For the sake of all the Alliance men and women who had died fighting. All those fighting still.

For the sake of the ogres who had been ruthlessly exploited and experimented on.

And for the sake of the Mongavarian citizens like the woman who'd helped them and who wanted to believe that her kingdom could be better than it was now.

Fieran's magic burned in his chest and through his veins in a way it never had before. This was a soul-deep righteous fury unlike anything he'd ever felt. Hardly knowing what he was going to do, Fieran shared a look with his dacha, finding there the same burning anger. "We need to end this."

With a firm nod, Dacha stabbed his swords into the ground at the edge of the road, kneeling as he did so. His words were a declaration, a death knell. "Then we will end it, sason."

Dacha's magic burst outward, crackling down his arms, over his swords, and into the ground. Fieran caught his breath at the sheer force of Dacha's power as it pummeled his chest.

Fieran copied his movements, kneeling and stabbing his swords into the dirt. Closing his eyes, he sank deep into the storm of his own magic and released it. All of it. He didn't try to hold back or control it in the ways he had before. Instead, he embraced the magic and let it take over until he was subsumed into the scorching force of it.

This was the full force of the magic of the ancient kings, only unleashed by the depth of the wrath Fieran felt. At that moment, he very likely would have registered as a 20 on the Marion Scale. He could only guess how high Dacha's magic would register. The taste of it seared against his in an immense power beyond anything Fieran had sensed before.

Neither he nor his dacha could have done this at the beginning of the war. If Fieran hadn't had the magical stamina or connection to his magic, then Dacha had needed the war to return to the warrior he'd once been instead of the husband and father he'd become. More, they hadn't been angry enough.

They were angry now.

His and Dacha's magic shot outward, covering not just the city, not just the surrounding urban sprawl, not even just the outlying farm fields. It surged mile after mile, crackling and powerful and yet not incinerating the people, the structures, the plants.

When that distant, rational part of him sensed the mechanisms of war—the metal, the gunpowder, the industry—only then did he exert enough control to consume or explode, annihilating whatever ability to make war that Mongavaria had left.

A hand came to rest on his shoulder a moment before a flood of a strangely cool but soothing magic washed over him. It twined through his magic, somehow not consumed as it followed the crackling tide outward.

Fieran peeled his eyes open and peered upward through a blue, crackling haze.

Aaruk stood there, a hand on both Dacha's shoulder and Fieran's, his eyes closed as he poured his magic over theirs. His mouth pressed into a tight line as he opened his eyes and met Fieran's gaze. "Destroy those machines. Don't let them keep the magic they stole. Avenge my people."

Maybe in the end, this was the pinnacle of purpose for a warrior of the magic of the ancient kings. They didn't just fight wars. They didn't just end them. They were the vengeance for all those who couldn't fight for themselves.

Fieran could only manage a tiny nod as his magic burned even hotter in his chest until he could barely breathe past the force of it. All he could do was drown in it as he let the waves crash across the Mongavarian landscape.

Where he sensed captured and twisted ogre magic, he released it or consumed it. Far away, aeroplanes lined up on an airfield exploded as they were incinerated. Artillery guns melted. Rifles disappeared in the power of his and Dacha's magic.

Then another magic burst outward, racing toward his and Dacha's across the land from a distance far closer than Fieran would've expected. An icy magic joined Adry's as Rhohen, too, poured his magic over the ground. Somewhere even farther away, Louise unleashed her magic.

Yet when their magic met, it didn't clash or spark as it always had in morning practices. Instead, the magic twined together until Fieran could no longer tell when his magic ended and his family's began. As the magic melded, it magnified into one massive maelstrom. Only Rhohen's remained somewhat distinct, not merging with the rest as fully.

This was something the world hadn't seen since the days of the ancient kings for whom this magic was named. Multiple warriors of the magic of the ancient kings wielding their magic together and unleashing a power that would destroy the world without an honorable heart to guide it.

Dacha spoke, his voice resonating in deep tones. "We are Laesornysh."

"We hold your kingdom in our hands." Fieran's own voice felt as ancient as his power as it clawed up his throat and reverberated in his ears. He dragged his eyes open, barely able to discern hazy shapes past the blaze of blue across his vision.

"Surrender. Now." Dacha's voice rang hard and sharp through the magic filling the air.

"Please, Your Majesty! We must consider terms of surrender!" One of the officials was on his knees. Many of the others were sobbing, pleading. "They will destroy us!"

Empress Bella's mouth worked. Was she still thinking about resisting even now?

Behind her, the government buildings crumbled, the roar of collapsing stone accompanied by a cloud of dust.

How much more destruction would it take before Mongavaria surrendered? The Alliance had battered Mongavaria to its knees. Would Fieran and his family have to level the entire kingdom before Empress Bella let go of her pride? Surely she couldn't be that heartless, right?

"There will be no one left to rule if we don't surrender!" Even protected within Pip's shield as he was, the crown prince had gone white and shaking, all defiance gone.

Would Fieran, his dacha, and his siblings do it? They held the lives of every man, woman, and child in

Mongavaria in their hands. Would they kill them all if that was what it took to keep the Alliance safe?

In that moment, Fieran couldn't be sure just how far he'd go. This war had stripped him of his naïveté, leaving a ruthless warrior behind.

Empress Bella swept a glance around, as if taking in her burning city, her fallen empire. She gave a shuddering sigh. "Mongavaria surrenders. Please present your terms."

Fieran breathed a magic-laced sigh, a sudden exhaustion pressing on him. How was he going to release all this magic without destroying everyone and everything?

Dacha's magic swept over his, as if gathering it up like a harvest. Fieran followed his dacha's nudging and sent his magic rushing toward the far Escarlish-Mongavarian border. Dacha's magic herded Adry's and Louise's magic as well. Rhohen's resisted a moment longer before he, too, sent his magic toward the border.

The residue of all the magic Dacha, Uncle Rharreth, and Uncle Weylind had poured into the Wall still remained, marking the location of the border. With Dacha's magic binding theirs into one great rush of magic, they slammed their unleashed magic into the ground. It sought the remnants of Uncle Rharreth's and Uncle Weylind's magic, anchoring it in place.

Perhaps it was Fieran's imagination, but the ground beneath his knees shook, even this far away. Or perhaps he was shaking as he released his magic, his limbs dissolving into the tired trembling of an exhausted body.

He slumped, his swords stabbed into the ground the only thing propping him upright. It took all his remaining strength just to crack his eyes open, his vision too blurry to focus.

Figures in gray and white uniforms were marching,

taking up positions around them. Voices spoke, an indistinct rumbling.

A hand settled on Fieran's arm, the grip as trembling as Fieran felt. "Sason."

"You're right." Fieran's words rolled slow and slurred off his thick tongue. "Draining your magic is uncomfortable."

Then Pip was there, kneeling before him, her hands cradling his face. "Fieran."

He couldn't seem to focus on her. Or keep his eyes open.

Another voice rang near Fieran's ear, and it took his sluggish brain a long moment to recognize his cousin Rokyd. "Let's get you aboard my ship. You look like you could use some rest. And a shower. Maybe not in that order."

"Can't argue with that," Fieran mumbled, not sure if anyone even heard him.

As strong arms lifted him, he tumbled the rest of the way into peaceful darkness.

THIRTY-TWO

Freshly showered and wearing a set of gray dungarees loaned to her by one of the female crew members, Pip sat on one of the beds in the female ward of the sick bay on Rokyd's ship.

One of the blue-garbed elf healers inspected the gash across Pip's upper arm before adding a hint more magic. "This is healing nicely. It will be fully healed by tomorrow night. You will need rest, both to assist healing and to replenish your magic."

Pip nodded, the exhaustion of the past day weighing on her. She hadn't slept the night before, she'd had her magic partially drained, and she'd held two shields in place for several minutes, then a single shield under the onslaught of whatever annihilating magic Fieran and his dacha had unleashed.

But she had no plan to rest until she'd seen for herself that Fieran was all right. He'd passed out and had to be carried by Rokyd onto the small motorboat and from there onto the ship.

Fieran's dacha had made it as far as the launch before he,

too, had collapsed. Prince Edmund had been in little better shape, also needing to be more or less carried to the boat and onto the ship.

At least Rokyd's shore party had assembled between the Mongavarians and Fieran, his dacha, and Prince Edmund so the only enemy who might have seen their weakness was the Mongavarian crown prince, whom they'd taken along as their prisoner to ensure continued cooperation until the official surrender terms could be signed.

Pip sat still while a nurse bandaged her arm, the picture of cooperation until the healers and nurses moved away.

Once no one was paying attention to her, Pip slid off the narrow hospital bunk and tiptoed to the door—hatch—of the female ward and peeked into the male ward, prepared to duck back if anyone inside wasn't fully clothed.

Thankfully, all four of the men on the beds were dressed. Prince Edmund lay on the bed in the corner to her left, wearing a hospital gown with a white blanket pulled up to his chest. He had an intravenous drip attached to his arm, and his wounds already appeared better than they had an hour ago.

Wearing a set of gray dungarees, Prince Farrendel sat on the next bed beside Prince Edmund's, facing him as the two of them talked in low tones. Prince Farrendel, too, had an intravenous saline drip.

Aaruk, the ogre lad that Prince Farrendel and Fieran had picked up during that long story she had yet to hear, was asleep on a bed across the way, tucked in beneath the blankets so that only his head was visible.

Fieran had the bed next to Aaruk's and across from his dacha's. He was also dressed in gray dungarees, his left arm held out stiff at his side because of his own saline drip. His eyes were closed, his chest rising and falling as if he was still asleep.

Prince Edmund's quiet voice held a trace of a chuckle. "It was rather convenient of them to bring me to their palace, right where I wanted to go. They provided a place for me to stay and everything. You'd think they would have learned after last time."

"That was quite foolish of them." Prince Farrendel nodded almost sagely, that too blank expression on his face that hinted at the humor beneath.

Pip remained where she was, pressed against the solid metal of the bulkhead. She probably shouldn't be eavesdropping, but she couldn't get her legs to move. There was something strangely comforting in listening to Fieran's dacha and uncle recount what had happened in such light tones.

"Yes. What else was I going to do but spy on them after they arranged everything so nicely for me?" Even after everything they'd been through, Prince Edmund's grin was wide, despite the healing bruises. "And they brought you right to the Ludin facility."

"They had me and Fieran pinned down to tables." The faint hint of humor vanished from Prince Farrendel's face.

"Ah." Prince Edmund's grin disappeared as well, something in his eyes holding knowledge—maybe a memory— that Pip didn't comprehend. "What else could they expect but utter annihilation after doing something so foolhardy?"

"Indeed." Prince Farrendel's tone held a dark trace of humor.

After all she'd been through in the past week—and throughout this war—Pip understood that dark humor more than she would have a year ago.

Finally forcing her legs to move, she stepped into the ward. Prince Edmund's gaze snapped to her while Prince

Farrendel craned his neck to look over his shoulder without moving his left arm with its intravenous needle too much.

Pip paused at their two beds and gestured to Prince Edmund. "Are you all right?"

"I'm fine. Or I will be in a day or two once the healing magic finishes." Prince Edmund settled back against the pillow with a sigh. "I love healing magic."

"And you? Are you all right?" Prince Farrendel regarded her with searching silver-blue eyes.

The old instinct to freeze swept through her, but it was only a heartbeat before the fatherliness in his gaze banished it.

Pip shrugged and rested a hand over the bandage on her arm. "I'm also fine. And also very thankful for healing magic."

"Speaking of magic…" Prince Edmund's grin returned in full force, cheery even with the blue-black bruises mottling his face. "You wouldn't happen to be interested in a more permanent job with the Intelligence Office, would you? Your magic makes you uniquely suited to the job."

More spying? No thank you. Pip resisted a shudder. She opened her mouth, trying to find the words to politely but firmly decline.

Prince Farrendel's arms moved, as if he wanted to cross his arms but remembered the needle in his arm. "No."

"You're just saying that because you want to hire her at the AMPC." Prince Edmund's grin didn't waver as he waved at Prince Farrendel.

"No, I do not want you corrupting my future daughter." Prince Farrendel's tone had returned to that hidden trace of humor once again.

Yet his words froze Pip in place as surely as the old hero-worship used to. Elves didn't have a word for *in-law,* and those married into a family were simply referred to the same as those born into it.

Elves were also incredibly hesitant to claim familial relationships. They usually waited to confirm a relationship until it was official, such as once a couple was betrothed or after they were married. Sometimes not even then, as was the case with her elven grandparents. To this day, they all but pretended Pip's mother didn't exist.

Her parents had defied both of their families to marry. They'd established a loving family despite all the hardships they'd faced. It was all incredibly romantic.

But there was also something special about not just finding a romance but also gaining a second family who embraced her as completely as her own parents and sibling did.

She probably should say something. Maybe hug Prince Farrendel. Something. Anything.

But she was still rooted to the spot. Nor, despite the claim, were either she or Prince Farrendel ready for father-daughter hugs just yet.

"Fine, fine. She's off-limits." Prince Edmund held up his hands, as if in surrender. Yet there was a twinkle in his eyes. As if he'd known his words would spur Prince Farrendel to such an admission and that, more than the offer, had been his point all along.

Pip cleared her throat, shifting a step back toward Fieran's bunk. "I'm honored, but I've had all the spying I can swallow."

"It isn't for everyone." Prince Edmund's grin slipped slightly, his eyes going distant.

Perhaps his mind had gone to Jayna, the way Pip's had. Pip halted in her retreat, lingering for one more question. "Do you think Jayna is all right?"

"Yes. She knows what to do." Prince Edmund said the words with the underlying desperation of a father trying to convince himself of that. Weary lines joined the bruising on his face as he settled more fully against the pillow.

She should let them rest. With one last glance from Prince Edmund to Prince Farrendel, she turned and crossed the small space to Fieran's bed.

As she approached, his eyes cracked open, his head turning toward her. When he spoke, his voice was laced with a hint of humor. "I was wondering how long you'd keep talking with my dacha and uncle before you actually got to me."

"I wasn't going to be rude." Pip halted next to his head, his expression sending a twisting through her stomach and a catch in her chest. "Especially since your uncle was offering me a job. Which I turned down. I've had enough spying."

"Good. You know I'll support you in whatever you want to pursue, but spying would be a tough one." Fieran's grin faded as he pointed to where she'd been shot. "How's the arm?"

"All patched up." Pip held her arm slightly stiffly at her side. "And you?"

"Apparently, cauterizing a wound with the magic of the ancient kings makes it harder to heal later." Fieran grimaced as he pressed a hand to his side before he gestured to the glass bottle holding the saline solution. "And it turns out that you can't cross a kingdom under the power of pure elfness without the consequences of dehydration and malnutrition. But why aren't you hooked up like the rest of us?"

"Since I was sitting around in a dungeon, I stayed properly fed and hydrated." Pip clasped and unclasped her fingers. Should she reach for Fieran's hand? "Although that would be Jayna's doing, not the guards'. If it was up to them, we would've been on one cup of water and a single piece of stale bread a day."

"Jayna was at Landri Castle?" Fieran's gaze snapped to Prince Edmund, although the prince had returned to his low conversation with Prince Farrendel. "I assumed she was somewhere in Mongavaria, but I never guessed that she was embedded so deeply."

"I hope she's all right. Things got rather chaotic there." Pip, too, glanced at Prince Edmund. There had been no time to find Jayna as they'd busted their way out of the castle, nor could they have talked with her without giving away that she was an Escarlish agent.

"I'm sure she is. She was raised by Uncle Edmund, after all." Fieran gave a little shrug, though the somber look in his eyes belied his easy words.

Pip eyed the space next to Fieran on the bed. There wasn't a chair to sit at his side, nor did just holding his hand feel like enough. She wanted to be held close and made to feel safe.

Perhaps Fieran understood or had the same craving for closeness. He held out his right arm, inviting her.

She clambered onto the bed, tucking herself next to him instead of merely sitting. His arm came around her, holding her close, as she rested her head on his shoulder.

Fieran heaved a sigh, his breath stirring her hair a moment before he pressed a kiss to the top of her head. "I was so worried about you when I realized we'd been separated. But my dacha reminded me that you are a strong, capable woman who can take care of herself. That helped. But I would've stayed worried if I'd realized that Uncle Edmund was getting you into his spy shenanigans."

Pip gave a somewhat hysterical, somewhat halfhearted laugh into Fieran's shirt. "I was fine. It wasn't like the shackles or metal bars could actually do anything but give me a lot of iron to work with. And it wasn't like the firing squad was actually a danger to me."

"Firing squad." Fieran's breath was half a laugh, half a sigh. "I definitely should've remained worried. But you're pretty amazing."

"Linshi." Pip snuggled more comfortably against him, letting her eyes fall closed and her body give in to the exhaustion. "You're pretty amazing yourself."

Fieran gave a wordless hum as a reply. His muscles relaxed, his breathing going more even. After long moments, so long that she'd assumed he'd fallen asleep, he murmured into her hair, "The next time we go on a dangerous mission, I want a heart bond. Relying on a telephone exchange of other people's heart bonds wasn't nearly good enough."

Pip propped herself up on her elbow and leaned her chin on her hand, her tone light and teasing. "Is that a proposal?"

Fieran gave another of those tired laugh-sighs. "No. Consider it a promise that I intend to propose sooner rather than later."

"Promises, promises." Pip relaxed once again, letting her eyes close again. "I'm going to hold you to it one of these days."

SHE WASN'T sure how long she'd been asleep, curled against Fieran's side, when she stirred at the feel of a blanket being settled over her shoulders. Somewhere in the background, a voice was saying something about surrender terms and Prince Edmund replied, his words indistinct in her sleepy brain.

She peeled her bleary eyes open, her vision blurry, her

eyelids gritty. Yet she could just make out the shortened strands of Prince Farrendel's hair as he spread the blanket over her and Fieran.

As if sensing her gaze, Prince Farrendel's silver-blue eyes met hers. He tipped his head to her. "Rest."

At another time, she might have been more embarrassed to have Fieran's dacha catch her and Fieran snuggle-sleeping like this. Tomorrow, she and Fieran would go back to boundaries and all that. Not that they were crossing any lines they were unwilling to cross, even now.

But for that moment, she was more than willing to stay right where she was and follow Prince Farrendel's directive.

Smile creasing her face, she let herself sink back into sleep.

"Should you be up and about this soon?" Pip clambered over the side of the small captain's boat, landing in the sand next to Fieran. Under the cover of darkness, seamen from the ship had rowed her, Fieran, Prince Edmund, and Prince Farrendel to a remote stretch of shore to the north of Landri Castle. Of all of them, she probably shouldn't be on this mission, but she was glad Prince Edmund had allowed her to come anyway. Her time in Landri Castle wouldn't feel complete without this.

"I'm fine now that the healer fixed me up." Prince Edmund grinned, the expression no longer horrific now that the swelling and bruising had gone down, as he slogged up the sandy beach toward the strands of sea grass and scrub brush.

Prince Farrendel made a noise in the back of his throat,

frowning at Prince Edmund. "The healer said this trip was inadvisable."

"But she didn't forbid me from going." Prince Edmund's grin remained, though it slipped as he struggled up the sandy beach.

Prince Farrendel gave a sigh, reached out, and gripped Prince Edmund's arm to steady him. "Not that anyone could have stopped you."

"No." Prince Edmund's grin disappeared as his voice became low, as if he wasn't talking to them any longer. He probably didn't even realize he switched to elvish. "She is my sena."

Fieran clasped Pip's hand as the two of them trudged up the beach. He leaned closer and whispered in her ear, "Apparently near-death experiences encourage my uncle and dacha to banter even more than usual."

"They are quite the pair." Pip leaned into Fieran more than necessary as the sand beneath her feet slid.

"They've had more than a few years to perfect their banter. Especially since they're stuck with each other at both sides of family gatherings." Fieran swayed into her as well, as if he, too, wanted to be as close as possible.

"They remind me of my mother and my Detmuk uncles." Pip would have leaned her head against Fieran's shoulder, but that would've made walking awkward.

"I can't wait to have the time to actually get to know your Detmuk side of the family." Fieran swung their clasped hands, grinning. "And see the dwarven mountains."

For a moment, Pip's heart sank. The dwarves weren't easy on elves, nor were the depths of the dwarven mountains. Her dacha tried, but he never fully fit with Clan Detmuk.

But Fieran wasn't fully elf. He was half human. He

wasn't bothered by stone, nor would he feel the lack of green, growing things any more than she did. With his loud, boisterous personality, he'd get along with the Detmuk dwarves like he was one of them.

She grinned up at him, something going light in her heart. "My clan will love you. And you'll love the mountains."

While her parents loved each other very much, she had seen how hard it was when a spouse couldn't adapt. They'd moved to the western rail terminal, isolated from both dwarves and elves alike, because they couldn't fit anywhere else.

Yet Pip had fallen in love with someone who could actually navigate her messy dual heritage and dual families alongside her. She wouldn't be alienated but would remain connected to all the pieces that made her whole.

Fieran, too, wouldn't have to give up either side of his heritage. She was as adaptable as he was. They fit together, no matter where life took them.

Prince Edmund and Prince Farrendel ducked into the darkness beneath the scrub trees at the edge of the beach, and Pip and Fieran followed a moment later.

In the gloom in a cluster of trees, Prince Edmund made a low hooting sound, like that of an owl.

A rustle came from deeper in the trees a moment before a figure stepped into the space, her hair especially black in the darkness. She dropped something heavy onto the ground before flinging herself into Prince Edmund's arms, her voice low despite the emotion in it. "Dacha!"

"Sena." Prince Edmund wrapped her in a hug, holding her with even more exuberance than he had when in the dungeon.

Jayna, too, held herself differently, as if both she and

Prince Edmund had been aware of their masks while in Landri Castle, even when the three of them had been alone. Only here, away from the castle, could they fully let down their guard.

"Are you all right? When I heard they were going to execute you…" Jayna's voice choked off for a moment. "It was so hard not going to you."

"You did so well, sena. Above and beyond what I should ever ask of you." Prince Edmund's hug remained tight, his own voice ragged and strained.

Pip looked away, and beside her Fieran shifted. Prince Farrendel went so far as to spin away. They were intruding, even if Prince Edmund had invited them to come.

After another long moment, Prince Edmund partially released Jayna from his hug. "You don't have to go back, sena. The war is over. You can come back with us. You can come home."

Jayna sniffed and swiped a hand over her face. Then she straightened her shoulders and shook her head with a sharp, determined motion. "No, I can't leave. Not yet. If I simply disappear when you do, it will cast suspicion on my cover and all my contacts. I need to take a few months to lay out an exit. On top of that, Mongavaria is in a perilous place. It's tipping toward an implosion, and losing the war might just be the thing that sends it over the edge. You'll need the information I provide in the next few months."

Prince Edmund pulled Jayna in for another hug. "My brave girl."

Jayna hugged him before stepping back. "Just following in my dacha's footsteps." She picked up the leather bag once again. "Here's all the information Pip and I gathered."

"Linshi. This is going to be key for the eventual peace treaty." Prince Edmund took the bag from his daughter. "I'll start laying the groundwork on my end for you to come home. Just a few more months, got it?"

"Got it." Jayna nodded, smiling, before she turned to where Pip, Fieran, and Prince Farrendel stood. Hurrying forward, she gave her uncle a hug. "Uncle Farrendel!"

"It is good to see you safe and well, neshena." Prince Farrendel patted her back in one of his awkward hugs.

Pip stifled a smile. Good to know the awkwardness wasn't just for her.

Jayna moved from Prince Farrendel to give Fieran a hug. "Good to see you alive, cousin. I've heard lots of frightful rumors and stories over here in Mongavaria. And I know Pip was very worried for you."

"And I was worried for her. Thanks for looking after her." Fieran gave Jayna a returning hug. "Keep looking after yourself."

"Always." Jayna released Fieran and turned to Pip, sharing a grin. "Well, we did it."

"Yes, we did." Pip hugged Jayna, standing on her tiptoes because the other girl was so much taller than her.

Jayna stepped back, still grinning. "I'll try to return in time for your wedding. I wouldn't want to miss it."

Fieran coughed, as if he was choking on his own spit.

Pip's face heated, and she couldn't bring herself to look at either Fieran or Prince Farrendel. "Well, uh, we haven't… we aren't even…"

"I know. Don't rush things, all right? I need a few months." When Jayna smirked, the expression was the exact mirror of her father's.

Pip looked up, meeting Fieran's gaze. He reached out and clasped her hand again, smiling.

No, Pip didn't intend to rush. She wanted to savor every step, every moment, especially now that she and Fieran wouldn't have a war hanging over their heads. Someday, likely sooner rather than later, she and Fieran would have that dream wedding. But Pip wanted every other dream along the way, no shortcuts.

As Jayna turned to say farewell to her dacha, Pip leaned her head against Fieran's arm. "Let's go home."

THIRTY-THREE

Fieran stood beside Pip on the deck of the ship anchored in the harbor beneath Landri Castle.

Ahead of them, a table had been laid out beneath the warship's turret in the shadow of the long guns stretching toward the bow of the ship. Dacha, Prince Edmund, and Admiral Brynjar Vulred—supreme admiral of the Kostarian Fleet and shield brother to King Rharreth—stood on one side of the table as the representatives of each kingdom in the Alliance. On the other side, Empress Bella glared, flanked by her son.

With a booming voice, Admiral Vulred read the contents of the surrender out loud, his voice piped through the ship so that anyone not assembled on deck would be able to hear. A nearby radio sent his words to all the ships in the fleet, both those in the harbor and stationed in a cordon farther out to sea.

Fieran gripped Pip's hand and tried to take in the words, but the unreality of it sent the sounds ringing in his ears without processing in his brain.

After all the fighting, the deaths, the blood on Fieran's hands, the war would end today.

When he'd finished reading it, Admiral Vulred placed his piece of paper on the table once again, lining it up with the other three copies of the surrender that lay there.

Uncle Edmund held out a pen to Empress Bella, holding her gaze.

For long, tense moments she kept glaring, unbending, unyielding. Then she took the pen and stiffly signed each of the four copies of the surrender terms.

Once she'd signed all of them, Uncle Edmund, Dacha, and Admiral Vulred signed the surrender, making it official. As Admiral Vulred scrawled his signature on the final piece of paper, Fieran released a long breath and squeezed his eyes shut.

Shouldn't he feel giddy? Happy? Relieved? Right now, there was just a strange numb incomprehension. He couldn't quite process that the fighting was over.

Perhaps the relief would come later as the reality settled in.

For this moment as the guns of the fleet boomed a salute and the six aeroplanes led by Rothilion flew overhead, Fieran merely clasped Pip's hand and breathed deeply of the salty sea breeze.

It was done. The war was over.

Fieran leaned on the metal railing at the prow, the light spray splashing him with chilly droplets.

In the sea around the ship, other smaller warships created a protective formation. Farther out, several submarines ran on the surface while overhead four airships provided air cover. All this extra precaution was to guard the three copies of the surrender that were currently locked in Rokyd's safe.

Scuffing boots sounded behind him a moment before Capt. Rothilion appeared beside him. Rothilion gripped the rail, a green hue beneath his silver skin tone.

"Got your gear stowed?" Fieran raised his eyebrows. Rothilion had come aboard before their ship had left the rest of the fleet, having been rowed over from a strange-looking ship patrolling in the center of the Alliance Fleet. The ship had a huge, flat top with five aeroplanes parked on top.

Rothilion's aeroplane was currently tied down at the end of the rather unwieldy-looking ramp hastily built over the bow gun turret and stretching over Fieran's and Rothilion's heads even now. The ramp wasn't long enough for a landing, but they could launch the aeroplane in case of an attack.

"Yes." Rothilion leaned farther forward as if he was debating upchucking over the side of the ship.

"So…the flat top. Your secret mission. You flew off a ship. I thought that was impossible." Fieran edged farther upwind. Hopefully if he got Rothilion talking, he would be distracted from his seasickness.

"Apparently the engineers figured out more or less how to balance a flat top on a ship's keel. They are still fine-tuning it." Rothilion sucked in a shaky breath and didn't vomit. "They realized that the size was not that much different from the landing strips in the trees that we elves have been using. The new aeroplanes have enough power to actually take off, and they rigged a similar root catching system for landing. It is a more efficient way of creating a mobile aeroplane airstrip since a seaborne ship has more capacity than an airship."

"They gave you command of that small squadron of

aeroplanes." Fieran gestured back toward where the main fleet was now out of sight, still holding station before Landri. "Yet you're giving it up?"

Rothilion huffed a mirthless laugh and released the railing long enough to wave at himself. "As my current state demonstrates, I am not well-suited to life onboard ship."

"True." Fieran told himself sternly that he wasn't going to laugh at the sight of a motion-sick elf. He hadn't thought Rothilion, of all elves, would have a flaw like seasickness. "We'll be glad to have you back in the Half-Breed Squadron."

"It will be good to be back, for as long as the squadron remains together." Rothilion sighed, staring at the horizon. "Once a peace treaty is signed, there will be no more need for integrated Alliance units. My half of the squadron will return to Tarenhiel, and yours will remain in Escarland."

A lump formed in Fieran's throat at the thought. Rothilion was right. Once a peace treaty was formally signed to negotiate the final and official end of hostilities, the Alliance would downsize from a war footing. Many of the pilots would be let go. Whole squadrons might be disbanded. As the only squadron formed of both elves and humans, the Half-Breed Squadron would likely be the first to disband, unless joint ventures were determined to still be useful.

Fieran swallowed and clapped Rothilion on the shoulder. "We will always be the Half-Breed Squadron, no matter where we go from here. That won't change."

"No, it will not." Rothilion somehow managed a smile as he clapped Fieran on the shoulder in return.

As much as Fieran had longed for the end of the war, it was strange to be melancholy about the changes peace would bring.

Yet no matter what, the Half-Breed Squadron was a badge all of them would wear with honor for the rest of their lives.

AFTER SEVERAL DAYS of navigating up the waters of the Hydalla seaway between the various islands and shoals, the ship anchored alongside one of the deepwater wharves jutting from below the bluffs of Fort Defense.

Overhead, aeroplanes bearing the elf ears of the Half-Breed Squadron soared in one last salute before they tipped their wings and headed for a landing on top of the familiar bluffs overlooking the docks. They'd been providing an escort in the sky from the moment the fleet had entered their range, and the sight of his squadron overhead brought a smile to his face and a warmth to his chest as they guided him, Pip, and Rothilion home.

The gangplank lowered, linking the ship to the pier.

Fieran stood off to the side, his hand clasping Pip's, as they waited for the official honor guard to disembark with the locked box containing the three copies of the signed surrender.

As the honor guard marched down the gangplank and disappeared down the wharf, a woman with her red hair and blue skirt flapping on the breeze stepped into sight.

Mama.

Behind her, Louise gripped Ellie's hand while Adry held Tryndar on her hip.

Before Fieran could go more than a couple of steps in that direction, Fieran's dacha all but dashed past him, taking the gangplank in three strides. He swept Mama into his arms, holding her close and murmuring words into her hair. She buried her face against his shoulder, her shoulders shaking as if she was crying.

Fieran swallowed. All through the war, his mama had been such a rock. Only now that the war was over did she let herself cry in front of them.

Mama lifted her head, and Dacha kissed her. Right there in front of all of them.

Fieran glanced away, just as another three people strode up the pier.

Pip yanked her hand free of his and raced down the gangplank, flinging herself into a group hug with her muka, dacha, and brother.

As Fieran followed at a much slower pace, Tryndar wiggled out of Adry's grip and leapt the distance from her to Dacha and Mama, giving a shout. Dacha reached out and caught Tryndar without even looking, letting the kiss linger another moment before he and Mama pulled back.

As Dacha greeted Tryndar, Fieran reached the rest of the family, exchanging hugs with Adry, Louise, and Ellie. Thankfully his wound had fully healed, so he was in no danger of flinching and having to explain that he'd been hurt.

It was good to see them all alive and well. Adry had been fighting on the front these past weeks, and Louise, Ellie, and Tryndar had been in some kind of danger.

They'd all have stories to tell. But for now, Fieran was more than content to simply hug his sisters and enjoy having their whole family together again for the first time since he joined the army.

Strange how he'd gone through this whole war only to realize he'd already had what mattered most in life. Loving parents. Close siblings. A loyal friend. A life that was rich and full.

That life would be even more rich and full now. More friends. More family. And now he knew never to take them for granted.

To one side, Uncle Edmund swept Aunt Jalissa into his arms, the two of them laughing and crying as if they were the only two standing on that pier.

Mama reached up and touched the shortened strands of Dacha's hair. "What happened?"

"I cut it." Dacha leaned his forehead against hers, placing an emphasis on the words that Fieran didn't quite understand as he repeated, "*I* cut it."

Tryndar placed both hands over his head, as if to protect the long strands of his hair. "Am I going to have to cut my hair?"

Dacha laughed, the sound lighter and more unburdened than Fieran had heard in a long time. Adjusting Tryndar in his arms so that he was facing him more fully, Dacha shook his head. "No, sason. You do not have to cut your hair if you do not wish to do so."

"But..." Tryndar glanced from Dacha to Fieran and back, his bottom lip sucked into his teeth.

Dacha shot a glance in Fieran's direction, meeting his gaze briefly, before he focused fully on Tryndar once again. "You, sason, are both an elf and a human. You may choose to wear your hair short to honor your human heritage, as Fieran does. Or you may choose to wear your hair long in the style of the elves. Either way, your macha and I will not be disappointed with you."

That longtime ache deep within Fieran's chest gave one last healing throb as a lump formed in his throat. Perhaps his dacha, too, had grown these past few months.

"But you cut your hair?" Tryndar's forehead furrowed,

his hands still pressed protectively to his hair. "And you are an elf."

"Yes, an elf's long hair is a symbol of his honor, especially for a warrior." Dacha's gaze remained fixed on Tryndar. "But long hair is only a symbol; it is not honor itself. Sometimes it is necessary for an elf to sacrifice long hair for something more important than a mere symbol. Do you understand, sason?"

Tryndar blinked at Dacha for a long moment before he shook his head.

Fieran laughed under his breath. Trust Dacha to confuse Tryndar more by the usual elven tendency toward cryptic statements.

Whatever else Dacha said was drowned out in Uncle Edmund's inarticulate shout and laugh as he spun Aunt Jalissa around. When he set her down, he turned to the rest of them, a huge grin on his face as he called out, "We're expecting! I'm going to be a father again!"

Mama laughed and hurried to Uncle Edmund and Aunt Jalissa, giving them hugs. "I knew it."

Fieran grinned, and he would have joined the celebration except that there was a drumming of running boots on the wharf and shouts of "Fieran!"

Fieran turned just in time as the flyboys mobbed him, with Stickyfingers and Lije leading the charge. The flygirls and elven pilots followed at a somewhat more sedate pace, although even the elves were smiling.

Laughing, Fieran found himself backslapped and brother-hugged and exuberantly pummeled in greeting. Lije, Stickyfingers, Tiny, Murray, Aylia, and all the other familiar faces.

Just when even Fieran was at the edge of overwhelm, he

spotted Rothilion edging down the gangplank, as if he was hoping he wouldn't be noticed.

Fieran pointed in his direction. "Look who I picked up on the trip back."

The flyboys glanced over their shoulders before several of them shouted, "Rothilion!"

Rothilion froze with wide-eyed terror as the whole mob descended on him, giving Fieran a moment to breathe.

He turned and found Pretty Face standing there, hanging back from the others. He was once again dressed in a pristine Escarlish Flying Corps olive-green uniform, although it hung on his still gaunt frame.

"You made it." Fieran pulled Pretty Face into a backslapping hug.

"Yeah, so did you." Pretty Face returned the backslap before he stepped back. "They haven't cleared me for duty yet, but they at least allowed me to rejoin the squadron."

Behind Fieran, there came more excited shouting, which included Pip's name. He could only guess that Rothilion had sicced the pack of flyboys on Pip.

Pretty Face grinned, nodded to Fieran, and ambled around him, headed in the direction of the excited babble. His trajectory changed as Aaruk tiptoed down the gangplank, as if the ogre wasn't sure if he should get off the ship.

Lije broke away from the rest of the gaggle around Pip. "Aaruk! How did you get here?"

"Lije?" Aaruk grinned as he exchanged handshakes with Lije, and then Pretty Face, the three of them talking over each other.

And then Merrik was there, strolling down the wharf with green magic glowing through his right pant leg, his shoulders straight, his head high. He carried himself with a confidence Fieran hadn't seen before. The weeks of command had done him good.

Grinning, Fieran pulled Merrik in for another backslapping brother hug. "You led them well. Linshi."

"I have not told you what happened in the past weeks." Merrik laughed as he slapped Fieran's back in return.

"You don't have to. They're all here, and you're alive. That's all that matters." Fieran stepped back, though he kept a hold on Merrik's shoulders in an elven hug a moment longer. "When did all of you return to Fort Defense?"

"As soon as you Laesornysh warriors ended the war. Rather spectacularly, I might add." Merrik clasped Fieran's shoulders. "Do not do that again."

"Adry passed out too, didn't she?" Fieran glanced over his shoulder to where his sisters were exchanging hugs with Dacha.

"Yes. It was horrible." Merrik's mouth pressed into a thin, unamused line that matched his tone. "But after that, the higher-ups decided that Adry and the Half-Breed Squadron had fought enough, and we were sent back here to rest. Although, it was a bit of a downgrade after the various mansions we stayed in while at the front lines."

"They still haven't built barracks for us, have they?" Fieran shook his head.

"Nope. We are back to tents. At least our platforms in the trees were still there." Merrik sighed, a smile curving his mouth.

Before Fieran could say anything else, a small figure with silver-blond hair came hurtling at him from the side. He turned barely in time to catch Tryndar as his little brother shouted, "Fieran!"

"Hey, monkey." Fieran hefted Tryndar more securely into his arms.

"You came back." Tryndar wrapped his arms around Fieran's neck, not even protesting the nickname like he usually did.

"Yes, I did." Fieran patted Tryndar's back. "I heard you were in danger."

"It was scary," Tryndar mumbled into Fieran's shirt before he lifted his head and made the bursting motions with his hands that always signified magic. "But then Louise came, and she was all *pffew-pffew,* and the bad guys were all screaming and then it was all better."

Fieran's throat tightened, and for a moment all he could do was hold his little brother, thankful he was safe. He wasn't sure he wanted to hear the full story.

Time for a subject change. He didn't want Tryndar dwelling on those bad memories a moment longer.

"Hey, would you like to fly in my aeroplane?" Fieran grinned at Tryndar.

"Yes!" Tryndar pumped his fists.

"Can we come?" Ellie hurried toward where Fieran and Merrik stood, trailed by Merrik's little sister Kari. Uncle Iyrinder and Aunt Patience had joined Dacha and Mama, and the four of them were slowly strolling in this direction.

Merrik sighed, although he smiled as he turned to their little sisters. "Yes. I'll fly you. I think the two of you can squish into the back seat of one of the two-seaters."

He was going to fly again. Fieran's heart beat harder as he eyed Merrik. "Is my aeroplane here?"

"Yes, we made sure it got back to Fort Defense with us." Merrik shook his head, even if his smile remained. "It's ready to fly whenever you are."

Perfect. Fieran turned to his parents. "We're taking Tryndar, Ellie, and Kari flying."

"Be careful." Mama shot him a stern look, although she was still smiling. "Don't crash."

"I won't." Fieran stepped in to give her a quick, one-armed hug while still holding Tryndar with the other.

Dacha eyed Fieran and Tryndar, as if he was debating whether to forbid the whole thing.

Before he could, Fieran raised his voice and waved to get the attention of the squadron. "Who wants to fly?"

"Yes!"

"Let's go!"

"Flying with Laesornysh again!"

The flyboys, flygirls, and elven pilots stampeded along the wharf, headed for the tram that would take them up the bluffs toward the sprawling hangars and airfield complex.

As they ran past, Stickyfingers slapped Pretty Face's back. "I'll fly you in one of the two-seaters."

"And you can ride with me, if you want to come." Lije motioned to Aaruk, who seemed a bit bewildered to find himself towed along in the tide of flyboys.

Pip hurried to join them. "I'll check the aeroplanes over. I need to make sure their maintenance is up to my standards."

"Hey, what are you implying? I was one of those maintaining them." Mak fell into step with her, giving her a teasingly hurt look.

"I'm sure whatever you did is acceptable." Pip bumped Mak's shoulder before she waved to Tryndar as she strolled past.

"I'll come too." Louise dashed past Fieran to fall in step on Pip's other side. "I knew my place was at the AMPC, but it would be nice to get a glimpse of what it was like in the field."

"I suppose I'd better supervise." Adry trailed after Pip, Mak, and Louise, gathering Ellie and Kari as she went. "And once the two of you get back from flying, the three of us can have a tea party. Maybe we can even convince Merrik to join us."

"Yes!" both younger girls yelled at once as they each grabbed one of Merrik's hands and dragged him along.

Still grinning so widely his face hurt, Fieran turned in that direction as well, shifting Tryndar so that his brother was perched on his shoulders.

Within short order, Fieran had Tryndar buckled in on his lap in his aeroplane as it rolled forward, headed for the airfield. He'd even managed to get official clearance to take his squadron up on a flight, although Colonel Dentley was unaware that three children and a civilian ogre would be going along.

Tryndar had a much-too-large flight cap pulled over his head while the band of the goggles he wore had been tied in the back to make them small enough to fit his head. Fieran wore his own flight cap and goggles, and he'd tucked Tryndar partially into his flight jacket to keep him warm enough.

Turning the aeroplane's nose to line up on the airfield, Fieran glanced over his shoulder at where Merrik had positioned the two-seater in the wingman position. Ellie and Kari were crammed side-by-side in the back seat, buckled in together and also wearing spare sets of goggles and flight caps.

Merrik waved, his teeth showing in a wide grin.

Fieran grinned back and faced forward as he sent the aeroplane hurtling down the airfield.

Tryndar shrieked and cackled, his silver-blond hair flapping free and into Fieran's face.

As the aeroplane grew light, Fieran pulled back on the control stick, and the aeroplane rose into the sky. Just behind them, Merrik's aeroplane soared as well, taking up that familiar position at Fieran's tail.

When the aeroplane gained more altitude, Fieran sent it into a gentle curve, tipping it on its wing. On the airfield, the rest of the squadron was taking off two by two, rising into the sky to join him and Merrik.

By the hangar, Pip, Mak, Adry, Louise, Dacha, Mama, Uncle Iyrinder, and Aunt Patience had lined up, shading their eyes as they peered upward.

Fieran tapped Tryndar's shoulder and pointed. "Look. They're watching. Wave."

Tryndar leaned in that direction and waved. Fieran matched his gesture, not sure if those on the ground would be able to see it from that far away.

Yet moments later, the whole line of those watching waved back.

As he returned his hands to the control stick, Tryndar placed his smaller hands over Fieran's, as if he wanted to help fly.

Another glance around showed that the squadron was assembling behind him. Rothilion with Aylia as his wingelf. Stickyfingers in a two-seater with Pretty Face in the rear seat. Lije, with Aaruk in the second seat of his two-seater, and Tiny. All the other men and women, both elf and human, who had formed the Half-Breed Squadron.

Fieran gave a whoop and laughed at the sheer rush sweeping through him.

The war might be over, but he still had his aeroplane. He had his squadron. And he had the bright blue sky stretching before him. Nothing was going to hold him back.

FIERAN SAT on the edge of the wooden platform beside his tent at Fort Defense, the setting sun warm against the back of his neck, the eastern horizon lit with the blue glow of the new Wall he, Dacha, Adry, Louise, and Rhohen created after flooding Mongavaria with their magic. Perhaps, once the official peace treaty was signed and the tensions finally eased, the Wall would retreat into the ground, as it had been in Fieran's childhood.

With a sigh, Merrik slowly lowered himself to sit on the platform next to Fieran.

A long, comfortable silence settled between them, filled with the steady hum of large vehicles, distant voices, and tromping boots. All the familiar sounds of an army base.

Fieran released a sigh, not daring to look at Merrik. "Do you regret it?"

He wasn't sure what he meant. Joining the army. The things they'd done. The people they'd killed. All that the two of them had lost along the way.

He wasn't even sure if he regretted those things or not. Yes, they held a weight. There were things he wished he had done differently. Tragedies he wished he could have prevented. He'd live with that weight for the rest of his life.

Merrik shifted his right boot, as if thinking of what joining the Flying Corps had cost him. "No. And yes. If that makes sense."

"It does." Fieran braced his hands behind him on the platform.

They lapsed into silence once again. This time the weight between them was that of long friendship, the brotherhood they'd forged during this war, and the brothers in truth they would become someday.

"Here you are." Adry's cheerful voice rang out a moment

later before she appeared around the corner of the nearest tent. "Pip thought we'd find you here."

"It's like I know him well or something." Pip laughed as she strode between the tents behind Adry. Her brother Mak trailed after her a moment later.

Adry settled in beside Merrik, clasping his hand, while Pip took the seat next to Fieran.

He put his arm around her, and she leaned into him. He didn't even feel too bad about snuggling in front of everyone, even when Mak sat on the next platform over since there wasn't enough room on this one.

The other flyboys drifted between the tents until Lije, Stickyfingers, Pretty Face, and Tiny were lined up on the platforms on either side. Even Rothilion and Aylia made an appearance. Aylia lounged on another platform over although Rothilion remained standing, leaning against a tree.

Stickyfingers picked up a pebble and gave it a half-hearted toss. "What was the point? To the war? All of this? Everything is just going to go right back to the way it was."

"Is that a bad thing?" Lije shrugged, leaning his elbows on his knees.

"No, but..." Stickyfingers sighed and threw another pebble. "The entire war was fought so that the border could remain exactly where it was. The Alliance didn't gain anything. No one gained anything."

"The last war resulted in the Alliance. It meant something. At least, that's how it sounds in stories." Tiny rolled a ball of ice around in his palms.

"We gained the alliance with the dwarves." Lije pointed toward Pip. "That means something."

"My dwarven kingdom, at least." Pip shrugged within

the circle of Fieran's arm. "But it isn't the close alliance like the one between Kostaria, Tarenhiel, and Escarland."

"It could become that. The first Alliance started with a mere defense treaty." Lije grinned, displaying the gap between his front teeth.

"True." Pretty Face gripped the edge of the platform, his shoulders somewhat hunched as if he was still curled within himself. Recovering from what he'd experienced would take time. "And this war will make a difference for the ogres. Perhaps Escarland will be able to strengthen ties with them."

"Most of all, this war proved the worth of the Alliance." Rothilion spoke in a low tone, his arms crossed. "There has always been some doubt on how well our kingdoms would be able to fight a war while so integrated. Mongavaria assumed we would fall apart into internecine fighting. They were counting on it."

"It was not an unreasonable assumption." Aylia's somber expression quickly disappeared into one of her cheerful grins. "But we did not. We won. The Alliance survived Mongavaria's attempt to destroy us. And now the Alliance is stronger than ever."

"We survived. That is the meaning." Merrik's voice drew attention. He gave a rolling shrug, even as he stretched out his prosthetic leg. "History books will likely list all those things as the result of this war. But for us right here, right now, all that matters is we survived."

"And we have each other." Fieran tucked Pip closer, even as he nudged Merrik with his other arm. "That's what we gained by the war, awful as it was. We have the Half-Breed Squadron and always will."

As his friends cheered their agreement and the sun set behind him, Fieran held Pip close, his best friend at his side, ready to face whatever future came their way.

EPILOGUE

*S*everal *months later…*

Fieran dashed along a thin branch in the upper reaches of the treetop palace of Ellonahshinel, his swords in his hands, his magic twining down the blades. The dwarven bracers were laced around his wrists, the dwarven-forged iron within them playing with his magic. He leapt, flipped over his swords, and landed lightly on the branch, spinning to face the other way.

Farther along the branch, Dacha mirrored his actions, facing Fieran with his magic-laced swords in his hands.

Fieran stepped into a thrust, the space between them large enough that there was no risk of hitting Dacha. Dacha too stepped into a thrust before sweeping his sword in an arc. Fieran wove his sword in a matching sweep, sinking into the peace of the graceful movements.

It was only the two of them this morning. Adry had a final drill with the elven army before she was officially discharged into the reserves while Louise had a break-through on the mechanical problem she'd been working on so she'd disappeared into the workshop first thing. Or perhaps she'd never left last night. Fieran wasn't sure.

He was glad of the quiet moment with his dacha, the stillness broken only by the crackle of their magic and the faint scuffing of their feet on the branches. This was the only chance Fieran would get to talk to his dacha alone before Fieran left with Pip's family, first for the western rail terminal and from there to the dwarven mountains.

The Half-Breed Squadron had remained on station at Fort Defense ever since the war had ended, spending the winter in a snug new barracks the army had finally gotten around to building.

Almost before the ink had dried on the surrender and long before an official peace treaty could be signed, Mongavaria had descended into chaos. The entire Mongavarian royal family, including Empress Bella, had been shot and killed by rebels.

Things had somewhat stabilized this spring—Jayna had a hand in that or so he'd heard—and the Alliance had finally given his squadron leave for well-deserved rest.

For several more minutes, Fieran and Dacha whirled and stabbed, thrust and spun, in a pattern as familiar as breathing, as soothing as a song, and as deadly as the magic both of them wielded.

They were Laesornysh, and they were ready to defend their kingdoms should the need arise.

Perhaps someday they wouldn't be needed. Maybe by the time Dacha placed swords in Tryndar's hands, the gesture would be more symbolic than preparation. Maybe Fieran's younger siblings would be free to walk in the footsteps of their Dachasheni Ellarin, acting as peacemakers rather than warriors, creating art rather than death.

But that wasn't Fieran's destiny. He was a warrior, like

his father before him, and he would guard his kingdoms with all the power of his magic and blades, on the ground and in the sky.

After one last swipe, Fieran raised his sword, saluted his dacha with it as Dacha saluted him, and cut off his magic at the same time as Dacha did.

As he sheathed his swords, Fieran couldn't quite bring himself to meet Dacha's gaze. "I'm going to propose to Pip."

Dacha made a noise in the back of his throat, but that was it.

After several heartbeats, Fieran forced himself to look up. Dacha stood there, regarding him with a look he couldn't decipher. Part sorrow, part joy, part something else that couldn't be named.

Clearing his throat, Dacha stepped forward and gripped Fieran's shoulders. "I am happy for you, sason. She is good for you, and you are good for her."

"Yeah, she's pretty great." Fieran grinned, gripping his dacha's shoulders for a moment. Then he stepped back, already starting to turn. "I need to talk to Merrik before I leave."

"Go on." Dacha smiled, making a motion toward him.

Fieran grinned and dashed along the branch toward his family's set of rooms in one of the far-flung branches of Ellonahshinel. The main room sat at a slightly lower position on a larger branch while six rooms were grown into various branches, connecting to the main room with various stairs and bridges.

While Fieran could hear voices and laughter coming from the main room, where his mother and younger siblings would be gathering for breakfast, he bypassed it and headed straight for the lift set on the far side. Stepping inside, he used the button to engage the small magically-powered engine. With a hum, the lift lowered through the broad leaves and tangled branches of Ellonahshinel toward the lush green of the elven forest floor.

It settled with barely a whisper on the thick grass. To one side, Dacha's workshop rose from the forest floor, grown in place, with a second, smaller lift resting on a platform built into the roof.

To the other side, Uncle Iyrinder and Aunt Patience's elven house grew from a small maple tree. In a normal forest, this tree wouldn't have survived, shaded by the upper canopy of Ellonahshinel as it was. But this was an elven forest where magic laced through every tree and plant.

Uncle Iyrinder and Merrik were strolling toward the tree-house cottage from somewhere deeper in the forest, likely from their own morning practice session. Or perhaps theirs, too, had turned into a talk session instead, given the looks on their faces.

After saying something to his dacha, Merrik turned and headed in Fieran's direction. "I can see you are eager to leave."

"Yes, but it isn't only that." Fieran rocked back and forth on his heels, barely holding back his magic. "I'm going to propose to Pip while we're there."

"Good." Merrik matched his grin, a glint in his eyes. "I'm going to propose to Adry."

Fieran exaggerated a gasp as he pressed his hands over his heart. "Going behind my back? Again?"

"I would not do so, except that *someone* is leaving on a long trip and will not be back for at least a month, perhaps longer." Merrik crossed his arms, his grin now more a smirk. "And maybe it makes me impatient, but I am unwilling to wait until you return."

"I don't blame you." Fieran clapped Merrik on the shoulder, that fizzing excitement still burning in his veins. He might need a second practice session today at this rate. "So, let me guess. You got Ellie a book for the gift. Tryndar is easy. He will be happy with just about any toy you get him. A new tool for Louise, probably for Dacha as well. A new mug for Mama or maybe a new flavor of hot chocolate. But I'm very curious what you got me."

In the elven tradition, a male elf would give gifts to the family of the female he was courting to gain their blessing before he proposed. The gifts would demonstrate to the family how well he knew them and cared for them, and thus for his prospective bride. An elf would propose after that, although for elves that could be months afterwards, if not years. Merrik wouldn't wait that long.

"I thought about a tool belt so that you could carry around Pip's tools. Or a new set of flying goggles. But then I decided that I already had the best gift." Merrik's smirk glinted in his eyes as he gestured at himself. "You are getting me for a brother."

Fieran tipped back his head as he barked a laugh. "Yes, you're right. That is the best. And you know you have my blessing."

"Linshi." Merrik's smirk softened slightly. "I still got matching tool belts for you and Pip, but I will give them to you once the two of you are engaged."

"You know you have her blessing as well." Fieran stuck out his hand, letting just a hint of his magic wrap around his fingers. "Brothers?"

Merrik let some of his own magic twine around his fingers before he clasped Fieran's hand. Their magic fizzled and popped in their palms for a moment as they shook. "Brothers."

The handshake wasn't enough. Fieran pulled Merrik in

for a quick, backslapping hug before he released Merrik. "We really should have thought of that new handshake long before now."

"It is far superior to the spit handshake." Merrik shook his head. "Although, we could not have done it before we came into our magic."

"True." Fieran took a step back in the direction of the lift. He needed to grab breakfast, shower, finish packing, and say goodbye to his family before he joined Pip and her family at the train station. "Well, I need to go. I want to hear all about how it goes when I get back. Just leave out the kissing parts."

"Same. And best of luck impressing the dwarves." Merrik was already starting to turn, heading for his own breakfast.

Fieran laughed and waved as he jogged toward the lift. "Thanks. I'm going to need it."

Pip leaned close to the window as the elven train glided to a halt on the spur track on one side of the western rail terminal. The familiar buildings spread before her beneath the spindly arms of the nearly bare trees, the first buds of spring dotting the ends of the twigs.

Home.

A lump formed in her throat. It had been nearly a year since she'd last seen it, and now she was returning only to say goodbye to it once again. This place that had shaped her, that held all her childhood memories, would never be her home again.

"Are you all right?" Fieran placed an arm around her shoulders, tugging her close.

"I'm fine." The words were hoarse, her throat so tight it hurt. But she didn't cry. Not yet, anyway. "It's just...change is hard."

"Yeah." Fieran's grip tightened around her as he enfolded her into a full hug.

She wrapped her arms around him and leaned into him, soaking in his warmth and strength. The next couple of days would be hard. Good, but hard. At least she would have Fieran at her side, bolstering her up.

Dacha, Muka, and Mak gathered their bags and climbed off the train.

Pulling herself together, Pip released Fieran, stepped back, and picked up her bag. She could do this. Surely saying goodbye to her childhood home wouldn't be as hard as many of the things she'd done in the past year.

After Fieran had slung his own bag over a shoulder, his twin swords hanging off the side, he held out a hand to her. "I can't wait to see where you grew up."

She clasped his fingers, her smile feeling somewhat more genuine and less forced. As long as she focused on showing her home to Fieran, hopefully the coming farewell to it wouldn't sting so much. "Come on."

She tugged him from the train and gave him a tour as they meandered through the terminal. Fieran asked questions and made suitably impressed comments as she pointed out the parked trains, the open-sided buildings to park trains out of the weather, the turntable for turning around both elven trains running on roots and human trains running on metal rails. Even as they wandered, a train rumbled across the arching metal bridge spanning the Milnissi River, likely holding dwarven raw materials hauled across the Afristani Plains.

The elves, half-elves, trolls, half-trolls, and half-humans, even the occasional full human, bustled between the parked trains, storage sheds, and open-sided buildings grown between the lofty trees. The workers shouted and waved to her, and she and Fieran paused to talk to several of them.

At the far side, they reached the longest building, which held the main office and the large mechanics shop where the more complicated repairs were done.

Beyond that long building, her family's cottage was grown into a grove of five trees, its sides and roof a living tangle of branches so that it almost looked like a giant, house-shaped beaver dam.

As she and Fieran strolled closer, they had to dodge around more workers hauling in packing crates, already getting started on the work of packing up her family's belongings. Inside the main room that filled the entire first floor, her muka and dacha stood in the center of the space, directing workers to set down the crates and what to pack in them.

Pip would have frozen right there in the doorway, but Fieran tugged her to the side before she could get bowled over by two men carrying a crate, who likely wouldn't have seen her.

Dacha glanced at her before he wound his way through the chaos to reach her side. Even across the room, he likely had seen how close she was to tears.

As Fieran stepped a few paces away, giving them space, Dacha clasped her shoulders. "I know it is hard to say good-bye. But this change will be good for your muka and me. The western rail terminal was the haven we needed to raise you and your brother in a Tarenhiel that was not ready for a dwarf-elf couple. But it is time to stop hiding here and use our talents in new ways, as you are doing, sena."

"What your dacha means is that it's time he started

pursuing his dreams and talents again." Muka strode forward and grabbed Pip out of Dacha's elven hug for a squeezing, rib-crushing dwarf hug instead. "He spent decades here so that I could do my mechanics. It's time he became Inawenys once again. And the dwarves need me to learn to be an ambassador as well as a mechanic."

When Muka released her, Pip gasped in a deep breath.

Dacha smiled down at Muka a moment before he leaned down and brushed a light kiss on her mouth.

Pip looked away for a moment. Her parents were happy. Yes, they were all mourning having to say farewell to this place, but this change would be good for them as well.

Almost as soon as the war ended, King Weylind offered her dacha the job of the government official in charge of dwarven affairs, which included his prior role as ambassador to the dwarves that he had given up when he married Muka and moved here. The king of Dalorbor had requested that Muka act as the dwarven ambassador to Tarenhiel, at least temporarily. On this coming trip to the dwarven mountains, her muka would consult with the king to see if she was going to be the permanent ambassador or if she would instead be aiding the actual ambassador.

Either way, both of her parents were needed in Estyra, although they would continue to travel to the dwarven mountains and to Aldon in Escarland as needed.

They'd spent the past few months training their replacements. But now it was time to pack up their things and clear out this house for new occupants.

"And we were not going to remain here when neither of you would be here." Muka glanced over her shoulder as Mak joined their huddle.

Mak, too, had decided to move to Estyra now that the army had downsized the Ordnance Corps and he'd been discharged. With the new airstrip, the resumption of the tourist airships, and the trains, there were plenty of opportunities for a mechanic with his skills and magic. Muka, too, would find a place to tinker if she grew bored with being an ambassador.

"We are so proud of the both of you." Dacha rested a hand on Muka's shoulder as he faced Mak and Pip. "It is time for all four of us to stop hiding and start pursuing our talents and abilities more fully."

Pip stepped into her family's group hug, her throat tight again. Perhaps her whole family had outgrown this place. It was time for all of them to move on and establish new lives elsewhere.

Once her family released her, Mak gave Pip a nudge toward where Fieran was loitering at the base of the stairs. "Go on."

With one last glance at her family, Pip smiled and hurried to Fieran's side, taking his hand again. The two of them climbed the stairs and reached the small circular landing at the top. Doors led into rooms around the landing.

"That's the guest room where you'll be staying." Pip pointed to a room on the far side of the stairs. Then she headed for the room directly ahead of them. "And this is my room."

She pushed the door open and stepped inside for the first time since she'd left for training at Fort Linder.

Everything remained as she'd left it. Her quilted bedspread lay pristinely over the mattress on her metal-framed bed, the headboard against the wall by the door. Curving shelves held a few knickknacks, mostly consisting of various wooden items Mak had made for her throughout the years. A cupboard next to that held the items of clothing she hadn't taken along when she joined the mechanics auxiliary while broad windows looked out into the forest, a glint of the river just visible through the trees.

One wall was mostly open and decorated with various posters and artwork she'd collected over the years.

The poster…

Tossing her bag onto her bed without even looking, Pip flung herself across the room and pressed her back to the wall, trying to hide the poster plastered there. Not that she could block it fully. The poster was too large and stuck to the wall too high up.

Fieran laughed and crossed the room at a slow, almost stalking pace. He nudged her gently aside before he regarded the poster with another chuckle. "I had forgotten just how academic Dacha looks in this poster."

With a sigh, Pip turned to face the poster, standing shoulder to shoulder with Fieran.

The poster was nearly three feet and by two feet. The black-and-white sketch showed Prince Farrendel with a set of goggles on his forehead and a book in his hands, his long hair flowing around him.

Pip groaned and dropped her face in her hands. "This is so embarrassing. I should have gotten rid of this poster years ago. But I guess it's beyond time to throw it away." She reached for the poster.

"No, don't!" Fieran halted her with a hand between her and the poster. "Don't just rip it up and toss it. This poster meant too much to you. Let's take it down carefully. At the very least, you can store it rolled in a box so we can take it out to laugh about it and our first meeting."

Pip released a breath, something easing in her chest. Perhaps she hadn't been as ready to just pitch it as she'd thought. "Yeah, let's do that. Linshi."

Fieran started working at the top corners while she eased

the bottom corners from the wall. The tree sap was still rather sticky, given that her dacha had helped her stick this poster here. He'd also laced the paper with his magic to preserve it.

Her younger self, who'd spent so many years staring at that poster and dreaming, would never have believed where she was now. That elf prince who inspired her so much was going to be her dacha someday, and she no longer froze up around him. Most of the time, anyway.

In her bag rested a copy of her hiring contract for her new job at the AMPC. As Fieran had predicted, the moment the army had downgraded her to the reserves with only the demand of a few weekends and weeks of duty here and there, Lance Marion had presented her with that hiring contract. Once she and Fieran returned from this trip, she would start the new position, working directly with Lance Marion, Bennett, Louise, and Prince Farrendel. Until she and Fieran married, she'd room with Louise in the apartment at the AMPC.

Fieran, too, had new orders. The Alliance had, indeed, sent each Flight of the Half-Breed Squadron to its own king-dom, stationing Flight A in Estyra under Rothilion's command and Flight B in Aldon under Merrik. Yet the squadron hadn't been fully disbanded, even if it was stationed in two different places. Fieran would travel between Estyra and Aldon as needed to oversee the squadron, and he planned for the whole squadron to meet up several times a year to train together. Rothilion and Merrik, too, would travel back and forth frequently to become familiar with both Flights and consult with Fieran. The hope of the higher-ups was that the Half-Breed Squadron would continue to train elven pilots and human pilots to work together.

Living in Aldon, Pip would be separated from the rest of her family. But Estyra was a much shorter train ride than the western rail terminal, and the trip would be even shorter if Fieran could requisition a two-seater and fly them. Besides, Fieran's job would demand travel back and forth, as would her parents' jobs. And when they were pressed for time, they could always meet up halfway in Bridgetown and Calafaren. While she might live away from her family, she wouldn't be cut off from them.

After the two of them eased the poster from the wall, Fieran carefully rolled it for her while she found a ribbon to tie around it.

As they finished, there came a knock on the open door. A worker stood there, holding a crate. "Where do you want it?"

"Just set it there by the door." Pip pointed to the open space on the floor.

Once the worker left, Fieran helped her pack the crate with the things she wanted shipped to Aldon. As they did, Pip found herself talking about the miscellaneous items, reliving her childhood even as she dismantled it.

Yet Fieran listened with a smile, laughing at the right moments, giving her space to cry when needed. Holding her close when she wanted.

As they finished packing the bulk of it, her muka's shout drifted up the stairs. "Supper is ready!"

Fieran grabbed his bag from where he'd set it on her bed next to hers. "Good. I was beginning to worry."

"No need. Dwarves never skimp on food." Pip straightened, brushed her hands off on her trousers, and crossed the room to him. "You can drop your bag off in the guest room, then we can head down."

"Actually, I need...I need to take my bag to dinner.

It's…" The tips of Fieran's ears turned pink as he looked away from her, hefting the bag higher on his shoulder.

Oh. Pip's face heated. He was going to do it. Tonight. The elven gift-giving tradition where he asked her family for their blessing on his coming proposal.

"I see." Pip took his hand and tilted her head toward the door.

As she and Fieran left her childhood room, her heart was far lighter than it had been a few minutes ago.

Yes, she was shutting the door on her childhood. On life in this home. But a new future stretched before her, bright and happy, filled with family and friends, mechanics and magic, new dreams and new adventures. All with Fieran at her side as she was at his.

FIERAN SAT on the roof of Pip's family home, the sun rising at his back and casting long shadows through the trees and over the broad, rippling waters of the Milnissi River. His swords rested in their sheaths across his back, a familiar and comforting weight.

He'd come up here to work off his restlessness this morning, only to realize that his exercising would likely wake everyone still sleeping in the rooms below. Yes, he had elven grace. But even that grace couldn't prevent the thumps of his weight landing on the roof branches.

Instead, he'd forced himself to simply sit and breathe, releasing the restlessness into the peace of the morning.

A faint scuffing and scratching came from below a moment before Pip's head appeared above the roof. She grinned at Fieran as she clambered the rest of the way onto the roof. "I thought I'd find you here."

"You know me well." Fieran returned her grin, shifting to the side to provide more space on the seat of interlacing branches. This nook formed a surprisingly comfortable seat, almost as if someone had purposely crafted it to be that way.

Pip settled in next to him with a slight sigh. After a moment of silence, she gripped the edge of the branch beneath them. "A year ago, I sat in this very spot and decided to join the Mechanics Auxiliary. Well, Mak convinced me I should."

"Something he might mildly regret, but I'm glad he did." Fieran smiled at her, but he resisted the urge to reach for her hand. Not yet.

Instead, he slipped a hand into his pocket, fingering the object there. His heart pounded harder in his chest, his magic burning inside him, as he gathered his courage.

"He regrets it less now that the war is over, and I'm no longer in danger." Pip propped her elbows on her knees, her gaze focused on the river and the western plains spread before them. She shot him a smile. "I certainly don't regret it."

"Good. That's...good." His voice was tight in his throat.

Pip looked at him, her brow furrowed. "Are you all right?"

"Fine. I'm fine." He swallowed, grasping the item in his pocket in his hand. This shouldn't be scary. Especially not after asking her family for their blessing the night before. It wasn't like this would be a surprise, nor would Pip say no.

Yet his heart was throbbing in his chest, his magic crackling through his veins. With his palms sweaty, his fingers shaky, he had images of dropping the ring and losing it among the network of branches on the roof.

Perhaps proposing here wasn't the smartest idea. But this seemed like the moment. He just had to go for it.

"Pip..." He clasped her hand with his free one as he turned toward her. "I love you. I've been falling in love with you from the moment we met. You are the most talented, amazing, lovely woman, and I want to spend the rest of my life with you."

Pip pressed her free hand over her mouth, a small squeak escaping her, as she gazed up at him.

That trusting, hope-filled look in her dark brown eyes strengthened him as he held her gaze. "I want to celebrate your every achievement and dream alongside you. I want to look to the sky with you as we build a life together."

Somehow, he didn't fumble the ring as he pulled it from his pocket and held it out between them. The three gems—a diamond, a ruby, and an emerald—winked in the morning sunlight where they were set in a silver band etched with the same dwarven designs as the dwarven bracers she'd purchased for him.

"Will you marry me, Pip?" He held her gaze, his heart there between them in that ring.

She made another inarticulate noise in the back of her throat, but other than that she didn't move or speak.

He managed a slight smile, despite his hammering heart. "Just to be clear, this *is* a proposal. And an answer is generally expected eventually."

"Yes!" The word was a high-pitched squeak. Pip flung herself across the space between them, wrapping her arms around his neck. "Yes, yes, yes! Of course I'll marry you!"

Fieran wrapped one arm around her, keeping a hold of the ring in his other hand.

Before he could gather his thoughts enough to speak, she pulled back, holding out her hand between them. He slipped the ring on her finger, and she reached up to touch the wrench necklace he'd given her with her non-ring hand. "It matches."

"Hope that's okay?" Fieran didn't release her hand.

"Yes. I love it. It's perfect." Pip's smile beamed in the morning sunlight, her eyes twinkling.

Fieran might have murmured something mushy about how she was perfect. Then he was kissing her, cradling her face as the light of dawn highlighted the strands of her dark hair and played across her skin.

Before them spread the western plains and beyond them, the far dwarven mountains. Adventure lay before him as wide and enticing as the trackless blue sky arching overhead, yet everything he could ever want was already in his arms.

Thanks so much for reading *Storm to Victory!* I hope you enjoyed the ending and were satisfied after all the ups and downs this series put you through!

If you want more, never fear! I plan to write a book featuring Lije, Pretty Face, and Stickyfingers getting up to adventures in Groyria. And the second sequel series, Elven Legacy, which includes a book for Merrik and Adry, will begin releasing next year!

If you'd like some War of the Alliance bonus content, including a short story of Pip and Fieran's wedding, sign up for my newsletter and download *Soar to Destiny* today!

Sign up for my newsletter now

A downloadable map and Fieran's family trees are available on the Extras page of my website.

If you ever find typos in my books, feel free to message me on social media or send me an email through the Contact Me page of my website.

If you want to learn about all my upcoming releases, sign up for my newsletter, buy signed books directly from me, and get a full list of my books, head over to www.taragrayce.com.

Acknowledgments

Thank you once again to you readers who keep picking up the books and loving them! A special thank you for reading and loving this series!

A very special BIG thank you to my brother Andy for reading this book over for me! I would have REALLY embarrassed myself in this book without you! Any mistakes portraying the military side of things are my own.

Thank you to my family for all your support and encouragement, especially with this series and how intense it has been doing this rapid release!

For all my nieces and nephews, I hope you enjoy seeing your names in books!

Thank you to my friends Bri, Paula, and Jill. You girls are the best! For my author friends, but especially Molly, Morgan, Addy, Savannah, and Sierra, THANK YOU for all the encouragement and commiseration!

Thank you to Bethany and Deborah for your proofreads and copyedits that polish up these books and make them shine! I appreciate both of you so much!